ABOUT THE AUTHORS

Amy McGavin is the pen name of a Scottish wife-and-husband writing team whose real names are . . . Amy and Gavin.

The couple's contemporary romance novels are set in the Highlands. Each story is crafted with humour and heart, with a wee bit of heat thrown in.

The pair live in Glasgow with their daughter and very lively cocker spaniel. When they're not writing, they enjoy exploring Scotland's breathtaking hills, glens, and beaches, then treating themselves to coffee and cake afterwards.

To keep up to date with all their publishing news, and gain access to exclusive bonus content, join their newsletter by visiting amymcgavin.com.

Newsletter

The Scottish Single Dads Series

Captain of My Heart

Built for Love

Catching Feelings

The True Scotsman Series

The Highland Kiss

The Highland Fling

The Highland Crush

The Highland Game

The Highland Bad Boy

For the most up-to-date book list, visit amymcgavin.com.

The
HIGHLAND
GAME

The True Scotsman Series

AMY McGAVIN

GRUMPY GROUSE
PRESS

ISBN 978-1-916734-07-4

Published by Grumpy Grouse Press

The HIGHLAND GAME

CHAPTER ONE

JAMIE

Together the warrior and mage trudge up the mist-shrouded hill, the mage's glowing staff casting faint halos in the swirling haze.

"It's been too quiet for too long," the warrior mutters.

"You're right." From beneath the mage's hood, a stray lock of fiery-red hair escapes, the colour a stark contrast to the grey all around the pair. "Stay on guard. I've a funny feeling you'll be using that sword of yours soon."

The two press on warily until the dark shape of a standing stone emerges from the gloom, looming tall and ominous before them. The warrior can just about make out others beyond it. A stone circle? He rolls his shoulders, a sharp crack breaking the stillness. "Looks like this could be a boss's territory. Are you ready, Sass?"

The mage smirks and twirls her staff with a flourish. "Always ready to save your kilt-clad arse, Lochie."

The warrior draws his broadsword from its sheath and continues towards the circle. He manages three steps before an unearthly howl shatters the quiet. The sound comes not from straight ahead but to the warrior's right. He turns to look, and the mist there coalesces into a monstrous form. A massive spectral wolf materialises, its eyes glowing like twin moons, its ghostly fur rippling as though stirred by a wind neither adventurer can feel.

"Oh, balls!" the mage curses. "That's the Cù Sìth. If that thing howls three times, it's instant death for both of us—game over. And the howl count is already at one."

The warrior settles into a fighting stance, his broadsword raised and ready. "Then we'd better put down this overgrown pooch pronto."

With a bone-chilling snarl, the Cù Sìth lunges forwards, its massive paws leaving scorched earth in their wake. The warrior meets its charge head-on, his broadsword clashing against the beast's infernal claws. Sparks fly as steel meets unholy energy.

"Incoming!" the mage shouts, and a volley of fireballs narrowly whizz past the warrior's head, striking the hellhound.

"Bloody hell, Sass, you nearly hit me!" The warrior blocks another claw swipe with his sword. "I can't focus on fighting this thing *and* dodging your pyrotechnics."

"Oh, please. If I'd been aiming at you, you'd be a smoking crater by now."

The warrior grins despite himself, parrying another blow from the Cù Sìth. In response the creature rears back and releases an otherworldly howl that echoes across the misty landscape.

"Shite, that's two!" the warrior yells. "We've got to take this beastie out before—"

Suddenly a horde of goblins charges out of the fog, their caps soaked in crimson blood, their rusted blades held high. The mage, already several paces behind the warrior, retreats to safety, but the warrior is quickly surrounded, and the redcaps cackle madly as they close in.

"We don't have time for this!" The warrior swings his broadsword in a wide arc, cleaving through three of the goblins in one stroke. "A little help here, Sass?"

"What's the magic word?" the mage teases, even as she raises her staff high.

"Please don't let me die a gruesome death at the hands of these ugly wee bastards?"

"Close enough!"

With a flourish, the mage slams her staff into the ground. A shock wave of force ripples outwards, scattering the redcaps like leaves in the wind. Several smash against the standing stones with sickening crunches.

"Show-off," the warrior mutters, but there's admiration in his voice.

Their reprieve is short-lived. The Cù Sìth lunges forwards once more, jaws snapping inches from the warrior's face. He stumbles backwards in the nick of time, but before he can steady himself, a surviving redcap pounces at him, its jagged blade tearing into his side.

"You wee gobshite!" The warrior drives his sword through the goblin's chest then kicks its dying body aside. Grabbing a small vial from his belt, he uncorks it with his teeth and downs the healing potion in one gulp. That's when he spots another sneaky redcap creeping up behind the mage. In a single smooth motion, the warrior draws his flintlock pistol, takes aim, and fires. The goblin's head snaps back like it's been yanked by an invisible string, and with a final gurgle, the creature crumples to the ground, very much dead.

"Saved your arse again, Sass!" The warrior turns back to the

Cù Sìth, only to find it bearing down on him, a snarling blur of fur and fangs. "Oh, crap!"

At the last moment a shimmering wall of golden light flashes into existence before the warrior, and the wolf slams into it with bone-rattling force. Shooting a glance over his shoulder, the warrior sees the mage lowering her staff and sporting an insufferably smug grin.

"You watch my back, Lochie, and I watch yours. That's what makes us a good team."

The warrior nods and returns his attention to the boss. The wall of light is still protecting the pair, for now, but it's already beginning to dim. That spell never does last long.

"I'm growing tired of this Big Bad Wolf, so let's end him before he howls a third time." The warrior wipes goblin blood from his blade. "Any bright ideas for taking him out, Sass?"

"I've always got a plan, Lochie—you know that. But you're not going to like it."

The warrior sighs. "Just tell me what it is."

"Simple, really. You lure Growly McGrowlface into the middle of the standing stones, and I'll handle the rest."

"Right, so I risk life and limb while you stand back and wave your magic stick around? Why does that feel so familiar? Oh aye, because it's your strategy *every bloody time*."

There's no opportunity to quibble further because the wall of light flickers one last time and then vanishes completely, leaving nothing but empty air—oh, and a gigantic monstrous wolf not of this world. The creature's lips curl back into a snarl that reveals far too many teeth.

The Cù Sìth pounces and the warrior drops into a roll, diving beneath its colossal paws just before they crash into the earth with enough force to shake the standing stones themselves. Scrambling upright, the warrior delivers a quick slash across the beast's flank—not that it does much more than piss it off.

"Here, boy!" he calls. "This way, you ugly mongrel!"

The warrior bolts towards the centre of the stones, sword in a white-knuckled grip, and the beast gives chase with terrifying speed.

"All right, that's him between the stones!" the mage calls. "Now keep him there. I only need a minute."

"A *minute*?" The warrior ducks as the Cù Sìth swipes at him, its claws slicing through the air where his head was but a moment before. "Sass, do you have any idea how long sixty seconds is when you're being chased by a homicidal ghost mutt?"

"Quit whining and keep it busy!" The mage's staff glows brighter as she chants in Gaelic.

The warrior dodges another swipe then, with a grunt, takes a swing at the beast. "Oh aye, sure. I'll make small talk with ol' Fluffy here while you recite a wee poem. Fantastic idea."

He reaches for his flintlock pistol, levels it at the fiend, and fires. The shot echoes through the stone circle, but the Cù Sìth shakes off the impact like it's no more than a bothersome fly. The wolf then circles the warrior with slow, deliberate steps, ghostly fangs bared, silvery drool dripping from them.

"That's it," the warrior growls under his breath. "Keep your eyes on me."

The mage's chant intensifies, her voice ringing out. Runes carved into the ancient standing stones pulse with light and grow brighter with each syllable. Suddenly beams of energy shoot from the stones, converging on the Cù Sìth. The demon hound roars in agony, the magical net constricting around it, holding it in place.

"Now, Lochie!" the mage shouts. "Finish it!"

"Gladly!" The warrior charges forwards, ducking under the beast's snapping fangs and then, with herculean strength, driving his broadsword upwards, piercing the creature's jaw and plunging deep into its skull.

For a heartbeat, everything is still. Then, in a blinding explosion of light, the monster shatters into nothingness. As the mist on the hill clears, the warrior and mage stand gasping for breath, the ground around them littered with the fading corpses of redcaps.

A golden text box appears: *The Cù Sìth has dropped the Claymore of the Clan Chiefs!*

◆　◆　◆

The Claymore of the Clan Chiefs? Finally! I've been hunting for this legendary sword for weeks. My fingers dance over the laptop keys.

LOCHNLOAD

Yas! Hope you're not too jealous, Sass.

I click the NEED button next to the claymore, indicating I want it. But to my surprise—and annoyance—SassyLassie's character portrait also appears beside it, signalling she's done the same.

LOCHNLOAD

What the hell, Sass? It's a massive two-handed sword. There's no way a mage could wield it—not with your puny wee twig arms.

So? I could sell it. Or maybe I just like big swords. ☺

I snort, the sound carrying through the snug. That's what we call the Bannock Hotel's small drinking area, where I'm currently "working" behind the bar. It's quiet tonight, as it often is. The only patrons here are two local men nursing pints at the far table. They cast curious glances my way.

"Sorry, don't mind me." I gesture to my laptop. "Just a funny moment in the game I'm playing."

They nod, clearly not interested, and return to their conversation. However, Bruce, the resident black Lab, rises from his dog bed, stretches, then pads over to see me, tail swishing lazily.

"Hello, mate." I reach down to ruffle the fur on his head, and he leans into my touch, his whole body wiggling with happiness. I give him a good scratch under the chin, earning myself a lolling tongue and a doggy grin.

After a bit more petting, Bruce gives my hand a lick then wanders back to his bed. He circles once, twice, then flops down with a satisfied grunt.

It's a dog's life, all right. Then again, I don't have it too bad either. Playing a video game while on the clock? I can hardly complain.

In the bottom-right corner of my screen, a playful animation pops up, adding a bit of levity to *Highland Legacy's* otherwise gritty game environment. A chibi version of my muscled Highland warrior, rendered in comically exaggerated proportions with bulging arms and a jutting jawline, grips one end of a rope. The other is held by Sass's tiny mage avatar, all oversized eyes and fiery hair. The rope jerks back and forth as numbers flash above the characters' heads—random game-generated rolls that take no account of the fact that, in a real tug-of-war event, my warrior would whoop Sass's ass.

I score a respectable sixty-one, but Sass rolls a total of seventy-three. With a final heave, her chibi mage yanks the rope so hard that my warrior goes flying. Her mage does a little victory dance, then the animation disappears and a text box declares: *SassyLassie wins the Claymore of the Clan Chiefs!*

LOCHNLOAD

Bollocks. This is an outrage. That was mine!

SASSYLASSIE

Aw, don't be a sore loser, Lochie. Why is a massive sword so important to you anyway? Compensating for something? 😕

LOCHNLOAD

Oi! Nothing to compensate for here. Anyone who's peeked under this kilt has been VERY impressed.

SASSYLASSIE

Sure. Keep telling yourself that.

LOCHNLOAD

I actually can't believe you rolled for the claymore. We've been questing together for months now, and we always distribute loot fairly. Never expected to be stabbed in the back by you.

SASSYLASSIE

Wow, keep your kilt on! I wouldn't want your wee dagger getting chilly (and even smaller).

LOCHNLOAD

You're unbelievable.

I blink, taken aback. Sass is steering our conversation towards some very unfamiliar waters. We don't normally talk to one another like this. Jokey banter? Absolutely, par for the course. Saucy confessions? Nope, that's new.

She and I chat about all sorts: anime, fantasy books, music, biscuits (she claims custard creams are the best, which is absolute madness, of course). In some ways I know a lot about Sass—what she likes, what she doesn't—but when it comes to the important stuff, I'm clueless. I mean, I'm certain she's Scottish, like me, but I've no idea what town or city she lives in. And I don't even know her real name. As for her voice? Never heard it. We exclusively communicate via text chat when we play together.

"Oi, Jamie! When you're done googly-eyeing your computer, a couple more pints, please."

I glance up to see that one of the two men—Roddy—has walked over and placed a couple of empty glasses down on the bar. So wrapped up was I in my digital world, I didn't even notice him approaching.

"Coming right up." I grab a glass, tip it under the tap, and let the golden liquid flow. "This should help you and Hugh tolerate each other for another hour or so."

Roddy shakes his head. "Jamie, it's a good thing we come here for the peace and quiet and not your patter. Though I suppose it's marginally better than your pouring skills."

"Ouch!" Grinning, I pass him the first pint then pour the second. "And here was me thinking it was my sparkling wit that brings you two old buggers here every Monday."

"Absolutely not!" Hugh calls from the table. "I've seen graveyards with a better atmosphere than this place. Still, at least we can hear ourselves think here. The same can't be said for the Pheasant on quiz night."

The Pheasant is the pub just down the road, and Hugh's right: it's no doubt as busy right now as the snug is quiet.

Roddy heads back to his table with the drinks, and I return my attention to my laptop. A new message has come in from Sass.

SASSYLASSIE

Cat got your tongue? Too scared to reply?

LOCHNLOAD

I can't tell if you're pulling my leg or if you're being serious.

I tap my fingers against the edge of the bar, weighing my options. Aye, Sass and I have never veered into this kind of territory before, but I'd be lying if I said I wasn't intrigued. And I really want that bloody sword.

Sod it.

A smile tugging at my lips, I lean forwards, fingers hovering over the keyboard. Here goes nothing.

CHAPTER TWO

MAISIE

Well? I'm waiting. Or should I just hang on to this claymore?

I bite my lip, the irony of my digital dare not escaping me. I've lost count of the number of times I've had to fend off creepy male gamers when they've initiated completely inappropriate chats with me. And yet here I am asking Lochie to open up about his sexual appetites.

Maybe I'm crossing a line in our virtual friendship, but I've been playing with Lochie for a few months now, and I reckon he's not the type to take offence easily. Either he'll answer my question or he won't. Whatever happens, I'll give him the sword—I've no use for it, and besides, he and I are a team. That being said, if I can have a bit of fun with him first, all the better.

Well . . . since you're twisting my arm, I'm sort of interested in power dynamics. Any game involving a blindfold is always fun to play. 😉

A burst of laughter escapes me, echoing off the walls of my empty flat. "Lochie, you dirty wee scamp!" I say out loud, amused by his candid admission and also oddly pleased that he actually opened up to me.

Nudging my finished dinner plate to the side, I pull my laptop closer and tap out a reply.

SASSYLASSIE

> Oh, spicy! I wouldn't have guessed that about you, Mr Muscles.

LOCHNLOAD

What can I say? I'm full of surprises. Your turn now, Sass. Fair's fair.

SASSYLASSIE

> Nope! That was NOT the deal. The deal was you answer my question, and I give you the Claymore of the Clan Chiefs. So here you go.

I navigate through the game menu and initiate the item transfer.

LOCHNLOAD

Cheers! You've just made my day. Though I can't help but feel a wee bit disappointed that I don't get to hear your kinky confessions. 😅

SASSYLASSIE

> Ha! Sorry, but my secrets are staying secret. For now, at least . . . 😌

LOCHNLOAD

You know what's weird? If I'd told someone
that in real life, I'd be beetroot red right now.
But with you, I don't even feel embarrassed.
It's like . . . you're a stranger and an old
friend rolled into one. Does that make
sense?

I know exactly what he means. The bond we've forged
through countless hours of gaming together feels . . . significant. Aye, we may spend most of our time ribbing each other,
but Lochie has also become my virtual confidant, a friend I
trust implicitly, even though I've never seen his face or heard his
voice.

SASSYLASSIE

Makes perfect sense. I always suspected
the mighty LochNLoad was a big softie,
really.

LOCHNLOAD

Softie? I prefer "emotionally well-rounded".
It's all part of my charm.

A knock at the door jolts me from my virtual world.

"Maisie?" a familiar voice calls.

"Iona, is that you?" I grab my dinner plate and dump it in
the sink. "It's open. Come in!" Sliding back into my chair, I
hastily type out a goodbye.

SASSYLASSIE

Sorry, gotta go!

LOCHNLOAD

Later, Sass.

I log off just as my friend Iona walks in, her blonde hair in its trademark messy bun, her puffin-print dress a testament to her love of animal-themed outfits.

She smiles. "There you are! Your da sent me up to fetch you. The pub is heaving and everyone is waiting for our quizmaster to show up. That's you!"

I check the time and wince. "Shit, sorry. I didn't realise it was so late."

"You lose yourself when you're gaming—kind of like how I get when I'm deep in a romance novel. Is this the *Highland Legacy* video game I've heard so much about?"

I've been returned to the title screen, where a gameplay montage showcases epic battles, scenic environments, and key NPCs. "Aye."

Although not a gamer, Iona *is* a fan of the *Highland Legacy* TV adaptation, and I can't help but remember the girls' night last year when she and I spent a little too long dissecting it. Or, more accurately, dissecting the famous scene in which lead actor Ronan Dunbar bares all. We both owned up to rewatching that bit more times than we cared to put a number to. Now *there's* a man who doesn't need to compensate for anything with some oversized sword—not with the "natural weaponry" he's been blessed with.

"You know," Iona says, "I'm pretty sure I've seen Jamie play this game."

Jamie is the younger brother of Lewis McIntyre, Iona's boyfriend and childhood sweetheart. Iona recently moved in with Lewis into the small hotel he manages, which is just along the road from here. It being a family operation, Jamie stays in the hotel too, and so he's now a housemate of sorts of Iona's.

"Aye, well, it's a pretty popular game," I say.

"You should look Jamie up and play together with him sometime."

"Absolutely not!" The words are out of my mouth before I can think better of them. "Not that there's anything wrong with Jamie," I hurriedly add, to be polite—even if, truth be told, he isn't exactly my favourite person. "What I mean is . . . gaming is my escape, you know? Like books are for you. Down in the pub, I'm constantly nattering with Bannock folk, filling them in on my life and catching up on theirs. Don't get me wrong, I love the chat, but it's also nice to have a bit of me-time, a chance to recharge my batteries. That's why I game with people I don't know. Playing with locals?" I shake my head. "That just wouldn't be the same."

"I get that. Sometimes you need a break from the familiar faces, eh? Well, if ever you change your mind, Jamie's username is Locked and Loaded or something like that."

My brain buffers for a moment. Locked and Loaded? That sounds an awful lot like . . .

No. No way. Jamie McIntyre couldn't be LochNLoad, could he? Surely not. I mean, what are the chances the stranger I've been playing with for the last few months is someone from my own Highland town? Minuscule, right? Practically nonexistent.

And yet . . .

I want to ask Iona a few questions to try to get to the bottom of this, but she's already moving towards the door.

"C'mon, let's go! We've blethered long enough. If we don't go down now, your da will think we've both gone missing."

"Right, aye, the quiz." My mind still glitching like a buggy software update, I follow Iona to the stairs. If Jamie is LochN-

Load, then that means . . . oh God, I just asked him about his kinks. And he answered!

Da and I live in the flat above our pub, so my "commute" takes all of a few seconds, leaving me no time to ponder LochNLoad's identity any further. Instead, shaking off my gaming persona, I summon my brightest smile and step out into the lively chaos of the Pheasant.

"Hold the search party!" Scott, one of our regulars, bellows from a corner table. "She's finally here!"

A chorus of laughter erupts, and heads swivel in my direction.

"About time!" Eileen, another local, adds. "One more minute and I'd have subjected everyone to a quiz about my garden gnome collection."

"Sorry, all!" I say, navigating through the crowded room. "But you know me: I like to make an entrance. Besides, I had to make sure my material was top-notch—I've got standards to uphold. I can guarantee there are no questions about garden gnomes, although I have popped in a few about Scott's love life. Look out for them in the fiction round."

As laughter ripples through the pub, I head over to the bar, where Da is pouring a pint. My smile wavers when I notice the pallor of his skin and the slight tremor in his hands, but I quickly plaster it back on. I'm good at keeping up appearances.

"Everything all right, Da?" I ask quietly.

"Never better," he says gruffly. "Now get on with the quiz before this lot start a riot."

"Will do. But first, if you've not taken Hamish's order yet, let me serve him while you sit down for a moment. I bet you've been run off your feet down here." Before Da can object, I grab a glass and say to Hamish, who's probably our most loyal patron, "The usual?"

He nods and I pour him his drink.

"I don't need you fussing over me," Da grumbles. "I'm okay."

"I know you are, Da. I'm just trying to help."

This isn't the time to bring it up, but I'll have to try chatting with Da again about getting an extra pair of hands around here. Just the thought of his predictable response—something about him having managed fine with our current staffing levels for decades, so there being no need to change things now—already has me wanting to bang my head against the bar. I love my da, but he's proud and stubborn, and he outright refuses to acknowledge he's no longer as fit and healthy as he once was.

After I pass Hamish his pint of bitter, I grab the mic then step out from behind the bar. "All right, ladies and gents, sharpen your pencils and your minds because it's time to prove who's got the brains and who's just here for the beer!"

There's a ripple of laughter and then the buzz of conversation dies down, eager faces turning my way. It's a full house tonight, and the familiar crowd is a welcome distraction from my equally familiar worries about Da.

"You know the drill: no devices, no shouting out answers, and no bribing the quizmaster. Though I might be persuaded by a wee dram."

As the crowd chuckles, I scan the room and spot Iona at a table with her mother, Elspeth, and—oh, great—Lewis. Not that there's anything wrong with Lewis, other than the fact he looks rather a lot like his brother Jamie. Who may or may not be LochNLoad.

Nope, don't think about that! I tell myself. *The virtual world is for upstairs. Right now you've got a pub quiz to run.*

So, waking my phone—where I've noted tonight's questions—I clear my throat. "Okay, here we go. Question one . . ."

CHAPTER THREE

MAISIE

It's a perfect spring day in our wee town, and Bannock's Main Street looks idyllic in the sun. The old stone buildings, weathered but proud, are brought to life by the cheerful splash of yellow daffodils spilling from flower boxes. As pretty as the sight is, I'm too preoccupied to properly appreciate it. I can't stop thinking about LochNLoad. The idea that my gaming buddy might be Jamie bloody McIntyre is doing my head in.

"Maisie! Wait there a moment!"

I glance across the street and see Elspeth Stewart waving at me. She's walking Bruce, Iona and Lewis's dog, and when the big black Lab spots me, his tail wags so furiously it sends his whole body into a joyful, wiggling frenzy. Elspeth and Bruce cross over to join me.

"Hiya, Elspeth. And hi, Bruce, you big sook." I bend down to scratch Bruce behind the ears. "How are you both?"

"Oh, can't complain." Elspeth's hair, once as blonde as her daughter's, has softened into a crown of silver, framing a face gently etched with laughter lines. "But how about you? You're looking very pensive today. Everything all right?"

I force a smile. "Aye, just a lot on my mind."

She nods sympathetically. "I hope this isn't prying, but the reason I stopped you is because I was actually wanting to ask you about your father. He didn't look himself at the quiz last night. Is he feeling okay?"

I consider brushing off her concern, but Elspeth, with her gentle demeanour and connection to Iona, feels safe. So instead I let out a small sigh. "Honestly? I don't think so, but he's too stubborn to admit it."

"Ah. Men, eh? That sounds like Bryce, all right."

Bruce's ears perk up at the name, and his tail thumps against Elspeth's leg.

"I said *Bryce*, not Bruce, you silly boy." Elspeth chuckles and pats his head. "Although to be fair, your name and Maisie's father's do sound very similar."

The dog tilts his head quizzically, and Elspeth and I both laugh.

"Anyway, your da should really go see the doctor and get himself checked out," Elspeth says.

"I've tried telling him that but he won't listen to me. Maybe if *you* said something . . ."

Elspeth reaches out and squeezes my arm, the contact warm and comforting. "Leave it with me. I'll have a word next time I see him. With both of us on his case, he might just cave, eh?"

"Thanks, Elspeth. I appreciate it."

We chat for a few more minutes before parting ways. I continue down the street a short distance then head into Bannock Stores, the bell above the door jingling as I step inside.

I grab a basket and pick up a few supplies—bread, milk, custard creams (an essential purchase on every visit)—then I go over to the drinks fridge, my eyes scanning the shelves for Gaelic

Fire, my favourite energy drink. I've been hooked on it since LochNLoad mentioned it during one of our late-night gaming sessions. There's a single can left, and I'm just about to take it when my phone pings.

I return my phone to my pocket then reach for the Gaelic Fire, but as I do, someone else goes for it too. Warm skin brushes mine as both my hand and the other person's close around the cool metal can. Startled, I glance sideways and come face to face with—what are the chances?—Jamie McIntyre. Okay, more like face to chest because he's so bloody tall. My gaze travels upwards until it locks on to those hazel eyes flecked with gold and brimming with far too much mischief.

"Great minds drink alike, eh?" he says in his low voice.

His chestnut hair is a charming mess, as though he's just rolled out of bed. I definitely don't want to ruffle it—just as I don't find the tiny freckle at the corner of his left eye utterly adorable, and just as I have no wish whatsoever to trace the faint stubble along his jawline with my fingertips.

Get it together, Maisie. Jamie McIntyre is an arse. Don't forget that.

But, seriously, how come someone so irritating looks this good? It's not fair. Like, not at all.

He arches a brow, his lips curving into a slow, maddening grin. "Er . . . your hand is touching mine. Are you going to let go of the can?"

"What?" I splutter. "*You* let go of it! I grabbed it first."

"Nope, pretty sure I did."

It's like Jamie has a special talent for pushing my buttons. I've barely said two words to him and already my blood is simmering.

"Ever heard of chivalry?" I huff. "How about being a gentleman and letting the woman have it?"

"Ever heard of *you snooze, you lose*?" he shoots back. "You were standing texting—you've only got yourself to blame. Now, I've got places to be, so if you don't mind." He nods at the can. "Hands off."

"Places to be? Like where? The Bannock Hotel's snug? Wouldn't want to keep all those empty barstools waiting, right?"

I swear Jamie McIntyre brings out the worst in me. Working in the Pheasant, I talk to people day in, day out— locals, tourists, sweet old ladies, lively lads on stag dos, you name it. I get on with everyone: I can always find some common ground for a conversation. But Jamie? No. He's like a scratchy label in my favourite jumper—forever rubbing me the wrong way.

"Ouch." With his free hand, Jamie clutches his chest in mock offence. "That cuts deep, Maisie. But you're right: the snug *is* always dead. That's why *I* need the energy drink. Without it, I'm at risk of dozing off. But the Pheasant? It's always lively in there, so there's no risk of you falling asleep."

"You *could* argue," I say through gritted teeth, "that since the Pheasant actually has customers—and I have to, you know, *work*—I'm the one who could do with the caffeine boost."

"An interesting perspective. Anyway, as fun as this exchange has been, I'd say possession is nine-tenths of the law, so . . ."

With a mischievous smirk, he yanks the can right out of my hand. "Better luck next time."

I gape at him, too stunned to respond. He winks at me then saunters off with the Gaelic Fire, whistling a jaunty tune. He is *unbelievable*.

There's absolutely no way that Jamie McIntyre, the utter *arsehole*, is the witty and considerate gamer I've been playing with these last few months. LochNLoad wouldn't dream of snatching something from a woman's grasp. He's a decent bloke, not an overgrown child.

But then again . . . Gaelic Fire is LochNLoad's drink of choice, and apparently Jamie's too. Bloody hell. I want to write this off as a coincidence, but the universe seems hellbent on forcing me to face facts. Sure, Bannock is small, but what are the chances of both of us being here at the same time, same place, and reaching for the same energy drink—the very day after Iona dropped the bombshell about Jamie's username? It's like some higher power is saying to me: *You can't go on denying it. It's him and, deep down, you know it is. No amount of wishful thinking is going to change that.*

Apparently, Jamie only came in for the can of Gaelic Fire. In the time I've been standing here, silently seething, he's already paid for it and he's now strolling for the door. Right before he leaves, he meets my eye and gives me a smug, triumphant wave goodbye.

The *bastard*. Please, universe, let this be some colossal misunderstanding. Don't let him be LochNLoad. I don't think I could stand it.

Although, at this stage, I reckon I need to know one way or another. I *could* hurry down the street after him and ask him to his face. Or . . . I could take the coward's approach.

I opt for the second option.

I move closer to the shop window, so I can keep Jamie in my line of sight, then pull out my phone. The plan is simple. I'll send Lochie a message via the app we use to organise gaming sessions and chat outside of the game. Then, as I await his usually speedy reply, I'll watch Jamie like a hawk. If a response comes in from Lochie while Jamie's hands aren't anywhere near his phone, I can breathe a sigh of relief.

SASSYLASSIE

Feel like venturing into giant territory tonight? It'd give you a chance to swing about that big sword of yours. 🗡

No sooner have I hit send than Jamie slows to a stop, fishes something out of his pocket, and glances down at it. Seconds later a reply comes in from Lochie.

LOCHNLOAD

You're on! And I'll bring along the Claymore of the Clan Chiefs too. ☺

Well, shit.

The pieces click into place with brutal finality. There can be no more denying it. LochNLoad—my ally, my friend—and Jamie McIntyre are one and the same.

Of all the gamers in all the world, I had to befriend him.

CHAPTER FOUR

MAISIE

I push open my bedroom door, the familiar creak a welcome sound after the long day. With a groan, I flop onto my bed, the springs protesting as I sink into the mattress. It's not time for sleep yet—I'm still dressed and haven't brushed my teeth—but . . . I just need a moment.

What an absolutely shite day.

It was busy in the pub, and at one point Da went missing for a suspiciously long time. I found him struggling with a keg in the cellar, his face red with exertion, his breathing laboured. "I've got it," he insisted, even as his arms trembled under the weight.

"Da, let me—"

"I said I've got it!" he snapped, then immediately looked contrite. "Sorry, Maisie. I just . . . I can manage."

But he couldn't, not really, and we both knew it. When I offered to take over, he bit my head off. I know it's not me he's angry with—it's his own body betraying him. Doesn't make it any easier to deal with, though.

At least there's a silver lining. Da's finally made a doctor's appointment. Not because of my constant pestering, mind you. Oh no. Apparently, all it took was a wee word from Elspeth. I'm grateful, of course, but is it bad that I feel a bit put out? I've been on at him for ages and he's ignored me. Then Elspeth makes a suggestion, and suddenly he's all ears.

Anyway, throw in the whole Jamie-is-LochNLoad debacle and you've got yourself a recipe for utter exhaustion. Physical and emotional.

As if on cue, my phone pings.

LOCHNLOAD

Gaelic Fire: consumed. Giants: quaking in their oversized boots. The only thing missing is my favourite mage. You ready to cause some mayhem, Sass?

I groan. Any other night, I'd be logging in to *Highland Legacy* faster than you can shout "loot drop!" After a day like today, there's nothing I'd love more than to lose myself in a virtual world where my biggest worry is whether I've packed enough health potions.

But I can't play tonight. Not now I know the brawny warrior I've been battling alongside for months is Jamie sodding McIntyre. I'll need to come clean and tell him who I am, of course, but I don't have the energy at the moment for that particular revelation. And I can hardly keep playing with him without telling him the truth, can I? That'd be . . . weird. Really weird.

With a sigh, I type out a reply.

SASSYLASSIE

Sorry, not feeling great tonight. Think I'm gonna have to bail.

I brace myself for some quip from Lochie about how he'd been looking forward to whipping out his massive sword and having a bit of fun with it. Why? Because that's exactly the kind of thing Jamie would say.

LOCHNLOAD

Oh shit, you okay?

I blink at the screen. That's . . . unexpectedly sweet.

Although . . . *is* it? Because it's what I'd have expected LochNLoad to say—he knows when to joke about and when to be serious. It's Jamie McIntyre who hasn't figured that one out yet.

Except . . . LochNLoad *is* Jamie McIntyre. Ugh, this is doing my head in.

LOCHNLOAD

Anything I can do? Want to talk about it?

SASSYLASSIE

I'm all right, just tired. Nothing a good night's sleep won't fix.

LOCHNLOAD

Fair enough. Take care of yourself, okay? I'll be here if you need anything. Even if it's just to listen.

Bloody hell. Where's this version of Jamie whenever he and I are face to face? How can the same person who snatched that Gaelic Fire right out of my hand be so . . . nice?

SASSYLASSIE

Thanks. Night, Lochie.

LOCHNLOAD

Night, Sass. Hope you feel better soon.

I turn off my phone, cutting off any chance of another message from Lochie—or anyone else, for that matter. But even as I set the device aside, I can't stop thinking about the enigma that is Jamie McIntyre.

How is it possible that the same guy who's nothing but a pain in the arse in person can be so supportive online? I mean, look at what happened today. We'd barely locked eyes in the shop before we were at each other's throats. Although . . . okay, maybe that wasn't *entirely* his fault. Maybe I'd been quick to snap too.

But there's history between us. Okay, "history" might be a bit of an exaggeration. We're not talking about stolen kisses in darkened corners or breathless encounters against a wall. No heated whispers; no hands slipping under clothing; no tangled sheets; no wild, desperate moments that leave you wondering how you'll ever look someone in the eye again. Not even close. No, my big drama with Jamie McIntyre? I asked him to dance with me at a ceilidh, and he said no.

I know how it sounds. *Maisie, you daftie, it was just a dance. Get over it already!*

But here's the thing. I'm good at chatting with folk—it goes hand in hand with my job in the pub, after all. But when it comes to relationships? Let's just say I'm not exactly fighting off suitors with a stick. Maybe it's because I still live with my da, which isn't really a selling point. Or maybe it's because while I can banter with the best of them, actual flirting? That's a whole other kettle of fish.

So, asking Jamie for a dance at a ceilidh—specifically, the engagement ceilidh of his eldest brother, Ally? That was me putting myself out there. And he said no.

Which is . . . fine. That's his right. But then he came back later and asked me for a pity dance because Emily, Ally's then fiancée and now wife, guilt-tripped him into it. Talk about adding insult to injury.

Still, I could've got over that if it weren't for the fact that Jamie is just so . . . Jamie. Always joking, always teasing, never knowing when to quit. It's not just me: everyone in his family—no, everyone in the *town*—moans about him. He lives to wind people up, to make them squirm.

So now, whenever I interact with him, it feels like he's laughing at me. Like he's thinking, *Remember when you asked me to dance and I said no? Wasn't that hilarious?*

But do you know what the worst part is? Two years later, and I still find him attractive. It's maddening. You'd think by now I'd have developed an aversion to his stupid handsome face. And maybe if I lived somewhere bigger and with more single young men, I would have. But no, I'm stuck in Bannock, where the dating pool is about as deep as a puddle. And so my traitorous eyes keep drifting back to Jamie.

So there you have it. I'm attracted to a relentless tease who winds me up something chronic, and I can't seem to get over it.

God, I could *really* do with killing some monsters right now.

Seeing as logging in to *Highland Legacy* is off the table, I decide to resort to my other tried-and-true coping mechanism—dyeing my hair. For me, nothing screams "I'm in charge of my life" like a dramatic change in hair colour. It's previously been purple, teal, cherry red, and green, although the green didn't work out so well. Most recently I went fuchsia, but it's now a rather faded pink.

Usually, I change my hair to mark some kind of big moment. Well, finding out that the charming, witty LochN-

Load is actually the most annoying person in Bannock? That qualifies as a big moment in my book. What I'm feeling now? It's grief, pure and simple. LochNLoad was my friend—until I found out who he really is.

I've had my heart set on navy blue for ages and even bought the kit a while back. I was just waiting for the right time, and this is it. Let's do this.

◆ ◆ ◆

I stare at my reflection in the bathroom mirror, tilting my head left, then right. My hair is now a deep inky shade of blue that shimmers under the light like magpie feathers.

Bold. Dramatic. Perfect for a woman having a crisis in the wee hours of a Wednesday morning.

The crime scene around me tells its own story: navy splatters across the sink, streaks on the floor tiles, and . . . oh no. My poor, poor white towel. R.I.P., little guy. You were too pure for this world (and for navy dye).

I'll have to clean this all up before bed, but still, it was worth it. This change isn't just cosmetic—it's symbolic. Like shedding an old skin.

Tomorrow—well, later today, really, as it's after midnight— I'll deal with Jamie McIntyre. I'll seek him out and tell him what's what, face to face. It's going to be shit but it has to be done.

At least I'll get to wind him up about his power-play kink. In this life you have to look out for the silver linings. Sometimes they're the only things that get you through.

CHAPTER FIVE

JAMIE

I pause at the summit of Ben Garve and, panting lightly, take in the view, Bruce wagging his tail beside me like he's just conquered Everest. The morning sun filters through patchy clouds, lighting up the endless green below in bursts of gold. In the distance a cluster of Highland cows graze lazily in a field, a scattering of ginger dots against the lush grass.

Okay, the scenery in *Highland Legacy* looks amazing, but I've got to admit, it's nothing compared to the real deal. There are no dodgy frame rates here, nor wonky textures—just raw beauty. And the air has that perfect, crisp quality that makes you feel like you're doing something healthy simply by breathing it in. Plus, unlike in the game, there are no goblins lurking behind boulders ready to ambush me. Although, to be fair, that does add a certain thrill.

I take a few moments to catch my breath, then Bruce and I head back down, Bruce occasionally heading off to sniff furiously at some mystery scent that has caught his attention. Rabbit tracks, maybe? On the horizon, a few darker, more ominous clouds gather. With any luck, I'll be back at the hotel before they crash the party.

Near the bottom, the hill is dotted with free-roaming sheep, so I clip Bruce's lead on—just in case he fancies himself a sheepdog and decides to do a bit of herding. Barely a minute later, his body goes rigid, like he's caught wind of something *very* important. His ears perk up, his nose twitches madly, then his tail kicks into overdrive—wagging so fast it practically blurs.

"What is it, boy?" I say, following his line of sight.

And that's when I spot her. A woman cresting one of the dips in the hillside and heading our way—her face familiar, though her hair now a striking shade of navy blue. That's new.

When we get closer to one another, I groan and say—loudly enough for Maisie to hear—"Typical, you come out here to escape everything, yet you end up bumping into someone you know."

She rolls her eyes. "I *would* say it's nice to see you, Jamie, but, well . . ." She crouches down and fusses over Bruce. "It is, however, wonderful to see *you*, you gorgeous boy. Lucky me meeting you two days in a row, eh? What a friendly dog you are—so unlike the man walking you." She scratches behind his ears, and Bruce melts under her touch, the big traitor that he is. "Have Lewis and Iona palmed you off on this grump today? Och, that's a shame. Elspeth is a better dog walker, isn't she? Oh, yes she is."

"If you're going to take a dig at me, at least do it to my face rather than through Bruce. What's the matter, anyway—have you not had a Gaelic Fire today? Oh wait"—I gasp and slap a hand over my mouth—"that's right, you were too slow to grab one yesterday. You poor thing!"

Straightening, Maisie fixes me with a steely green-eyed glare.

"Still can't believe you snatched it out of my hand. Who does that?"

"A dashing rogue with lightning-fast reflexes and impeccable taste in energy drinks?"

"Hmm, if 'dashing rogue' is code for 'insufferable prat', that sounds about right."

I smirk. "Touché! Anyway, there's something different about you today, but what is it?" Stroking my chin like some cartoon villain plotting world domination, I let my gaze travel up and down Maisie's figure, taking in her oversized open zippy hoodie with sleeves bunched up to the elbows; her cropped stripy T-shirt, which shifts as she moves, offering fleeting glimpses of pale skin that are rather distracting; her black skinny jeans with a tear across one knee; and her scuffed blue trainers.

A faint—and kind of cute—blush rises to her cheeks, and she crosses her arms defensively, though it just makes me notice how the cuffs of her hoodie are frayed, like she's spent countless hours absent-mindedly tugging at them. Lowering her eyes, she pushes a strand of navy-blue hair behind her left ear, briefly revealing a small Celtic knot tattoo on her neck that I've never noticed before.

"Is that . . . a new hoodie?" I say eventually.

Her eyes fly back up to meet mine, and she lets out an exasperated huff. "It's my hair, you muppet. It's blue now."

"*Really?*" I tap my chin. "No, I could have sworn it was blue yesterday as well."

"Do you never get tired of constantly being a pain in the arse?"

"I think we both know I'm delightfully charming."

"Nope, far from it. *Anyway* . . . I'm a little surprised to see you out in the open air. Word on the street is you spend most of your time in the snug, ignoring the few customers you have and tapping away at a laptop."

"Aye, well, Lewis gave me two options this morning: either walk Bruce or sort through a bunch of invoices from suppliers. It was a close call but I decided to give the great outdoors a whirl. And I've actually really been enjoying the view—so serene, so timeless, so utterly ruined by someone who looks like they lost a fight with a blueberry pie."

"*You* . . ." Maisie splutters then shakes her head. "I have no words. I just—no words. Anyway, there's no point dragging this out longer than necessary so let me cut to it. When you're on your laptop, you play games, right? Iona mentioned you play *Highland Legacy*?"

"Er, aye. Why?"

"Well—"

Suddenly Bruce lunges forwards with a force that nearly yanks the lead out of my hand. "Oi, Bruce!" I yell, stumbling after him. "Heel!"

He's spotted a rabbit—a small brown blur that's darted out from the undergrowth. Apparently, bolting after it is a lot more important than listening to me. The daft dog drags me right into Maisie's personal space, at which point the rabbit abruptly changes direction, looping back towards the undergrowth.

"Wait! Bruce, no—" My words are useless. Single-minded and oblivious, Bruce follows, his lead wrapping around Maisie and me and then pulling taut, yanking us together so that Maisie's slender frame presses flush against me, our legs caught in a tangle, her fingers digging into my biceps, gripping them for balance.

I gulp. "Er . . . well, this is kind of intimate, eh?"

All right, Jamie, definitely don't think about how her head fits perfectly under your chin like it's meant to be there. Just focus on untangling the lead.

But before I can figure out how to do that, Bruce delivers another powerful tug, and with my legs tied together, I don't stand a chance of remaining upright.

"Shit!" The world tips, then my back slams into the ground, knocking the wind out of me—then *she* lands on me with a startled yelp, her face barely an inch from mine.

Her wide eyes stare down at me, and it's like she can't decide whether to laugh or kill me. Meanwhile, I can't help but be acutely aware of every point of contact between our bodies, and of her hair brushing my cheek, and of her lips so close I can feel her breath warming my skin.

For the love of God, Jamie, get a grip! Don't be some weirdo perv.

Okay, but what do I do? Maybe crack a joke?

No! For once in your life, don't do that. How about apologising? Asking if she's okay?

I clear my throat. "You know, if you'd wanted to throw yourself at me, you could have just asked."

"Ugh! *You*," Maisie hisses, "are the absolute worst!" She pushes herself upright—not an easy feat when, thanks to Bruce, it's like she and I are in some three-legged race that has gone horribly wrong. As she wriggles and squirms to free herself, her knee digs into my stomach, forcing a grunt out of me, but if she notices, she doesn't care.

"This is just . . . argh!" Maisie tugs frantically at the lead while very deliberately avoiding eye contact with me and grumbling curses that would make even a sailor blush. And, talking of blushing, I can't help but notice her face has turned a rather bright shade of pink.

She finally manages to untangle herself then scrambles to her feet. Dusting off her jeans, she glares at me, muttering something I don't quite catch—which is probably for the best.

As I attempt to wrestle the lead off of me, Bruce pads over with what can only be described as an apologetic grin and proceeds to smother my face with enthusiastic, slobbery licks.

"Oi, Bruce! Stop—" I sputter, trying and failing to push him away.

Eventually I manage to free myself, from both the lead and Bruce, but as soon as I stand up straight, a sharp pain shoots through my left thigh. Aw, shit. The fall must have caused my old injury to flare up. Before I can stop myself, I let out a hiss through gritted teeth.

"Are you all right?" Maisie's lips twitch with amusement. "Did I land on your balls or something? Is that why you're pulling that face?"

"Nope, my balls are fine, thank you very much." I keep my tone breezy and plaster on what I hope is a neutral expression. But bloody hell, my thigh feels like someone has taken a hammer to it. *Don't wince, Jamie!*

"Shame. I was hoping for a bit of karmic justice after your blueberry pie comment."

I manage a half-smile but I've lost the mood for banter. Honestly, I'd almost rather she *had* squished my nuts. Better that than this, I reckon.

It's an obvious thing to say but real life isn't like a video game. In *Highland Legacy* injuries can be healed by downing a potion or asking a friendly mage to cast a spell, but in reality old wounds come back to haunt you, no matter how many years have passed. Isn't it enough that my injury robbed me of the one thing I actually wanted to do with my life? Does it have to go on claiming even more from me? I *hate* feeling weak and vulnerable, but that's exactly how I feel right now.

Despite my best efforts to play things cool, Maisie's face melts into concern—which is *so* much worse than her teasing me. I can handle her taking the mick. What I'm not okay with is her feeling sorry for me.

"Are you all right?" she asks. "If you're actually hurt and I was messing around, I'm so sorry. Do you want to sit down for a bit? Or can I help you back to the hotel, maybe?"

Jesus Christ! I don't want her pity.

"I'm fine," I say, my voice sharper than I intended. She flinches at my tone. Aw crap, I'm making a mess of this.

I take a deep breath and try to soften my voice. "Look, I'm going to go. Sorry about Bruce and the fall and . . . you know, the comment about your hair. It was a stupid thing to say. It's nice—really. But . . . well . . ." I'm not sure what else to add so I simply say, "See you later, okay?"

And with that, I turn from her and set off with Bruce.

"Wait!" she calls after me. "There's something I want to say to you. Why don't we walk down together and we can chat on the way?"

Shit. No, I need to get away from Maisie right now, not spend more time with her. I just . . . need to be alone. Ideally at home, where I can pop a few painkillers then lose myself in a virtual world where injuries don't linger. But since I'm no good at explaining that, I resort to old habits.

"You know," I say, turning back, "I was only being polite about your hair. It looks like Smurf cosplay gone wrong. Honestly, it's a bit tragic."

Maisie blinks in stunned silence, her mouth opening like she's about to fire something back—but nothing comes out. She just stares at me, her cheeks flaming.

Shit. That was too much.

But instead of apologising, what do I do? I ram one hand into my pocket, tighten my grip on Bruce's lead with the other, and mutter over my shoulder, "See you around."

I don't dare look back.

CHAPTER SIX

MAISIE

When I arrive back at the Pheasant, my mind is still reeling from the encounter with Jamie on Ben Garve. It's barely past noon and the pub isn't open yet. Outside of the summer high season, we don't open till four on weekdays.

"Da?" I call out, my voice echoing in the empty pub.

"In the back!" comes the reply.

I find him in the small office behind the bar, doing some paperwork. Literal paperwork. Sometimes I think he's allergic to anything with a power button.

He looks up, faint lines of exhaustion framing his green eyes and a slight tremor in his hands betraying itself as he sets down his pen. He's always been the strongest man I know—my rock. But rocks wear down eventually, don't they? Which scares me more than I care to admit.

"How'd it go at the doctor's?" I perch on the edge of his desk. "I still wish you'd let me come with you."

Da waves a dismissive hand. "Och, I'm a grown man, Maisie. I can handle a wee doctor's appointment on my own."

I bite my tongue, resisting the urge to point out that he's

been putting off this "wee appointment" for months. "So, what did they say?"

He sighs, leaning back. "Well, the doc reckons it might be rheumatoid arthritis. She wants to do some more tests to be sure."

"Rheumatoid arthritis?" It's a relief to have a name for what's been plaguing Da, but it doesn't make it any easier to hear. "What does that mean, exactly?"

"It means I'm getting old," Da says with a wry smile. "But it's nothing to fash yourself about. Once they've got the diagnosis confirmed, there's medication I can take to ease some of the symptoms."

I nod. "And . . . maybe there should also be some lifestyle changes? Did the GP talk about slowing down at all? Resting more?"

Da picks his pen back up and fiddles with it. "Well, she might have said something about that—about 'recognising my physical limitations'—but I reckon once the medication is doing its job, I'll be just fine."

I see an opening and decide to take it. "Maybe this is a good time to think about hiring some extra help? It'd take some of the pressure off you, and—"

"Maisie," Da cuts me off, his tone sharp. "I've been running this pub for longer than you've been alive. A little arthritis isn't going to stop me."

"I know, Da, but—"

"But nothing. We've managed fine until now. We don't need to be wasting money on additional staff."

My frustration bubbles up. Our tiny team just isn't enough. A couple of chefs covering evening meals between them. One extra pair of hands behind the bar on weekends. And a cleaner coming in only a few hours a week. "It's not a waste if it helps you, Da. And it's not just about you. The pub—"

"The pub"—Da's voice rises—"is my responsibility. I'm the manager here, Maisie, not you."

I bite my lip, hard. The urge to argue with him is strong but I swallow it down. "I'm only trying to help," I say eventually.

Da's expression softens. "I know. But I've got this under control. You don't need to worry."

But I *do* worry. I worry every time I see him wince as he lifts a crate. Every time I catch him massaging his hands when he thinks no one's looking. Every time I have to cover for him because he's too proud to admit he needs a break.

"All right, Da." I stand. "Just . . . promise me you'll think about it? Please?"

He's already turning back to his paperwork. "Aye, I'll think about it."

I leave the office, closing the door behind me, and rest my elbows on the bar, where I drum my fingers on the well-worn surface as though that might drum some sense into him by proxy. I love my Da, I really do. But sometimes he can drive me absolutely mad.

Right, tea. A good cuppa can solve everything, or at least that's what my maw always used to say. She passed away when I was nine, but her wisdom lives on.

I climb the stairs to the flat and, once inside, make straight for the kettle. As it boils, I replay the morning's events in my head. Most of the time Jamie had been his usual irritating self— utterly insufferable—but there *had* been a moment when he'd apologised to me and actually seemed sincere about it. He'd even complimented my hair. And then, just seconds later, he'd delivered that cutting remark about me looking like a Smurf. Talk about emotional whiplash.

Besides, Smurfs have blue skin, not blue hair. In fact, Smurfette is a bloody blonde! If you're going to throw out an insult, at least get your facts right.

I pull down a mug, toss in a teabag, top it with steaming water, then add a splash of milk. Ugh, men! Jamie is all smug one-liners, Da all unbending stubbornness. Honestly, how do they not wear themselves out? Just being around them is exhausting.

Through in the living room, I curl up on the sofa with my tea. I reckon I could do with a dose of girl power right now, so I lift my phone and open the "Scottish Sirens" group chat—a sacred space for me and my two besties, Iona Stewart and Cat McIntyre.

MAISIE

Ladies, I am having A DAY. Someone please distract me with some classic Siren shenanigans.

Within moments the words *Cat is typing . . .* appear.

CAT

Caught two students making out in a supply cupboard yesterday. Naturally, I yelled, "This is NOT Love Island!" The lad turned bright red and tried to explain they were practising "dialogue" for Romeo and Juliet . . . while his hand was on her arse.

MAISIE

LOL! I mean, at least they're committed to their roles, right?

Cat is a bit of a party animal. Until last year she lived down in Glasgow with Iona, where she enjoyed all that city life has to offer. Now, though, she's stuck up north in a town that's even more remote than Bannock. She's slogging through her probationary year as a secondary school English teacher, and with just a few months left on her contract, I'd bet good money she's counting down the days until she can escape.

Growing up, I thought of Iona as the Hermione Granger of Bannock, minus the magic wand. Her nose was always buried in a book—when she wasn't hanging out with her best friend, Lewis McIntyre, of course. It wasn't until she moved back last year and we grew closer that I discovered her professional exterior as a farm vet hides quite the naughty streak.

Cat is the baby of the McIntyre clan, the only girl among

four siblings. Ally is the eldest brother, Lewis the middle one, and the youngest is . . . Jamie.

My thumb hovers over my phone. I do have goss I could share—the rather colossal revelation that my mysterious online gaming buddy is none other than Cat's brother Jamie. But . . . I can't drop that bombshell quite yet. He may be an infuriating arse, but even so, Jamie deserves to be the first to hear that.

But there's nothing stopping me from telling the girls about the little run-in I had with him earlier.

Rolling my eyes but secretly delighted by her enthusiasm, I snap a quick selfie and fire it off to the group chat.

IONA

Maisie, you look incredible! 😍

CAT

Oh my God, YES! That colour is stunning on you. It's perfect!

MAISIE

Thanks, girls. I needed that boost. Because Jamie told me I look like a Smurf. 🙄

CAT

He did WHAT? Just when I think he's hit rock bottom, he grabs a shovel and keeps on digging. Want me to kick him next time I'm home? Because I will. Happily.

IONA

Even by Jamie's standards, that's completely out of order. I'll have a word with Lewis—he'll sort Jamie out.

MAISIE

No, honestly, it's fine. I'm used to his nonsense by now. Just wanted to vent.

CAT

Fair enough, but I'll kick him next time I see him anyway. 😊 Remember, you're a queen and that hair is hot! 🔥 👑

As I'm about to reply, another notification pops up. Speak of the devil . . .

I decided yesterday that it'd be too weird to go on playing with LochNLoad, but attempting to tell Jamie my identity in person was a complete disaster. Talking with LochNLoad online, on the other hand? That's something I've always found easy to do, so maybe that'd be a better way to approach this.

I reply in the affirmative, tell the girls I have to go, then grab my laptop and set it up on the kitchen table. When I log in, LochNLoad's warrior avatar is already waiting near the portcullis of a crumbling stone keep that's perched atop a misty cliff. My own character materialises by his side.

Okay, okay, I'll tell Jamie who I am in a moment, but after his comments to me earlier today, I reckon I'm entitled to tease him a little. It's only fair.

Actually, Iona once let slip that Lewis is rather blessed in that department—but that doesn't mean his wee brother is too.

I blink at the screen. Wait, is he talking about me? Before I can stop myself, I type:

LochNLoad fires back his single-word response without even a moment's hesitation. Which is weird because Jamie's never shown any sign of being attracted to me in real life. Could he have made a fool of himself in front of two women today? Is it the other one he thinks is pretty?

My fingers hover over the keyboard. I'm honestly not sure what to say next.

LOCHNLOAD

Hello? Sass? You still there? Don't tell me
you're jealous.

SASSYLASSIE

LOCHNLOAD

Uh-oh. Sounds serious. Should I be
worried?

SASSYLASSIE

CHAPTER SEVEN

JAMIE

I'm back in the snug, nursing a pint and staring at my laptop screen. It's just me and Bruce in here, and he's sprawled out on his dog bed, snoring gently, his paws twitching as though he's chasing rabbits in his dreams. Rain patters against the window.

Painkillers downed, I've logged in to *Highland Legacy*, Sass is here too, and it's time for a bit of escapism. Although . . . I'm less interested in escaping the ache in my thigh and more interested in escaping the chaos running riot in my head. There's the obvious regret over being such an arse towards Maisie. Seriously, what is wrong with me?

But there's also the memory of us crashing into each other and her landing on top of me. I can still feel the heat of her body against mine, the softness of her slim curves. It's been ages since I've been that close to a woman, and the encounter has stirred up feelings I'm not entirely sure what to do with. I can't decide whether I want to push them away or . . . well, dwell on them obsessively.

I take a swig of my beer and focus back on the chat with SassyLassie. She asked if the girl I made a tit of myself in front of was pretty, and I typed "Aye" without even needing to think about it. Because Maisie *is* pretty. More than pretty, if I'm being honest.

God, why did I have to go and insult her hair? I really am an idiot.

Anyway, Sass has gone a wee bit quiet on me, so I decide to be just a little mischievous.

LOCHNLOAD

Hello? Sass? You still there? Don't tell me you're jealous.

SASSYLASSIE

In your dreams. Although . . . actually, there's something we need to talk about.

LOCHNLOAD

Uh-oh. Sounds serious. Should I be worried?

SASSYLASSIE

Er . . . well . . .

LOCHNLOAD

Oh! I know what this is. You're going to tell me your secret kink, right? Because I told you mine and I've been waiting for you to confess yours.

Fine, there's no point trying to deny it: I've got sex on the brain today. And not even *Highland Legacy*—the one thing that usually works—seems capable of distracting me.

SASSYLASSIE

No, it's not that. It's something else.

LOCHNLOAD

Aw, c'mon! Why don't you tell me your secret kink first, THEN you can tell me the other thing?

I don't usually take things in a sexual direction when I'm winding up Sass—I don't want to be that guy who makes women regret gaming online. But she kicked off the whole secret kink chat—and she was literally *just* ticking the piss about the size of my dick—so I reckon fair's fair.

SASSYLASSIE

This is important, Lochie.

LOCHNLOAD

And your secret kink isn't?

I find myself wondering what SassyLassie looks like. It's not the first time I've pondered this, of course, but now the curiosity is more intense. Seeing Maisie so close, with every little detail of her face laid bare, has sparked something in me, like a match striking against tinder.

SASSYLASSIE

Lochie!

LOCHNLOAD

Okay, okay, but . . . c'mon, I told you mine days ago. Now it's your turn!

SASSYLASSIE

. . .

LOCHNLOAD

Go on, throw me a bone here! Just tell me something you find kinda hot. It's only right!

SASSYLASSIE

. . . I suppose that is fair. If I tell you, will you
actually listen to what I need to say?

LOCHNLOAD

I promise.

SASSYLASSIE

All right, well, you know the Highland
Legacy TV series? The one you refuse to
watch even though you're obsessed with
the game? Season two, episode seven.
That's all I'm saying.

LOCHNLOAD

God, that isn't the one where Ronan Dunbar
gets his willy out, is it? Everyone is always
going on and on about that. It's part of the
reason I've never watched the show.

SASSYLASSIE

Nope, that's season three, episode four,
thirty-two minutes in.

LOCHNLOAD

Bloody hell! You know the timestamp?

SASSYLASSIE

Clearly. But as for what happens in season
two, episode seven . . . if you want to know,
you'll just have to watch it for yourself.

LOCHNLOAD

Tease! But all right, I'll accept that as an
answer. Now spill—what was it you were
going to tell me?

Just as I'm about to find out what Sass's big revelation is, Lewis strolls into the snug, followed by Emily. She's the wife of my eldest brother, Ally. A petite brunette, she's currently five months pregnant with nephew number two. She helps Lewis with the running of the hotel.

"Er, guys, do you mind?" I joke, gesturing around the empty snug. "I'm trying to work here."

Lewis and Emily exchange a look that screams, *We are not amused.*

"We need to talk," Lewis says.

Bloody hell, what is it with people needing to talk to me today? Before SassyLassie can hit me with whatever life-changing bombshell she's typing, I fire off *BRB* then snap my laptop shut.

"I'm all ears." I take a sip of my beer then gesture to the barstools opposite me. "Go on then, take a seat. What's this about?"

Lewis eyes my pint glass. "You're drinking on the job again? And this early?"

"I need to serve *someone*, don't I? Else I'd go mad. I *had* been thinking of pouring myself a whisky, but I reckoned I'd knock that back in no time then pour myself another, so instead I'm slowly sipping a beer. This is me being responsible."

Just as Lewis is about to unleash what I'm sure would be a spectacular bollocking, Bruce lets out a loud yawn and stretches. Distracted, Lewis glances down at the dog, who trots over to him with his tail wagging like a furry metronome.

Lewis just can't help himself. He drops to one knee and fusses over his pet, and Bruce rolls onto his back, paws in the air, begging for a belly rub. Lewis happily obliges, of course. "Who's a good boy?" His voice jumps an entire octave—proof his balls have temporarily vacated the premises. "You are! Yes, you are!"

Emily catches my eye and we share a smile. The way Lewis dotes on Iona is sickening. The way he dotes on Bruce? Barely any better.

When Lewis eventually straightens, the fire has gone out of his eyes—at least for now. "All right, where were we? Oh aye, we were about to sit down." He eyes Emily's bump. "Is the bar okay, or would you rather a table?"

"The bar is fine," Emily insists. She and Lewis settle onto the stools.

"So . . . the snug," Lewis says.

I lift my beer and take a slow sip, partly to see if I can get under Lewis's skin again, but he doesn't take the bait. "What about it?" I ask.

Lewis rubs the back of his neck. "Well . . ." With his other hand, he taps a finger on the bar. "Er . . ."

Emily steps in. "Lewis and I have been looking at the profitability of different aspects of the business. And there's one part that isn't doing as well as we'd like."

I know the answer but I ask the question anyway: "And that is . . . ?"

Emily presses her lips together, while Lewis shifts on his stool. The silence stretches just long enough to make its point.

"But everyone loves the snug!" I protest, even though the empty chairs and tables don't exactly support my case. "You're not thinking of closing it, are you?"

Lewis pulls a face, his features twisting into something awkward and vaguely apologetic. "We've not made any final decisions yet, but having you run the place is a significant investment of time and money, and . . . we're not sure it's pulling in enough to justify the cost."

Emily says, "We need to consider whether this space could better serve the guests—and maybe generate more income at the same time." Her tone is gentle but practical.

"Of course, we won't be getting rid of a bar entirely," Lewis adds. "For events like wedding receptions, we'd absolutely still have you serving drinks, either here or maybe we could set up something in the function room instead. But I just don't know that we can continue having the snug open on days like today when it's so very . . . quiet."

Crap. I can't deny it's a cushy job. Lounging in an empty bar, messing about on a video game, and drinking beer—which, let's face it, the hotel is technically paying for—isn't exactly strenuous, but . . .

"Hey, someone's got to keep Bruce company, right?" I say.

Lewis's expression hardens. "This is a business, Jamie. And sure, it's a family one, and I'm very happy for you to work here but . . . you're twenty-five now. At some point you're going to have to start pulling your weight a bit more. We can't drag you through life indefinitely, doing all the hard work while you just sit here playing games."

His words hit home hard, largely because they ring true. I hate that he has a point.

Before I can respond, Elspeth sticks her head into the snug, wiping her hands on a tea towel. "Oh, should I be at this meeting?"

"Er, no," Lewis says. "Always nice to see you, Elspeth, but this meeting is about the snug. It doesn't really impact your side of things."

Elspeth has been the chef at the hotel's wee restaurant since before I was born. She was my maw's closest friend, and since I lost my parents when I was eighteen, she's looked out for me and my siblings, in addition to always being there for her own two, Iona and Aidan.

Despite Lewis's comment about the meeting not being for her, Elspeth steps into the snug properly to give Bruce a quick pat, earning herself a tail thump against the floorboards. "Well, don't be too hard on the lad," she says to Lewis and Emily. "Someone's got to keep that stool warm, eh?" With a wink at me, she leaves just as quickly as she arrived.

I tap my finger against the rim of my pint glass and glance around the snug—the low wooden beams, the mismatched chairs, Bruce curled up on his dog bed like he owns the place. Quiet? Aye. But this is a special spot. It's not just some old room in a hotel that can be changed to something else willy-nilly. It's mine in a way I can't quite explain, a place I've always felt at home. Growing up, Da and I used to watch rugby together here, for God's sake. I had my first drink here. We can't just close the snug. This is where I sit, and if Lewis and Emily think I'm giving up this stool without one hell of a fight, they've got another thing coming.

Okay, maybe I haven't been pulling my weight—they're right about that. And maybe, just maybe, I haven't minded the lack of customers all that much. It does mean fewer interruptions from *Highland Legacy*, after all. But damn it, I *can* try harder, can't I?

"What if I turn this place around?" I blurt out. "Make it busier? If we're raking in more cash and it feels less"—I wave a hand at the empty chairs—"like a funeral parlour, would you consider keeping it open?"

Lewis arches a sceptical brow. Emily casts him a sidelong glance.

"Well . . ." she says slowly. "If you could make this place more profitable and . . . livelier, then yes, I suppose we'd reconsider. Right, Lewis?"

He nods. "But, Jamie, that'd involve you actually doing a bit of hard graft. You're not going to change the snug's fortunes by sitting on your arse playing games. Emily and I aren't going to do the work for you, so if you're serious about turning this place around, you'll need to put together a plan showing us how. You'll also need to prove to us you're willing to roll up your sleeves and get stuck in. If, in a few days, nothing has changed and you're still just pissing your life away in some virtual world, Emily and I will push ahead with our own ideas."

"Warning received loud and clear." I lift my glass in a mock toast to them. "You know, I've been waiting for you two to give me a kick up the arse. It's about time you got your act together."

Lewis groans. "Aye, *we're* the ones who needed to get our act together. Right."

"I'll be rooting for you, Jamie." Emily's lips twitch with the hint of a smile and she leans forwards. "I'd love for you to prove us wrong and show us how amazing this place can be."

"You can have the rest of the week to mull it over, but I want to hear at least one good idea from you by Monday." Lewis stands, his chair scraping against the floorboards, loud enough to make Bruce lift his head briefly before settling back down again. "If not, it's goodbye to the snug."

"Challenge accepted."

After they're gone, I rake a hand through my hair and wonder just what I've got myself into. Then, remembering SassyLassie had something important to say, I flip my laptop open again. I'm still connected to the game and my last message, *BRB*, sits there unanswered. Looks like she's been waiting for me to return before spilling the beans.

LOCHNLOAD

Sorry about that! Just had an "interesting" meeting. Long story short, it looks like I'll have less time for gaming going forward — real life is calling.

I need to step up at work, bring in more customers, maybe even poach some from the competition down the road. 😂

Anyway, what was it you wanted to tell me?

CHAPTER EIGHT

MAISIE

The message stares back at me like it's a ticking bomb I'm utterly unequipped to defuse.

I read it once, twice, three times. With each reread, it hits me a little harder, like someone squeezing my chest tighter and tighter. "The competition down the road" can only mean one place: the Pheasant. The snug and the Pheasant are the only two drinking establishments in Bannock itself. Sure, there's the Glen Garve Resort a few miles out with its posh cocktail bar, and the distillery nearby with its tiny tasting room, but here in town? It's just us and them.

Which means . . . Jamie is planning to steal customers from the Pheasant? From me and Da?

My thoughts trip over each other. Is telling him who I am really such a great idea when he's just announced he has plans to sabotage my business? Maybe I should try to find out more first.

SASSYLASSIE

> That's a shame you won't have as much time for gaming. Interesting about your work, though. How are you planning to bring in new customers?

There. Casual. Breezy. Totally not fishing for information.

LOCHNLOAD

> LOL. Will need some time to think about that. Also, we don't normally share personal details like that, remember? Just our secret kinks. 😁

SASSYLASSIE

> Right. Of course.

LOCHNLOAD

> So . . . the news? The big deal? What is it? I'm braced for a bombshell.

Oh God. Right. That.

I chew on my bottom lip so hard it's a miracle I don't bite clean through. Shit. He's got me there. I *did* say I had something to tell him—and now he expects me to deliver.

SASSYLASSIE

> Oh . . . never mind. Wasn't important after all.

LOCHNLOAD

> What? But you said it was important. You were literally worried about how I was going to react.

Crap, crap, crap, crap, crap.

I was just being dramatic. You know me! It honestly wasn't such a big deal, really.

???

My conscience shrieks at me: *Maisie! Tell him who you are. Be honest!*

But then another voice chimes in, a more pragmatic one: *You've just found out he wants to take customers away from the Pheasant. Are you sure telling him is wise right now?*

Before I can decide which voice is right, a loud crash echoes up from downstairs. What the hell was that?

Sorry, something's come up IRL. Got to go!

I don't wait for his response before logging off then rushing downstairs and into the pub.

A battered cardboard case lies on its side near the bar, whisky pooling out from it. My nose smarts at the heady mix of sweet malt and oak.

Da and Kyle from the distillery stand on either side of the dropped case. Da's face is redder than the tie he wears every December, while Kyle looks equal parts baffled and exasperated, clutching his delivery clipboard like it's a shield against Da's wrath.

"You said you had it!" Kyle insists.

"No, you let go too soon!" Da's hands tremble slightly but his voice is firm.

Kyle blinks at him. "With all due respect, Bryce—"

"Are you really going to pin this on me?" Da interrupts. "I'm clumsy, am I? Is that what you're saying?"

"No," Kyle replies carefully, looking like he wishes he were literally anywhere else.

I step forwards before this can escalate any further. "Right, what's going on here?"

Both men turn to me. Kyle's expression brightens like I've just handed him a get-out-of-jail-free card, while Da scowls like I've suggested pairing a single malt with Irn-Bru.

"Well . . ." Kyle gestures to the mess on the floor. "The crate, er . . . slipped."

"Because *you* let go too soon," Da says. "My daughter and I will not be signing for a box of broken whisky bottles."

Bloody hell. Between being called a Smurf, discovering Jamie might be planning to steal customers from us, and now this mess, I think it's clear the universe is out to get me today.

"Da." I look him squarely in the eye and soften my voice. "Why don't you go sit down for five minutes? Let me handle this."

"There's nothing to handle," he huffs. "We're not signing for whisky we can't sell, and that's final."

I try to summon the same patience I use when handling drunken pub-goers. "Please, Da," I say, my tone even gentler now.

His jaw tightens as if preparing for battle, but then something in my expression must get through to him because he finally relents.

"Fine," he mutters. With one last glance at the whisky puddle on the floor—a mistake that'll likely cost us as much as a whole month of grocery shopping—he stalks off to the office.

"Sorry about that," I tell Kyle once we're alone. "I'll sign for the bottles."

"You don't have to do that. I'm sure we can work something out, Maisie."

"It's fine." I hold out a hand for the clipboard, attempting a casual smile. The distillery is an important supplier and we need to maintain good relations with them. Besides, although Da would rather swallow glass than admit it, I reckon the rheumatoid arthritis may have played a role in this. It's not fair to expect the distillery to cover the breakage.

"Look," Kyle says, "here's what I'm going to do. I'll charge you for the broken crate at cost price. When you order a replacement, I'll give you that at cost price too. All right?"

I'm not too proud to turn down this offer. "Thanks, Kyle." It's still a costly blunder, but that does take the sting out of it a wee bit.

We sort out the paperwork then Kyle makes to leave. "Oh, by the way, you should have got an email about it, but we're doing a tasting event for clients at the distillery soon. You or your da should come along."

"Aye, sounds good. One of us will be there." In my head I'm already debating whether it'd be riskier to send Da or leave him here unsupervised. Neither option seems great.

Once Kyle's gone, I haul the dripping, soggy crate to the bin then grab the mop and bucket from the supply cupboard. I'm halfway through cleaning up when Da reappears, hands shoved into his pockets, jaw tight.

"I'll take over," he says gruffly.

"It's fine, Da." I wring out the mop and focus on wiping the floor. "I've got it."

"I'm not over the hill yet, you know."

I pause and look up at him. "I never said you were."

He gives me a curt nod then steps behind the bar and busies himself rearranging glasses, even though they're probably already perfectly aligned.

As I pour the bucket into the sink, it's hard not to think of the money going quite literally down the drain. I think, in future, it'd be better if I handled deliveries, but that discussion will have to wait until another day. He's just told me he's not "over the hill" yet—I'm not about to bring up anything he might consider an attack.

My mind wanders back to Jamie—LochNLoad—and our unfinished conversation. The thought of him trying to poach our customers on top of everything else . . . it's too much. Don't get me wrong, I *want* to tell him who I am but . . . maybe it'd be smarter not to rush things? I mean, if I can use our online friendship to figure out what he has planned, then . . . that just makes sense, doesn't it? It'd be better to be prepared for what might be coming. I'm only looking out for me and Da.

I *will* tell him soon. Just . . . not quite yet.

CHAPTER NINE

JAMIE

My shift at the snug over, I make my way upstairs. The hotel has settled into its usual nightly hush, just the occasional creak of old wood and the faint hum of the boiler keeping me company. Once in my room, I kick off my shoes, ready to unwind.

My head has been spinning with ideas. I've had a few decent ones, but none of them feels like *the one*—the idea that will wow Lewis and Emily and turn around the snug's fortunes. On the bright side, the ache in my thigh has finally eased up. Small mercies and all that.

I check my phone but there's still nothing from Sass. I've not heard from her since she abruptly logged off before we'd even made it into the keep. I fired off a message to her a few hours back to suggest we give the quest another go tonight, but . . . no reply.

It was kind of odd that one moment there was something she really wanted to tell me, then the next her big news suddenly wasn't important anymore. What was that about?

I don't want to hound her but I shoot her one more

message in case she missed the first one. Just a quick note to say I'm up for gaming tonight, if she fancies it. This might sound a bit tragic to anyone whose idea of "gaming" starts with Scrabble and ends with Monopoly, but trust me, you really do feel like something is off when your favourite teammate goes AWOL.

Staring at my phone and willing it to light up with a response is obviously a pointless exercise. But when I tear my attention away from it, my gaze lands on the *Highland Legacy* figurine perched on my shelf. The red-haired woman holds her staff high, ready to cast a spell on anyone who calls her an action figure instead of a collectible. Of course, her uncanny resemblance to SassyLassie's in-game character had nothing to do with why I bought her . . . honest.

Okay, okay, I'm lying. In actual fact, I couldn't believe my luck when I spotted her in a *Highland Legacy* merch drop, and I knew I had to have her. I've never actually admitted to Sass that I own a physical representation of her, and I never will. I mean, it's possible she'd find it endearing, but it's also possible she'd find it creepy. Better not to take that risk.

I force my eyes away from the figurine, but there's sod all else in my room to distract me. My other shelves groan under rows of sci-fi and fantasy books, while a weathered paperback copy of *Dune* sits on my desk beside what might be the world's most chaotic tangle of charging cables. But I don't feel like reading right now, and there's no point gaming without Sass because I'd just spend the whole time wishing she were there beside me.

But . . . there *is* something else I could do.

I grab my laptop then settle on my bed. If Sass isn't around for some virtual adventuring, maybe it's time I finally dipped into the *Highland Legacy* TV series. Everyone's been raving about it for years but somehow I've never got around to watching it. Probably because no adaptation could ever live up to the game. Still, Sass said if I wanted to understand her secret kink, I should watch season two, episode seven, so that's what I'm going to do.

Sure, I *could* start at the very beginning—season one, episode one—and work my way up to that particular episode, but I'm nowhere near patient enough for that.

I find the episode on a streaming service and click play, settling back against my pillows as brooding choral music swells through my tinny speakers. The opening shot pans over a mist-shrouded battlefield strewn with broken spears and shattered shields, corpses lying in grotesque disarray—some human, others twisted remnants of reanimated flesh. A lone wolf howls in the distance—because of course it does.

The scene shifts to a dimly lit castle chamber, where a towering Highland warrior (shirtless already for no good reason) is deep in conversation with an auburn-haired woman. They're discussing their next move: gathering forces for another clash at dawn. Apparently, the earlier bloodbath wasn't enough.

I've no idea who these two are. In the game, players design their own unique avatars for the adventure, so there are no set "heroes". The show's creators must have come up with an original cast of characters to drive the narrative, though I have heard that a few NPCs from the game make an appearance.

I watch about ten minutes, in which various other characters are introduced, but since I've no idea who's who, it's a tad confusing. I give up trying to follow the story and scrub through the episode instead. And then . . . bingo. This has to be it.

The Highland warrior and auburn-haired woman are back, this time in a smaller chamber. Swords and axes hang on stone walls alongside banners embroidered with Celtic designs. Torches flicker, their light glinting off steel and painting the room in a warm amber glow.

The warrior is still shirtless, his breeches riding dangerously low on his hips. His companion, meanwhile, has traded her earlier leather coat for something far thinner: a gauzy chemise that clings to her curves in a way only a TV wardrobe department could pull off.

"Let me mark you for battle," the man says, dipping his fingers into a bowl of thick blue pigment. His voice is low and rough—like he gargles gravel every morning—and his muscles shift under skin so bronzed, it's as if Scotland suddenly relocated to the Mediterranean.

I snort softly as I settle further into my pillows. Body painting before battle? Pretty sure they're off by a few centuries with that. Mind you, given they're preparing to fight an army of the undead, I suppose I shouldn't worry too much about historical accuracy. And there's something about the way he leans closer to her that draws me in despite myself.

His hand moves slowly across her cheekbone, leaving trails of cobalt over pale freckled skin as she watches him with wide green eyes—a mixture of nerves and something hotter simmering below the surface. Every stroke is deliberate, like the warrior is not just painting her face but committing it to memory in case fate isn't kind when the sun rises. And given the way they occasionally glance towards the weapons on the walls, perhaps they know it won't be.

The camera lingers as his hands shift lower—from her jawline to her neck, tracing swirls across her collarbone where firelight makes her skin glow molten gold. Neither of them speaks, but Christ almighty, you don't need dialogue when the tension between them is thick enough to choke on.

Without a word she takes the bowl from him, dipping her fingers into its depths before gliding them over his chest, drawing slow spirals across taut muscle. Her hand trails lower until it hovers just above the point where those breeches rest so precariously on his hips.

The music swells, a tempest of strings and mournful harmonies. Clothes come off piece by piece. First his breeches slowly slide down, and Jesus Christ, that's a whole lot more Highland warrior than I needed to see. Then her chemise slips free until bare breasts gleam under firelight. Fuck, her tits are gorgeous.

The warrior takes the bowl back and continues painting her. His fingers move over her skin, leaving strokes of azure across the gentle swell of one breast before circling her nipple, lingering too long for it to pass as innocent artistry. When she lets out a shaky breath, he stills for a moment, as if trying to rein himself in.

She then takes charge again, decorating the rest of his body like she's conjuring some ancient spell to seduce a god. By the time she reaches his thighs—and yes, she gets scandalously close to brushing his cock—I'm watching in stunned disbelief because somehow this man's penis remains soft through all of this. How? HOW? Meanwhile, my jeans are starting to feel uncomfortably tight, and I'm just watching this unfold on my laptop screen. Honestly, if this actor doesn't win a BAFTA for restraint alone, there's no justice in the world.

The firelight flickers, casting shadows that move almost as sensuously as the characters do. It's ridiculous how much chemistry these two have. Somehow their connection feels . . . real.

The warrior pins the woman against a wall, her painted body arching towards his as though they've forgotten everything except each other. His hand slides down her thigh, his strong fingers lifting her leg, then he presses himself even closer to her. Her head falls back, exposing the delicate curve of her throat, which he descends upon with his mouth—biting softly first, then suckling hard. The guttural sound she makes when his hips roll against hers is so raw and feral it sends a shiver down my spine.

Fuck me if this isn't hot as hell. I can't believe I put off watching this for so long.

I unbutton my jeans and tug them down past my hips then let out a breath I didn't realise I was holding. Sweet relief. My cock wastes no time expressing its gratitude—it twitches in my boxers like it's giving me an approving nod for finally using my brain. Not that my brain has much to say right now.

The woman's hands claw at the warrior's shoulders, her desperate movements urging him closer, deeper into the molten pull of their shared need. He growls low in his throat then loops an arm around her waist and lifts her effortlessly—as though she weighs nothing at all—and strides to an ancient wooden table nearby. With one sweep of his free arm, scrolls, goblets, and more crash to the floor, then he's laying her down, her hair spilling out over the dark wood.

His hands map her curves while his hips press insistently between her thighs. The firelight catches their every movement:

muscles flexing, breaths quickening until they sound less human and more animal—raw and unrestrained.

Finally she shudders violently against him with a gasp so sharp it could slice through steel, dragging him right over the edge with her. His roar crashes against the stone walls like a thunderclap. Afterwards, as he struggles to catch his breath, his chest rising and falling, he gazes down at her as if she's some rare treasure he can't quite believe is real. "You're . . . everything," he murmurs, the words slipping out like they've been waiting a lifetime to escape.

Cut to: an exterior shot of the lone wolf howling again.

I pause the episode and run a hand over my face, willing myself to get a grip. What is wrong with me? The whole show is ludicrous—essentially a soft porn disguised as historical fantasy. And yet my cock is standing to attention like it's just heard the first bars of "Scotland the Brave." I kick my jeans off entirely, yank my polo shirt over my head, then flop back onto my bed in nothing but my boxers—although my dick is quite clearly straining to be free of them too. Phew, I reckon I need to cool down a bit.

My eyes catch on the *Highland Legacy* figurine—the one that looks so much like SassyLassie—and I swear to God, her tiny painted face is smirking at me. My gaze then drifts to my phone. Hmm. I probably shouldn't send her *another* message. But sod it.

LOCHNLOAD

Bloody hell, Sass. Just watched THAT scene. You weren't kidding—it's hot as fuck.

I'm not expecting a response anytime soon—not after she

ghosted my last couple of messages. But then—*bam!*—out of nowhere a reply comes in.

SASSYLASSIE

Patience really isn't your virtue, is it?

My stomach does this weird little swoop thing. It's good to hear from her.

LOCHNLOAD

Sorry! But just to clarify, are you talking about my relentless messaging or the fact I skipped ahead to S2E7?

SASSYLASSIE

Both

LOCHNLOAD

Fair enough! But I have to ask . . . body painting? That's your secret kink? Want to, er, discuss it in more detail? ☺

SASSYLASSIE

Nope

I frown at my phone. That's not the response I was hoping for. Where's the fun in that?

LOCHNLOAD

Okay, although . . . with her auburn hair, that actor didn't look a million miles away from your avatar. Just saying!

SASSYLASSIE

Lochie! Let's change the subject 😳

Interesting. I've never known Sass to get flustered before. It's kind of cute.

LOCHNLOAD

Okay, sure. How about instead you tell me the big news you were going to tell me earlier?

SASSYLASSIE

No, let's not talk about that either. That's . . . not relevant anymore.

LOCHNLOAD

Mysterious, but NP. I won't ask you about that ever again . . . so long as you tell me one SPECIFIC thing you liked about the body-painting scene.

What is it about it that gets you going? The intimacy? The build-up of sexual tension? The mess? 😛

SASSYLASSIE

OMG, stop! This is embarrassing. 🙈

LOCHNLOAD

Ah, I get it. *strokes imaginary beard* You want someone to paint YOUR boobs like that. Well . . . *heroically grabs nearest jar of paint*

SASSYLASSIE

Oi, watch it! I am THIS close to blocking you. You have been warned!

LOCHNLOAD

Okay, backing off now, promise! 😬

But seriously, everything good? You logged off pretty suddenly earlier. Not trying to pry, BTW—just looking out for my favourite quest partner.

SASSYLASSIE

All fine here. Just . . . been a funny day, you know?

LOCHNLOAD

Aye, I have them too. Think everyone does.
Fancy a game?

SASSYLASSIE

Not tonight. I'm tired but I wanted to check
in before bed. Talking of which . . . 😴 I'm
off to hit the hay.

LOCHNLOAD

Night, Sass. Sweet dreams . . . preferably
involving blue paint. 😊

SASSYLASSIE

You just can't help yourself, can you? Night,
Lochie.

I toss my phone onto the bedside table. I'm glad Sass broke her silence, even if that conversation wasn't *quite* as fun as it could have been.

All right, I'm too wired to sleep so . . . what to do with myself?

My gaze slides to my laptop, which is still open on my bed, the paused video glowing faintly in the dim light of my room. I reach for the touchpad, hesitate a moment, then . . . aye, I rewind it.

Back to *that* scene because apparently one viewing wasn't enough to properly appreciate its "artistic value".

I hit play then glance at my hand, which is resting oh-so-innocently on my thigh.

"Looks like it's just us again, mate. No offence but you're not exactly my first choice. But beggars can't be choosers, eh?"

JAMIE

It's been five days since Lewis dropped his bombshell about potentially closing the snug, and I've been racking my brains for ideas to save my wee bar. I've been taking the whole thing very seriously—so seriously I've resisted going back to season one, episode one of the *Highland Legacy* TV show. Why? Because if I do, I'll probably end up bingeing the entire series, and I'm trying to impress Lewis and Emily, not swap one time-sucking habit for another.

My phone buzzes.

SASSYLASSIE

Good luck with your presentation!

LOCHNLOAD

Aw, thanks! Not really a big deal, though 

Sass and I haven't gamed much over the last few days, but we've chatted a bit instead, which is . . . fine? Except it hasn't been as fun as usual because she's ditched the banter about boss fights and secret kinks in favour of asking dull questions—like about my work. I've kept things vague, obviously. Who wants to chat about their job when they're supposed to be relaxing? But she's persistent. I told her I had some ideas to pitch to my brother just to get her off my back.

Is this her way of trying to make us "closer" somehow? No clue. Women are hard enough to figure out when you actually know them. When you've got no idea what they look like or even their real name? They're complete enigmas.

Anyway, whatever, right now there's no time to dwell on Sass because bigger things are at stake—like convincing Lewis and Emily not to close the snug.

I take a deep breath outside the door to the hotel office and straighten my shirt. Bloody hell, what's wrong with me? Why am I worried about looking smart for these two? And, more importantly, why do I feel nervous? God, is this what happens when you care about something?

Well, screw that. I don't have time for nerves. I need to show Lewis and Emily I mean business. It's showtime.

I burst into the office with all the bravado of LochNLoad charging into battle. "Prepare to have your minds blown!"

Lewis glances up from his computer and arches an eyebrow. "Er, hi, Jamie. Nice to see you too."

Emily sits beside him, one hand resting lightly on her neat baby bump. She smiles, amused but clearly also bracing herself for whatever is about to come out of my mouth.

"Well?" Lewis leans back in his chair. "What have you got for us?"

"Right." I roll my shoulders and crack my knuckles for dramatic effect. "Picture this. It's a scorching hot day in Bannock—"

"Scorching hot? In Scotland?" Lewis cuts in instantly.

"Maybe let him get through more than two sentences before interrupting?" Emily suggests.

Lewis shrugs but waves me on like he's some benevolent laird granting me an audience. How magnanimous of him.

"It's sunny," I clarify with exaggerated patience. "Guys are wearing shorts; women are in sundresses. People are even complaining it's *too* hot. It happens every once in a while, believe it or not. Now, imagine you're a tourist who's just hiked up a mountain or a local looking to catch up with mates after work. You're parched. Desperate for a cold pint." I lean forwards as if sharing a great secret. "Do you really want to trudge into the dark, stuffy Pheasant?"

They exchange wary glances—the kind that says they expected some half-baked suggestion about the snug but not whatever tangent they think I've wandered off on.

"Don't get me wrong," I say quickly, holding up both hands like I'm pleading my case in court. "The Pheasant is great when it's pissing down outside or blowing a gale. It's charming—traditional—I'm not denying any of that. But when the sun finally decides to bless Scotland with its presence, do people really want to be cooped up in some old pub where natural light is practically outlawed? No, they want to be right here at the Bannock Hotel's brand-new . . . drumroll, please . . ." Neither of them obliges. Tough crowd. "Beer garden!"

I throw my hands out like a magician finishing his trick. *Ta-da!* Sadly, there's no applause, but Lewis leans forwards slightly while Emily's eyebrows lift in curiosity. At least they haven't kicked me out yet.

"I thought you were going to talk about saving the snug," Lewis says slowly.

"Aye, and I am!" I nod eagerly. "Just hear me out. The snug

is brilliant, but it's small. That's literally why we call it the snug—it can't hold that many people. But if we convert part of the garden into an outdoor bar during summer? Boom! We double—nah, triple—our space."

My enthusiasm snowballs faster than Lewis can chug a protein shake (and trust me, that man downs them fast).

"We'd pull in everyone craving a pint in the fresh air—locals, tourists, you name it. And once people get a taste for hanging out at the Bannock Hotel, they'll hopefully keep coming back, even when the rain is coming sideways. *That* is how we make the snug busy. It could bring in new crowds too, like hikers or cyclists in need of a pit stop. Oh, and families!"

"Families?" Lewis repeats sceptically.

"Aye, imagine a wee play area for kids so parents can relax with their pints without feeling guilty. Nothing massive, just a slide or some swings tucked into a corner somewhere. And ice cream! That'd be popular. We could stock locally made stuff. Maybe also string up fairy lights for the evenings. Oh! And fire pits—everyone seems obsessed with cosy vibes nowadays."

Smiling, Emily scribbles hurried notes onto a pad, and that little boost sends me soaring even higher.

"And events!" I exclaim triumphantly. "Barbecues! Live music! Things to bring people through the doors."

Lewis's mouth twitches into something that might just be approval. "You've really thought this through," he admits grudgingly.

"You're damn right I have. Turns out there's more than just gaming strategies rattling around up here." I tap my temple.

"Well, what do you think, Emily?" Lewis turns to her. "As our official event planner?"

She considers this. "We'd have to plan it carefully, of course.

Wedding clients love using the garden for photos, and their guests enjoy mingling there after the ceremony with a glass of champagne in hand. Whatever we do would have to add to the garden's charm, not detract from it. But honestly? This could totally work! The garden space is beautiful but it's not being used to its full potential right now."

"What about alcohol licensing for a beer garden?" Lewis asks cautiously.

Lucky for him—and thanks to ten minutes on Google—I've got that one covered.

"We'd need an amended licence," I tell him. "But since, like Emily just said, we already serve champagne out there for weddings, it shouldn't be too complicated."

Lewis presses his lips together, his expression thoughtful, but before he can say anything else, Elspeth pops her head around the door with her trademark knack for inserting herself into discussions no one invited her to.

"And what about *me*, eh?" she asks before narrowing her eyes at Lewis in mock outrage. "Another meeting where my opinion doesn't count?"

Lewis lets out a long-suffering sigh, although there's a twinkle in his eye. "It's not about missing you out," he says diplomatically. "This doesn't affect the restaurant—you're running things perfectly there already! Guests are always raving about your food."

Elspeth gives an emphatic nod. "Aye, and don't you forget it. Although . . . I overheard something about a beer garden. Answer me this: who's going to feed the hungry hordes if they show up expecting pints *and* pork chops, eh?"

Lewis blinks. "Oh, fair point. Well, take a seat, then. I suppose this meeting does involve you after all."

We briefly fill Elspeth in on what we've discussed so far, and once she's up to speed, she fixes me with a gaze that's equal parts curiosity and mischief. "Look at you, Jamie, actually using that brain of yours for something useful. Maybe there's more to you than just cheek and charm after all."

"Aye," Lewis agrees. "It's amazing what happened when I finally gave him a boot up the backside. I should have tried it ages ago."

I shoot him finger guns with zero shame because—let's face it—he's not wrong.

"Jamie, you do realise this would mean a lot more work for *you*, right?" Emily asks.

"Aye, I get that, but I *want* this to be my thing—my own wee project to sink my teeth into. Maybe I *have* been coasting a bit, but if you give me the green light, that'll change. I'll work hard at this because I know it could be something really special."

Lewis snorts softly, though there's no malice in it. "Didn't think I'd live to see the day Jamie volunteered to take on extra responsibility."

Emily nudges him. "Don't scare him off now. But seriously, Jamie, if we say yes to this, are you sure you're ready to take it on?"

"A hundred per cent. Also, the distillery is putting on an event for local businesses soon. I thought I'd pop along, chat to a few people, and see if I can't work out some kind of deal with them that benefits both sides. We could maybe promote their tours more actively to our hotel guests if they can give us an exclusive offering. The beer garden idea might just be the beginning. I may have more than one trick up my sleeve!"

"Another suggestion that's not half bad," Emily concedes.

"Not half bad?" I mock gasp. "Come on now, it's at least three-quarters genius!"

"I'll give you a quarter genius," Emily deadpans, though a smile tugs at the corners of her mouth. She turns to Lewis. "I think a beer garden could work."

Lewis rubs his jaw, mulling it over. Eventually he nods, not enthusiastically—let's not get carried away—but it's definitely a nod. "Jamie, you might be onto something."

"It's like I always say, miracles do happen," Elspeth offers.

"Thanks for that stunning vote of confidence, Elspeth." I wink at her then flick my gaze between Lewis and Emily. "So . . . does that mean you're signing off on this? Like, I can get started?"

"Just so we're clear," Lewis says, "before you tear up the garden, there are things you'll need to do, like speak to the council about adjusting the alcohol licence. You'll also need to work out the costs for everything you've just suggested. Keep Emily and me updated at every stage, and bear in mind that some of your grand plans might not make the cut if the budget doesn't stretch. That being said . . . aye, I think this is worth exploring, so go ahead and take it to the next stage."

"Yes!" I punch the air then wipe an imaginary tear from my eye. "I'd like to thank the academy, my family, and of course, my undeniable brilliance."

"Any more shite jokes and I might change my mind," Lewis warns.

"Understood!" I clap my hands together then rub them gleefully like an old-timey villain plotting dastardly deeds. "We're really going to cause the Pheasant some problems, aren't we?"

"Oi!" Lewis says. "We're not setting out to cause trouble for any other businesses—that's not how we do things in this town. We're just trying to sort out an aspect of our own operation that isn't performing as well as it should be."

I scoff. "If that's how you want to think of it, fine. Me, though? I like a bit of competition. I can't wait to see Bryce and Maisie's faces once they discover what we've got planned. But let's keep it on the down-low for now, eh?" I tap my nose and wink.

CHAPTER ELEVEN

MAISIE

My fingers drum a restless rhythm against the bar as I watch Da attack his glass-polishing like each tumbler has personally insulted him.

"I still don't see why *you* need to go to the distillery event," Da grumbles, setting down a freshly polished glass with more force than necessary. "I've always handled these things. This isn't about that dropped crate of whisky the other week, is it? You're not still holding on to that?"

"No, Da. It's not about that."

He huffs out a breath and studies me, his eyes narrowing. "Then what is it? You think I'll mess something up? Cause problems?"

"Of course not!" I can see where this is going—all wounded pride and stubborn determination.

"Feels like you're trying to push me into the background," he says gruffly. "A secondary role in my own business. A business I've built up with these two hands and have dedicated decades of my life to."

The accusation stings, and heat rushes to my cheeks.

"That's not it at all! I just . . ." I bite my lip, trying to keep my emotions in check.

"You just what?" Da presses, his tone sharper now.

"I just . . . *care* about you, you daft old man!" I've no wish to spell it out any further than that. But honestly? I think the long event may be a bit much for him at the moment.

Da's shoulders sag and he sighs, running a hand through his thinning hair. "All right, all right. I'm sorry," he says softly. "I know you mean well. Anyway, enjoy yourself at the event. I heard Jamie McIntyre is going along too."

I've heard the same and I reckon this could be an opportunity to suss out what Jamie is up to with the snug. And this time, I can just be myself rather than SassyLassie, which should make things a whole lot simpler. Besides, my attempts at coaxing useful info out of LochNLoad haven't exactly borne fruit. Plus, that time he chatted with me about the body-painting scene . . . well, things got a little uncomfortable. I mean, he did crack a joke about grabbing a jar of paint and decorating my boobs.

Aye, I've previously teased him about his sword fixation, suggesting—not too subtly!—it's actually about the size of his dick. I can't be too miffed at a bit of boob banter. But . . . let's just say the whole keeping-my-identity-a-secret thing is starting to weigh on me.

"Aye, I might see if Jamie wants to share a ride," I say nonchalantly. "Save on petrol and all that."

Of course, if I'm stuck in a car with Jamie—just the two of us and no distractions—I might just be able to tease out some info from him. I've not told Da that the Bannock Hotel is up to something. He's got enough on his plate without me adding to it.

Before heading out to ask Jamie if he fancies playing chauffeur, I fuss over my reflection in the mirror until I catch myself. What am I doing? I *could* try and claim I'm just making sure I look polished for the distillery event, but that's nonsense. This is about looking good for Jamie, which is ridiculous because it's not like I care what he thinks. Besides, he's made it abundantly clear he has zero interest in me. He called me a bloody Smurf!

Still, I inspect the hair he found so offensive—it's now up in a simple twist at the back. Then I tug at the hem of my navy corduroy pinafore dress, which is short enough to show a bit of leg but not so short as to cause gossip. I've paired my outfit with my black-and-white checked Converse trainers—the only ones in my collection that aren't completely knackered—and a white T-shirt. Smart casual, but cute.

With one last glance in the mirror, I grab my bag, call goodbye to Da, pray he'll be all right working the bar himself this evening, then head out to Main Street. I stride along it with a spark of determination in my stride. Today I'm less small-town bartender and more covert operative on a mission. Move over, James Bond. There's a new secret agent in town, and she's armed with sass, wit, and a sixth sense for sniffing out secrets.

I enter the hotel then step into the snug, which—unlike the Pheasant—is already open. Or at least, it's *supposed* to be open, but there's no buzz of conversation or clink of glasses. In fact, there's not a soul in sight except Jamie. Whatever his grand scheme is, it clearly hasn't kicked off yet. This place is dead.

Jamie is wiping down a table, a tea towel slung over one

shoulder. Gone are the usual jeans plus casual shirt or polo. He's wearing a crisp white shirt with the sleeves rolled up and a pair of navy chinos that hug him in all the right places. His outfit highlights his lean frame in a manner that's maddeningly appealing.

His head lifts just as I'm taking in the way those chinos fit a little too snugly across his thighs. Our eyes meet for a split second, and my stomach does an awkward wee lurch. Oh God, did he just catch me gawking? He raises one brow ever so slightly, as if to say, *Gotcha!* I quickly avert my gaze, pretending to suddenly find the floorboards fascinating.

Luckily, Bruce ambles over to say hello before my face can reach tomato-level redness, and I turn my attention to him.

"Hiya, pal." I crouch and give him a thorough scratch behind his ears. "See? This is what a proper welcome looks like. Take notes, Jamie."

Bruce chooses this moment to give my hand a big slobbery kiss.

"Oh?" Jamie comments. "*That's* a proper welcome, is it? Noted. Next time you come by, I'll drop to all fours and give you a good lick."

I snap my head up and gape at him. "Jamie!" My brain scrambles for a clever retort but it's gone completely blank. I wasn't expecting him to say that.

"What?" His eyes gleam with mock innocence but he can't hide the laughter bubbling behind them. "Just following your lead."

"You—" I splutter, pointing a finger at him like it might help me find words. "That's not what I meant and you know it!"

He shoots me a cheeky grin. "Anyway, what can I do for you, Maisie?"

"I"—I clear my throat—"heard you're going to this event at the distillery too."

"Aye, I am."

"Well," I say in what I hope is a breezy manner, "I was thinking, why don't we go together? Seems daft taking two cars when we live so close."

Jamie's grin shifts into a devilish smirk. "Ah, so that's how it is, eh? First you're throwing yourself at me on Ben Garve, and now you're angling for a cosy wee car date?"

"I threw myself at you? You're the one who couldn't keep this dog under control!" Glancing down at Bruce, I murmur to him that he's a perfect wee angel.

"That's not how I remember it. Pretty sure you just couldn't keep your hands off me. If we go to the distillery together, what's to stop you 'accidentally' spilling your drink on me so you can help me out of my shirt?"

I roll my eyes. "Is there an off switch for your crappy banter? Asking on behalf of everyone who's ever met you. And seriously, Jamie, don't flatter yourself. If I wanted to ogle a topless man, I'd just google Chris Hemsworth. Anyway, thanks for reminding me how utterly insufferable you are. I thought I'd give you a second chance after your Smurf comment, but this was obviously a mistake. I'll make my own way to the distillery."

Spinning on my heel dramatically (because a good exit deserves a bit of pizzazz), I stride off. But just as I'm about to step outside—and leave Jamie McIntyre's maddeningly punchable grin behind—brisk footsteps catch up with me.

"Maisie!" His hand lightly brushes my shoulder. Glancing

back, I see his eyes have lost their usual mischief, replaced by something gentler and almost . . . regretful?

"Hang on a minute." He drops his hand and shoves it into his pocket, while the other rubs awkwardly at the back of his neck—the universal sign for *This Idiot Knows He Messed Up*. "Look, I was only pulling your leg. Sorry if it went a bit far. Of course I'll drive you to the distillery, and, er . . ." He hesitates, clears his throat, then looks me squarely in the eye. "That Smurf joke? It was out of order—not funny at all." A pause stretches between us, thick and awkward, before he adds quietly, "Your hair is brilliant. And . . . you look good. Really good."

Jamie's words hang in the air between us, and I feel my resolve weakening. It's infuriating how he can go from irritating to endearing in the blink of an eye.

"Thanks," I manage. "And I'll accept the lift. Although if you bring up Smurfs again, just know that my revenge will be swift and creative."

A small smile tugs at the corner of Jamie's mouth. "Deal. Now, shall we get going before they drink all the whisky without us?"

He lets his brother, Lewis, know that he's off, then we make our way to his car, which is parked around the back of the hotel. Settling into the passenger seat, I'm acutely aware of Jamie's presence beside me. It's almost like the car shrinks around us, the space becoming surprisingly intimate. Jamie's arm brushes mine as he clicks in his seat belt, and a flicker of heat dances across my skin.

I will myself to focus on the task at hand. I'm here to gather information, not get distracted by Jamie's proximity or the way his aftershave seems to fill the vehicle (it's woodsy and warm, like cedar and sandalwood, with the faintest trace of smoky peat).

We leave Bannock then take the winding country road through Glen Garve, the late afternoon sun glinting off Jamie's windscreen. The road snakes through a patchwork of emerald fields dotted with woolly white sheep. Towering hills frame the glen on both sides, while a meandering river cuts through the valley floor, its gentle flow flashing into view now and then like a shy guest at a party.

I steal a glance at Jamie, only to catch his eyes flicking away from me, as if I've caught him doing something he shouldn't. Was he just checking me out? Is it because I made more effort than usual today? Did he actually mean it when he said I looked good?

I can't resist testing the waters so, after staring resolutely out the window for a little while, I dare another peek. This time, his eyes collide with mine, holding steady rather than darting away. And then it happens—a smile blooms on his face, slow and unguarded, soft enough to make my stomach flip like an acrobat on a trampoline. And then . . . the moment is over and his gaze shifts back to the road.

God help me. Why did he smile at me like that? And why do I feel like I might melt into this seat if he does it again?

Sitting up straighter, I force myself to concentrate on what I'm here for: information about the snug. Not Jamie's smile . . . or how annoyingly good those chinos look on him . . . or how they seem to fit extra snugly around his—*oh, for crying out loud, Maisie. You're not a hormonal teenager. Get a grip!*

"So," I say, trying to sound casual, "how are things going at the hotel?"

"All good." His tone is easy, though a flicker of something unreadable passes across his face.

"All good? That's all I'm getting? Come on, it's not like you're guarding state secrets over there."

His lips curve into a grin that manages to be both irritating and stupidly attractive all at once. "Maybe I am."

"Right." I huff out a breath and lean back in my seat. "You know what? Forget I asked. You're impossible."

"Impossibly handsome," he corrects, glancing my way and waggling his eyebrows.

"Impossibly delusional, more like. I suppose you're not *bad* looking—if you squint a wee bit and have low standards."

Lying through my teeth, obviously. The truth is, Jamie's annoyingly good-looking. Those hazel eyes with that cheeky freckle at the corner of the left one? Absolute menace. And don't get me started on that messy chestnut hair just begging to be messed up further.

I flick my gaze back to the road ahead before he can catch me staring, but my mind is less cooperative. Because now all I can think about is running my hands through that tousled hair until it's a complete disaster. And maybe . . . just maybe . . . letting my hands wander elsewhere on his body too.

Didn't I tell you to get a grip, Maisie Kerr? Well, get a grip!

"Low standards, eh?" Jamie says. "Ouch. And yet something tells me you don't mind me nearly as much as you pretend to."

Our gazes meet and he winks. Oh God.

Determined to wrestle back some control over whatever strange energy is swirling between us, I decide to throw him off balance.

"You know, it's good you're going to the distillery. Word

around Bannock is your social life could use a wee boost. Remind me, apart from Bruce, who are your mates again?"

Jamie's eyes dart towards me and then back to the road, but not before I catch something—just a flicker—a shadow of vulnerability that vanishes almost as quickly as it appears.

Crap, was that too harsh, what I just said? But come on, it's Jamie! He dishes it out constantly. Surely he can take a little teasing in return? Still, I can't help wondering if that hit closer to home than I intended.

A pause stretches between us then he says, "Well . . . there's this gamer I play with online."

My pulse skips.

"She just gets me, you know?" His voice is uncharacteristically soft—thoughtful—and it throws me completely off kilter.

Oh no. *Oh no.* He's talking about me. SassyLassie. His gaming partner. Me . . . and yet *not* me.

"That's the great thing about the internet," Jamie continues. "Before it, people could live their entire lives in a town without finding anyone who truly gets them. But now? I can chat with this gamer, even though . . . well, there's no one in Bannock quite like her."

The unintentional irony of his words makes my stomach squirm. It's not like I'm *technically* lying to him, but withholding the truth isn't exactly honest.

I glance out the window to steady myself. As beautiful as the glen is, the view does nothing to untangle the mess in my head.

"You're quiet over there," Jamie remarks after a beat.

"Aye, well . . . I'm just thinking how weird it is that there's someone out there who actually tolerates your nonsense."

God, why is this so complicated? It's supposed to be a

simple mission: find out what Jamie is up to with the snug and use that information to protect the Pheasant. End of story. And once I've done that? I'll come clean. Of course I will.

But as I steal another look at Jamie—relaxed, disarmingly handsome, utterly infuriating—I realise there's nothing simple about this at all.

CHAPTER TWELVE

MAISIE

The malty aroma of whisky permeates the air of the Glen Garve Distillery's event room, where thirty-odd representatives from local pubs and hotels mill about, chatting and networking. It's a testosterone-heavy crowd, mostly men in crisp button-down shirts or branded polos that scream hospitality industry. There's a scattering of women too, although we're definitely in the minority.

I've been here about five minutes, making small talk with a man from Inverness, who's giving me a blow-by-blow account of his pub's new menu. He's lovely but I'm only half listening. Jamie and I split up when we arrived, to mingle, but my attention keeps drifting back to him. He's a few feet away, deeply engrossed in a discussion about beer kegs. Hardly edge-of-your-seat material, but you never know when he might let slip his plans for the snug, and it bothers me that I'm only catching bits and pieces of what he's saying.

The Inverness publican eventually clocks my wandering gaze and toddles off with a cheerful "nice to meet you". I'm about to sidle over to join Jamie's conversation, ready to feign a deep interest in beer kegs, when I'm intercepted by Johnny MacDonald, an old school friend who works at the nearby Glen Garve Resort.

"Maisie! How are you doing?" Tall with long dark hair tucked behind his ears and piercing blue eyes, Johnny is drop-dead gorgeous. He's kind too—but alas, he's not on the market. He's head over heels with David, a lovely bloke who moved up from London two years back. And honestly? They might just be the cutest couple in Bannock.

"Johnny! Good to see you." I pull him into a hug.

"Is your da here?" Johnny asks me after I've released him.

"No, he's manning the fort today. Are you here by yourself too?"

"No, I've got Robbie with me. He understands whisky. Me? I happily drink it, but I haven't got a clue. I thought Glenfiddich was a character from *Lord of the Rings* until about two years ago."

Johnny nods to the far side of the room, where his brother, Robbie, is inspecting a display cabinet of rare whiskies, his tattooed arms folded over his broad chest. While Johnny works in management at the Glen Garve Resort, Robbie is part of the hotel's maintenance team—the brawn behind its operations. The brothers share the same colouring and tall stature, but that's where the similarities end. Where Johnny radiates easy charm and friendly smiles, Robbie has the kind of brooding presence that could darken a sunny day.

Jamie's rich, throaty laugh draws my focus. He and the bloke he's been chatting with are now clapping each other on the back. Beer keg conversation apparently wrapped up, Jamie heads over to me and Johnny, his lopsided grin as annoyingly attractive as ever. He offers Johnny a handshake and the two of them exchange a few words.

Robbie makes his way over next, nodding briefly in my direction before shaking Jamie's hand too.

"McIntyre," Robbie rumbles.

"MacDonald," Jamie replies.

What is it with men and addressing each other by their surnames? Is it some ancient ritual? A chest-thumping display of male camaraderie? Or just a convenient way to avoid the disaster of forgetting someone's first name? Honestly, it baffles me, and yet I can't deny there's something ridiculously hot about how they do it, all gruff and gravelly.

"You keeping well?" Robbie asks.

Jamie shrugs affably. "No complaints."

"Glad to hear that," Robbie says, his tone surprisingly genuine.

I blink. That's . . . strange. I can't remember ever hearing Robbie MacDonald ask after, well, anyone. He doesn't really do small talk or pleasantries. Also, there's bad blood between Jamie's family and Robbie, or at least I thought there was. And yet here these two are, talking to each other like civilised human beings.

At the front of the room, Kyle from the distillery claps his hands together loudly. "If everyone could please take their seats." He gestures to the round tables that have been set for the tasting.

Floorboards creak and chairs scrape. Soon Johnny, Robbie, Jamie, and I are all sitting together at a table, each of us with six small tulip-shaped glasses in front of us.

Kyle kicks things off with an enthusiastic introduction and overview of the plan for the evening, which will basically consist of a guided whisky tasting followed by some more mingling.

"If you need them," Kyle continues, "there's a spittoon in the centre of each table. Remember, we want everyone to have a safe journey home!"

"Ach, I'll be making use of that, then." Jamie leans back and gives me a sideways smirk. "Lucky you. You get to swallow."

My mouth falls open, but I quickly snap it shut again. I'm thrown by the sheer audacity of the double entendre—and by the fact he has absolutely no shame about it. And this on the heels of his earlier quip about getting on all fours and giving me a good lick. Truth be told, a tiny part of me wants to laugh, while another part wants to smack that smirk clean off his face. But I refuse to give him the satisfaction either way.

"Wow, Jamie. Subtle as ever. Do you use that line on all the ladies, or am I just lucky today?"

Thankfully, before Jamie can come out with anything else, a staff member comes over to pour us all our first whisky, and that shuts him up. At least, for now.

"All right!" Kyle says. "Let's kick things off with our first dram, a twelve-year-old aged in sherry casks. First things first, we nose the whisky." He models how to do so.

I swirl my glass then take a slow inhale of the amber liquid. The scent is rich—sweet yet earthy.

"Anyone care to share what they're picking up?" Kyle prompts.

I raise a hand, but Jamie says aloud, "Apples and . . . maybe a touch of caramel?"

Damn it. I was going to say caramel.

Kyle nods, his smile widening. "Excellent! Spot on. The

caramel comes through subtly—that's a great nose you've got, Jamie. And now to taste."

He models the technique and I follow suit, taking a small sip and letting the whisky coat my tongue. It's smooth and velvety at first, but then comes the warmth—the almost fiery burst of flavour. I take my time, swirling it in my mouth, trying to pinpoint the layers hidden within.

"Any comments on the palate notes?" Kyle asks once everyone has swallowed or used the spittoon.

"There's definitely a spice there," someone at another table says.

Kyle nods. "Is anyone able to identify a specific spice?"

The moment it clicks, I part my lips to speak, but—

"Cinnamon!" Jamie blurts, snatching the word right off the tip of my tongue.

"Not just cinnamon," I say, unwilling to let him steal the spotlight again. "There's a touch of nutmeg in there as well."

"And if you *really* focus on the finish," Jamie adds, swirling his glass like he's in the running to be crowned Scotland's Next Top Whisky Guru, "there's clove too. It's *very* subtle, though." His eyes lock onto mine, daring me to rise to the challenge.

"Actually—" I begin, but I'm cut off by Kyle.

"Thank you, both! Excellent observations—very thorough." He gestures towards another table. "Let's hear from the rest of the room now."

Jamie smirks triumphantly, basking in the victory of having the last word. I shift my attention to the other speakers. Better than looking at his smug face.

The second whisky, an eighteen-year-old single malt aged in bourbon barrels, is even more intriguing than the first. I savour the velvety warmth as it blooms through me, then my tongue darts out to relish the lingering traces on my lips.

That's when I notice Jamie's gaze on me—specifically, on my mouth. Just like earlier in the car, he averts his eyes the moment he realises I've caught him looking.

I'm not sure why my pulse skips, but I hurriedly announce to the table, "I'm getting raisin. Anyone else?" I look pointedly at Johnny and Robbie.

"No, not raisin," Jamie states with confidence. "More like . . . dates."

This forces me to turn my attention back to him, and I narrow my eyes. "I'm pretty sure I know what I'm tasting, Jamie."

"Well, I got dates too," Robbie grumbles.

Jamie grins, entirely too pleased with himself. Honestly, what *is* it with this guy? One moment he's all flirty banter. Then I catch him staring at me like he's savouring the sight of me just as much as the whisky. And then he's goading me! It's like trying to dance a reel with someone who keeps changing the steps. I can't keep up.

I briefly consider telling him to shove it. But instead I tip back the rest of my dram—far too quickly, as it turns out. The whisky rushes down my throat with a fiery kick, and I can't stop myself from coughing.

"You all right there, Maisie?" Johnny asks, concern evident in his voice.

Jamie pours me a glass of water. "Careful. If you're this flustered after two drams, I hate to think what you'll be like after six."

I glare at him then take a sip of the water. Across the table, I swear I see a flicker of amusement cross Robbie's usually impassive face.

"Don't worry about me, Jamie." I set the glass down. "I can handle a dram—or ten—better than most men in this room."

Or so I claim, but as the evening rolls on, a pleasant languid sensation unfurls through me. Then, during the sixth and final sampling, something unsettling happens. I catch Jamie tipping his head forwards to spit into the spittoon. I've been trying to avoid it all evening—it feels oddly intimate, almost too personal for public scrutiny—but now that I've seen it, I can't help but notice the curve of his jaw, the flex of his throat . . .

It shouldn't be hot. And yet, somehow, it absolutely is.

A flicker of heat blooms low in my belly, and before I can stop it, a tiny sound escapes my lips—something between a sigh and a gasp.

Jamie glances my way. "Did you say something?"

"Just clearing my throat," I manage, reaching for the jug of water to top my glass back up, my cheeks burning.

Despite my earlier bravado, it's clear the whisky has gone to my head. Sure, the tasting samples are smaller than your typical measure, but there have been a fair few of them. It also doesn't help that I've not eaten in a while—total rookie mistake, and especially embarrassing considering I work in a pub.

Kyle wraps up the tasting session, inviting people to come up to speak to him or the rest of the distillery team with any questions. Folk push to their feet, and the room quickly fills with chatter. Jamie is off like a shot, apparently very keen to talk to someone. I'm determined to follow him, not wanting to miss anything that could be important, but the moment I stand, a wave of light-headedness hits me. The ground doesn't exactly shift beneath my feet, but for a second everything feels off. I clutch the back of my chair and take a steadying breath. I'm *really* regretting not having an early dinner now.

Once I feel stable again, I assure a concerned Johnny that I'm fine then slip my bag over my shoulder and straighten up. Kyle's voice carries faintly over the hum of chatter—he's talking to some folk by the far wall—but it's Jamie I focus on. He's already deep in conversation with a man who works for the distillery—Oliver, I think his name is. Acutely aware that Jamie's plans for the snug might involve the distillery, I make my way across the room. I need to get close enough to eavesdrop but not so close as to arouse suspicion. This is where my secret agent skills come into play, if I actually have any. And if they work when I'm drunk.

As it turns out, I do a pretty damn good job, if I do say so myself. I have a chat with Claire, who works here and is a Bannock girl, while at the same time keeping half an ear tuned to Jamie's conversation. I pick up bits and pieces, but nothing that sounds particularly important—at least, not yet.

The problem is that, between the whisky drinking and the water I've been guzzling, my bladder has reached critical capacity—the kind of fullness that simply cannot be ignored. Do real-life spies have to contend with this? What happens when you're in the middle of a mission and the need to go hits you? Because, knowing my luck, the moment I nip off to the bathroom will be when Jamie spills all his secrets.

I hold out as long as I can—a valiant effort, really—but eventually I just can't put it off any longer without compromising basic human dignity. And so I have to ask Claire where the toilets are.

Right, I'll be quick. I probably won't miss a thing.

Except . . . there's a bloody queue! Of course there is.

Because life as a woman involves queuing for loos like we're waiting to enter some exclusive nightclub instead of just desperately needing to pee. And there weren't even that many women at the event! Did our bladder alarms all go off simultaneously?

Oh, to be a male secret agent! Twenty seconds at a urinal, *shake shake*, job done, then straight back in the game. It's *so* unfair.

When I return (ah, the relief of an emptied bladder—truly one of life's uncelebrated joys), Jamie is having a serious chinwag with Kyle. His gestures are purposeful, his hands slicing through the air as Kyle nods along intently. There's something about their body language—a gravity in Jamie's movements, a focus in Kyle's posture—that screams this isn't just casual chitchat. This is important. Big, even.

Damn it!

I edge closer, hoping to pick up at least a snippet of what they're saying, but before I can get within earshot, Kyle shakes Jamie's hand and claps him on the back.

Conversation over. And . . . I missed it entirely.

To really rub it in, when Jamie spots me approaching, he flashes that insufferably charming smile of his and says, "Oh, there you are! Good timing. You ready to go?"

No, Jamie. Not good timing. Very bad timing, in fact. I just missed the one thing I was really hoping to get out of this event.

But biting back my frustration, I plaster on a smile and say, "Sure."

So we head outside, and it must be the rush of fresh air, but suddenly it's like someone has cranked up the volume on my drunkenness. Everything feels a touch too wobbly, and walking in a straight line is a lot harder than it should be.

"You all right?" Jamie asks, his voice tinged with amusement.

"Of course!" I wave him off with barely concealed indignation. "I told you. I can handle my drink."

But then we reach a short flight of steps leading up to the car park—there are literally just five of them. I ignore the hand Jamie offers me, successfully navigate the first three, then promptly lose my balance.

It happens so fast it doesn't feel real—the backwards tilt, the yelp that never quite leaves my throat—but . . . I don't hit the ground. No, instead I fall back against a solid wall of warmth, then arms wrap around my waist, locking me in place.

Jamie's breath fans the side of my neck in quick bursts as if even he's surprised by how fast he reacted. And then there's everything else: his hands on me, strong and steady; his chest rising and falling against my back; and, oh God, my backside snug—far too snug—against his groin. Every point of contact between us fires off sparks as though someone's dropped a live wire into my bloodstream.

Mortification bubbles up inside me, and yet I make no effort to squirm out of his grip. The two of us remain frozen in this wildly inappropriate position, neither of us moving or speaking. The air hangs thick and charged around us, crackling with something too dangerous to name.

"I've got it from here," I blurt out abruptly.

"You sure?" Jamie's words tickle my ear, his breath hot against my skin.

"Yes!"

His hands slowly retreat from me, but even after they're gone and I've managed to make it up the last few steps in one piece, the memory of his touch lingers.

CHAPTER THIRTEEN

MAISIE

The car rumbles along the winding road back to Bannock, and I'm feeling pleasantly warm and fuzzy from all the whisky we sampled at the distillery. My head is swimming a bit, soft and floaty in a way that makes everything feel as if it's wrapped in cotton wool—safe, hazy, untouchable. Embarrassment? What's that again? Yes, I stumbled back against Jamie, and my body ended up pressed *very* close to his, but I can't seem to summon a single ounce of shame about that anymore. It's just . . . gone. Blame it on the drink.

I sneak a glance at him. He's focused on the road ahead, and the golden light of the setting sun catches his profile—strong jawline, straight nose, thick lashes casting shadows across his cheeks. It's unfair, really. He was handsome enough when I was sober, but now? Ugh, he looks even better somehow. How does that work?

"So," I say, aiming for casual but probably missing by a mile, "what were you and Kyle chatting about? Looked very important."

Jamie doesn't take his eyes off the road but one corner of his mouth curves up. "Did it now?"

"Aye, it did. Come on, spill."

"My lips are sealed." There's a teasing edge to his tone that makes my curiosity itch even more.

"Seriously?" I huff, crossing my arms. "You're not going to tell me anything?"

"Nope." He pops the *p*, all smug and self-satisfied.

I make a scoffing noise and shoot him my best *you're ridiculous* glare, but my eyes have other ideas. They drift south, lingering on the way his shirt stretches across his chest before sliding lower . . . to those chinos. Specifically, that area where they're doing some very intriguing bunching around the crotch. Damn their perfect tailoring and their suggestive folds that send my tipsy brain cartwheeling straight into Dangerous Thought Territory.

I can't help but remember how, when Jamie caught me, my arse landed squarely against *that area*. And let me tell you, the sensation was . . . well, let's just say it wasn't forgettable. Because ladies and gentlemen (drumroll please), there had *absolutely* been something substantial beneath those trousers.

This, of course, raises questions—important questions! Like: just how substantial? Sadly, the encounter was too brief to allow me to answer that, so clearly further investigation is required. I never did do well in science at school, but honestly, if *this* had been in the curriculum, I'd have graduated top of the class. Hmm, how would a proper scientist go about gathering more data for a study?

What if—hypothetically—a sharp turn or pothole sent me toppling conveniently across Jamie's lap? That could work! I'd pop a hand down to steady myself, and it might land some-where . . . enlightening. Cue an entirely accidental grope-and-grab as I push myself up, followed by a dramatic gasp as I realise what I've got a hold of. "Oh my God, I'm so sorry!" And . . . voilà! Mystery solved. Give it an apologetic pat then let it go. No harm done.

Is it just me, or is that plan foolproof? Like, what could possibly go wrong?

I'm so deep in this questionable train of thought—definitely not my finest hour—that I don't notice Jamie glancing my way until it's too late. When I look up and our eyes meet, his brows rise in amusement and . . . oh hell, is that suspicion?

Oh no. Oh God. Does he know I was ogling his crotch?

I need to deflect. Fast. "Er, you've got a bit of something on your trousers," I blurt out. Good save, right? Totally convincing. Then, for reasons I cannot explain even to myself, I add, "Here, let me get it for you."

What am I doing? But now I've said it, I can't back out. So I lean over and swipe at his thigh. Repeatedly. In a very deter-mined fashion. You know, just to make sure the imaginary fluff is well and truly gone.

And . . . with dawning horror I realise that my hand is now perilously close to his crotch. Mere centimetres away from a region I'd just been mentally plotting to investigate. My pulse quickens as the tipsy devil on my shoulder whispers, *You're already in the neighbourhood. What's one little nudge? A quick brush with your fingertips—accidentally, of course. Go on! You can say, "Oopsie, how clumsy of me!"*

The angel on my other shoulder pipes up: *Don't listen to her! You cannot grope a man's crotch just because the thought popped into your whisky-addled brain. That's not cheeky—it's wildly inappropriate. Criminal, even!*

Thankfully, even drunk Maisie understands boundaries. It was one thing to amuse myself with the ridiculous idea of copping a feel—and let's face it, the idea *was* hilarious—but there's no way I'm actually going to do this. Nope. Uh-uh. Time to take my hand back.

It's at this exact moment we go over a bump in the road and—oh God—my hand slides onto Jamie's crotch. My palm meets warmth and . . . a very distinct shape.

We both freeze.

For what feels like an eternity but is probably two seconds tops, nothing happens except for me developing sudden tunnel vision as all my senses zero in on The Thing Under My HandTM. Turns out my earlier suspicions weren't exaggerated—if anything, they were woefully underestimated. It's quite the package. We're talking first-class freight delivery here. And sweet baby Jesus, it isn't even hard. What kind of monstrous proportions are we talking about when it is?

Jamie lets out an incredulous laugh that sounds half amused and half . . . something else entirely. "Er . . . Maisie?"

I finally come to my senses and snap my hand away so fast you'd think his trousers were made of molten lava. "Oh my God. Ohmygodohmygodohmygod!" My voice comes out in a high-pitched squeak, and I clutch both hands to my chest like I'm auditioning for a Victorian melodrama.

Jamie's shoulders tremble with suppressed laughter, his eyes crinkling at the corners. "Maisie, what the hell was that?"

"Nothing! Absolutely nothing happened! Don't even know what you're talking about." I'm talking way too fast and my cheeks are on fire.

"You just groped me."

"I did *not* grope you! It was the car's fault. The bump in the road—it threw me off balance!"

"Hmm. Is your face always that shade of red?"

"It's not red! It's . . . warm in here! My colour is totally unrelated to me accidentally touching your . . . er . . . you know . . ." I don't even know what to call it. Cock? That's the word I use in my head, but saying it out loud might make it sound like I've wandered into the pages of *Fifty Shades*. Willy? Too playground. Penis? Nope, too clinical. Todger? Good God, no. ". . . thingy."

He loses it then, laughter spilling out of him until he has to swipe a hand across his eyes.

"It's not funny," I mutter miserably.

"It's absolutely funny," he counters with maddening cheerfulness. "One of the funniest things that's ever happened to me, in fact."

He is *impossible*. Still, at least he's chuckling and not giving me a lecture on appropriate car etiquette or declaring he'll never let me near him again for fear of further unsolicited crotch encounters. Trust Jamie to find this funny—he turns everything into a joke. God forbid he take anything seriously for once in his life. No, he'd much rather have a giggle at my expense while I quietly try to die of embarrassment over here.

"If you could stop laughing sometime soon," I grumble, "that'd be great."

"Aw, come on now." He wipes at his eyes again before glancing my way with a lopsided grin. "Lighten up! It was an accident . . . wasn't it?" He lifts an eyebrow suggestively.

My jaw drops. "Of course it was an accident! What are you suggesting, I had some master plan involving rogue bumps and intrusive hands?" (Okay, so maybe I *did* have a plan like that, but I never actually intended to put it into action!)

Jamie chuckles again, utterly unbothered by my indignation as though winding me up is some kind of sport to him, and one where he receives bonus points for every shade of pink my cheeks turn in rapid succession.

Shifting slightly in his seat, he casts me a sideways glance so sly it ought to come with its own theme music. "Oh, Maisie, you've actually got something on your arm."

I frown down at the aforementioned limb, which is completely clean. Not so much as a speck of lint in sight.

"Let me return the favour," Jamie continues with mock chivalry, lifting one hand off the wheel and reaching towards me oh-so-casually. "Though, fair warning, if we hit another bump, I may accidentally graze a boob."

"Jamie McIntyre!" I shriek, crossing both arms firmly over my chest. "Don't even *think* about it!"

He shoots me a grin that's all devilry and places his hand back on the wheel. "Relax. I just wanted to say the phrase *graze a boob*. I wasn't actually going to do it. Unlike some people, I know how to keep my hands to myself."

The joke breaks the tension—until, all nonchalant-like, he reaches down and tugs at his chinos. He's clearly trying to act casual, but given my unhealthy level of crotch-awareness this entire journey, I catch it right away. He's shifting things around down there. Is he . . . getting hard? From just the *idea* of grazing my boob? Or maybe it's a delayed reaction to my earlier wandering hand?

"Are you . . . okay there?" I ask, aiming for breezy but landing somewhere between breathy and barely functional instead. Damn whisky. Why did it have to turn me into such a liability?

A moment passes, then, "Aye," he says with just enough rasp to make my pulse trip over itself. "All good."

Uh-huh. Sure you are. And I'm totally not imagining how good you'd look without your trousers right now. Except I absolutely am because apparently this is who I am as a person—a whisky-addled pervert who, having already placed my hand on his crotch, now wants to see it out and standing to attention. Possibly even pet it like a prize-winning Highland cow, murmuring "Good lad" with tears of pride glistening in my eyes.

Okay, no, that's just ridiculous, Maisie.

But then, through the fog of idiotic drunken thoughts, a cold, hard truth smacks me in the face. Jamie has no idea I'm SassyLassie. *Abort mission!* I cannot—absolutely cannot—let this veer into spicy territory when I'm harbouring a secret like that. It wouldn't be fair. I need to shut this down immediately. Stop whatever is stirring in his chinos before it's up and saluting. Toss a metaphorical bucket of icy water over his lap. Deploy every unsexy word in the dictionary.

Quick, what's the least erotic thing I could say? *Flaccid!* Can I drop that in without sounding suspicious, though? *Oh, look, what a flaccid sunset!* Does that work?

No, Maisie, you eejit, of course that doesn't work.

God! Right, tomorrow I'll come clean, but right now I need to steer this ship back into safe, unsexy waters. Somehow. I just need some better ideas.

At this point it starts to rain, droplets peppering the windscreen like tiny liquid bullets. Jamie makes a noise low in his throat then reaches for the wipers and flicks them on. "This wasn't forecast."

"It'll probably pass," I say optimistically, delighted that Mother Nature has provided me with this opportunity to segue into a completely non-sexy topic: weather. "So, tell me, Jamie . . . what's your favourite weather? Like, if you had to choose. Not that you'd have to choose—obviously there's no weather competition or anything. But—"

"My favourite *weather*?" Jamie stares at me for a beat, one eyebrow hitching up like I've just asked if he prefers his eggs scrambled or on fire.

"Aye," I say brightly, plunging forwards because retreat isn't an option now. "You know, sunshine? Rain? Maybe you're a big fan of fog?"

Jamie turns his attention back to the road and shakes his head slowly, lips twitching like he can barely hold back another laugh. "Jesus Christ, Maisie."

"What?" I snap a little defensively. "Okay, fine. If you don't want to talk about the weather—clearly too controversial a topic—let's talk about . . . oh, I know, your gamer friend. You know, the one you were telling me about on the way out?"

Quick Jamie crotch check and, yep, it's definitely bulgier than normal down there. *C'mon, Maisie, you need to get that thing back to its usual (far from insignificant) size!*

"What about her?" Jamie asks.

I shrug as casually as I can manage. "Hmm, how about . . . what's her name? Where does she live? What does she look like?" Okay, *I* know the answers to all those questions—Jamie doesn't—but I'd quite like to hear what sort of opinion he's formed of my online identity.

He frowns. "I don't know. Well, she's Scottish, but I don't

know whereabouts in the country she lives. Otherwise, I only know her username: SassyLassie."

That's me, pal! But I don't say that, of course. Instead I say, "You don't even know her real name?"

"Nope." Jamie's jaw tightens ever so slightly. He adjusts the windscreen wipers again. The rain is coming down harder now, lashing against the glass.

"But you've spoken to her, right? Like, with a microphone or something? You'd recognise her voice if she walked into a room?"

Jamie shakes his head. "We've only ever used text chat."

"*Really?*" I lay on the pretend incredulity pretty thick. "So how do you know she is who she says she is? Or even a *she* at all? For all you know, SassyLassie could be some balding guy with a beer belly, parked in front of his computer in a stained vest and manky boxers. Right?"

Jamie mutters something under his breath that sounds suspiciously like *bloody hell*. His grip on the wheel tightens, tension rippling up his forearms as he peers through the rain obscuring the road ahead.

Another glance at Jamie's lap, and hallelujah! Things are settling down. The disturbing mental image of Beer-Belly SassyLassie—the ultimate anti-aphrodisiac—must have sent Jamie's trouser department an urgent memo: *Stand down, lad. This mission is a no go.*

Well, go me! If penis pacification were a sport, I'd be an Olympic champion. Gold medal and everything. Don't know if that's something to be proud of, though.

Eventually Jamie says, "She's not some guy. I trust her."

He trusts SassyLassie? That's kind of adorable, and maybe it ought to stir up some guilt about the whole hiding-my-identity thing, but I can't resist teasing him a wee bit more. I blame the whisky.

"But you don't *know*, do you? Not really. She told you she's a lassie and you believed her, but what if she's really . . . I don't know . . . Big Davie from Glasgow? I can picture him right now. He's sat there, stroking his nipple, whispering, 'Call me SassyLassie again.'"

"Maisie . . ." There's an unmistakable warning note in Jamie's voice now, a low rumble that tells me I'm inching perilously close to some invisible line he doesn't want me crossing. "Could you hold your tongue for a minute? I'm trying to concentrate here."

But do I stop? Of course not.

"Tell me you haven't sent Big Davie any sexy messages. Please, for the love of all things holy, say you haven't!"

His reaction is instant—and epic. He tenses all over, a muscle ticking in his jaw. Ha! What must be going on in his head right now? Because he *has* sent Big Davie—I mean, Sassy-Lassie—racy messages. About how he enjoys a bit of power play.

The rain turns savage, pounding the car with a vengeance. Fat droplets streak across the windscreen in chaotic rivulets, smearing the world into a blurry mess of grey and green. The wipers swipe furiously in what feels like an act of futility. Bloody hell, it's as if some weather god just flipped the switch from "moderate" to "full-blown apocalypse". Even for the Highlands, this is next-level. I'm talking biblical flood vibes here—"build an ark" territory.

Even so, I can't resist carrying on with the ribbing. Jamie still hasn't answered me and I'm terrible at letting things go, especially when winding him up is so much fun. So I press him again.

"Come on, Jamie!" I say in a singsong lilt. "Fess up! Did Big Davie get a saucy little message? What did you say to him? You can tell me! Or—oh God—you didn't send him a naughty photo, did you? Tell me Big Davie doesn't have a cheeky pic of your, *ahem*, thingy?"

"Bloody *hell*, Maisie!" Jamie's voice cuts loud and sharp through the deafening staccato of rain. Is he . . . breathing harder? Because from where I'm sitting, it sure looks like his chest is rising and falling faster than before. Oh wow, am I really working him up *that* much?

"Can you *please* just stop talking?" he says.

I should. I really should. But I don't.

"What's the wildest thing you've said to her—I mean him—I mean . . . whoever? Don't tell me you went straight for 'Sit on my face.' Classic amateur mistake."

Tyres screech against wet tarmac, their high-pitched wail slicing through the downpour, then my seat belt slams into my chest as the car jerks to an abrupt halt.

For a few awful seconds, neither of us speaks. The only sounds are the frantic *whirr-thwack-whirr* of wiper blades and the rain hammering against metal and glass.

I turn to Jamie, every inch of me prickling. "Why did you stop? Did you see something?"

But he doesn't answer. He's leaning back, breathing hard through his teeth, sharp tendons flexing in his neck like he's trying to hold himself together and it's taking every ounce of effort he can muster.

"Jamie?" My voice wavers slightly, uncertainty creeping in around the edges. He finally looks at me, and I wish he hadn't.

There's something dark and raw in his eyes, some unspoken storm that rivals the one raging outside.

"Get out," he says quietly. The words are calm enough on the surface but hum with a force that punches straight through me.

I blink at him, stunned. "What?"

His grip tightens on the steering wheel until his knuckles are bone-white. Rain pummels the roof, but even that can't drown out the tension crackling in the cramped space between us.

"I mean it." His tone is low with a razor edge I've never heard from him before. "Get out."

I gape at him, struggling to process what's happening. "Jamie, come on! You can't be serious." My laugh comes out high-pitched and hollow—more plea than humour. "I was just having a laugh! Don't tell me you're actually mad about—"

"*Maisie!*" he snaps, cutting me off so sharply I flinch. He lets go of the wheel and rakes a hand through his hair, then he exhales harshly through his nose like a bull preparing to charge. He fixes his gaze straight ahead on the rain-streaked windscreen. "Just . . . go."

His words land with the force of a blow, hard and unforgiving.

"You're really kicking me out?" I gesture wildly to the chaos outside. "In *this* weather?"

His jaw tightens further, something I didn't think was possible.

"This is ridiculous!" I protest. "It's absolutely *pissing* down out there! Jamie—"

"GET OUT!" His voice cuts across mine like a whip crack.

Swallowing hard, I fumble with my seat belt. It takes me

three tries to unclip the bloody thing. The storm is roaring against the car like some primal beast desperate to get at us—or maybe just at me. It sure feels personal when I finally shove open the door and all hell breaks loose.

Rain lashes sideways into the car interior before I've even got both feet on solid ground—or on soaking wet tarmac, more accurately. With teeth clenched so hard my jaw aches, I step out fully into the downpour. The rain punches through my dress in seconds, drenching me to the bone with merciless efficiency.

This is madness. Surely Jamie isn't going to make me walk back? Even through the deluge, I can tell where we are—it's a ten-minute walk back at most—but I am *not* dressed for a rainy hike. Surely any second now he'll shout out, *Maisie, I'm joking. Get back in!* And even though I'll want to throttle him for being such an arse and pulling such a mean prank, I'll swallow my pride and climb back in. Because at least then I'll be somewhere dry.

But no such miracle comes.

Instead Jamie sits stiffly in his seat, staring straight ahead as though all this—the weather, *me*—isn't worth sparing another glance for.

I slam the door shut but Jamie doesn't even flinch. He's nothing but a shadow behind the wheel now, his profile illuminated by the cold glow of dashboard lights. I will him to look at me, to realise what an absolute dickhead he's being, but he doesn't. Instead he shifts into gear and—*vruh-vrrroooomm!*—the car lurches forwards and speeds off, its taillights smearing red streaks through the curtain of rain and the stinging wetness in my eyes that is most definitely not tears.

"You bastard!" I yell, the words ripping from my chest, a half-sob, half-battle cry.

My whisky haze is gone—not just lifted but ripped away by pelting rain and the searing sting of humiliation. In its place, something raw and electric sparks to life: fury.

I march forwards, my soaked trainers squelching with every step.

And to think I was going to tell Jamie tomorrow that I'm SassyLassie. There's no bloody way that's happening now, not after this. This is war, and I'm not above fighting dirty.

CHAPTER FOURTEEN

I collapse into my gaming chair, desperate to escape into *Highland Legacy* and forget about my day. The familiar loading screen illuminates my shadowy room, its soft glow soothing my frayed nerves. Gaming is my sanctuary, the perfect way to shut out the world. Tonight I need it more than ever.

After slogging through endless paperwork and mind-numbing budget spreadsheets for the beer garden—because apparently dreams come with a whole load of soul-sucking admin—the distillery event was meant to be a bit of light relief. A fun break. And it *had* been fun—at first. Maisie and I were on fire, locked in a ridiculous battle of whisky trivia, each trying to outdo the other. Then things took an interesting turn when we were leaving together and she fell, her arse somehow landing perfectly against my crotch in a way that made my brain short-circuit and my lungs forget how to function.

Wow, that had been hot. But things only got hotter. In the car, after that bump in the road, her hand landed square on my dick. Like, right on it. By accident . . . I think? No, definitely an accident. Her eyes went huge, her cheeks flushed pink, and her mouth made an *o* of mortification. There's no way she meant to do it. And yet . . . for whatever reason—maybe she was frozen in shock or something—she didn't move her hand straight away. Nope. There were a few seconds of hand-on-dick contact before she finally snatched it back.

Was it shock, I wonder. Or did she think to herself: well, seeing as my hand is here anyway, I may as well cop a wee feel. Because let's be honest, if my hand had accidentally landed on her boob, I wouldn't have been in any rush to move it either.

A rough breath escapes me. God, just thinking about it has me half-hard again. Brilliant. I scrub a hand over my face and try to pull myself out of the memory because this really isn't helpful right now. Not given what happened next—me chucking her out into that storm like an absolute bastard.

Outside, the rain picks up again, lashing against my window like a hundred tiny fists demanding answers. Unease prickles in my chest, and I crank up the volume of my head-phones until the game's soundtrack drowns out the noise entirely.

Fucking rain.

I only wish I could drown out the guilt so easily. If I'd ever had even a fraction of a chance with Maisie—and let's be honest, I probably didn't—I've ruined it now. Completely bollocksed it up. What sort of man throws someone out of their car in a storm? Only a complete knobhead would do something like that. Not just a knobhead—a dickhead of the highest order. Top-tier arsehole energy right here. *Well done, Jamie. You've really outdone yourself this time.*

These waves of shame are, of course, the ultimate cold shower. The situation down there de-escalates in record time.

My avatar materialises on screen: the kilt-clad hulking

Highland warrior with muscles rippling beneath fur-lined armour. He stands in his usual battle-ready stance, unyielding gaze fixed ahead. LochNLoad, the epitome of rugged masculinity. If only I were half as put together as him in real life. Or even a quarter.

Right then. Time to lose myself in this world and forget everything else. For a little while, at least, I can be bold and indestructible.

I check my quest log. Rescue this. Slay that. Retrieve some lost heirloom for an NPC who couldn't be arsed to keep track of their own belongings. Classic stuff. But tonight calls for something meatier—something distracting enough to drown out both guilt and accidental gropes.

Having spawned near the tavern in Torlannach, I make my way to the square, which is bustling with activity: townsfolk haggling at market stalls, children chasing chickens through the mud, and one particularly angry goat harassing a flustered blacksmith. The details never fail to impress me.

Near a well stands a crooked wooden noticeboard, plastered with yellowed parchments curling at the edges. I review them until one catches my attention: *A forgotten village calls for vengeance! Clear out the bogborn horde plaguing its ruins.*

Ah yes, the bogborn, *Highland Legacy*'s favourite swamp-dwelling nuisances. I can't quite remember their lore—something about ancient curses and mud magic or whatever nonsense some overzealous developer cooked up at three in the morning. There's even a cheeky handwritten scrawl at the bottom of the poster: *Warning: they reek worse than yer da's feet after a ceilidh.*

Charming.

Venting my frustrations on some mucky monsters sounds

like exactly what I need right now, so I open the map and fast travel to the quest location—because who has time to hike when you can teleport?

I appear at the edge of the ruins. Cottages that were once homes are now just piles of stone draped in ivy and moss. Thick mist swirls across the ground like something straight out of a cheesy horror film. Man, do the game devs love a bit of mist.

And then they shamble into view: the bogborn, mud-caked monstrosities with half-melted faces that drip black sludge from empty eye sockets. Their limbs end in claws that make Edward Scissorhands look amateur. Definitely not something you'd want sneaking up on you in the dark—or at all, really.

The closest bogborn lurches towards me with an ungodly gurgle, and I waste no time pulling out LochNLoad's broadsword, its blade gleaming impossibly bright against all this murkiness.

"Let's do this," I mutter.

LochNLoad's blade slices clean through the first creature, and that's the signal for the rest to charge. They swarm me but I'm ready for them. I hack and slash at them, timing my dodges perfectly, claws swiping inches from my face but finding nothing but air. One by one they collapse into filthy heaps at my feet, splattering mud everywhere.

There's a strange satisfaction in the madness of it all—side-stepping claws and striking with precision—but no matter how many bogborn fall, the guilt remains, a constant hum beneath the clamour of the skirmish.

Focus, Jamie! Lose yourself in the fight!

I take a couple of hits and my health bar dips—it wouldn't be fun if there weren't some stakes—but it shoots back to full after I chug one of those violently purple potions every fantasy RPG seems to think counts as medicine.

Eventually the last bogborn dissolves into a sticky pile of sludge. A triumphant note blares through my headphones and bold text flashes across the screen: *Quest complete! Return for your reward.*

The victory music fades and . . . it doesn't leave behind the satisfaction I'd hoped for. The thing about games is how simple they make everything—clear quests, claim rewards. Real life just isn't like that. There's no objective marker guiding you to fix the stupid mistakes you've made.

Before I can decide whether or not to bother collecting the bounty (spoiler alert: it'll probably be disappointing), a notification appears in the top-left corner of my screen: *SassyLassie has logged in.*

Maisie's comment about Big Davie sitting in his vest and boxers pops into my head, but I know I can trust Sass. She's been my partner-in-crime in *Highland Legacy* these past few months, always ready with a cheeky quip or a daring strategy. I type out a quick message.

LOCHNLOAD

The monsters wail, they're out of luck—
Sass is back to run amok!

There's a longer pause than usual before her reply appears.

SASSYLASSIE

Hey.

Just *hey*? Well, that's a bit disappointing. Maybe she's just warming up. She usually riffs off my greeting with something equally ridiculous.

Up for slaying some beasties together? We never did do the Dun Speir quest. How about it?

Another pause, then:

SASSYLASSIE

That's the keep on the clifftop above Loch Dread, right?

LOCHNLOAD

That's the one. Word is the boss is a nightmare, and I've not fancied going in solo without your spells to back me up. 😬

SASSYLASSIE

Fine. But no chatting tonight. I just want to play.

LOCHNLOAD

Oh . . . okay. Sure.

No chatting? That's unusual. Sass is usually the queen of banter, and her playful quips are a big part of the reason I enjoy playing with her. Well, that, and the fact she's saved my arse from certain doom more times than I can count. Without her spells, I'd just be a reckless idiot charging into battle like a kilt-wearing kamikaze. The idea of playing with her without chatting feels . . . off, like putting a shoe on the wrong foot.

Still, if that's what she needs tonight, fine. I fast travel to Dun Speir, appearing just beyond the shadow of the crumbling fortress. Moments later Sass materialises beside me, her scarlet mage robes fluttering in the wind. I would ask if she's ready, but . . . no chatting . . . so I head towards the entrance, and she follows.

As we approach the rusted portcullis, it creaks open, seemingly of its own accord. Sass and I go through it and into the courtyard beyond, where cracked flagstones are scattered with bones and weeds, while ivy snakes up walls that look ready to topple under their own weight.

Dark shapes lurch into sight from behind chunks of fallen masonry and overturned carts. Wretchlings: gaunt, skeletal figures draped in shrivelled strips of flesh that flap around them like tattered sails in a storm. I've fought these guys before. Their right forearms are grotesquely warped into jagged blades that they swing in sweeping, vicious arcs. They've also got a very nasty habit of snapping off fragments of bone from their own bodies to hurl as improvised projectiles.

The wretchlings stagger towards us, disturbingly quiet—no snarls, no roars, just the clatter of bone against stone. Sass ducks behind a cart for cover, her scarlet robes blending surprisingly well with the blood stains on its wood. She fights with cool efficiency, fire magic streaking from her staff in searing bursts, each blast slamming right into a wretchling's ribcage. Meanwhile, I charge straight in, broadsword gleaming as it cleaves through brittle skeletons with satisfying crunches, fragmented bones raining around me like confetti at some deeply unsettling party.

Normally, Sass would poke fun at my complete lack of tactics. Something along the lines of: *Wow, top marks for subtlety! Why not close your eyes next time for extra chaos?* But tonight? Nothing.

The silence feels heavier than any blow a wretchling could land.

I try to lighten the mood because clearly I'm incapable of

just leaving things alone. After cleaving a wretchling's skull from his body, I type out one of my classic dad jokes.

LOCHNLOAD

> What do skeletons say to each other before a meal? Bone appétit!

And . . . nothing. Not even one of Sass's signature eye-roll emojis.

You know that sinking feeling when a joke bombs so badly you worry even imaginary video game monsters might start heckling you? No? Just me then? Luckily, rather than throwing a tomato at me, Sass shoots a fireball past me to incinerate a wretchling that was about to slice my back.

"Thanks," I mutter aloud. Hey, if I can't talk to her, I can at least talk to myself, right?

We clear out the rest of the wretchlings without much trouble, although I do take one bad hit due to mistiming a dodge. With the courtyard secure and no new horrors emerging from the shadows (yet), I down a health potion then we approach the massive oak doors leading into Dun Speir's central tower. They groan open dramatically—because why wouldn't they?—revealing shadowy corridors lit by flickering green torches whose flames sputter unnaturally against invisible drafts.

Here we go again.

Inside is exactly what you'd expect from a cursed fortress: ancient staircases spiralling upwards towards God knows what; tattered tapestries hanging limply, their faded patterns barely visible; and an ambient hum that sounds suspiciously like someone whispering ominous obscenities directly into your soul.

More wretchlings spawn as we ascend, now with armour

pieces strapped haphazardly across their fragile frames, but their strategy isn't any different from before, and they're no match for me and Sass.

I try another joke as we climb the tower because clearly I haven't learnt my lesson.

LOCHNLOAD

> What's a skeleton's favourite musical instrument? The trombone!

Still nothing from Sass. Damn it, I thought that one would have at least got a groan. It was truly awful. She was being serious when she said no chatting.

We advance through Dun Speir's endless maze of stairs and hallways until we reach what must be the boss chamber: enormous double doors etched with glowing runes that pulse faintly like a heartbeat.

Before heading in, I try one last time to chat with Sass. Silent treatment or not, we need a game plan. This isn't going to be some minor scrap with a few wretchlings. This is a boss fight, and *Highland Legacy* boss fights are always brutal.

LOCHNLOAD

> I think I should use the Claymore of the Clan Chiefs. That'll leave me exposed, though.

The weapon Sass won after we defeated the Cù Sìth, and which she gifted to me after I admitted my interest in a bit of power play, is a massive two-handed sword. It's practically guaranteed to inflict devastating melee damage on the boss, but using it means no shield, no pistol, and—worst of all—no health potions. Yes, for some sadistic reason the game doesn't let you heal yourself when you're using a two-handed weapon, and there's rarely a chance to switch gear in the middle of a boss battle.

After a pause so long it makes me wonder if she's gone AFK, a reply pops up.

Just "k"? Not "Don't worry", not "Got your back", just . . . "k"? Wow, she's *really* sticking with this whole "no chatting" thing. Usually we'd spend ages hashing out our approach. She'd poke holes in my harebrained plans, I'd try (and fail) to defend them, then we'd inevitably go with her idea.

There's no opportunity to dwell on her uncharacteristic coldness because she sprints ahead and opens the massive double doors.

"Fine then," I mutter, once again to myself. I follow after her.

The chamber beyond is vast, and more green torches line its stone walls, casting shadows that dance across the floor. In the very centre of the room stands our opponent, lit by moonlight that spills from a crack in the far wall.

The thing is enormous, easily three times my avatar's size, with twisted antlers that curl out from a cracked skull. Its body is translucent and vaguely humanoid, but it shifts and flickers like smoke trapped within an outline of armour. One of the wraith's hands grips a wickedly curved glaive that glows with a sinister green light, while the other holds spectral chains that drag noiselessly across the floor as it takes a menacing step towards us. The monster lets out a bone-rattling howl.

LOCHNLOAD

All right, big guy. Let's dance.

No response from Sass, not even a sarcastic "Wow, original" like she'd usually throw at me for such clichéd bravado. She simply takes position behind me and charges her staff with fiery energy.

I edge closer to the wraith, for once resisting the urge to rush in without thinking. A crucial part of any *Highland Legacy* boss fight is figuring out the thing's attack patterns. Skip that step and you don't stand a chance. The key to survival in the opening minutes is observation, not unloading every attack in your arsenal.

The wraith and I circle each other cautiously as I wait for an opening. When Sass sends a series of fireballs its way, I see my chance and lunge towards it, but it darts sideways with surprising speed for something so massive, then lashes out with a wide swing of its glaive. I *just* manage to dodge the weapon itself, but the blade sends green shock waves outwards that chip away at my health bar. Great start.

Crap, I need to be more careful. I move further away from it, trying to stay just outside its reach while studying its movements.

Sass casts another fiery barrage at the wraith that lights up the chamber like a miniature fireworks display. One fireball slams into the monster's chest plate, momentarily dispersing some of the smoke from its body. But, like fog drawn into a vacuum, it re-forms. The wraith lets out a piercing shriek and turns towards Sass, brandishing its chains high.

Not today! I dart forwards, drawing its attention back to me, then roll under a swipe of its glaive, but the pulsing shock waves again catch me, dropping my health bar even further. Shit! But at least it gives Sass an opening. She unleashes a crackling inferno that sends flames licking up the wraith's antlers.

The blast draws the fiend's focus back to Sass, which in turn gives me the perfect chance to strike. I swing the Claymore of the Clan Chiefs in a wide arc that carves straight through its smoky midsection. For a moment it looks like it's had no effect, then crimson damage numbers flash above its head: 1200 . . . 1400 . . . 1600. *Hell yes!*

Confidence surges through me. We've got this in the bag! Or so I think. Those spectral chains whip forwards and coil around my legs, yanking me off my feet and slamming me to the ground, taking a massive chunk out of my health bar.

"Oh, come on!" I complain to my screen as LochNLoad scrambles back to his feet, the flashing red warning at the bottom of my display screaming danger.

I wait for Sass to cast a healing spell, but instead she lobs another volley of offensive spells at the boss. What is she playing at?

LOCHNLOAD

Heal!

I dodge another devastating glaive attack by sheer luck rather than skill—that would have been the end of me—but again I'm caught by those bloody shock waves, knocking my health down ludicrously low.

LOCHNLOAD

HEAL!!!

Still nothing! What is she doing?

And then: another swing of the glaive—another desperate dodge—but the shock wave slams into me anyway, draining the last of my health. LochNLoad staggers and drops to one knee, the claymore slipping from his grasp. Then . . . he crumples forwards, faceplanting onto the stone floor.

My screen fades to black, and bold white letters declare: *You Have Died*. A moment later the game really twists the knife in: *Experience Lost: 9450 EXP*.

"Brilliant," I groan, leaning back and rubbing both hands through my hair. "Just bloody brilliant." Nearly ten thousand experience points gone, just like that. That's everything I earned since I last levelled up.

Admittedly, it *is* possible to disable the lose-EXP-on-death setting for a less brutal gaming experience, but any self-respecting gamer knows that's just not how it's done. Dying is *supposed* to sting. And sting it does, because everything I've accomplished today—clearing out the bogborn infestation in the ruined village and taking down wave after wave of wretchlings in Dun Speir's courtyard and tower—has been for nothing. Every bit of experience I earned? Gone.

I respawn all the way back at Torlannach Tavern. Sighing, I type out a simple message.

LOCHNLOAD

WTF, Sass?!

Naturally, she doesn't reply because why would she? Tonight she's not chatting—nor casting healing spells, apparently. And she's not sticking around either. A notification pops up: *SassyLassie has logged off*.

I rip off my headphones and toss them down on my desk,

muttering a string of curses under my breath. Outside, the relentless rain continues its assault on my window.

My gaze shifts to the *Highland Legacy* figurine perched on my shelf, the one with the uncanny resemblance to SassyLassie. I narrow my eyes at it and grumble, "What had your knickers in a twist tonight?"

But then, closing my eyes, I press my fingers to my temples and take a deep breath. As frustrating as that was, I hope everything is okay with Sass.

CHAPTER FIFTEEN

JAMIE

Seven years ago

The windscreen wipers thud a frantic rhythm, hopelessly battling the relentless Highland rain. From my spot in the back seat, I watch droplets chase each other across the window, merging and splitting like tiny streams. Beyond them lies a grey smear of hills and trees, their familiar shapes distorted into something almost unrecognisable. It really is coming down heavily out there.

"You'll have them eating out of your hand tonight, son," Da says, his voice rumbling over the hiss of tyres on wet tarmac. He hunches over the steering wheel as we round a bend. "All that charm of yours, plus a bit of rugby chat? They'll be throwing their wallets at you."

"Aye, well, Coach reckons I need to improve my tackling if I want to make it to the next level." I tug at my shirt collar. The thing feels like it's strangling me.

"Tackling?" Da scoffs, shooting me a quick look in the rear-view mirror, his eyes bright with that unmistakable glint of pride. "Jamie, you're not there to tackle. You're there to sprint past every poor sod on the pitch and score tries like your life depends on it. And that just happens to be something you do fucking brilliantly."

"Angus McIntyre!" Maw's black velvet dress catches the glow of a passing car's headlights. "Must you swear every time you praise him? Honestly, the boy's ego is big enough without you throwing f-bombs at it."

As we round another bend, the car jolts slightly. Da steadies us then leans forwards a little more, squinting at the road ahead. "He's eighteen now, Mairi—a man! If he can survive being smashed into the mud by blokes twice his size every weekend, I think he can handle hearing an f-word or two from his da. Besides, I've seen old men at matches clutching their hats and muttering swear words they haven't used since National Service all because of Jamie. The lad's got so much raw talent it'd make any rugby fan curse out loud. He's already better than some of the professionals out there, if you ask me."

A flush creeps up my cheeks. "I'm not sure about that, Da."

"*I* am. That try in your last game against Moray? You dodged one of their players, sidestepped another, then took off like a rocket. Nobody stood a chance of catching you!"

"It wasn't *that* impressive," I mutter, even though inside my head I'm now replaying the try, and . . . okay, sure, I don't want to blow my own trumpet, but it was pretty good.

"It was *bloody* impressive, son. Mark my words, in a few years you'll be playing for Scotland. I can see the headline now: *Jamie McIntyre storms past English defence at Murrayfield. Scotland crowned champions!*"

"Aye, right," I say, but I can't hold back a small grin. It's impossible not to when Da's so certain about things like this. Mind you, when a strong gust of wind batters the car, my smile falters and I grip the door handle, as if clutching it will somehow keep us anchored.

"This weather!" Maw says. "Are you sure you can see where you're going okay, Angus?"

"Of course, Mairi."

"Okay, well, just watch your speed." Maw cranes her neck to give me a once-over in the back. "As for you, young man, even if you're not leading Scotland to glory quite yet, I must say, you're looking very handsome tonight." She reaches back to fix my tie like I'm six years old again.

"Maw," I groan, releasing the handle to swat her fussing hands away. "As Da said, I'm eighteen now. I can sort my own tie, you know."

"Och, you'd best get used to women fawning over you, son," Da quips. "Once you're scoring tries on TV, there'll be a lot more of that, I reckon."

I let out a small laugh but there's a tightness in my chest, like a coiled spring ready to snap. It's daft, really, pinning so much on tonight's casino-night fundraiser at the rugby club. It's just a bit of fun for charity, nothing to lose sleep over. Except . . . coaching staff for the Scotland under-20s team are going to be there, and that makes it a pretty big deal. Especially as there have been whispers lately. Nothing official, just vague rumours about "certain people" keeping an eye on me.

The rain hammers down harder, furious now, like the sky has decided to wring itself dry all at once. The wipers screech frantically as they fight a losing battle against the onslaught.

When another gust of wind hits us, Maw draws a sharp

breath. "Maybe we should pull over?" Even over the roar of water on the roof, the worry in her voice is unmistakable.

Da doesn't answer straight away. Instead he leans even further over the wheel, his shoulders bunching beneath his tweed jacket. "The weather is fierce," he admits at last. "But we're nearly there now. Just need to get past this stretch."

I peer out of my window. The trees that whip past are nothing more than inky streaks against the raging night.

And then suddenly it happens: a sudden shift in the car's movement. The tyres stop gripping properly. They slide, like they can't find purchase on the slick surface below. My pulse spikes.

"Angus!" Maw says urgently.

"I've got it," Da replies, though there's a waver in his tone. He tries to correct our path but the car doesn't respond like it should. It lurches and skids sideways with an awful inevitability.

"Jesus!" Maw shrieks.

The world outside spins in sickening flashes. My fingers dig into the door handle. We veer towards a hulking shadow—a tree—and then—

A deafening crunch reverberates through my body as metal crumples like tin foil and my head slams forwards into something hard.

◆ ◆ ◆

I wake up thrashing, my hands clawing at my duvet, which is twisted around my legs like a restraint, my body jerking as if still trapped in the crash. For a few seconds panic clouds everything—the darkness too thick, my chest too tight. I reach out blindly and frantically until I finally find the switch for my bedside lamp. Light spills across my room, washing over familiar shapes: my shelves crammed with geeky books; my perpetually messy desk; the gamer chair that probably needs replacing but feels like home.

Fuck. I'm safe. Alive.

Unlike—

I press the heels of my hands into my eyes, hard enough to see stars behind closed lids, as though I may be able to block out that tree or the awful sound of metal folding in on itself. In daylight those moments stay locked away in some shadowy corner of my mind, one I can't access, like my brain knows I'm not strong enough to face them. But in dreams like that one? They tear through me with a ferocity that leaves me gasping for air.

For a while I just lie there, my chest heaving as I fight to slow my breathing, the sheet beneath me clinging uncomfortably to my sweat-soaked back. Eventually, with a groan, I force myself upright and swing my legs over the side of the bed. That's when it hits—the sharp, stabbing ache in my left thigh.

"Bloody hell," I hiss, rubbing at the spot like that'll do anything. It's been seven years since they shoved the titanium rod into my femur—seven years since *that night*—and although I've recovered well, the pain still comes back sometimes. I can understand it when I take a tumble—like when Bruce turned me and Maisie into human dominoes a couple of weeks back— but on occasions like this, when I haven't done anything physical to trigger it? That's the worst. "Psychosomatic pain", my doctor called it. But knowing that it originates in my mind doesn't make it any less real.

I drag shaky hands through sweat-damp hair then, bracing

myself, get to my feet. I hobble over to a chest of drawers, where I always keep a bottle of whisky stashed. Well, I didn't get to swallow the drams at the distillery, did I? So I shouldn't feel guilty about having a wee nightcap. Not that I usually need an excuse. Thus the bottle in my bedroom.

No glass required. I tip the whisky straight from the neck, letting the fiery liquid burn its way down. It's not exactly smooth, but right now that roughness is just what I need: a distraction, a small comfort wrapped in heat.

I take a second swig for good measure then shuffle into my en suite bathroom, the tiles cool underfoot. When I click on the light, the brightness stings my eyes. I grip the edges of the sink and examine my reflection: shadowed eyes, hair sticking up in tufts, skin pale except for blotches of heat blooming on my chest and neck, courtesy of the adrenaline still surging through me.

Twisting on the tap, I splash cold water over my face, the icy shock chasing away some of the memories and anchoring me back in the here and now. Then, peeling off my boxers, which are damp with sweat, I wet a cloth with warm water and wipe down my armpits and chest, then the lower regions too. There's nothing quite like giving your balls a scrub at three in the morning to really hammer home that you're winning at life, eh? Not exactly glamorous, but better than sitting around drenched in sweat and smelling like a bogborn. Obviously, a shower would be better still, but no, thanks. Not right now. Too much like rain.

Fucking rain.

Back in my room I pull on joggies and an old T-shirt then slump into my chair and flip open my laptop. Sleep, I know, is a lost cause. Even with the whisky warming my insides, my heart is still racing and my thoughts still spinning. I need . . . I need to not be me for a while.

I log in to *Highland Legacy*. SassyLassie won't be online at this hour, and even if she were, she's giving me the cold shoulder at the moment. That's okay. I think a solo quest is exactly what I need right now.

CHAPTER SIXTEEN

MAISIE

My head pounds in time with every wet swish of the mop across the Pheasant's wooden floor. The hangover gods have outdone themselves this time. My brain feels like it's hosting a bagpipe concert, with each note more discordant than the last.

Still, I soldier on and attack a patch of gunk. *What even is this?* I wonder. Something sticky. Whatever it is, it's stubborn and obnoxious, not unlike a certain man I spent some time with yesterday—and who had the audacity to chuck me out of his car into rain so torrential it could've been the final scene in a disaster movie.

Bloody Jamie. Just the thought of him has me gripping the mop so tightly it's a wonder I don't snap it in two. What makes everything worse—what I *really* can't wrap my head around— is that, before I was sent out into the storm, I was actually enjoying myself with him. There were . . . moments. Like when I caught him watching me during the tasting, his eyes lingering on mine a second too long before he looked away. Or when he steadied me as we were leaving, his chest solid and warm against my back. And as for the drive home, well, let's just say it's hard to square the obvious contempt he has for me (enough to banish me into a monsoon) with the . . . enthusiasm I noticed in his trousers.

Sure, I might have poked the bear a bit right before he kicked me out, but come on, this is Jamie McIntyre we're talking about—the king of inappropriate banter. If you can't take it, don't dish it, right? The whisky must have dulled my awareness of just how wound up he was getting, but still, his reaction was wildly over the top. Is SassyLassie really that sacred to him? Was suggesting she might in fact be some guy called Big Davie such an unforgivable crime?

At least I got revenge, of sorts, in *Highland Legacy*. After months of healing LochNLoad's sorry arse, buffing his stats, and saving him from death on practically every quest, it felt bloody brilliant to abandon him, just like Jamie abandoned me on the road home. And look, I'm not unhinged—it's only a game—but . . . watching that wraith finish him off? Deeply satisfying. I know, I know, but I'm only human! Afterwards, I teleported myself to safety—perks of being a mage—and logged off.

Still, if I want to use my online alliance with LochNLoad to suss out Jamie's intentions for the snug, betraying him might not have been my smartest move. I'll have to message him, smooth things over, grovel a bit.

Although . . . now that I've had time to dry off and think about it, isn't all this sneaky scheming a bit much? Aye, Jamie was an arse yesterday—an utter prick, in fact—but should I maybe be taking the moral high ground here? Don't get me wrong, there's not a chance in hell I'm about to confess to keeping certain details from him longer than was strictly necessary. I'm hardly going to admit to a failing and offer an apology when what he did was so much worse. But . . . maybe I could just block LochNLoad and never play with him again? Clean break. No drama.

When my phone vibrates, my first thought is it's probably him, wondering what that was all about with the wraith fight. But no, it's Cat in the Scottish Sirens chat. She's sent a photo of herself glaring at an Everest-sized stack of essays with a caption that reads: *Send help!*

> **IONA**
>
> 💙 💙 💙 Maybe just write "Needs Improvement" on each of them and call it a day?
>
> **CAT**
>
> 🌍 I wish! Trying to pass my probationary year here.

God, it'd be such a relief to tell them both everything. But how would that conversation go?

Hey! Funny story. I've been secretly playing this online game with Jamie to spy on his plans for the snug. He has no clue it's me! 😂 *I suppose you could say I'm trying to sabotage the Bannock Hotel? Aye, I'm aware how much the place means to you both. Oopsie!* 🫢

Hmm, what else? Oh aye, I kind of touched Jamie's 🍆*. By mistake, I promise! Although . . . before it happened, I HAD literally been thinking about doing it. Make of that what you will. LOL!*

Anyway, just wanted to keep you both in the loop! 💙

God, when did things spiral this far out of control? After I found out Jamie was LochNLoad, I fully intended to tell him I was SassyLassie. I really did. I tracked him down on Ben Garve, but then Bruce tangled us in his lead and tugged us over, and after that Jamie's mood completely changed, and he stalked off before I could tell him. So then I thought, fine, I'll do it in the game instead. But that's when he casually announced his grand plan to "poach" some customers from "the competition" (a.k.a. me and Da).

At the time, keeping quiet for just a wee bit longer seemed harmless enough—a way to get the inside scoop. Not once did I think my choice might lead to unintentional penis petting, abandonment in a biblical downpour, or the staging of a virtual murder. I'm in too deep to come clean now.

So instead I send an image of a Highland cow in oversized sunglasses with the caption: *You've got this!*

Total cop-out.

I finish off mopping the floor then head down to the cellar to do a stock check. Clipboard in hand, I count bottles and kegs, my pen scratching against the paper as I tick off items on the list. If it were up to me, we'd use a digital system, but Da is a firm believer in "if it ain't broke, don't fix it". And what Da says goes.

When I reach the section where we keep *Golden Stag Lager*—a local craft beer that practically sells itself—I stop short. Two kegs left. *Two.* That won't get us through Friday night, let alone the weekend.

Great.

I trudge back upstairs and find Da hunched over a mess of papers at his desk. The office, as always, smells faintly of lemon cleaner and stale coffee.

"Da, when is the Golden Stag delivery due?"

He lifts his head and frowns slightly. "It should be coming in on . . ." Trailing off, he glances down at the cluttered desk as if the answer might be hiding there somewhere. "Wait, didn't it come in on Monday?"

"Nope." I lean against the doorframe and cross my arms. "We're down to two kegs."

"That can't be right." He rifles through a precarious stack of invoices and receipts. Flipping one over, he squints at it then grabs another slip from the pile. Finally he lets out a low groan and slumps back in his chair. "Aw, shite."

"What?"

He tugs a sticky note free from the chaos on his desk—a crumpled square with scrawled reminders—and holds it up between two fingers like damning evidence. "Looks like I meant to place the order last week but forgot."

I chew my bottom lip. "Da . . ."

"It's these tablets the doctor put me on," he says gruffly. "They make my brain all fuzzy."

"It's okay, Da. I'll sort it."

"No." He straightens stiffly. "I'll phone them right now." He reaches for the landline on his desk.

I nod and leave the office, shutting the door quietly behind me.

He won't admit it but he's struggling, I know he is. First the stiffness in his movements, now forgetfulness? Keeping this place running is taking its toll on him but he refuses to step back, as though sheer willpower alone can make up for what's slipping through the cracks. And maybe it could, once upon a time, but not anymore.

I let out a slow breath and glance around the empty pub. It's on me to keep things steady, isn't it? To pick up the slack where I can and stop mistakes like this one from happening again. Because we can't afford more mistakes, not when Jamie is cooking up a scheme to poach our customers.

Sitting myself down at a table, I pull out my phone. Am I proud of being neck-deep in virtual espionage against Jamie? No, of course not. But since I've already waded this far into the muck, I might as well see it through. As much as I hate the secrecy of it all, knowing what Jamie's planning could give me an edge when it comes to protecting the Pheasant. Knowledge is power, right? And not knowing—sitting here stewing in uncertainty—is torture. At least with answers, I can come up with a plan of my own.

First step: apologising to LochNLoad for yesterday's mid-battle betrayal. This is not going to be fun.

SASSYLASSIE

> Hey. So, about yesterday . . . sorry for how I acted. I was dealing with some stuff IRL. I wasn't quite myself.

Of course, the things I was dealing with in real life involved Jamie, not that he has any idea. Honestly, I'm not sure this apology is going to cut it. He probably lost a shitload of EXP yesterday. If I were him, I'd be raging.

His reply comes in surprisingly quickly.

LOCHNLOAD

> No worries. Wasn't my best day either.

Wait, what? He's not going to berate me? Make me grovel? Demand I transfer him in-game currency in compensation?

LOCHNLOAD

> Hope everything is okay your end. Always here if you need someone to talk to.

I blink at my phone. I just . . . don't get it. How can someone who'd abandon a person in a storm be capable of such easy kindness? The two sides of Jamie don't match up at all.

Wow, it looks like getting back in his good graces might just be a lot easier than I was expecting. I fire off a reply saying I'll see him online tonight.

◆ ◆ ◆

Later, after the last punter has stumbled out of the Pheasant and Da has gone to bed, I settle in front of my laptop. My hair is still damp from my shower, and I'm wrapped up in my comfiest jammies. It's just me, the glow of my screen, and a whole heap of questionable moral decisions.

As soon as I log in to *Highland Legacy*, a message pops up.

We both fast travel to the forest, then I guide Lochie through the towering trees, past bubbling streams and crumbling ruins overtaken by ivy, to our destination: the base of a roaring waterfall. The water tumbles into a crystal-clear pool, sending up sprays that catch the sun and scatter tiny rainbows across my screen.

LochNLoad stops beside me.

Instead of answering, I walk straight through the curtain of water. Lochie hesitates for a moment before following. There's something satisfying about knowing something he doesn't—not that it happens often.

Beyond the waterfall lies, not a dark cave, but a hidden grove bathed in eternal sunshine. Flowers in every colour ripple across the grass like a living tapestry. Butterflies weave lazy circles through the air. The location practically oozes serenity—a stark contrast to *Highland Legacy*'s usual vibe of misty landscapes and looming danger.

I pause a moment before opening my inventory and selecting the item I crafted on my break using some ridiculously rare materials. The Eidolon Plate glows faintly with blue magical patterns that counter ghostly attacks. Clicking GIVE, I transfer it to Lochie.

SASSYLASSIE

For you. To properly apologise for
yesterday.

LOCHNLOAD

Wait, is this what I think it is? Wraith-
resistant armour?! No way.

SASSYLASSIE

Aye! To be clear, it won't save you if he
cleaves you in half with his glaive, but it
should protect you from those pesky shock
waves. 😊

LOCHNLOAD

You've brought me to a secret location AND
given me an epic gift? Hang on, are our
characters on their first date? LOL.

My hands hover over the keyboard for a stunned second before I type like a woman possessed.

SASSYLASSIE

Date?! No! Definitely not!

But Lochie—*Jamie*—is undeterred.

LOCHNLOAD

Really? Because look around, this place
screams romance vibes: sunshine, flowers,
butterflies doing mating dances or whatever
it is they're up to.

Oh God, he's doubling down on this madness.

SASSYLASSIE

I crafted the wraith armour for monster
slaying—not matchmaking!

But Lochie moves towards one of the flower patches dotting the grove. Kneeling, he picks a single white bloom then walks back over to me with it.

I groan. This is *not* what I intended. I'm just trying to apologise and get him to trust me again so I can . . . what? Spy on him some more? Christ, when did I become this person?

Why the hell would I want to trigger a candlelit dinner cinematic with another player—or worse, one of the infamous fade-to-black "romance" cutscenes that everyone goes on about?

Come to think of it, maybe I should've put my quotes around "fade-to-black" rather than "romance". Because by all accounts, the in-game movies only actually dissolve to black after first "rewarding" players with a glimpse of bare boobs and a thoroughly unaroused penis. Apparently, that's the developers' idea of keeping it classy—*no vaginas or erections in our game, folk*. Truly masterful restraint.

Well, no, thank you. I'm not here for Sass's bounce physics or Lochie's sad sausage. I'm here to hurl fireballs in trolls' faces.

I blink at my screen, impressed and surprised by how quickly he dropped the notion. The Jamie who abandoned me in the rain yesterday feels worlds apart from this considerate guy who immediately ditches a topic at the first sign of reluctance. Honestly, it'd be so much easier to hate him if he were some creep who couldn't take no for an answer, like half the blokes online. Why does he have to show glimmers of goodness and make me feel guilty about my deception?

I reread Jamie's last message, the cheerful emojis mocking me from the screen. The realisation hits me so hard it's like I've stepped on a rake and the handle has smacked me right between the eyes. Sunshine, good company—and that bloody massive garden behind the Bannock Hotel.

Oh shit. Jamie is working on a beer garden.

CHAPTER SEVENTEEN

JAMIE

The snug is dead this afternoon. Obviously, my goal is to address that, but right now it suits me just fine. My laptop is propped open on the bar, and I'm fiddling with table-and-chair arrangements for the beer garden. Our application is in with the council, so it's mostly a waiting game now, but that doesn't mean I can't keep tinkering. Small tables or long communal ones, or maybe a mix of both? Should I swap out some chairs for benches to squeeze in a few more arses?

After a few more minutes of rearranging virtual furniture, I sit back and scrutinise the beer garden mock-up. Not bad. Not bad at all. It's been ages since I put this much effort into anything at the hotel. Most of the time I just coast through, barely exerting myself. Something has definitely changed. Even Lewis has noticed I'm more invested in the business.

Bruce, meanwhile, is on his bed, dead to the world, legs flung out like he's just collapsed after a marathon. A marathon of what, though? Wagging? Sniffing things? Making every human he passes on his walk tell him he's a good boy?

Chuckling softly at the sight of him, I turn my attention

back to my screen and toy with the idea of dragging one of the tables closer to the flowerbeds. This project has been a welcome distraction, keeping me from stewing too much over how I made a complete arse of things with Maisie the other day. Normally, in Bannock, something like that would be all over town by now, but for some reason Maisie's kept schtum about it.

It's strange, really. She works in a busy pub and so is surrounded by folk who'd love a juicy story like how I booted her out of my car in the middle of a downpour. One well-placed comment and she could've had the whole town sharpening their pitchforks for me. But no, it's like she hasn't said a word to anyone. I don't know why she's spared me that humiliation. Maybe because she's worried, if she opens her mouth, I'll tell people about her hand's accidental cock inspection? I'd never do that. It was obviously a mistake, and she was utterly mortified by it. It'd be cruel to embarrass her even more.

Whatever her reason, I owe Maisie for her silence. I'd rather not have the whole town gossiping about that incident and guessing at my reasons.

A familiar figure makes his way into the snug, breaking my train of thought. It's Aidan Stewart, my brother Ally's oldest mate. Behind him comes Grace, his partner, with their wee girl, Callie, balanced on her hip.

"Hiya, Callie." I give her a quick wave from behind the bar, but she barely notices me.

"Boose!" she squeals, pointing at the dog with her tiny finger.

Bruce snorts awake, lifting his head, and Callie—on a mission now—wriggles in her maw's arms. Laughing softly, Grace places her on the floor and steadies her as she wobbles her way over to Bruce, who's already up and stretching, tail wagging.

"Boose!" Callie cries again, reaching out for him.

"Gentle hands, sweetheart, remember?" Grace says.

Whether Callie understands is debatable. She plants both hands on Bruce's head and proceeds to pet him like she's kneading dough. He takes it like a champ, though, his tail thump-thumping on the floor.

Aidan watches his two lassies for a moment then joins me at the bar. "All right, Jamie?" He leans over and swipes a packet of peanuts.

"Oi, only *I'm* allowed to do that!"

He shrugs, rips the packet open with zero shame, then flicks a peanut high into the air and catches it neatly in his mouth.

I'll give it to him. It's impressive. And he's never exactly been shy of helping himself around here. I suppose that stems from the fact that, growing up, the hotel was practically a second home to him and his sister, Iona. But with Lewis watching the budget like a hawk, I'd rather not be giving away bar snacks at the moment, especially since a few packets of salt and vinegar crisps may have mysteriously vanished while I was creating my digital seating plan.

"We're just popping in to see Maw," Aidan says, "but I hear you're thinking of opening a beer garden. Great shout. Could be a big hit come summer."

"Er . . . thanks, but it's not public knowledge yet. I take it your maw told you?"

Even though I've asked Elspeth to keep it under her hat, it wouldn't surprise me if she's blabbed to her son.

"Nope." Aidan tosses up another peanut and again catches

it with ease. "Heard it from Maisie. She's going round asking folk to sign a petition opposing your plans."

"*What?*" The word bursts out of me so sharply that Grace, Callie, and Bruce all glance over at us.

Aidan lifts his hands in surrender, his blue eyes dancing with a mix of amusement and apology. "Hey, don't shoot the messenger."

My pulse drums in my ears as I shove my stool back with a grating screech and march towards the door.

"See you later, then!" Aidan calls.

Ignoring him completely, I stride past reception and straight out into the bright afternoon sun. The cheerful chirping of birds grates on my taut nerves. It takes me less than two seconds to spot Maisie outside Bannock Stores, clipboard tucked under one arm as she chats away with Tom from the Coffee Bothy. I storm towards her.

Tom looks up as I approach, his weathered face creasing into a smile. "Afternoon, Ja—"

"One sec," I cut him off, my focus laser-locked on Maisie. "What the hell are you doing?"

She doesn't so much as flinch. "I'll be with you in just a moment," she says sweetly. "If you could kindly let me finish this conversation, I'd very much appreciate it. Thank you."

I ball my hands into fists at my sides. Is there anything more infuriating than being dismissed like you're an impatient child? I'd *never* speak to someone like that (my recent treatment of Tom notwithstanding).

Maisie turns back to Tom as though I'm about as threatening as Bruce rolling over for a belly rub.

"So," she resumes smoothly, her tone all poised professionalism, as if she isn't actively trying to sabotage my life right now, "as I was saying, if you're concerned about excess noise or anti-social behaviour, or just how drastically this beer garden could change the character of Bannock, I'd really appreciate your signature." She holds out the clipboard to Tom, who—annoyingly—accepts it.

Before Maisie can hand him her pen too, I snatch it from her fingers.

"Actually," I tell Tom through gritted teeth, fighting to keep some semblance of politeness in my voice, "you might want to hold off on that. Feel free to forget everything you've just heard because it's not remotely true."

Maisie's eyes flash dangerously in the sunlight. "Jamie, this is a private conversation between Tom and me, so if you don't mind . . ."

"The council haven't even released the plans yet," I explain to Tom, ignoring Maisie entirely. "Once they do—and once everyone knows the *actual details*—there'll be plenty of time to raise objections if needed. But signing some half-baked petition now isn't going to help anyone." I wave vaguely at Maisie like she's a nuisance fly buzzing around on a summer day. "This is just . . . scaremongering nonsense."

Maisie's nostrils flare.

Tom, clearly deciding he wants nothing more to do with either of us, makes his excuses before beating a quick retreat to his café.

Now it's just Maisie and me standing toe to toe on Main Street, surrounded by quaint painted shopfronts and an annoying amount of picturesque charm for what feels like an all-out war zone.

"You and I need to chat." I nod at her clipboard like it's a weapon she hasn't quite holstered yet. "What the hell is that?"

"A petition." She lifts her chin defiantly. "And clearly you already know what it's for."

"Oh, come *on*." A bitter laugh escapes me before I can stop it.

It feels dangerous being this close to her. The memory of her hand on a rather intimate spot flashes uninvited through my mind, but I chase it away. I need to focus on what matters: winning this argument and stopping her from ruining all my hard work with that bloody clipboard.

"You don't actually care about Bannock's 'character'," I say. "You're worried about how the beer garden might affect business at the Pheasant."

Her lips curve into a slow smile that somehow manages to look both smug *and* infuriatingly attractive all at once. It sets my teeth on edge.

"How did you even know about my plans anyway?" I demand, taking a step closer.

Maisie shrugs like butter wouldn't melt in her mouth. "It's a small town. Word gets around."

Someone at the council must have blabbed. Either that or one of the contractors I've been speaking to let something slip over a pint at the Pheasant. Bugger.

"Anyway," she continues nonchalantly, brushing nonexistent dust off her jumper as though we're discussing something far less incendiary than weeks of planning going up in flames. "It was a cute idea, Jamie, but there's no chance it'll happen. Best save yourself some embarrassment and give up now."

Anger surges hot through my veins. I step even closer to her until we're practically nose to nose.

"The beer garden *will* open," I say.

This close up her eyes are dizzyingly distracting—and absolutely deadly.

"Oh aye?" Her voice drops to a mocking whisper. "Well, after you kicked me out of your car in the middle of a rainstorm, I say, bring it on! I'm more than happy to fight you. Also, what sort of man is so insecure that he has a wee tantrum when someone jokes that their gamer friend is really an old guy called Big Davie?"

I frown. "Wait—"

But she doesn't wait. She's already talking over me. "We live in a democracy. A free country," she announces with enough conviction to rival someone delivering their closing argument in court. "And I have every right to tell people what you're up to. So, goodbye."

She turns on her heel and stalks off, leaving me standing there like a right eejit.

She thinks *that's* why I kicked her out of the car? Christ, I'd barely even registered half of what she was saying by that point—I'd been too busy gripping the wheel and trying to keep the panic at bay as the rain hammered against the windscreen and memories threatened to overwhelm me.

Shit, even though I *never* talk about this stuff with anyone, I really should clear this up, as painful as this is going to be. I need to explain things.

"Maisie!" I take a step after her.

She whirls around like she's ready to go ten rounds in a boxing ring. "What? Unless this is an announcement that you're moving out of Bannock altogether—which honestly would solve a lot of my problems—I can't imagine there's anything you could say that would improve my afternoon. So, if you're planning to offer me some half-arsed excuse for your behaviour, don't bother. I've no interest in hearing it. Why don't you stick to what you're good at? Oh wait, what *are* you good at? Winding people up and generally being an arse? Nah, don't do that. Just . . . piss off!"

The words I *had* been going to say die in my throat. Instead my temper flares back up—hot and irrational but impossible to ignore. Sod it. If she wants a fight, fine. Let's have one.

"If you had any decency at all," I spit, marching closer until there's barely a foot of space between us, "you'd hold off on this petition nonsense until the council releases the actual plans. You don't even know what you're objecting to yet! You're asking people to sign something based on rumours at best and outright lies at worst—and that's not fair, and you bloody well know it."

Maisie draws in a sharp breath like I've slapped her, then blows it out again with an exaggerated huff that sends stray wisps of navy-blue hair flying around her face. For one maddening moment she doesn't reply. She just stands there glaring daggers at me while I glare right back at her.

"Fine!" she finally snaps, throwing up her hands in exasperation. "I'll hold fire for a few days if it'll stop you moaning, but don't think for a second this changes anything. The moment the plans go public, I'll be back out here collecting signatures faster than a bairn running to the ice cream van."

She spins away again before I can respond, so I don't get a chance to argue more or even to grudgingly thank her. Worse still, I'm *really* struggling to come up with an ice cream-related comeback to shout after her. Something about her being a flake? Nah, that's naff. Oh, she needs to chill out? No, too obvious. And . . . I've left it too long. If I say something now, it'll seem like I'm trying way too hard.

I head back to the hotel. When I pass the bakery, Morag emerges, wiping floury hands on an apron that looks like it's seen better days.

"Jamie, I must say, I was really disappointed to hear about this beer garden idea." She doesn't bother with pleasantries because apparently we've skipped straight to *public scolding*. "The last thing this town needs is folk getting rowdy outside our windows at night when we're all trying to sleep."

"What exactly has Maisie been saying to you?" I complain. "The whole point of a beer garden is it's a place to sit outside during the day when the sun is out. We're not going to be conducting late-night raves there. Maisie's made it sound like I'm planning something totally different from what I'm actually trying to do. All I want is to create a wee spot where folk can relax, have a natter, and soak up a bit of sun on a nice day."

"Oh," Morag says after an awkward pause in which I'm pretty sure half my brain cells shrivel from stress alone. "Well . . . that doesn't sound so bad." She sounds almost reluctant admitting it.

"Right?" I run both hands through my hair, probably making it stick up in a way that suggests I've lost the plot entirely. "So maybe people should wait until they've seen the full plans before deciding whether they object or not, eh?" I shoot her a grin in an attempt to take the sting out of my words. Getting tetchy with folk isn't going to make launching this beer garden any easier.

Back at the hotel, I find Lewis and Emily chatting in the office.

"You'll never believe what Maisie's been up to!" The words burst out of me before I've even crossed the threshold. I jab a thumb over my shoulder. "She's going around town with a bloody petition. A petition! Getting folk to sign it before they've even *seen* the plans for the beer garden. Can you believe it?"

Lewis and Emily exchange a look, then Emily slides out a chair and pats the seat. "Why don't you sit down before you pop a blood vessel and fill us in?"

"Not happening. Sitting won't help." The energy coursing through me feels like it'll explode if I don't keep moving. My legs carry me back and forth across the office as if they've got minds of their own. "Maisie is unbelievable! She's out there gathering signatures like she's some kind of crusader for justice—which, by the way, she isn't. She doesn't even know what she's talking about. And now half the town thinks we're planning a bloody outdoor nightclub!"

I regale them with every maddening detail—her smug smile, her ridiculous "democracy" speech, her complete refusal to listen to reason. Naturally, they're on my side and concerned by this development, but I seem to lose them a little when I say, "Honestly, who even behaves like that? At the very least, you'd think people would hear someone out before tearing their idea to shreds, wouldn't you?"

Emily's lips twitch, and Lewis arches a brow. They meet eyes like they're having a silent conversation.

"What?" I bark. My heart is still hammering from the encounter with Maisie. "What's with the telepathic eyebrow dance? And can I point out how bloody weird it is for work colleagues to have their own silent language? Do Ally and Iona know about this?"

Lewis holds up his hands. "Whoa there, tiger. We're not the enemy here." He leans back in his chair with a hint of a smirk. "But tell me, doesn't any of this sound familiar? Maybe, oh, I don't know, like that report Emily and I put together for Ally a couple of years ago?"

I frown at him, completely lost. "What report? What are you on about?"

"You can't have forgotten! Back when Ally was still manager, Emily and I worked on a report, laying out plans to modernise and improve the hotel. Before I could present it to Ally, though, you grabbed a hold of it and showed it to him."

"I did?" It rings a vague bell, and to be fair, it does kind of sound like me.

"You tore my ideas apart in front of him before I could present them properly! Maybe this mess with Maisie is karma coming back to bite you."

"Nah, if I really did that—"

"You did."

"—I'm sure it was all in good, cheeky fun. Maisie, on the other hand? She's out for blood."

"You know, Jamie," Emily says with a measured tone, "just because you're having fun doesn't mean everyone else is. I recall Lewis being pretty ticked off about that at the time."

"Wow, will you two *please* focus on the real issue? This isn't the bash-Jamie show. It's the bash-Maisie show!"

"Why don't we arrange a meeting with Maisie and Bryce?" Emily suggests. "Sit down with them, listen to their concerns . . . it doesn't have to be a fight."

"Nope," I say. "Maisie's made it clear she wants to play dirty, so this is war. The beer garden *will* open, it *will* be successful, and she is going *down*."

It's been ages since I've felt this fired up about anything in the real world. It's like the buzz I used to get before a rugby match, only these days it usually takes a brutal boss battle to get my blood pumping. The beer garden is the first thing I've properly cared about in forever, and now Maisie is trying to sabotage it? It's no wonder I'm fuming.

"You're really fired up about this," Emily observes.

"Of course I am!" I go back to pacing, then an idea hits me and I whirl on Lewis so fast he actually leans back. "Your girlfriend is good friends with Maisie! Ask Iona to have a word with her and tell her not to derail our business ideas."

Lewis folds his arms across his chest. "I'm not going to ask Iona to take sides. That's not fair."

"Fine." I whip my phone out. "Cat is friends with Maisie too. I'll message *her* and tell her to—"

Lewis stands and plucks my phone from my hands. "You're not messaging Cat either. Emily's right: you're getting yourself worked up. Why don't you go play your video game and kill some monsters or something? Clear your head because, if you try to deal with this as you are now, you'll just make a mess of things."

"I don't think killing virtual monsters is going to cut it today."

"Well, I'm off to the gym soon. You're welcome to tag along, but I know it's not really your thing."

I mull over this offer for a moment. "Aye, I'll come."

"Really?" He looks so surprised it's kind of insulting.

"Aye. I think I need to do something physical. Punching something—or someone—would be ideal, but I'm willing to try lifting heavy stuff. A bit of exercise, then I'll set to work undoing the damage that Maisie's done."

"All right." Lewis gives me a brotherly clap on the back. "Let's go work off some of this anger before you do something daft."

CHAPTER EIGHTEEN

MAISIE

I drag the 1950s photograph of Bannock's Main Street into my PowerPoint slide. The image is pure vintage perfection: a couple of Morris Minors lined up neatly by the pavement and several women in headscarves chatting away to each other. It joins the other pictures I've found of Main Street from times gone by, each one a wee time capsule of a different era.

Satisfied, I lean back in my chair and crack my knuckles. My desk is chaos: two empty mugs, a crumpled biscuit packet, and an abandoned can of Gaelic Fire. Evidence of a morning (and much of an afternoon) spent hunched over my laptop, working hard. Honestly, I can't remember the last time I put this much effort into a pub quiz. Some weeks I don't even bother with a presentation.

The plans for the beer garden have been public for a month now, and tomorrow the council will deliver their decision. Even with all the rallying I've been doing, trying to win people over to my way of thinking, there are still plenty of folk who rather like the idea of pints in the sun. That's why tonight's quiz isn't *just* a jaunt through Bannock's history. It's also a chance to evoke a bit of nostalgia and community pride—and maybe plant a seed of doubt about anything that could threaten the status quo.

I kept my promise to Jamie. I didn't gather any more signatures until his proposal was officially announced. But as soon as it was, I came out swinging, petition in one hand, freshly printed anti-beer garden posters in the other—many of which are now proudly displayed around town, pinned to noticeboards and brightening up shop windows.

Jamie, of course, is livid with me, which only makes it all the more satisfying. This past month we've bumped into each other a number of times, and those encounters have been . . . charged. I can practically see Jamie's jaw clench any time he spots one of my PROTECT BANNOCK flyers or SAY NO TO THE BEER GARDEN posters, or when he catches me extolling the virtues of community preservation to another local.

Good. After he left me stranded in that rainstorm, he deserves every bit of the aggravation I'm causing him. I'm not easing up until his ridiculous beer garden idea is dead and buried. Once life is back to normal, then—and only then—I'll come clean to him about the small matter of me being SassyLassie.

How I'll tell him, I've no clue. Maybe I'll just rip the plaster off: *Hey, Jamie, remember when I took the piss out of you, saying you were probably talking to some pervy guy from Glasgow? Well, surprise! I'm Big Davie!*

Aye, I can't imagine he'll take it well.

I haven't actually played *Highland Legacy* since I took Lochie beyond the waterfall. Word around town is Jamie's traded his laptop for kettlebells, so I doubt he's had much time for gaming either.

The creaking of my bedroom door pulls me from my thoughts. Da.

"You still working on that thing?" He comes closer and squints at my screen.

"Aye. Nearly there, though."

"Hmm . . ."

"What?"

"It's just . . . your passion is impressive, Maisie. Really, it is. But even if this beer garden goes ahead, we'll be okay. A beer garden is seasonal, remember—something for the summer only. So don't get yourself in too much of a twist about this."

I force a smile, trying to keep my frustration in check. "But the summer is when the tourists come—and when we make most of our money. So even if it *only* affects us then, that's still a big deal."

Da gives a casual shrug. "I doubt we'll take much of a hit. Folk will still come to the Pheasant for what they always have— the food and the company. Anyway, I'll leave you to it, but don't spend too much longer on this, all right?"

The moment the door clicks shut behind him, I slump in my chair and blow out an exasperated puff of air. Da just doesn't seem to appreciate the impact this could have on us.

◆ ◆ ◆

Muttering a quiet prayer to the tech gods, I jab the cable into my laptop. I don't entirely trust the old TV above the bar— God knows I've had issues with it before—but thankfully my first slide flickers onto its screen. Phew.

A few patrons glance over before turning back to their

conversations. The quiz isn't due to start for another ten minutes or so. I'm just getting myself organised.

The place is buzzing—not quite at fire-code-breaking capacity, but close. The sight of so many locals crammed together tugs at something deep inside me. If tonight doesn't remind these people that the Pheasant is Bannock's heart and soul, nothing will.

"Hello, Maisie!" a voice says from behind me. "Bannock's history—what a wonderful theme for a quiz!"

I turn around to see Elspeth beaming at me, Iona by her side.

"Ladies!" I pull each of them into a quick hug.

"Right, well, I'll leave you two girls to chat," Elspeth says. "Iona, I'll go get us a couple of wines and have a wee blether with Maisie's father while I'm at it. See you in a few minutes!"

Elspeth moves along the bar to speak with Da, leaving me with Iona. She takes in my outfit—a red tartan mini dress over a white T-shirt—then says, "You look *amazing* tonight, Maisie."

"You don't think the fishnets are a bit much?" When I checked in the mirror earlier, I thought they looked good with my chunky black boots, but it's always nice to get a second opinion.

"They're great," Iona assures me.

"Thanks!" I shoot her a quick smile then tuck an errant strand of hair behind my ear. "By the way, I'm sorry I've been so scarce lately. Life has been . . . hectic."

"Of course." Iona returns my smile, then her gaze drops to the floor for a moment. When she lifts it again, her expression is unsure. "Are we . . . okay, Maisie?"

I blink. "Aye." I reach out and give her shoulder a wee squeeze. "Why wouldn't we be?"

She relaxes a little, although a hint of doubt lingers in her eyes. "I just don't want this beer garden getting in the way of our friendship."

I get what she's saying. Her life is tied to the Bannock Hotel and the McIntyre family, and that puts her in a slightly awkward position.

"It won't," I say firmly. "We Scottish Sirens stick together."

That does the trick: her face lights up with relief. "Well, this particular siren is parched. I'll leave you to finish setting up, and I'll go see Maw about that wine. Good luck tonight, quizmaster!"

A few minutes later, I grab the mic and turn it on. "All right, everyone, let's get this show on the road. Tonight's quiz is a special one. It's all about Bannock: its history, its charm, and why we're all so proud to call this place home."

Cheers and applause ripple through the packed pub, and I beam, soaking up the energy.

"Let's kick things off with round one: Famous Faces of Bannock Past." I tap a key on my laptop, and the next slide appears on the TV: an old black-and-white photo of a young man, all rippling muscles and smouldering confidence. He's topless, wearing only a pair of vintage boxing shorts and gloves, his fists raised like he's ready to knock someone into next week.

A wolf whistle rings out from the back of the room, followed by a peal of laughter.

I flash a grin then say, "Question one: which Bannock-born athlete went on to have a successful boxing career in the US?"

The room bursts into activity. Heads huddle together, people whispering furiously to one another, then pens scratch across answer sheets. There's a buzz of excitement in the air.

Forget Jamie's beer garden. *This* is what Bannock—and the

Pheasant—is all about. Tradition, community, and togetherness.

◆ ◆ ◆

I'm announcing the scores for the first round when who should walk in but the smug bastard himself: Jamie McIntyre. He props himself against the bar, all easy arrogance, and shoots me a smirk that screams trouble.

To make matters worse, he looks *good*. Annoyingly so, like he's made a genuine effort for once. His hair—usually ruffled from running his hands through it—is styled, and his stubble is deliberate rather than lazy. His black shirt is smart—sharp, even—and fits him *very* well. The sleeves are rolled up just enough to reveal surprisingly strong forearms, and the hem is neatly tucked into chinos. More specifically, into *those* chinos—the penis-petting ones.

"Er . . ." My voice comes out strained through the mic, and I hastily clear my throat. *Get back on track, Maisie. Don't let him distract you.* "There's still everything to play for, but right now in first place we have . . . the Boob Lovers!"

A stunned silence falls over the pub. And then, like a dam breaking, laughter bursts out—booming, gleeful, unstoppable. I glance down at my notes. Oh, shit. My cheeks flame.

"I mean, the *Book* Lovers!" I blurt into the mic. "The BOOK Lovers!"

The laughter only grows louder, and I swear someone at the back wheezes. Brilliant. Just brilliant.

My eyes, against my better judgement, find Jamie's. His trademark smirk has spread into a full-blown grin that practically screams, *I am never letting you live that one down.*

Damn him. That only happened because he made me flustered. What is he even doing here anyway? Surely he knows how inappropriate it is that he turned up? He probably came to throw me off my game. That's the only reason I can think of.

"Right," I say into the microphone. "That was quite the . . . *titillating* mistake, wasn't it? Let's swiftly move on before I make an even bigger boob of myself."

More laughter, and just like that, I've regained control of the situation. You don't get through as many pub quizzes as I have without learning how to control a crowd.

"So, once again, well done to the Book Lovers—some of whom, no doubt, are also rather fond of boobs—for taking an early lead. Before the next round, I have a bonus question for you, which is about . . ." I tap a laptop key while simultaneously gesturing to the TV. ". . . the Pheasant! Everyone's favourite place to relax and have a drink with friends." I flash Jamie a self-satisfied smile. "Pencils at the ready, please! Your bonus question is: when was the Pheasant established? This one is multiple choice, and your options are: 1775, 1825, 1875, or 1915."

Folk lean in close, exchanging furtive glances and muttered theories. And then Jamie—who isn't even on a team—asserts to a table near him, "It's 1825. Says so on the foundation stone outside. Although these days that's hidden by that ugly SAY NO TO THE BEER GARDEN poster, of course."

His voice is loud enough that several other tables hear him too, which spoils the whole format of the quiz. He's trying to get under my skin, and it's working.

"Some eejit over here has spoiled that question with his foghorn voice," I say. "If anyone didn't hear, the answer was 1825. At least no one will be finishing the quiz with zero points, eh? Anyway, if you'll excuse me for just one minute, I'm going to have a word with the eejit in question—outside."

Glaring at Jamie, I point to the door. With a cocky grin, he follows me through it onto Main Street. It's still light out, and the air is cool but pleasant. It's a perfect May evening, although—for me—it might as well be raining fire.

"So." Jamie casually leans against the wall of the pub. "Is this *really* about my loud voice? Or were you just wanting to gossip about the dreamy looks Elspeth and your da were giving each other? Because I thought Iona would be your go-to choice for that conversation, but if you'd rather chat with me about it, fine, let's do this. What's going on between those two? I'm desperate to know. Has your da, like, started putting a sock on his door? Because if so, that could be a sign they're banging."

I roll my eyes so hard it's a wonder they don't get stuck. "Ugh, what are you even talking about? Actually, don't answer that question—I've no interest in your teasing tonight. The one thing I *do* want to know is: what are you doing here?"

He stretches his arms overhead as though he hasn't a care in the world then lets them fall loosely by his sides. "What do you think? Having fun at a community quiz. Isn't that obvious? It's a really nice idea, by the way."

I scowl at him. "I know you're only here to distract me."

"Really? Oh dear, what gives you that impression?" That maddening twist of his lips says it all: he knows exactly how much he's needling me.

"How come you're looking so smug anyway?" I cross my arms. "Shouldn't you be nervous? I've done everything I can to push back against your proposal. I think it's very unlikely your beer garden will be signed off tomorrow."

"Oh, do you now?"

"Aye."

"Well, that's interesting." He pushes off from the wall and takes a step closer to me. "Because I have a feeling things will go quite differently. In fact, I'd bet good money on it."

Not to be undone, I take a step towards him. "Your confidence astounds me. What makes you so bloody sure of yourself?"

We're close now, close enough that I catch a whiff of his enticing woodsy scent. His eyes drop briefly to my lips then sweep down over my outfit, lingering on the fishnets. When they meet my gaze again, there's definite heat there.

And that makes me *furious*. How *dare* he look at me like that? Although . . . okay, maybe a tiny part of me is pleased my clothes are doing their job. But only the teeny tiniest bit.

He tilts his head to the side. "Did it occur to you that maybe, just maybe, I was informed of the decision a day early? Before the official announcement tomorrow?"

My heart stops. "What? No . . ."

Bollocks.

He doesn't say it, but I'm sure he's thinking it: *checkmate*. He just landed the winning move in a game I didn't even realise I was losing.

"Right then," Jamie says, "it's clear you don't want me here, so I'll be on my way. I should probably get an early night anyway. It's going to be a busy day tomorrow, what with setting things in motion to get my beer garden up and running."

His words hit me like a punch to the gut. With a wink, he turns and strolls away, leaving my mind spinning.

It's possible he's just winding me up. But while I'd like to believe that, I can't shake the gnawing feeling that he's telling the truth, that the beer garden really has been signed off. Which means all my hard work, all the support I've drummed up over the last month, has been for nothing.

Damn it! I suck in a deep breath, then another, trying to steady myself and stifle the rising tide of panic. This isn't the time to fall apart. There's a pub full of people waiting for me to continue the quiz.

Squaring my shoulders, I paste on the brightest smile I can muster and head back in, although every step feels perilous, like I'm made of glass and could shatter at any moment.

Faces turn to me. I pick up my mic and clutch it like a lifeline.

"Sorry about the short delay!" My voice comes out thin at first, but I force a cheery tone into it, hoping no one notices the slight tremble in my hand. "Right, where were we?" With a tap of a key, I bring up the next slide. "Ah yes, on to the next round, Local Folklore and Legends."

CHAPTER NINETEEN

JAMIE

The sun beats down on my neck as I adjust one of the wooden benches for what must be the hundredth time this morning. It's probably perfect already, but I can't help myself. Everything has to be just right for the opening. It's not just an event, it's *my* event.

"There," I mutter, stepping back to survey my handiwork.

The beer garden has transformed the Bannock Hotel's previously underused outdoor space into something I'm truly proud of. New decking stretches out from the French windows in clean, sharp lines, and solar-powered fairy lights crisscross overhead, ready to create a magical atmosphere when evening falls. The tables and chairs are arranged in clusters, with a mix of regular seating and longer communal benches. Flowers spill in vibrant cascades from hanging baskets hooked onto wrought-iron shepherd's crooks. There's colour everywhere: bright blossoms against freshly painted wood and deep green from the potted plants dotted around the space.

In one corner sits a kids' play area with swings and a slide—small but enough to give parents a moment of peace while they sit for a drink. Next to that are oversized garden games: Jenga, chess, Connect Four. I'd love to say I picked those because they'll be great for families, but honestly? I can't wait to have a go at giant Jenga after a pint or two. Meanwhile, a fire pit waits patiently for cooler evenings. I can already picture folk huddling around it, drams in hand and laughter in the air.

Jamie McIntyre: beer garden designer extraordinaire. Who knew?

In the end I did most of the work myself, to keep costs down *and* because I couldn't bear to let anyone else take charge. I've sweated over this too much to let someone interfere with my vision. And honestly? That only makes me prouder of how it's turned out.

For today's grand opening we've gone all out: there's a barbecue station set up near the decking, a bouncy castle and face painting for kids, an area designated for Kyle to run whisky tastings, and a small stage where a local band will play this evening. I'm sure I've thought of everything—even Lewis said so yesterday—and yet . . .

I run a hand through my hair, probably making it stick up at all angles, and let my gaze sweep over the space again. It looks good. Better than good—it looks amazing. A little corner of magic carved out here in Bannock.

But what if no one shows up? What if Maisie's crusade against my beer garden has ruined everything? Her flyers and posters were bloody everywhere—STOP THE BEER GARDEN plastered across town like she was rallying troops for battle rather than opposing the serving of drinks outside.

I shift a table an inch to the left. Then back again. Pointless, but I'm just trying to keep myself busy—standing around getting nervous isn't going to help. The physical work feels good, though. Between building this space and hitting the gym with Lewis (which has already become as routine as breakfast), I'm in better shape than I've been since . . . well, since before everything went sideways.

It still feels weird sometimes—that sense of energy buzzing through me again. It used to be second nature, back when rugby was my life. For years after the crash stole my shot at going pro, I gave up on keeping fit altogether, like if rugby wasn't an option, there wasn't any point even trying anymore. But lately? Lately things have shifted again—for my body *and* my brain—and working on this beer garden has helped more than I could've imagined.

My phone buzzes in my pocket. It's Lewis asking if we need more ice (we do). After firing back a quick yes, my thumb hovers a moment before tapping open my chat with Sassy-Lassie. Just in case. Maybe I missed a notification somehow? But no, the last message is still mine from days ago, checking if she's okay. It's been weeks since she last logged in to *Highland Legacy*. True, it's not like I've had much time to play myself, but that doesn't stop me from worrying about her.

The trouble with online mates is if they vanish, you're left with no way of knowing why. What can you actually do if you don't even know their real name? Maybe it's nothing—maybe just life getting in the way, as it has for me. At least, I hope that's all it is.

I shove my phone away and turn my attention back to the task at hand. Wandering over to the giant Jenga, I nudge back into place a piece that's sticking out. For some reason I immediately picture the tower toppling over onto some poor kid's head later this afternoon.

Brilliant. Like I didn't have enough to stress about already.

Keep busy, Jamie. Keep busy!

I adjust a plant pot, but the deep blue splash of delphiniums catches my eye and reminds me of something, or rather, someone. Navy-blue hair, stray wisps escaping in every direction . . .

And just like that, Maisie has stomped her way back into my brain without so much as a polite knock to ask permission.

Last night when I was walking Bruce, I wandered past the Pheasant and spotted her through the window. She didn't see me, which is probably a good thing, seeing as I was standing there like some sort of creep in the shadows, watching her work. She poured pints faster than you'd think humanly possible, without spilling so much as a drop, all the time chatting away with customers. That smile . . . so genuine, so effortless. But never directed at me, of course.

There's something about her that ties my brain in knots—and not just because we're currently at war over this beer garden. It's inconvenient as hell, if I'm honest. How am I supposed to hate someone when even thinking about her has a way of setting off memories I've no business dwelling on?

Like how her body felt pressed against mine on Ben Garve—slim curves leaning into me while Bruce wagged his tail like he'd done us both a favour. Or that moment outside the distillery when she stumbled into me after one too many drams at Kyle's tasting session, her arse flush up against me in a way that fried every coherent thought in my head.

And don't even get me started on the car incident. Bloody hell. Her hand slipping and landing squarely on my crotch . . .

That was two months ago now, yet somehow my brain refuses to let it go. Instead I've replayed it so many times I've started imagining all the ways it could've gone differently. Like what if, rather than yanking her hand away, she'd . . . kept it there? Curled those fingers around me? Maybe even . . . unzipped me?

Oh Christ.

I groan out loud because this is exactly what I need right now: getting hot under the collar over someone who can't stand me, right before an event I've been breaking my back over for weeks.

I shouldn't be thinking about Maisie. Not like this, not with everything riding on today. But guilt has a funny way of creeping in, even when you're desperate to shove it aside. Because, of course, it's not just about the attraction with Maisie—though that's a beast of its own, clawing at me when I least expect it. No, it's also about everything else. Like how I can't forget the way her eyes shadowed with fear the night before the council's decision, when I admitted I already knew what they'd say. She tried to hide it, but I saw. She's worried about the Pheasant—that much was clear. Her and her father's livelihood is tied up in that pub, and here I am, charging head-first at it like a battering ram.

But then again . . . she hasn't exactly made things easy for me, has she? The posters, the petition—her *crusade* against this beer garden. Glancing around at what I've built here—this space that made me sweat and ache and bleed—I know this is more than just some project to me. Losing rugby left a hole nothing could fill, until this. Until now. Don't get me wrong, I love *Highland Legacy*, but *this* . . . this is real.

A sharp pang hits my chest as my mind drifts back to that rainy night in the car. Kicking Maisie out like that was low—arsehole behaviour of the highest order—but what would she have thought if she'd seen me falling apart? If she'd sat there while my hands locked around the wheel in a death grip, shaking so violently I could barely breathe? Flashbacks are bad enough—they don't need an audience.

And yet, knowing all that doesn't make me feel any better about what I did.

I close my eyes briefly as vivid memories return: rain hammering against the windscreen . . . my chest tightening until it felt like my ribs might snap under the pressure . . . forcing myself to pull over just minutes after dumping her on the roadside so I could work through my breathing exercises. It had taken nearly twenty minutes for me to feel human again—and by then, Maisie was gone.

She still thinks I kicked her out because of some flippant joke about SassyLassie being an old pervert called Big Davie. Honestly, part of me wishes that *were* the reason—it'd be easier to explain than admitting I'm too broken to handle heavy rain behind a wheel without spiralling into a panic attack.

I should really tell her the truth. But every time we talk—or rather, argue—it feels like we're playing a game where neither of us knows the rules, but we're both sure we're losing. And naturally, that makes us bloody furious with each other. Besides, dragging up those memories isn't exactly high on my list of enjoyable activities. Even now, just thinking about them, my throat constricts.

Tomorrow, I decide. Tomorrow, after the opening event, I'll track down Maisie and explain everything. Hell, I'll try contacting SassyLassie again too, though I don't know if that'll do any good.

But today? Today is about the beer garden.

I check the time on my phone. Two hours until we open. The sun blazes above without a single cloud in sight, a stroke of luck in Scotland if ever there was one. Inside the hotel kitchen, Elspeth is busy chopping and prepping for the barbecue.

It's going to be fine. More than fine.

Closing my eyes for a second, I let out an exhale so deep it nearly doubles as a prayer. *Please let folk show up.*

◆ ◆ ◆

The afternoon sun hangs high above the beer garden, drenching it in warm golden light. The place is picture-perfect—no, better than that, it's *alive*. Every single seat is taken. Laughter ripples through the air, mingling with the lively buzz of conversation coming from all directions. Folk are gathered around tables dotted with half-empty glasses of beer and wine, while others stand together in loose huddles, their faces lit with animated expressions as they swap stories or catch up on gossip. Kids dart between the bouncy castle and the play area, ice creams melting faster than they can lick them. A few brave souls are locked in a battle over the giant Jenga tower, which sways precariously after each reckless tug at a wooden block. No casualties yet—thankfully—and I've mostly stopped envisioning it collapsing onto someone's head. Mostly.

The place is bloody packed. Families sprawl across tartan picnic rugs in the grassy areas; couples sip prosecco by the hanging baskets; and tourists stand about like they belong here, clutching pints as they soak up the sun and chatter away. It's surreal seeing strangers in this space I built with my own hands and knowing they didn't wander in by chance. They came *for this*. For something I created.

It's more than I could've hoped for when I first started putting this plan into motion, and so far everything is going brilliantly. No disasters, no complaints—hell, not even a hint of drama (which might be a first for Bannock). Elspeth and Lewis have the barbecue station running like a well-oiled machine, while the local teens I hired for face painting are crazily talented. And best of all? The tables I've been checking in on all afternoon keep saying the same thing: they're happy.

Not that I've exactly had time to kick back and bask in my runaway success. It's been nonstop since we opened—a blur of ferrying drinks, clearing glasses, and making small talk just long enough to seem welcoming without coming across as rude when I inevitably dash off mid-sentence to tend to something else. Emily's been helping out where she can, but right now she's taking a break at one of the tables. Seated next to her is Grace, and across from them are David, Grace's brother, and his boyfriend, Johnny MacDonald.

All four of them are laughing, each in their own way. Tears stream unchecked down Grace's cheeks, while David clutches Johnny's arm like it's the only thing keeping him upright. Johnny sits there grinning like he's seen it all before, quietly amused by their antics. And then there's Emily, chuckling softly as she strokes slow circles over her baby bump without spilling a single drop from her glass of lemonade.

As I weave past them on my way to the snug, to sort out yet another order, Emily fixes me with a mock-stern glare and tilts her head just so.

"Don't even think about telling me my break is over," she warns.

"Wouldn't dream of it," I shoot back, because honestly? Like hell am I going to boss around my very pregnant sister-in-law today. "Take as long as you need."

She gives me a sly smile before turning back to whatever

story David is telling that has Grace dissolving into giggles. I continue on to the snug but manage only six steps before someone else stops me.

"Oh, Jamie!" Cat calls out sweetly—the kind of sweet that sets alarm bells ringing if you know my sister even a little. She's down from Wick to support me for the beer garden's opening weekend. And by *support*, I mean catching up with her pals and soaking up as much free booze as she can.

Right now she's perched on the edge of a table, chatting away with Iona, who has Bruce with her. Cat looks like she hasn't got a care in the world, except clearly she wants something from me, and whatever it is, I can't imagine it'll make my life any easier.

"Aye?" I say warily, already bracing myself. "What is it?"

"Oh, nothing major," she says casually. "It's just, you see that table over there? They asked for five pints of Golden Stag, two glasses of house white, and one house red, while *that* table asked for . . ." She pauses then turns to Iona. "Hmm, what was it again? Can you remember?"

"Hang on!" There's an ache building behind my eyes, the kind that promises a headache later, but that's Future Jamie's problem. "Let me write down that first order before you try to remember the other one."

I take out my battered notepad, trying not to wince at the sight of three orders I haven't even started on yet. And now there's two more? Brilliant. With Emily on her break, it's just me holding down the fort, and while everyone is all smiles and easy-going vibes for now, their patience might not last. If I don't speed up, this chilled-out beer garden could turn into a riot of empty glasses and grumbling punters.

When people talk about being a victim of your own

success, is this what they mean? Because I *am* proud of how buzzing this place is, but it's got to be said, hanging about in an empty bar playing video games was a shitload easier than this.

"So," I mutter, "what was it again? Five pints of—"

"Six," Cat interrupts breezily.

I look up and narrow my eyes at her. "Didn't you just say five?"

"Oh, did I? Maybe that's because . . . I made those orders up." She flashes me a cheeky grin. "I just wanted to watch you panic for a minute."

I bite back a groan. "Cat!" My tone is full of warning.

She winks. "Seriously, though, give me a few pages from that notepad and let me help. You're looking pretty swamped."

I cock my head to the side and raise an eyebrow. "Did I hear that right? Did you volunteer to help? Like, without coercion? Without being bribed? What's going on?"

She rolls her eyes. "Consider this me earning the complimentary drinks I've been enjoying all afternoon. But the offer won't last, Jamie. Take it or leave it."

I quickly tear three pages from the notepad and hand them to her. "Taking it!"

Cat turns back to Iona. "Right, drinks to prep, but we'll catch up more later, okay? Oh, and you, me, and Maisie need to sort a Scottish Sirens meet-up while I'm down. A proper in-person gathering!"

At Maisie's name my brain threatens rebellion again—but no time for that right now.

As Cat strides off towards the snug—armed with my notepad pages and a level of confidence I can only hope isn't misplaced—I crouch down by Bruce for what feels like my first real breather since we opened. Petting dogs is supposed to reduce stress, isn't it? God knows I could do with that.

"All right, big man?" I scratch behind one of his floppy ears, but Bruce's soulful brown eyes are locked firmly on Lewis over at the barbecue station. Or, more specifically, on the sausages and burgers sizzling away under Lewis's watchful eye.

Can't say I blame him.

Lewis blows a kiss across the beer garden and, without missing a beat, I straighten up and snatch it out of the air like this is a routine we've perfected over years.

"Love you too, bro!" I call out loudly enough to turn a few heads.

Lewis glares at me, a faint flush spreading across his cheeks, then turns his attention back to the barbecue and flips another burger.

Beside me, Iona snorts into her glass of wine. "That was meant for me, you daftie."

"Was it?" I grin at her innocently. "Could've been meant for you . . . or Bruce . . . or me. We may never know."

She shakes her head in mock despair. "You might've pulled off something amazing here today, but you've not lost your bloody sense of humour."

"And thank God for that!"

I give Bruce one last ear scratch. He lets out a mournful whine and casts another glance at the barbecue, a string of drool hanging from his jowls.

"Right then," Iona says, "I'll see if Aidan and Callie can distract Bruce from those tantalising smells. But seriously, Jamie, good work here. You've done a cracking job with everything." She leads Bruce off towards her brother, who's currently hurrying after her adorable, pint-sized whirlwind of a niece.

Okay, what now? With Cat handling those orders, maybe I should do a quick circuit of the tables and check everyone is still happy? But before I can so much as take a step, Ally, my eldest brother, waves me over. Honestly, would it kill my family to cut me some slack today? I've got a whole crowd of customers to keep smiling. Still, I head his way to find out what he wants.

Ally lounges on a tartan blanket with Ru, his fourteen-month-old son, planted beside him. My nephew's face is painted like a tiger, although the stripes are a bit smudged now. Wide-eyed with wonder, Ru watches Callie's antics with a sort of adoration lighting up his wee round face.

Callie totters across the lawn with an air of determined mischief, her tiny feet surprisingly fast for someone so new to walking. Every wobble looks like it's about to end in disaster, yet somehow she powers on unscathed. And then she spots Bruce, coming over with Iona. Her face lights up like it's Christmas morning and she charges towards him, arms wide open. "Boose!"

Ru isn't walking yet—or talking either—but he's utterly enchanted by Callie. The tilt of his chubby wee face as he follows her every move says it all: he thinks she put the stars in the sky.

"Jamie, come sit for a moment." Ally pats the rug beside him.

"I'm kind of rushed off my feet here."

"It'll only take a minute." He fixes me with one of those big-brother looks that isn't really a request at all. "You've got time for your eldest brother and your only nephew, don't you?"

"All right, fine." I plonk myself down and hold a hand up to Ru for a high five. "How's it going, wee man?"

Ru studies me intently for a moment before offering a cautious slap against my palm. Then he goes back to watching Callie.

"So, what's up?" I ask Ally.

"I just wanted to say . . . I'm impressed by what you've done here. Really impressed."

The compliment—coming from him—warms my chest in a way I'm not sure how to handle, so naturally, my first instinct is to brush it off with humour. "Jesus," I mutter. "Becoming a da has made you soft."

Ally growls. "I was trying to be nice."

"Aha! There's the moody git I know and love." I wink. "Good to have you back."

He shakes his head. "Seriously, though, it really is amazing what you've done here—even if you do still have a bit of work to do on your personality." He ruffles my hair like I'm twelve. "But listen, even if it makes you squirm to hear it, I'm proud of you, Jamie. I really am. I remember waiting in the hospital after the crash, scared out of my mind for you, and now look at you. Look at what you've built. Well done."

My chest tightens at the mention of the crash, but I push the feeling aside. Today is too good to let those memories in.

"Cheers, Ally. Anyway, I best get on."

I get back to my feet and dive straight back into it. Orders need taking, glasses need clearing, and conversations need just enough charm from me to keep things upbeat. It's a rhythm now: check the tables, crack a joke here, share a quick smile there, mentally triage what needs sorting next. I've never worked this hard in my life, not even close, but because I built this place with my own two hands, I don't mind the graft.

As the afternoon slips into evening, the families peel away one by one. Ally and Emily head off with Ru slumped fast asleep against his da's shoulder, his tiger face paint even more smeared now but still very cute. Aidan follows soon after with Grace and Callie, who somehow still has energy left. The garden doesn't quieten down, however. Rather, it shifts gears, filling up with childless couples and lively groups of friends, all fresh-faced and ready for a good time. Conversations grow louder; laughter rings out sharper.

On the stage Neil straps on his accordion while Eileen tunes her fiddle beside him. Scott—sporting an impressive amount of facial hair, even by Bannock standards—adjusts the height of a cymbal from behind his drum kit. They're not big names or anything (not outside our part of Scotland anyway), but they're local legends, the sort of band that can get any crowd tapping their feet and nodding their heads within seconds of playing their first note.

Meanwhile, Kyle is already charming small groups into sampling the distillery's various whiskies, guiding them through each dram with the reverence of a priest delivering a sermon.

Even though I'm running on empty at this point, there's something magical about witnessing the vibe shift without the buzz fading.

"Jamie!" Lewis calls from behind the barbecue station, where he's still flipping burgers.

I let out an exaggerated groan then make my way towards him. "If you're about to tell me we've run out of sausages again—"

"No," he interrupts, shooting me a grin. "I wanted to congratulate you. You've exceeded my expectations today. Everything has gone really, really well."

I blink at him like he's sprouted antlers. "Sorry, what was that? Could you repeat it? Louder this time?"

He rolls his eyes but doesn't take it back. "Don't make me regret saying it." He nods towards the crowd instead. "Look at this place—it's packed! Folk are raving about the food, the drinks, the atmosphere. I didn't think you'd actually see this through when you first suggested it. Thought you'd lose interest or cock something up halfway through."

"Wow," I deadpan. "You really know how to deliver a compliment."

He smirks. "Okay, how about this: you smashed it. Everyone loves the place, and we must be taking in a good bit of money too."

Whoa, Ally *and* Lewis complimenting me on the same day? Is there a full moon or something?

Lewis continues, "Even some of the die-hard regulars from the Pheasant have shown up. Check out old Hamish over there at Kyle's tasting table. Never thought we'd see him, let alone on day one."

A pang of guilt sneaks in, unwelcome but insistent. Because if the Pheasant's regulars are here instead of there . . .

Nope. Not going there. I worked my arse off for this, and I am *not* going to feel bad about pulling it off. Instead I let myself bask in the moment, taking in the laughter, the clinking glasses, and the first notes of music drifting from the stage. This is what success feels like, and damn, it feels good.

CHAPTER TWENTY

Sunlight streams through the pub windows, highlighting the dust motes drifting lazily in the still air. The Pheasant is eerily quiet. Normally, on a Saturday evening in June, this place would be packed with a lively mix of locals and tourists. But tonight? Just three people are sipping drinks over at a table, and one of them is Da.

Bloody hell.

Sighing, I give the already spotless bar top another wipe.

Last night I prayed for rain—fat lot of good that did. It's an absolute stunner of a day, perfect for basking in the sunshine with an ice-cold beer, not for being cooped up in a stuffy pub.

Ugh!

I toss down my cloth. "Back in a second," I mutter to Da before heading outside. I lean against the wall of the pub and suck in a deep breath, hoping the fresh air will settle me. No chance. The laughter and cheerful chatter drifting down from the hotel are impossible to ignore. Of course Jamie's event is a success—how could it not be with weather like this?

A huge banner spans the front of the Bannock Hotel,

proudly announcing the beer garden's grand opening. Clusters of balloons jiggle in the breeze like they're mocking me. And the smoky scent of barbecue wafts through the air, teasing my empty stomach and making me hate Jamie even more.

A beer garden. Big deal! We've got real history here at the Pheasant—proper charm that you can't fake with a bouncy castle and overpriced burgers. But apparently, folk around here are easily swayed by shiny new things. Who knew? And also, doesn't loyalty count for anything anymore? Da's been pulling pints for the people of this town for decades. He knows their orders before they do! And now? Now they've all buggered off.

I pinch the bridge of my nose, fighting the knot of anger tightening in my chest. If folk *knew* that Da's health isn't what is used to be, maybe they'd rally around him instead of abandoning him when he needs them most.

But no, Da is as stubborn as an old ram. He'd sooner juggle chainsaws than let people think he's anything less than fighting fit.

I shove off the wall and head back into the quiet gloom of the pub. Behind the bar, I fiddle with a row of glasses, nudging them into an even straighter line, even though they're already lined up like soldiers at attention.

"Maisie, love." Da heads over carrying a half-finished pint. "Stop fussing and relax. A slow day won't kill us."

"Aye, one day won't. But what about tomorrow? Or next week? What if it stays this way?"

He sets his glass down. "Ach, novelty burns bright but fizzles fast. Folk will be back. Don't let it get under your skin." He rests a hand on my shoulder and gives it a gentle squeeze.

His confidence grates on me. I don't like him brushing away my worries like they don't matter. And maybe they don't—to him. Because he's got a pension waiting for him when he packs this in. Me? I'm twenty-seven years old and have no backup plan. This pub is the plan—it always has been. I'll be taking over when Da retires, so of course I'm keen to make sure it stays not only open but thriving.

"Bloody Jamie McIntyre," I grumble. "He opens his beer garden, and suddenly all our customers are following him like rats to the Pied Piper."

"You're awfully fired up about Jamie." Da takes a sip of his pint. "He's all you ever talk about nowadays. Is there something going on between you two?"

The question catches me off-guard, and I blink at Da. "Aside from him poaching our customers? Isn't that enough?"

He arches an eyebrow. "I meant something more . . . personal."

A flush creeps up my neck, hot and unwelcome. "No," I say quickly.

Because really, where do I even start with that question? Do I tell Da about how Jamie tossed me out of his car in the middle of a downpour? Aye, it *is* tempting to let that one slip—to Da, to Morag from the bakery, to anyone who'd listen. It'd be such an easy way to get folk turning their backs on him and his beer garden. But if Jamie decided to retaliate by sharing *his* version of events—a version featuring drunk me getting handsy with his unmentionables—well . . . no, thanks.

I've instead kept my mouth shut and shoved down all my feelings—which could be why I feel like I'm about to burst.

"No, Da," I reiterate. "There's nothing going on between me and Jamie."

Da squints at me like he can see right through me, but thankfully he drops the subject. He takes another swig of his beer then casts a glance towards our two customers. "Tell you what, once they're done with their drinks, let's call it a night."

"But we never close early!" My shoulders stiffen at the suggestion because it feels like an admission of failure.

"And we won't make a habit of it. But you could do with a night off for once—you've been running yourself ragged lately."

I huff out a resigned breath. "Fine. But just this once."

◆ ◆ ◆

After Da and I shut up shop, I can't help myself—I have to see what all the fuss is about. Which is how I find myself at the entrance to the beer garden, arms crossed as I take it all in.

The place is buzzing, alive with energy. Everywhere I look, people are grinning, chatting, clinking glasses. And as much as it annoys me to admit it, everything looks . . . good. Not just "meh, it'll do" good. Genuinely good.

The tables and chairs are solid wood—none of your cheap plastic rubbish—and they're arranged in a way that makes the most of the space. And the garden itself? Gorgeous. Vibrant colours everywhere you look.

Resentment prickles uncomfortably under my ribs, tangling messily with something else: reluctant admiration.

On the lawn, Morag and Elspeth are playing a game of giant Connect Four, wine glasses in one hand and game pieces in the other. Every time one of them slots a piece into place, they dissolve into fits of giggles so loud I can hear them from here.

Damn it. This is clever. There's something for everyone here.

I spot Kyle at a sampling table, surrounded by locals and tourists, all hanging on his every word as he pours whisky into tiny tasting glasses. Yet another clever move by Jamie—using the event to deepen ties with local businesses. It stings to see Hamish among the group. I can't remember the last time he missed a Saturday night at the Pheasant—until tonight.

The Glen Garve Distillery isn't the only local business Jamie's managed to rope in for the event. On a small wooden stage Thistle and Reel, a band who regularly perform at the Pheasant, are playing a lively jig. A few folk are twirling each other about in impromptu dances on the grass.

The contrast to the ghostly stillness of the Pheasant earlier couldn't be any more pronounced.

And then I see him.

Jamie stands in the middle of it all, deep in animated conversation with a group of guests. He's wearing a crisp white shirt with the sleeves rolled up to his elbows, paired with dark jeans that fit him far too well. His hair, which usually gives off "couldn't be bothered" vibes, is still slightly tousled but tamer than usual. And that's not the only change in him. His shoulders are broader; his stance more self-assured; and a faint tan warms his skin from all the hours spent working outdoors.

It's not fair. He's not supposed to look this good while destroying my family's business.

I'm ready, primed to march over there and give him what for, when someone tugs sharply at the back of my shorts. I whirl around, half expecting to come face to face with an overly friendly tourist who hasn't learnt boundaries (it wouldn't be the first time). But instead . . .

"Cat!" I exclaim, momentarily forgetting everything else.

The youngest McIntyre grins at me, her tiny nose stud

catching the evening sunlight. With her long auburn hair and delicate features, Cat is an absolute knockout, but somehow she carries it off without even a hint of smugness.

"Maisie!" She pulls me into a hug.

No sooner has she released me than Iona appears at her side. "Well, would you look at this? The Scottish Sirens together again in person."

"Oh, aye." Cat loops an arm around Iona's shoulders. "Though we might need to rethink the name now that one of us is all domesticated, eh?" She wiggles her eyebrows teasingly at Iona.

"Once a siren, always a siren," I say, but my eyes—traitorous things that they are—drift back to Jamie.

He hasn't clocked me yet. He's too busy holding court, all charm and easy laughter. Right on cue his audience erupts into fits at something he's said. When did he become this version of himself? *I'm* the one who chats effortlessly with locals and tourists alike while serving them drinks. Jamie's meant to sit awkwardly behind the bar in the snug, glued to his laptop rather than even pretending to be interested in his patrons.

I realise I've been staring too long when Cat nudges me with an elbow. "You all right there?"

"Aye, fine. Actually . . . we'll catch up properly in a bit, okay? I just need to . . . sort something first."

Ignoring their puzzled expressions, I stride—all right, stomp—towards Jamie before I can talk myself out of it.

His head turns as I approach, his eyes meeting mine and holding them. My stupid heart decides *now* is the time to somersault like it's auditioning for the circus. He says something low to his group then excuses himself.

"Maisie! Welcome." That maddening smirk is already tugging at the corners of his mouth.

"Jamie," I grit out.

"Let me get you a drink! On the house, of course. Something about sharing success makes it taste even sweeter." He winks.

I scowl at him. Like hell I'm accepting a free drink. But the problem with not replying straight away is it gives him time to trail his gaze over me, slowly and deliberately, setting off a creeping heat that snakes its way up my neck.

I shift my weight from one foot to the other, suddenly all too conscious of the way my denim cut-offs sit on my thighs—not scandalously short, but under Jamie's attention, they feel practically indecent. My off-the-shoulder T-shirt isn't helping. The warm breeze skims across the sliver of skin between its hem and my shorts, leaving me torn between tugging it lower and folding my arms across my chest.

When Jamie's eyes finally meet mine again, some of his playful confidence melts away into something softer . . . something dangerously sincere. "If we weren't business rivals," he murmurs, pitching his voice lower so that no one but me can hear, "I might say you look bonny tonight."

Bonny? Is he joking? With my hair scraped up into a messy blue bun that's more bird nest than intentional style? Aye, right.

And yet . . . Jamie keeps looking at me like he actually means it, with those intense eyes searching mine before flicking back down as though he can't help but take in my appearance a second time.

"Oi! My eyes are up here, McIntyre." It's not that I hate the way he's checking me out—if anything, it's unsettling how much I don't—but he's the enemy. I can't let him stand there giving me the once-over.

"Aye . . . sorry." A crooked, almost bashful smile tugs at Jamie's lips before his expression shifts into something more thoughtful. "I've been meaning to have a word with you. Planned to seek you out tomorrow, actually."

"Oh, aye? And what exactly did you want to chat about?"

"Er . . ." He scratches behind his ear. "Remember what happened on the drive back from the distillery?"

"Of course I bloody remember." My voice is sharp enough to turn more than a few heads. "It's not exactly the kind of thing you forget. You tossed me out of your car in the middle of a downpour and left me to traipse home in the lashing rain!"

A few more heads turn. Jamie's cheeks flush.

"You know what," he says, "at your Bannock-themed pub quiz, you asked me to step outside for a chat, and I reckon that was a good idea. Maybe we should do the same now. Fancy going somewhere quieter to talk?"

I shrug. "Whatever."

So I follow Jamie through a back gate in the tall hedge, which leads to a gravel driveway in which a couple of cars are parked outside a double garage.

"If you start shouting at me, how loud are you likely to get?" he asks. "I'm just wondering if the hedge is enough soundproofing, or if we should add a wall to be safe."

I give him a withering look. "I've been cooped up in an empty pub all day watching customers flock to *your* beer garden. Once I get going, no hedge in Scotland will be able to muffle me."

He half chuckles, half grimaces then jerks his chin towards the garage. "Well then, better safe than sorry."

Inside there are no cars, just paddleboards lined up against one wall and shelves packed with outdoor equipment: climbing harnesses, helmets, and other gear. Jamie's brother Ally must use this space for Bannock Adventures, the business he runs with Aidan Stewart. Still, there's plenty of room for Jamie and me to have it out.

"So." I cross my arms over my chest. "Decided to apologise, have you? Did you consider that maybe it's a bit late for that? Because now I've got more things to be angry about than just the rainy walk home."

Jamie breathes out heavily and rakes his fingers through his hair. For half a second I wonder if it feels as soft as it looks.

Not a helpful thought right now, Maisie. Come on!

"Er . . . aye." His Adam's apple bobs. "Look, this isn't exactly easy for me, but the thing is—"

"Da and I had to shut the Pheasant early because it was so bloody quiet!" I step closer to him, my voice shaking with emotion. "You've stolen everyone away. You've even poached our bloody band!"

"To be fair," Jamie replies with maddening calmness, "Thistle and Reel are hardly *your* band. They've done a few ceilidhs in our function room."

"Argh!" I curl my hands into fists at my sides because I can't grab his stupid crisp shirt and give him a good shake, as much as I might want to. "You're infuriating!"

"*I'm* infuriating?" Jamie's eyes flash as he steps closer too. "You're the one who went around town bad-mouthing my beer garden before it was even open!"

"I was simply doing my civic duty by giving people a heads-up."

"Civic duty?" Jamie scoffs. "You've seen how much folk are

enjoying the place—how it's brought everyone together. You think that's not good for the community?"

I let out a sharp laugh. "Oh aye, Jamie, because what this town really needs is fairy lights and giant Jenga."

Now it's Jamie's turn to cross his arms. The movement pulls the fabric of his shirt taut across his shoulders and chest, accentuating a physique I swear he didn't have a few months ago.

"People have been *loving* the garden games. You may want to give them a go—you might actually have fun. Sure, the chess is probably a bit above your head, but I'm sure you could manage Connect Four. It's nice and straightforward, and the pieces are in bright colours to help hold your attention."

I take another step forwards without thinking. It's automatic now, instinct driving me closer to him even as anger twists inside. "You think you're hilarious, don't you? Newsflash, Jamie, you're not. Your jokes are pretty terrible."

There's the tiniest flicker in his jaw—a pulse that tells me I'm striking a nerve. "Oh, aye? Well, you seem to think dyeing your hair a bold colour makes you interesting. *Newsflash*"—he does a high-pitched mockery of my voice—"it really doesn't."

I gasp as if he's reached out and physically prodded me.

"It does too!" Okay, so not exactly a winning comeback, but it's hard to think straight when we're so close now and my brain is busy cataloguing every little detail of him, like the little flecks of gold in his irises.

For a moment he doesn't say anything. His gaze locks on mine, steady and unreadable, then dips to my lips. My daft heart thunders in response, pounding so loudly I'm certain he can hear it. When he finally speaks, his voice is low and rough. "You're awfully close, Maisie."

His eyes drag back up to mine, but he doesn't move back. Doesn't even blink. "Sure you're just here to argue?"

"What else would I be here for?" My words come out steadier than I feel—a small personal victory.

Jamie's mouth curves into something wicked and impossibly sexy. "I can think of a few things . . ."

I gulp. "I hate you," I whisper hoarsely. And I really do—or at least I did. But right now? Right now my body is determined to betray every shred of logic screaming at me to step away.

"No," Jamie murmurs with maddening certainty. His hand finds my waist, and his thumb brushes over the bare skin where my top rides up. A spark ignites beneath his touch, hot and consuming. Then he dips his head, his breath a whisper against my lips. "You don't."

The moment stretches unbearably taut between us until finally—*finally*—it snaps.

I'm not sure who moves first, but the next thing I know, our mouths are crashing together like every sharp word and buried feeling has burst free in a collision of heat and frustration. His lips are firm against mine, carrying the faint taste of smoky whisky and something deeper, something intoxicatingly elusive that leaves my thoughts spinning.

I clutch at his shirt, twisting my fingers tightly into its fabric, while his hand curls possessively around my waist, holding me against him like he has no intention of letting go.

Whatever clarity I had left dissolves into nothingness as the kiss deepens, blotting out time and place, and any shred of common sense. I barely register that I'm moving until my back meets the rough surface of the garage wall. The jarring contrast—the cold bite of stone and the blistering warmth of Jamie's body—sends a shiver through me.

The scrape of his stubble against my skin . . . the way his lips move over mine like he's determined to leave no part unexplored . . .

For a few brief, blessed moments, there's only this—all heat and desperation. And *then* . . .

At first it's just the faintest hint of movement between us. But then I feel it again. *Him.* Unmistakable now, his cock pressing increasingly insistently against my stomach as it grows and hardens against me.

I know I should shove him away, should tell him off like I've been dying to all day. But instead . . . instead I press into him—into *that*—hip brushing hip, as if my body has decided to take matters into its own hands. The fact I shouldn't be doing this somehow only makes it all the hotter. I release a hold of his shirt and wrap my arm around him, inviting him closer to me, drawing his chest to mine. And now every shallow breath I take is matched by his deeper ones.

Laughter carries from the garden, mingling with the strains of music, but it seems so far removed from this moment that it could be happening in another world entirely.

Jamie's thumb brushes a slow circle just above my hip bone, leaving a trail of fire in its wake. I bury the fingers of my free hand into his hair, which is even softer than I expected, but I don't linger on that thought. Instead I give it a firm tug, and the sound that rumbles out of him—a low, guttural groan— vibrates straight through me.

With his lower body still pressed firmly to mine, he leans back just enough to meet my gaze, his eyes wild now, the gold flecks burning bright amidst the hazel. "Maisie." That's all he says—my name—but he says it in such a deep, gravelly tone, and with such desire, that it steals away what little breath I have left.

A faint voice of reason stirs somewhere in the fog of want, warning me to stop—to remember all the reasons this shouldn't happen—but Jamie doesn't leave room for coherent thought. He slides his hands down to grip my thighs then lifts me off the floor and pins me to the wall. For half a second, something flickers inside me—logic clawing at its final chance—then the hard ridge of his cock presses exactly where I need it, and any hesitation crumbles. Instinct overtakes me, and my legs lock around his waist, drawing him closer.

Jamie moves with purpose now, grinding against me in slow, deliberate rolls that have me biting back a moan. Our mouths collide again, but there's no finesse left in either of us— just heat and need and almost frantic desperation. He kisses me like he's trying to devour me whole, his tongue sweeping into my mouth with unrestrained hunger.

I should stop this—I know I should—but it's impossible when everything about him sets fire to my senses: the taste of whisky lingering on his lips; the woodsy scent of his aftershave; the way he growls low in his throat when I arch against him. My nails scrape along the nape of his neck lightly at first but then harder. Then he shifts just right and *oh*!

My head drops back against the wall with a barely contained whimper.

"Fuck," Jamie mutters, burying his face against my neck as though trying to steady himself—though judging by how tightly he's gripping me, steady isn't really an option for either of us anymore.

His hips move again, and dear God, if this keeps up much longer . . .

This is madness. Pure insanity.

And then—

"Jamie! Where are you, mate?" A sharp male voice cuts through the haze like a bucket of icy water.

Jamie freezes instantly, and suddenly we're both holding our breath as if staying perfectly still will somehow make whoever it is bugger off and leave us alone. We exchange wide-eyed glances, the heat between us still thrumming even though neither one of us dares move another inch.

"Shit," Jamie murmurs, a mix of frustration and regret lacing the word. His hair is sticking up wildly thanks to my wandering fingers; there's a flush on his cheeks; and his lips are swollen from our kisses. Oh, and he's very much still hard.

As much as I don't want it to, reality forces its way back in. The strains of ceilidh music; the chatter and laughter. The world is waiting just beyond these walls—a world where Jamie McIntyre isn't supposed to make me feel like this.

"Jamie," I manage finally. "You need to put me down."

For a moment he doesn't move. Hesitation flickers in his eyes, and his hands remain firm against my thighs. But then he exhales—something low and frustrated slipping between his teeth—and sets me carefully back on trembling legs.

The second my feet touch the floor, I stumble away from him like he's suddenly turned radioactive. My heart is pounding so hard it feels like it's trying to escape my chest entirely. And although I can feel his gaze boring into me—hot, heavy, searching—I don't dare meet it. If I do, God help me, I might lose whatever shred of composure I'm trying to cling on to.

"Maisie—" His voice is rough with something unspoken.

Regret? Frustration? Desire? Maybe all three, but I cut him off before he can say anything else.

"No." The word comes out sharper than intended. "I . . . I have to go." I move towards the garage door.

Jamie calls my name again, but I don't look back. I slip outside and drag in deep breaths of the evening air. Then, my legs feeling like jelly, I force myself to walk—fast, almost tripping over my own feet in the process.

What happened back there wasn't part of the plan. And it can never, *ever* happen again.

CHAPTER TWENTY-ONE

JAMIE

I fall back onto my bed, still fully clothed, and stare up at the ceiling. My entire body aches, like I've somehow managed to cram a week's worth of graft into a single day. And yet my mind refuses to settle. It keeps replaying everything—the success of the beer garden's opening event, the busy crowds, the laughter and music, all those smiling faces. Aye, it was a bloody good night.

But that's not what's stealing all my brainpower right now, is it?

No, there's only one moment I can't stop thinking about.

The kiss.

Christ above. That kiss.

One second Maisie and I were having a blazing row in the garage, and the next . . . well, I put my hand on her waist, which was pretty fucking daring. After that, I'm not sure who moved first. Did she lean in? Did I? Doesn't matter now. All I know is that suddenly her mouth was on mine and I was done for. She tasted of raspberry lip gloss and something else too. Something purely *her*.

The friction between us was enough to tear my sanity in two. My cock hardened almost instantly, straining against my jeans like they'd suddenly become two sizes smaller. But it wasn't just the pressure or the movement that unravelled me. It was the heat. It radiated through every layer of fabric between us, until it felt like my skin might catch fire just from being near her. Then she let out this sound—a soft little moan that was pure sin wrapped up in silk—and I swear I nearly lost it on the spot.

Almost before I knew what I was doing, I had her pressed against the wall and was grinding against her, deepening our kiss, gripping her tight to keep from flying apart. Even through my burning desire, I couldn't stop thinking about how perfect she felt in my hands. How perfectly she fit against me, like she belonged there.

Then she shifted—just slightly—but *fuck*, it was enough to hit all the right spots at once. My world tilted dangerously on its axis as white-hot pleasure spiked through me so sharply I nearly saw stars. For a second I thought I might embarrass myself completely and come undone right there in the garage like some horny teenager. And truthfully? Had it happened, I wouldn't have given a damn.

My body responds to the memory, and I squirm, adjusting myself down there.

But just as things were really heating up in that garage, we heard Kyle shouting from the beer garden, and Maisie bolted quicker than a ewe from a sheepdog. Just like that—gone.

I wanted to go after her. Hell, every fibre of me screamed to go. But Kyle was calling my name, and since the beer garden is my responsibility, I could hardly pretend not to hear.

Anyway, I had to linger in that garage for a few minutes to

cool off. Strolling back into the beer garden while pitching a tent in my jeans wasn't exactly the triumphant ending to the opening event I'd envisioned. I had to breathe deeply and recite my times tables until I could face people again.

After that, the rest of the evening passed in a blur: pulling pints, clearing glasses, smiling at jokes I wasn't really listening to. Even after we finally closed, my family kept me up for ages, going on and on about how proud they were of me. Any other time, I'd have been chuffed to hear that—though I'd have rather danced naked in a snowstorm than admit that to them. Tonight, though, I just couldn't focus. My head was somewhere else entirely.

Or rather, with someone else entirely.

I check the time on my phone: 12:54 a.m. Way too late to pop over to the Pheasant, even though part of me wants to. Maisie and I need to talk about what happened. I mean, you can't just kiss someone like that and not discuss it afterwards. Can you?

Groaning loudly, I drag myself off my bed and collapse into the chair at my desk. There's only one thing for it: *Highland Legacy*. As soon as the familiar loading screen appears, some of today's tension eases from my shoulders.

This is what I do when life turns messy: log in, kill some monsters, forget about reality for a while.

I spend a few minutes flicking through the available quests, searching for something that looks suitably mind-numbing. Then a notification pops up: *SassyLassie has logged in.*

What are the odds? I've barely touched the game in weeks, and she's been completely MIA. Yet here we are, online at the exact same time.

A pause stretches out—so long that I think she might not answer—then at last her reply comes through.

Okay, not exactly warm or welcoming, but fair enough. Everyone has their off days.

Still, desperate times call for desperate measures.

When I first started playing with SassyLassie, she was always upbeat and full of banter. Now, though? Even before she disappeared for ages, there was that time she let me get annihilated by the wraith. Something must be going on in her real life, but I've no idea what since we don't talk about personal stuff when we play.

But tonight I'm desperate to chat—because who else am I supposed talk about Maisie with? Not anyone in Bannock, that's for sure—not unless I fancy the whole town knowing by sunrise. But an online gamer who doesn't even know my real name? Aye, I can talk with her.

Pretty please? I kissed this girl today and I'm losing my mind trying to make sense of it. There's no one here I can talk to who won't blab within seconds.

But you're different. You're . . . safe.

Her reply takes longer this time, and when it comes through, it bruises more than expected.

SASSYLASSIE

Not in the mood to play agony aunt tonight.

Ouch.

LOCHNLOAD

All right. Anything I can say to change your mind? 🤐

SASSYLASSIE

I said no. This was a mistake. I'm going.

LOCHNLOAD

Wait, what?!

SASSYLASSIE

If you need to talk to someone this badly, pour your heart out to Bruce.

My fingers pause above the keys. Bruce? *My* Bruce? As in, Lewis and Iona's dog?

A cold prickle crawls across my skin. Did I ever tell Sass his name? Because I don't remember doing that. In fact, I'm almost certain I didn't.

Before I can question her about this, a notification pops up: *SassyLassie has logged off.*

A knot twisting in my stomach, I search our in-game chat

history for the word "Bruce". Nothing comes up. Maybe I mentioned him in the app we use to arrange gaming sessions? But no, a search there doesn't yield any results either. Which begs the question: how the hell does Sass know his name?

All those late-night conversations, the easy banter, the trust . . . hell, my confession about my "secret kink" . . .

On the drive back from the distillery, Maisie teasingly suggested SassyLassie might really be some creepy balding middle-aged bloke in a stained vest and boxers. At the time I paid her no notice, but . . . what if she was right?

Who the fuck have I been talking to all this time? And how the hell do they know things about me I've never shared?

CHAPTER TWENTY-TWO

JAMIE

I barely register the morning sun warming my face as I walk down Bannock's Main Street. The pieces of the puzzle that kept me up all night are finally clicking into place, and no matter how I arrange them, they all point to the same impossible, infuriating conclusion.

Maisie Kerr is SassyLassie.

It'd explain how Sass knew Bruce's name, but it'd also explain the other clues and coincidences I only spotted once I started looking. Like how that time in Bannock Stores, Maisie and I both reached for the last can of Gaelic Fire—the same energy drink I'd got Sass into months previously. Or the fact Maisie brought up gaming on Ben Garve—a conversation that was cut off when Bruce tangled us together.

There's also, of course, Maisie's curiosity about my "online friend" during the drive to the distillery, and then her teasing remarks about "Big Davie" on the way back. Maisie was practically waving a big neon sign in my face saying that not everything about SassyLassie was as it seemed, and I was too thick to catch on.

And it doesn't even stop there! Next there's the "coincidence" that the night SassyLassie let me get mauled by the wraith was the same night I told Maisie to get out of my car. Oh, and right after I confided in Sass that my big plan to improve things at my work involved "sunshine and good company", Maisie launched her petition against the beer garden. I thought that someone at the council must have let slip details of my plan, or perhaps one of the contractors I'd been speaking to. But no, *I* was the leak.

The more I think about it, the more glaringly obvious it all seems. Maisie is SassyLassie, and she's been playing me for months.

I pause outside the Pheasant, my heart thudding against my ribs. I'm not even sure what this feeling is. Anger? Nerves? Betrayal? Probably all three, garnished with a hefty dose of dread, because if Maisie really *is* Sass . . . well, I don't know what comes next. Only that there'll be hell to pay.

Taking a deep breath—and then another—I raise my fist and knock firmly on the door.

Some moments pass before Bryce opens it, and his expression darkens the instant he sees me.

"Well, well," he says in a low growl. "You best come in."

How come he's making me feel like *I'm* the one who's done something wrong? I do as he says, though, and step inside, then he closes and locks the door behind me.

"I hear you kicked my daughter out of your car. During a rainstorm."

Aw, shite. How did that get out? Ah, that's right: Maisie blurted it out yesterday in the beer garden. Word must have got back to Bryce.

"What sort of man abandons a woman in the middle of

nowhere?" Bryce's voice grows louder, his face turning a furious shade of crimson. "My Maisie! My *daughter*! Who do you think you are, treating her like that?"

"I—"

"First you try to poach our customers with that godforsaken beer garden of yours, and now I hear about *this*? I always had respect for the McIntyre family—your maw and da were good folk, and what happened to them was a tragedy. But abandoning a lass in a torrential downpour? That's just disgraceful!"

"I . . . well . . ." Talking about the crash is hard enough at the best of times, let alone when someone is yelling at me like they think they're William Wallace reincarnated.

"What's wrong? Cat got your tongue?" Bryce demands. "I don't know why Maisie didn't tell me about this sooner because, believe me, if she had, I'd have marched round to that wee hotel of yours and—"

His breath catches mid-sentence, his tirade coming to an abrupt halt. He drops a hand onto the nearest table, fingers curling stiffly around its edge, his knuckles gleaming white, while his other hand trembles at his side. A flicker of pain flashes across his face, but he grits his teeth and braces himself like a man determined not to give in.

"Bryce?" I take a hesitant step towards him. "Are you all right?"

"Of course I'm bloody all right!" he snaps, though there's less fire in his tone now. He straightens—or tries to—but even that seems to require more energy than he has to spare. "Just lost my temper, that's all."

"Aye," I say, unconvinced. "Maybe you should sit down for a minute?"

He brushes me off with a shaky hand. "Don't treat me like

some frail old codger! I'm perfectly fine on my feet, thank you very much."

"Da?" Maisie's voice rings out, and she appears in a doorway, freezing at the sight of me. "What's going—" Her words cut off when she takes in Bryce's pale complexion and stiff posture. Concern floods her face, and she hurries towards him. "Da! What happened? Are you okay?"

"I'm fine," Bryce grumbles. "Just . . . worked myself up thanks to this eejit." He gestures towards me.

Maisie glares at me with enough venom to fell an army. But then her gaze flicks back to Bryce, worry eclipsing fury once again. "I'll deal with *him* in a minute. Sit down, Da." She pulls out one of the pub chairs for him.

"I don't need—"

"Please, Da," Maisie says. "For me."

He relents with an exaggerated sigh and eases himself into the chair.

"There. Catch your breath, all right? I know you want to defend me—and believe me, I love you for it—but there's no point getting yourself into a state over this arsehole. Besides, I can handle Jamie McIntyre myself."

She turns to me. "You. Upstairs. Now."

It's not an invitation. It's a declaration of war. Without waiting for an answer, she spins on her heel and marches off. I suppose that's my cue to follow her.

I glance at Bryce for guidance—or maybe mercy—but get neither.

"You're lucky she intervened, laddie, because I wasn't done with you."

I nod then follow after Maisie, each step up the staircase feeling like a slow climb to my doom. She's clearly furious with me and wants to have it out, but shouldn't *I* be the one who's angry? I came here to confront her about being SassyLassie, after all.

She leads me into her kitchen, the cosy warmth of the space doing nothing to thaw the icy tension simmering between us. She gestures to the table, silently ordering me to sit, and I do. But Maisie? No, she stays standing, arms crossed over her chest like a shield. That's a power move if ever I've seen one.

So I get back to my feet too. No way am I letting her have the upper hand. And, aye, I cross my arms as well. Two can play at this game.

I lock eyes with her, but the fire blazing in her gaze throws petrol on memories I do *not* need right now. Like yesterday, her lips pressed to mine, her body grinding against me . . .

My idiot cock twitches at the thought, and that's enough to snap me back to the present. *Get it together, Jamie. You're here for answers. So what if her floaty forest-green dress brings out the colour of her eyes? That's not relevant right now.*

"Right, what's this about? Why were you hassling my da?"

"I wasn't hassling your da! I came here to speak to *you*. I wanted to ask you what the hell you're playing at, *Sass*."

I lift my chin a fraction. *There.* The challenge has been issued and I can't take it back.

Her expression doesn't change—not even a flicker of surprise. "Sass? What are you talking about?"

Damn, she's good. But she *is* SassyLassie, I'm sure of it.

"Oh, come on. You can drop the act. Do I really need to list every piece of evidence that links you to SassyLassie? How about we skip ahead to the part where you admit it?"

For a moment she just stares at me, her face unreadable

except for the tiniest twitch in her eye. Then, with a heavy exhale, she says, "Fine! Yes, I'm SassyLassie. What of it?"

"*What of it?*" How can she stand there so calm and collected, like this isn't the betrayal of the century? We're talking *months* of lies and manipulation here. The blasé nature of her confession hits me harder than the admission itself.

I step closer to her, my voice shaking. "What the hell is wrong with you, Maisie? You tracked me down online, toyed with me for hours on end, all to find out my plans for the snug? And now you say, 'What of it?'"

"Whoa! Maybe get your story straight before you throw accusations around. Am I SassyLassie? Yes. Have I known for a wee while you're LochNLoad? Also yes. But have I *always* known? No. And did I *track you down* to learn your plans for the snug? Don't be so bloody ridiculous. We'd been playing together for ages by the time you came up with the beer garden idea."

She too steps closer, her stance practically daring me to back down.

Her words leave me reeling for a few seconds because . . . all right, fine, logically that does check out. But still!

"You're seriously telling me it's pure coincidence we ended up playing *Highland Legacy* together, even though we live in the same town?"

"That's exactly what I'm saying. I'd no idea you were Lochie until Iona mentioned to me one day that you play *Highland Legacy*. That's when it all clicked."

"But you kept playing with me *after* you figured it out," I point out.

"I *meant* to tell you." She uncrosses her arms and gestures in frustration. "That day on Ben Garve? I went there specifically to come clean, but before I could, you stormed off in one of your moods!"

"Oh, come on—"

"And *then*," she barrels on, talking right over me, "I tried telling you online! But that was when you casually mentioned your intention to poach customers 'from the competition down the road', and I knew that meant me and Da. And, look, you saw him downstairs—he's not as fit as he once was, though he'd rather crawl over hot coals than admit it. He has enough on his plate right now without you piling more on. So, aye, I put my father and myself first. Who wouldn't have done the same in my place?"

I'd *love* to tell her I'd have done things differently in her shoes, but let's be honest, I probably wouldn't have. Anyway, that fierce determination blazing in her eyes? Her unshakeable loyalty to her father? Her refusal to back down? Damn, it's surprisingly hot. Not that I'm about to admit that out loud.

Instead I say, "You kissed me!"

That throws her for a moment, but then she says, "We kissed each other! Don't act like it was all me. And . . . it wasn't planned! It was a lapse of judgement."

She's right, of course. Something just came over us both. Anyway, *she* didn't lift *me* up and pin me to the garage wall.

"I trusted SassyLassie!" I blurt. Which is the truth. I did.

"Oh, aye?" She steps closer until there are only inches between us and jabs her finger hard against my chest. "Well, I trusted you to get me to and from the distillery safely. I suppose we both misplaced our trust, didn't we?"

Her words land like a well-aimed blow. I drag in a slow breath, doing my best to keep my tone even. "About that night . . . I owe you an explanation. I should've done this sooner—I did try yesterday—but, well, it's not exactly the easiest thing for me to talk about."

"Oh, isn't it? Why am I not surprised that saying sorry doesn't come easily to you? Smug one-liners, cheeky banter—no problem there—but actually being the bigger man? Nah. Definitely not your area of expertise."

I clench my teeth. "I get panic attacks when it rains like that, all right?" After a beat I add, "Especially if I'm in a car."

Maisie's anger falters, and although her expression remains guarded, there's a flicker of something else, like I've managed to throw her off balance. "Panic attacks?"

"Aye. Ever since . . ." I gesture vaguely towards the window, as though she'll understand what I mean without me having to say it.

And, of course, she does. Her eyes widen briefly before narrowing again in acknowledgment—because everyone in Bannock knows about *the crash*. About *my parents*.

"Oh," she says quietly.

"Aye. *Oh.*"

For once neither of us has a snarky comeback. We both find ourselves stranded in a silence that feels too raw to break. Maisie looks like she wants to say something—to challenge me or comfort me or maybe both at once—but instead she presses her lips together in a tight line and just stares at me.

My hand twitches at my side, itching to reach for her, to close the small but unbearable space between us. But I stop short because . . . well, because.

"You think I don't hate myself for telling you to get out of my car? But . . . I couldn't breathe, Maisie." My voice cracks slightly, and I hate that too. "I felt like my chest was collapsing in on itself and all I could see was twisted metal and broken glass and—"

"You could have told me!" she cuts in sharply. Fire flickers back into her eyes alongside something raw and pained. "Instead of abandoning me on the side of the road without a word, you could have explained. Do you know how humiliating it was? Standing there like an idiot while you drove off, leaving me to get utterly soaked, to have to trudge home in the dark?"

"I know," I say hoarsely.

"No, Jamie. You don't know." Again she jabs my chest with her finger, this time with so much force it's almost like she's trying to pierce through bone instead of just prove a point.

Her words hang in the air, sharp and biting, but underneath them I can hear it—the thread of hurt winding through her anger. And that's what undoes me. Not the raised voice, not the accusations, but the fact that I hurt her. That I made Maisie Kerr—this fierce, fiery woman who doesn't take shite from anyone—feel like she wasn't worth a bloody explanation.

It hits me so forcefully it's like the earth tilts under my feet. I reach out and grab her arm—not hard, just enough to make her stop jabbing me with that punishing finger. Her breath hitches at the contact, her lips parting in surprise. For a moment we stare at each other, the air between us crackling with a charge so intense it's like brushing against a live wire.

"Maisie," I murmur roughly, my voice cracking under the weight of everything I can't quite say.

And that's when she moves—or maybe I do. Just like in the garage, it's impossible to tell who starts it, but suddenly our mouths collide in a kiss that's wild and reckless.

Her lips are soft and warm, faintly sweet but with just

enough sharpness to leave me breathless. My hands move instinctively—one sliding into the silky waves of her blue hair, the other finding its place on her waist. I pull her closer, pressing her body flush against mine. Fuck, I'm already getting hard. This woman drives me crazy, and I can't get enough of it.

The kiss deepens, turning hungrier, fiercer—a heady mix of heat and desperation that sets my senses ablaze. Maisie makes a small sound against my mouth—a soft whimper that shoots straight through me—and the little control I've been clinging to frays at the edges. Her fingers trail down the length of my arm before boldly grabbing my hand and guiding it to her breast. The heat of her invitation is electrifying, and even through the fabric of her dress, I can feel the tight peak of her nipple pressing insistently against my palm. Christ.

These last few months I've tried not to stare too long whenever she wore low-cut tops or tight jumpers. I told myself to be a gentleman. But now, with one hand, I can confirm what I suspected: Maisie's tits are perfect. Small, soft, and perky beneath my palm—and so maddeningly hers I can hardly think straight.

I trace slow circles over her nipple with my thumb before gently rolling it between my fingers. Maisie gasps, a sharp little intake of breath that makes every muscle in my body tighten in response. My cock throbs against her belly as the sound loops endlessly in my brain like some kind of sinful soundtrack.

Something primal surges within me, and before I fully register what I'm doing, I scoop her up, just like yesterday. She immediately responds by wrapping her legs around me. Her thighs grip me tightly, like this is where they're meant to be. I hook one arm under her right leg while the other cups her arse—a perfect handful.

We're kissing again before I even have time to think about it, our mouths reuniting as though they've been starved for each other. Maisie presses herself close to me, and I swear I can feel her warmth radiating through every layer between us, tantalising and maddening.

But then she pulls back slightly, breaking the kiss with a soft pop. Her chest rises and falls with ragged breaths; her cheeks are flushed a delicious shade of pink; her swollen lips glisten from our kisses. God, she's bonny like this—untamed and unguarded in a way that knocks the wind out of me.

I swallow hard. "You all right?"

I'm braced for her to say we've gone too far again and I need to put her down. Instead she says, "Take me to my bedroom."

"You sure?"

She nods. "Aye."

That single word is all the encouragement I need. She directs me to her door, and I take her through it and to her double bed. We collapse onto it, her body soft beneath mine, our mouths fusing together once more. Then Maisie starts shimmying beneath me—not pushing me away but wriggling with purpose until something small and black slides down her legs. A tiny black thong.

My brain short-circuits for several seconds as realisation dawns: beneath this maddening excuse for a summer dress, Maisie Kerr is . . . bare.

Bloody hell.

"Need to see you," I rasp. Words are difficult as all the blood has rushed south.

I slide the fabric of her dress higher and freeze. Slick, glistening skin framed by soft golden curls. I'm so used to seeing

Maisie with bold hair colours I almost forgot she's a natural blonde.

The temptation to taste her is too much to resist. I place a hand on each of her thighs and lower myself between them, pressing a soft kiss just above where she's hottest. Her thighs twitch, a delicious reaction that spurs me to let my mouth wander a little closer.

Her scent hits me: sweet and musky with an edge so raw it goes straight to my head—and my cock. And when my tongue finally glides over her slick heat? Heaven. Absolute bloody heaven.

Maisie moans sharply at the first touch, one hand flying into my hair like it's the only thing anchoring her to this world. The sound drives me mad, and before I know it, I'm feasting on her like she's all I've ever craved.

My tongue works its way through every inch of her wetness, teasing and learning all at once until I find where she needs me most. When I circle that sensitive spot—not too hard but just enough—she gasps loudly, rocking against my mouth despite herself.

"Jamie!" She yanks on my hair, pulling me away from her pussy and dragging my mouth back up to hers, claiming it in a kiss that leaves us both breathless. It's messy, all lips and tongues and unspoken hunger, the kind of kiss that sets fire to your blood.

But then she's fumbling at my belt, her movements frantic and impatient, the metallic clink of the buckle ringing out in the charged air between us. She teases my jeans down over my hips and to my ankles, tossing them aside. Then she hooks her fingers into the band of my boxers, lingering just long enough for anticipation to spike through me. Time stretches unbearably thin . . . and then she yanks them down in one swift movement, freeing me completely.

I go in for another kiss, eager to devour her again, but she presses a hand to my chest, holding me just far enough away so she can look down. She studies me without shame or hesitation, not shy or uncertain at all. In fact, she's so bloody confident it ruins me. My cock twitches under her unwavering attention.

Slowly, deliberately, she reaches out and curls her fingers around it. I can't suppress the deep groan that rumbles through me. The heat of her palm against me is perfect—small but firm—and every nerve ending in my body lights up at her touch.

Her first stroke is slow. Teasing. Excruciating in the best possible way. She pumps me once, then twice, drawing out a rhythm so unhurried it feels like torture. My breath hitches when her thumb brushes over the tip, catching the bead of precum that's already glistening there.

She lifts her thumb to her lips, and all I can do is stare as her tongue darts out to taste me, unashamed and unapologetic about what she's doing or how much it's undoing me. Then her hand wraps around me again, only this time her grip is even tighter, enough to make my knees threaten to buckle. I'm hanging on by a thread here.

Her eyes find mine, burning hot and unrelenting, as if they're branding themselves into my soul. "Jamie, I need you, need *this*"—a firm, deliberate squeeze—"inside me. Right now."

The words hit me like a thunderclap. Blood roars in my ears, drowning out anything else I might have been capable of thinking. *Fuck.* There isn't a chance in hell I could deny her—

not when I'm so hard it aches, and definitely not when she's lying beneath me looking like sin incarnate in that floaty green dress bunched high around her waist.

"Er . . . protection?" I manage to rasp, though my voice barely sounds like my own.

"No need." Her tone is a delicious combination of impatience and desire. "I'm on the pill. Now stop wasting time and put it in already."

Her bluntness sends a fresh surge of fire straight through me. Still gripping me, she guides me down to where she's warmest, slickest—where she's waiting for me. But she doesn't let me in straight away. No, she slides the head of my cock along her silky heat, back and forth with unhurried precision, the soft sound of wetness filling my ears. Each pass sends a shudder through me, so sharp it's almost painful. My hands tighten on her hips as she teases us both, and Jesus, she's making me dizzy. But then, finally, she presses my tip right where she needs it most.

"Fuck," I groan. "You're going to drive me out of my bloody mind."

Her lips lift into a mischievous smile.

I press forwards slowly, achingly slowly, feeling every inch of the wet warmth that welcomes me as I push into her. She's tight—a heavenly kind of tight—and I have to grit my teeth against the overwhelming urge to thrust all the way in at once. Instead I hold as steady as I can, watching every flicker of emotion that plays across her face.

Her lips part, a low breathy sound escaping them as her legs shift slightly wider around my hips. The soft furrow of her brows tells me she feels the stretch of it, the size of me forging its way inside her.

"You good?" I murmur, my hand sliding up to brush against the side of her flushed face.

She nods. "Aye. Just . . . take it slow." There's something almost vulnerable in the way she says it, although the fierce determination never leaves her expression.

I obey, inching forwards with careful precision, each movement sending shock waves through me. Maisie gasps softly as I slide deeper still—then relaxes once I'm fully seated within her.

Her heat surrounds me entirely now, tight and velvety soft. My forehead drops to hers while we both catch our breath for a moment.

"You're big," Maisie says in a way that makes it sound like breaking news rather than something we're both acutely aware of right now. My cock pulses inside her like it's delighted by the compliment.

I draw back ever so slightly before easing forwards again, testing how we fit together now that we've adjusted to one another. "And you're fucking perfect."

The tentative rhythm begins there—a slow slide out followed by a deliberate glide back in. It builds heat between us until restraint slips away entirely. Soon our bodies move instinctively together: each snap of my hips met by Maisie's eager rise beneath me; each shuddering moan from her lips spurring me on harder and faster.

I grip Maisie's waist like it's the only thing keeping me tethered to reality, my fingers digging into her soft skin as though I might fall apart if I let go. I can't get enough. There's no air in my lungs—no space in my head for anything but her. The way she moves against me, the way she makes me feel like I'm completely hers in this moment—it's all consuming.

The bed creaks beneath us with each thrust, a rhythmic

protest that barely registers in the haze of sensation. Somewhere at the back of my mind, I notice a dull throb in my left thigh—probably from bracing against the mattress—but it's a distant ache drowned out by the overwhelming pleasure of Maisie's body pulling me deeper. Pain can wait until later. Right now, there's only her.

For months she's driven me mad with frustration and turned every conversation into an argument or challenge or game that somehow always left us both wanting more. And now? Now everything is boiling over—weeks of tension exploding into something raw and unstoppable. A force neither of us could walk away from, even if we tried.

Maisie's legs tighten around mine suddenly, her inner thighs gripping me with an urgency that sends a jolt of electricity straight through me. I feel it building before it happens—the way her body arches slightly off the mattress, the deep crimson flush painting her cheeks and chest, the soft whimpers spilling from her lips growing louder and needier. She's so close I can feel it like a live wire sparking between us.

"That's it," I growl, low and rough, driving into her harder like nothing else in this world exists but this moment. "Let go for me!"

Her hands claw at my shoulders, fingernails biting into my skin, a cry escaping her lips. The sight and sound of her coming undone in my arms sends me careening over the edge right after her.

My hips jerk involuntarily, my orgasm tearing through me, white-hot and all-consuming. I come hard inside her until there's nothing left to give. For a moment, there's no room for logic or thought—only this raw kaleidoscope of sensation that leaves me utterly wrecked in the best way possible.

"Christ," I mutter, the word dragged out on a breathless exhale as my head drops forwards to rest against hers.

A beat passes, a long moment where neither of us says or does anything except breathe together in sync, our chests rising and falling with ragged effort. Then I carefully withdraw from her and collapse onto the mattress beside her.

For a while longer neither of us speaks. We just lie there, catching our breath.

Eventually Maisie sits up. She reaches for her thong and slips it back on. Meanwhile, I stay flat on my back, utterly spent and completely incapable of moving. My eyes follow her as she smooths down the fabric of her dress, her movements brisk and efficient, as though she hasn't just rocked my entire world.

"Well," she says lightly, brushing her tousled hair out of her face. "That escalated quickly."

I let out an incredulous laugh despite myself because . . . aye, no kidding.

She stands, glancing at me quickly then looking away again. "I suppose we both needed to get that out of our systems."

I push myself up onto my elbows. "Er . . . come again? What do you mean?"

"This can't go anywhere, Jamie. You know that and I know it. I just want to be sure we're both on the same page."

"But—"

"There's no 'but'." Her tone is matter-of-fact.

I sit up fully. "Maisie, come on—"

"Are you planning to close your beer garden?"

I frown at the abruptness of the question. "No."

"Well, then." She shrugs as though that settles it. "You and I could never work."

"What are you talking about?"

"We're rivals, Jamie. You with your new beer garden, me with my da's pub. *That*"—she waves a hand vaguely between us—"was just . . . an opportunity for us to release some tension. Nothing more."

Suddenly I'm acutely aware that my lower half is still stark naked. Hoping this conversation might go better with some clothes on, I stand and pull on my boxers then reach for my jeans.

"Maisie—"

"I'll admit it," she continues as if I haven't said anything at all, "the opening day of your beer garden was a bigger success than I was expecting. But my da and I aren't going to go down without a fight."

There's fire in her eyes again, a look I'm very familiar with by now.

"In case it wasn't already obvious, our days of playing *Highland Legacy* together are over," she adds. "That can't continue."

This leaves me floundering for something to say. "Maisie, you can't just—"

"Please leave," she interrupts calmly but firmly.

I want to argue more, but something about her expression stops me in my tracks. Defeated, I do up my fly, fasten my belt, then make to go. But as I reach her door, some part of me rebels against walking away without saying anything more.

"For what it's worth, I really am sorry I told you to get out of my car that night."

Something briefly flickers in Maisie's eyes before her gaze turns cool and distant again.

"Goodbye, Jamie," she says simply.

And just like that, I'm dismissed.

I head downstairs feeling thoroughly disorientated—confused as hell and reeling from how quickly everything went sideways after . . . well . . . *that.*

But there's no time for wallowing because as I'm making a beeline for the exit—

"Well!" Bryce's voice fills the pub, loud enough to make me flinch, and he steps out from behind the bar. "Did you and Maisie sort things out?"

"Er . . ." My brain scrambles to form an answer, but after what just happened upstairs, all I can think about is how loudly Maisie's bed creaked and whether Bryce might've heard it. Christ. I've no interest in hanging around for a chat. I need to get out of here.

"Not exactly. Anyway, I've got to go. Bye, Bryce."

CHAPTER TWENTY-THREE

MAISIE

The Pheasant's tables are empty, chairs flipped upside down on top of them, except for the one at which Da and I sit. It's late morning on a Monday—the perfect time for a meeting, I'd say, but judging by my father's face, you'd think I'd dragged him here for a funeral.

"Right." I pull out my notebook and click my pen. "Let's talk about how we can make the Pheasant even better."

Da raises an eyebrow, making no effort to hide his scepticism. "Even better? What's wrong with the way things are?"

"Nothing is wrong. But with Jamie's beer garden now open—"

"Och, here we go."

"—we need to make sure we stay competitive."

Da leans back, arms folded defiantly across his chest. "The Pheasant's been here for decades, Maisie. Folk know us. Trust us. We've always done well."

"And we want it to keep doing well. That might mean trying out some new ideas so people have more reasons to come here—not just because they always have, but because they choose to."

He grunts, unconvinced but listening.

"In cities, pubs have to innovate all the time because of competition. We don't have as much of that here in Bannock, but that's changing now, thanks to Jamie."

"Fine." His tone says it isn't fine at all. "What exactly are you proposing, then?"

"I thought about promotional nights." I flip through my notes. "Reduced prices on certain drinks to get people through the door. Or—and this one is my favourite, I think—we expand our cocktail menu."

Da squints at me like I've suggested we start serving sushi instead of steak pies. "Cocktails? We already do a decent gin and tonic if someone asks. What more do they need?"

"Think mojitos, cosmopolitans—drinks people are used to seeing in city bars."

"And you think folk around here want that stuff? A pint of lager or a dram of whisky is what they're after. Maybe a glass of wine. Not some fancy concoction with umbrellas sticking out the top."

"First, you don't put umbrellas in mojitos or cosmopolitans. Second, it's not just about giving people what they already drink, it's about tempting them to try something new—and to pay a premium price for the experience. We could brand our cocktails as the perfect treat for a summer's day. That might just attract people here rather than to Jamie's beer garden."

He looks distinctly unimpressed.

"We could use local spirits and ingredients," I add. "That could be a real selling point. Our cocktails could offer a uniquely Bannock experience."

He scratches his chin thoughtfully but doesn't seem convinced yet. "Sounds like a lot of faff to me. Measuring fancy ingredients, shaking things around. No, thanks."

"How about I take full responsibility for the cocktails, then? You wouldn't have to lift a finger. You could just leave it to me."

There's a long pause while Da studies me, considering this offer. Finally he exhales and shrugs in reluctant surrender. "Fine, if you're that determined, try it out. But I *will* be leaving it to you."

"Agreed!" I say quickly before he can change his mind. "We could maybe even create a signature cocktail for the Pheasant—something unique that visitors will remember us by." I tap my pen against my notebook, thinking aloud. "Maybe something bright green? We could use Midori and whisky, then top it with a cucumber slice shaped like the Loch Ness Monster. Tourists might—"

"No! I'm drawing the line there. That's *way* too gimmicky."

"Okay, maybe it is a bit," I concede. "But there's got to be something we can come up with. Something that captures the spirit of Scotland and the Highlands without veering into tacky territory. Hmm . . . leave it with me."

"I intend to do just that." He pushes himself up from the table. "Look, you clearly want to try new things, and that's fine by me, but I'll be leaving the work to you. Me? I've been doing things the same way for decades and I'm not about to change now."

"Wait a second! I haven't even got onto the subject of social media yet. I was wanting to talk about our online presence because I'm sure there's loads more we could be doing. What do you think about—"

Da cuts me off with a laugh. "Maisie, social media? You're asking *me*? Lass, I can barely figure out how to turn on my phone most days. You're the brains when it comes to anything involving a computer. For the longest time we were the main boozer in town, so we never had to bother much with that stuff. But if you reckon it'll help us keep up with Jamie, go ahead. Just don't expect me to get involved."

I smile and nod. "Aye. Thanks, Da. I'll take care of it."

Unfortunately, after Da leaves, my thoughts stray straight back to Jamie. Jamie, who gets panic attacks when it rains heavily.

The whole point of the meeting with Da was to keep my brain occupied—anything to stop thinking about *him*—but now I'm alone, it's like trying to hold back a flood with a tea towel.

When he told me to get out of his car that night, it wasn't because of anything I said or did. It was solely about the rain. I should really have pieced it together sooner. Everyone in Bannock remembers the crash. Mairi and Angus McIntyre weren't just Jamie's parents, they were part of the fabric of our community. Their sudden deaths shook us all. But I'd no idea that Jamie—the perpetual joker—carried a mental scar that could be triggered by something as simple as a change in the weather.

I shake my head, willing these thoughts away. I can't let myself get sidetracked.

Even if knowing about that vulnerability does endear him to me more than I'd like. Even if yesterday's sex was . . .

Christ. No. Not going there.

I refuse—outright refuse—to think about the rough

warmth of his hands as he gripped my waist. Or the woodsy, masculine scent of him that seems to have taken permanent residence in my senses. Or the way he filled me perfectly, stretching me open as his hips drove into mine like he was staking some primal claim. Or that low, needy groan he made just before he let go inside me. Or how his face tightened as he came—jaw clenched, eyes squeezed shut like he couldn't bear how good it felt . . .

Ugh! Seriously? Now? Thanks, brain. He's supposed to be my competition—not my weakness.

In an attempt to distract myself, I grab my phone and check the Pheasant's social media accounts. They're nothing to be proud of—a handful of half-hearted posts, the most recent one from a few weeks ago when I ran the Bannock-themed pub quiz. Da's right: up until now social media has never exactly been a priority for us. But it's time to change that.

I'll admit, my expertise with technology leans more towards conquering virtual dungeons than crafting a killer marketing strategy, but . . . maybe some of the skills are transferable?

While I put together tonight's quiz on my laptop, I play videos on my phone about growing a social media presence (multitasking for the win). Even after we open for business and regulars start trickling in—more, thankfully, than on the beer garden's opening day—my mind keeps wandering back to what I've learnt. It's not about shoving promotions down people's throats. "Sell, sell, sell!" doesn't cut it anymore. It's about creating content people actually want to engage with.

But what kind of general-interest content can you create for a small Highland pub? *Here's another photo of someone holding a pint!* Hardly riveting stuff . . .

As a test, I record a few videos—shots of food being served and locals laughing—but not anything worth posting.

The problem niggles at me all night, lingering through last orders and beyond, as I scrub tables and sweep floors. It beats thinking about Jamie anyway.

Freshly showered and tucked up under my duvet, I watch yet another research video on my laptop, jotting down ideas in a notebook. Showcasing local suppliers? Highlighting quirky regulars? Sharing cocktail tutorials? By the time I finally set my notebook aside, I still don't feel like I've cracked it.

As if on cue, my phone buzzes with a message in the Scottish Sirens group chat.

IONA

Anyone else staying up for tonight's episode of Highland Legacy?

God, it's already 1:57 a.m.! Just three minutes until the new episode drops in the UK to match its US broadcast time. (Because even though the show is filmed in Scotland with a cast full of British actors, its creators are, naturally, all about reeling in that huge American audience.) Normally, I wait until morning to watch, but tonight? I'm too wired with new ideas to think about sleeping anytime soon.

MAISIE

I am! Also, there's something big I've been keeping from you and Cat—proper juicy gossip—but I'll tell you tomorrow.

IONA

Don't leave us hanging!

Cat doesn't respond. She's probably fast asleep already. That's got to be a first, her being the sensible one of the three.

The episode opens with calamity: waves crash against a besieged coastal village as a massive kraken coils its tentacles around rooftops and fishing boats. Callum, the roguishly hand-some fire mage introduced this season, charges into action to help Isla, the enigmatic but powerful water mage. As they fight side by side, their elemental magic collides spectacularly: blis-tering flames meeting rushing waters in a clash that sends steam billowing through the air. Through it all, it's impossible not to notice how sexual tension crackles between them like another force of nature.

It's an exciting start, but things really escalate halfway through the episode when we finally get *the* scene, the one fans online have been speculating about for weeks. We all knew it was only a matter of time before Callum and Isla surrendered to the desire they obviously feel for one another.

Under a pale moon in an ancient stone circle, they meet again, only this time it isn't a common enemy that brings them together but raw need. Things begin slowly, charged glances melting into tentative touches, until restraint shatters entirely and clothes fall away. The show delivers on its usual no-holds-barred nudity policy, and let's just say both actors are easy on the eyes—with their clothes on and without.

The man playing Callum is objectively attractive, like the human embodiment of a Greek statue come to life. But, to me at least, he just doesn't compare to Jamie. And so, instead of appreciating what's right in front of me, my traitorous mind drifts back to yesterday. To Jamie's hands sliding over me, his body pressing close, solid and scorching-hot against mine . . .

Argh! Stop it, brain!

I force my attention back to the screen, and thankfully it doesn't take long for *Highland Legacy* to pull me back under its spell. Because what's more impressive than the actors' physiques is the way their magic comes alive as their passion crescendoes. Callum's ribbons of fire twist through Isla's streams of water in an otherworldly display above them, sparks hissing and crackling while glowing golden symbols form on the mages' flushed skin. Steam rises from them both, coiling into the night air as guttural moans echo off the towering stones surrounding them.

Thanks to Callum's fire magic, it's easily one of the hottest scenes *Highland Legacy* has ever aired—pun very much intended. In fact, it might even give the infamous body-painting scene a run for its money. But just as I'm about to crown it the steamiest moment in the show's history, something unexpected steals my attention. That stone circle . . .

As the camera pans out in a wide arc, capturing the fiery and watery tendrils entwining above, I realise I know the place. Not just from TV but from real life. It's barely a half hour's drive from Bannock. Oh my God, did they really film this scene there?

I grab my phone and go onto social media. Unsurprisingly, viewers (mostly American at this hour) are already losing their minds over the scene. #HighlandLegacy is trending, and my feed is flooded with posts, many featuring blurry screenshots marked *NSFW: Click to reveal.*

Wow. How do actors do it? Strip down, bare it all—literally

everything—and know that within seconds of broadcast their bodies will be screenshotted, GIFed, zoomed in on, and shared across every corner of the globe? Fame must come with an extraordinary level of fearlessness.

But I put a full-blown analysis of celebrity courage on hold because an idea flickers to life in my brain, a suggestion for marketing content that might actually *work*. Something people may just stop to watch. Something that could give Jamie's beer garden a run for its money.

In my head, it's like Callum's fire colliding with Isla's water: a spark here, a sizzle there, until suddenly I've got a bold, exciting plan that I can't wait to try out.

CHAPTER TWENTY-FOUR

JAMIE

The beer garden is heaving again, every table packed with tourists and locals basking in the kind of sunshine that feels like a miracle this far north. We've been blessed with a streak of golden days, perfect in every way—and perfectly timed. Three days since the grand opening, and each one has been bustling with life. The hum of chatter fills the air, glasses clink like a merry symphony, and shades, sunhats, and wide grins complete the scene. It's everything I hoped for. Everything I should be proud of.

But I can't savour it. Because Maisie's on my mind. Again.

The sex? Phenomenal, obviously. But that's not what's got me in knots. Not entirely anyway. Have I replayed that encounter more times than is healthy? Sure. But it's all the other stuff that takes up more space in my head.

I keep circling back to all those gaming sessions with Sassy-Lassie—how easy it was to chat with her, how she made me laugh harder than anyone else ever has, how she *got* me in a way no one else seems to. And now, to find out she wasn't some anonymous online gamer but was actually Maisie from down the road the whole time . . .

Bloody hell, it's a lot to wrap my head around. Realising that she knew who I was—for at least part of that time—and didn't tell me stings more than I'd like to admit. It feels like a betrayal. But then there's the other side of it, the one I keep coming back to no matter how hard my pride tries to steer me away. Because isn't it kind of amazing? The one person who sees me for who I am has been right under my nose all along. That kind of thing shouldn't happen in real life, and yet somehow it has.

It's not that I never noticed Maisie before. I've always thought she was cute—gorgeous, even—but it wasn't her looks that drew me to her when I met her online. Back then, she was just a fiery-haired mage with an annoying knack for outsmarting me at every turn. It was her sharp tongue that got to me: her wicked humour, the way she could cut me down and make me laugh in the same breath.

I miss the banter she and I used to have. But more than that, I crave it in real life. I crave *her* in real life.

But Maisie has made things very clear: nothing can happen between us so long as this beer garden remains in operation. She's drawn her line in the sand, and I'm standing on the wrong side of it. If I want there to be an "us"—if I want even half a chance to see where this could go—I have to walk away from everything I've worked so hard to build.

What kind of choice is that?

I head into the snug to prep a drinks order, still mulling over all things Maisie, when Emily ambles in behind me, one hand resting on her bump. "There you are! Have you seen what Maisie has done?"

I freeze, a pint glass poised under the tap. "What?" The word comes out sounding far too interested—at least to my ears—so I clear my throat and pour the lager with forced nonchalance. Just a bloke pulling a pint. Nothing to see here.

Emily, apparently oblivious to my overreaction, taps her phone a few times then slides it across the bar towards me. "Watch this."

Maisie's head and shoulders fill the small screen. Her hair is different now, a vibrant red streaked with orange and yellow highlights. What a striking contrast to her green eyes. She looks bloody incredible—like she's been kissed by flames—and I have to throw every mental bucket of cold water I've got at the reaction that surges through me.

But as stunning as she looks, my gaze catches on the username laid over the social media clip: SassyLassie. Her gaming alias. Now Maisie in the flesh mirrors the blazing hair she always had in the game, the fire spells she'd unleash . . .

"Want to know a secret?" Maisie raises an eyebrow at the camera before it pans out dramatically to reveal she's wearing a cropped tartan top and a denim skirt and is standing in a circle of standing stones. "That steamy scene in last night's episode of *Highland Legacy*? The one where Callum and Isla finally gave in to their desires?" She winks, and it's the kind of wink that could bring grown men to their knees—God knows I'm one of them. "It was filmed right here!"

A wistful Celtic melody plays in the background as Maisie continues. "The stones you see around me have stood here for over four thousand years. Some say they're buzzing with natural magical energy. I can't promise you'll see fire and water collide like in last night's episode, when our favourite mages decided to, ahem, *combine their powers*." She smirks. "If you're as big a fan of *Highland Legacy* as I am, though, you'll want to visit this place. And while you're at it, don't miss the charming wee town of Bannock just down the road."

The video transitions smoothly from the timeless mystique of the stone circle to the unhurried rhythm of Bannock's Main Street. Maisie now stands in front of her and her father's pub.

"Pop into the Pheasant for a true taste of Highland hospitality."

Quick cuts show off its cosy interior: laughing locals, plates of hearty food being served. All familiar sights until Maisie appears again behind the bar, holding up a vibrant red cocktail garnished with a chilli pepper.

"And if you're feeling adventurous, try our brand-new cocktail menu—we're putting the finishing touches to it now. My personal favourite? The Highlander's Secret. It's as bold and spicy as last night's episode." She raises her glass. "*Sláinte mhath!* See you in Bannock!"

For several seconds after the video ends, I just stand there like someone switched off my brain and forgot to reboot it.

Emily says, "Check out how many views she's got. She's gone viral! The latest episode of *Highland Legacy* has social media in a frenzy, and Maisie's video dropped at exactly the right time. Talk about clever. And look! You have to see some of the comments people have been leaving her."

Emily scrolls through them, and I read a few as they briefly appear on her screen:

Love the Pheasant's vibe! And your smile is contagious.

Your accent is adorable! Can you narrate my life, please? 😂

Loving the Highland Legacy references, but I'm more interested in the person behind the bar. Single? 😉

Your energy is infectious! Makes me want to book a trip to Scotland right now.

OMG, your style is so unique. Love it! 🔥

Bloody hell. That question about whether she's single hits me right in the chest.

"Also, a cocktail menu?" Emily says. "That's new. Looks like Maisie is upping her game, fighting back against the beer garden already. Maybe we should get you on social media too, shaking up some fancy cocktails."

I run a hand through my hair, messing it up. "Er, not sure about that. I doubt people would be as keen to watch me as they are Maisie. She's kind of . . ." I gesture at Emily's phone. ". . . nice to look at, you know?"

A slow smile spreads across Emily's face. "Oh, is she now?"

Heat creeps up my neck. Damn it. I walked right into that one.

I finish the drinks order then get on with my day, trying to focus on work, but every time I get a moment to myself—which, admittedly, isn't often given how busy we are—I find myself reaching for my phone to watch Maisie's video again. The view count keeps climbing higher and higher, and I'm not even a little bit surprised. There's something magnetic about her, something that draws you in and makes you want to stick around.

The easy confidence, the playful smile, the way she makes everyone feel like they're in on some delicious secret. It's exactly how she is behind the bar at the Pheasant. She's got a gift, one I've never quite mastered myself. Sure, I can pull a decent pint, but Maisie? She makes people feel like they belong.

Every time I check the video, more folk have left comments.

Jealousy coils in my stomach because SassyLassie used to be mine—our conversations, our adventures, our inside jokes. Now she belongs to the world, and Christ, they love her. How could they not? That fierce determination of hers blazes as bright as her new hair, and watching her take on this challenge, seeing her fight back against the beer garden with such style . . . it's sexy as hell. The same fire I saw in her when she played *Highland Legacy* burns even brighter now I'm seeing it in real life.

As I'm preparing another round of drinks in the snug, my phone buzzes with a notification: *SassyLassie has posted a new video.* (Yes, I've followed her. How could I not?)

I have work to do, and I've already spent more than enough time thinking about her, but I hit play before I can stop myself. Maisie's face appears on my screen, and just like that, I'm a goner. That smile of hers? Lethal.

"I'm blown away by the reaction to my last video!" she says. "I went for a wee nap after posting it—I was up late last night watching the new episode, after all. So when I woke up and checked my phone . . . well, let's just say I had to pinch myself!"

She goes on to talk about her plans for future content, mentioning other *Highland Legacy* filming locations she's thinking of visiting, but I'm caught on the way she tucks her red hair behind her ear, revealing that small Celtic knot tattoo.

"Oh," she continues, "and one more thing: I'm actually a huge *Highland Legacy* gamer. Have been for ages. Would you guys like to see some gameplay footage? Or should I stick to tours around Scotland? Either way, let me know in the comments, and you can help shape what I post here. And, of course, don't forget to follow me and stick along for the ride!"

◆ ◆ ◆

As the golden hues of late afternoon melt into evening, I'm doing my rounds of the tables, ensuring everyone is happy (they are) when Lewis steps out into the beer garden with Emily in tow. He scans the crowd, spots me, and jerks his head towards the hotel. "A word, Jamie? Shouldn't take long."

I follow the two of them into the office, where Lewis perches on the edge of a desk and Emily settles into a chair.

"Emily's filled me in on Maisie's video and this new cocktail menu at the Pheasant," Lewis says. "I thought the three of us should have a quick chat. First off, let me say again, you've done an incredible job with the beer garden—completely surpassed our expectations. But what's your take on this move from the Pheasant? Should we be concerned? Do we need to step up our social media presence?"

"I mean . . ." I lean against the wall, thinking—or rather, trying to think. The problem is, my brain is a lot more interested in a certain fiery redhead than business strategy right now.

"Are you all right?" Emily asks.

"Aye. Just . . . mulling things over," I mutter. Like how, in those videos, Maisie looked like she was made for the spotlight. Or how different things might be if the beer garden weren't standing between us.

I wonder how Lewis and Emily would react were I to suggest shutting it down. Not well, I bet.

When I remain quiet, Emily turns to Lewis. "You know, Jamie let slip earlier that he thinks Maisie is easy on the eye."

"He did?" Lewis hoots with delight. "She's the competition, Jamie. Falling for her might not be the smartest business move, eh?"

"I didn't *let slip* anything," I grumble. "I was just stating a fact. You can hardly expect me not to notice when someone looks . . . well . . . like *that*."

"Like what, exactly?" Lewis teases. "Come on, Jamie. Enlighten us."

I cross my arms. "Can we please drop this?"

But Lewis doesn't let it go—of course he doesn't. "So, has anything happened between you two? A sneaky wee kiss, maybe? Or . . ." He wiggles his eyebrows suggestively. "More than a kiss?"

"No," I lie, too quickly.

"Why the red face, then?" Lewis fires back. "Because that only happens when you're embarrassed."

"I'm not embarrassed! I'm just . . . argh!" The frustration spills over before I can stop it. Unable to think of a convincing excuse, I opt for brotherly violence instead. I give him a hard shove, and he flails dramatically, almost sliding off the desk entirely.

"Oh-ho! That's how we're doing this, is it?" His grin turns feral. "Come on then, little brother."

Before I can react, he lunges at me, hooking an arm around me in an attempt to wrestle me into a headlock. But I duck out of his hold and jab him in the ribs with my elbow. He yelps—dramatic as ever—and retaliates by grabbing my shirt and yanking me towards him.

"You've got it bad for her!" he crows, flicking me on the forehead, a move he immediately follows by poking me in the stomach. "The joker's finally fallen for someone. Admit it!"

"Oi! Very pregnant woman here!" Emily's voice slices through our increasingly childish squabble. "If either of you clowns tumbles into me, Ally will be down here in five minutes flat to knock your heads together. You have been warned."

That gets our attention. Lewis lets go of me, but then he says, "So . . . was it game over back when she had the blue, or did the flaming hair seal the deal?"

And with that, I shove him again—but away from Emily, which I think makes it okay.

"That the best you've got, wee man?" he jeers, crouching like he's about to charge me.

"You two are as bad as bairns!" Elspeth appears in the doorway, radiating disapproval, her hands planted firmly on her hips. "May I remind you both that you're supposed to be professional young men running an actual business?"

Lewis straightens and flashes her his most charming grin. "How come you always know when there's a meeting happening you weren't invited to? It's uncanny."

"This is a meeting, is it? Sure doesn't look like it." Elspeth steps into the room like she owns it, even though technically Lewis is the boss around here.

"Aye, well, we *were* talking about Maisie's social media efforts and the new cocktail menu at the Pheasant," Lewis says. "But it . . . sort of dissolved into me and Emily teasing Jamie about having feelings for Maisie."

"Absolute lies!" I protest loudly. "I don't have feelings for her."

"Oh?" A sly smile tugs at the corners of Elspeth's mouth. "And yet what's this I hear about you going up to Maisie's flat with her the other day? And your hair being more dishevelled when you came back down than when you went up?"

My jaw drops. What bloody sorcery is this? How does she know about that?

Lewis and Emily exchange a look, their eyes lighting up like kids spotting a pile of presents under the Christmas tree. Two seconds later, Lewis doubles over with laughter while Emily leans back in her chair, both hands cradling her baby bump as if it might pop from all the shaking.

Meanwhile, I'm left gaping like a fish out of water. "How . . . how do you even know about that?"

"Oh, Bryce mentioned it yesterday when we were having a wee chat."

Bloody hell. Can't Maisie's da keep his mouth shut?

"It wasn't . . . . it wasn't what you think it was!" I stammer, even though it was *exactly* what they think it was.

God, my pulse was already racing from having to fend off Lewis and Emily, but now Elspeth too? This is too much.

"Does anyone else fancy wandering in and joining this meeting uninvited?" I say bitterly, glancing at the door as though daring fate to test me further.

Of course, fate takes me up on the offer.

Iona steps into the office right on cue, still dressed in her farm vet gear, smelling faintly of hay and antiseptic.

Lewis gives her a quick kiss then grins like he's about to spill the juiciest secret of the century. "Guess what? Jamie has a thing for one of your mates!"

"Oh?" Iona blinks with surprise. "Funny, I thought *I'd* be the one delivering that piece of goss to you. Maisie already spilled the beans."

My stomach drops. "Maisie told you . . . what exactly?"

"Everything," Iona replies in an infuriatingly smug tone.

Lewis perks up like a dog catching the scent of bacon. "Everything? Such as . . . ?"

I throw up my hands, desperate to shut this down before it spirals any further. "Right, that's enough. We don't need to—"

"They hooked up on Sunday," Iona says with all the tact of an air horn.

Kill me now.

"I did not hook up with Maisie!" My protest bursts out with far too much force, making everyone's eyebrows shoot up in unison. Scrubbing a hand over my face, I try again in a calmer—though no less panicked—tone. "Can we please all watch what we say? This is how rumours start."

Iona arches an eyebrow. "Well, that's an interesting take, considering Maisie was quite clear about what happened. And she was, you know . . . there."

My face heats with the kind of mortification I didn't think it was possible for a grown man to experience. Normally, I'm the one dishing out the teasing and revelling in other people squirming. How the tables have turned.

Before I can salvage what's left of my dignity, Lewis breaks into raucous laughter, a deep belly laugh so loud it seems to shake the walls. This sets off Emily, her giggles punctuated by barely disguised snorts. Elspeth cackles softly while Iona tries— not very hard, mind you—to hide her amusement behind her hand.

And then—oh God—they start chiming in with jokes and prying questions, the kind only nosy family members or highly unprofessional colleagues would dare ask. They keep at it until something inside me finally gives way.

"All right! That's enough!" My voice cuts sharply through the laughter, silencing them all.

I force myself to meet their gazes one by one, then I take a deep breath and lay it all out. "Maisie said nothing can happen between us unless I shut down the beer garden."

As my words sink in, their grins fade away.

"Oh," Iona says quietly. "Maisie didn't mention that bit."

"Well, she really should have because it's a pretty important point. Maisie and I don't have a future—not unless I'm willing to torch everything I've built."

CHAPTER TWENTY-FIVE

JAMIE

Rain pelts the snug's window, each drop a mocking reminder that my beer garden—my pride and joy, my brilliant idea—is sitting empty. Not just empty: abandoned. Chairs tucked neatly under tables, parasols furled, looking about as inviting as a dentist's waiting room.

Earlier, Lewis and I discussed using the hotel's restaurant as a spillover space for the snug. Back then, I'd been anticipating the same kind of crowds we've had these past few sunny days. But no. The snug is as dead as it ever was.

I mean, what did I expect? You can hardly sit outside drinking pints in weather like this.

My phone sits on the bar in front of me, taunting me. I've lost count of how many messages I've drafted to Maisie, each one deleted before sending. Because what can I say? *Sorry for building a beer garden that threatens your and your da's business, but fancy giving us a shot?* Aye, that'll work.

Christ, I need to pull myself together. The whole thing has done my head in, if I'm honest. First, finding out that Sassy-Lassie—my gaming buddy, the person I trusted most—was actually Maisie. Then falling into bed with her only to be dismissed by her immediately afterwards. And now the entire bloody town knows about it. Word spread fast after Lewis, Emily, Iona, and Elspeth found out. Now Ally keeps giving me these knowing looks, and every now and then Aidan or Grace will make a gently teasing remark.

Right. Enough. Time to focus on something productive. Maisie's made her position clear: we're opponents, not anything else. So be it. She's got her fancy social media presence and her cocktail menu, and me . . . well, I've got other ideas, not just the beer garden. Ideas that'll keep the snug buzzing, rain or shine. Further collaborations with the distillery, for one. Kyle seemed keen when we spoke at the opening event.

I pull up my email on my laptop and start drafting a message to Kyle. I'm halfway through when my phone pings with a notification: *SassyLassie has posted a new video.*

Don't watch it. Focus on the email.

My finger hovers over the notification.

Don't.

I tap it.

Maisie appears on screen, looking particularly stunning today. Her flame-coloured hair is loose around her shoulders, and she's wearing this wee smile that makes my stomach flip.

"Hello, my lovely followers!" She holds up a cocktail glass filled with something blue and decorated with a tiny paper umbrella. "Today I want to introduce you to my newest creation: the Rainy Day Rescue. Perfect for those days when you were hoping to relax outside in a beer garden . . ." She pauses dramatically then winks at the camera. ". . . but it's really not the weather for it."

The cheeky wee—

I bash out the rest of the email to Kyle, clacking the keys hard, then fire it off, probably with a few typos in it. But sod it. Some things are more important than perfect spelling—like putting Maisie in her place.

I march out to reception, where Lewis is behind the desk. "I'm heading out," I say. "You'll need to keep an eye on the snug."

"Er, you do realise I'm the manager, don't you? I'm the one who gives the orders."

"It's dead in there. I'm sure you'll manage."

"Jamie—" he starts, but I'm already tugging my jacket on.

Time to pay Maisie a visit. If I'm honest with myself, I've been looking for an excuse to see her again.

The rain drums against my hood as I make my way along Main Street. The Pheasant's windows are lit up like a beacon, and through them I can see it's packed. Folk are huddled around tables, laughing and chatting, sheltering from the weather. I spot a number of faces that were in the beer garden over the last few days. Now that the sun has gone away, they've returned to their old haunt.

I push open the door, warmth hitting me along with the familiar scent of beer and whisky. My gaze sweeps the room, searching for Maisie, but she's nowhere to be seen. Bryce is, however, behind the bar, pulling a pint.

My steps falter. Last time I was here, Bryce had a go at me. Mind you, that was when there was no one else around. Now the place is heaving. He wouldn't try anything with all these witnesses, would he?

I approach the bar, keeping my movements slow and casual, like I'm trying not to spook a wild animal. "Er, is Maisie around?"

"Upstairs." Bryce's tone is gruff. "She's not feeling too great."

"Really?" I frown. "But she just posted a video."

"Aye, well." Bryce hands the pint he's just poured to a customer then turns back to me. "You going up to see her, then?"

"If that's all right?"

He shrugs. "You're both adults. Just remember there are folk down here with ears."

Heat creeps up my neck. "Right. Well. I'll just . . ." I gesture vaguely towards the stairs up to their flat then make a quick escape.

I take the steps two at a time, my mind already forming the perfect comeback to her video. Something witty. Something that'll get under her skin. If history repeats itself (and here's hoping it does), our inevitable argument will just be foreplay for us tearing each other's clothes off and her wrapping her legs back around me. I mean, obviously that wouldn't solve anything, but—

I find her curled up on the couch, swaddled in a blanket like a burrito, a hot water bottle clutched to her stomach. She's pale, there's a faint sheen of sweat on her brow, and there's no sign of the usual fire in her eyes.

"Great timing, Jamie," she says, her voice as sharp as ever despite her obvious discomfort. "Come to gloat about me being under the weather?"

All my clever words evaporate. "I . . . er, are you all right?"

"Just peachy." She shifts slightly under the blanket. "Crippling cramps are exactly what I needed to brighten my day."

"Oh. Right. But . . ." My gaze darts to her hot water bottle, noticing it's not actually pressed against her stomach but a bit lower. I quickly lift my eyes back to her face. "You literally just posted a video, and you were smiling in it. Being cheeky! Making fun of the way heavy rain messes with my head."

Her eyes widen. "Oh shit, it was a poke at the beer garden, not at—"

"I'm winding you up." I hold up my hands in a gesture of peace before she injures herself trying to explain. "But seriously, no one watching would've guessed you're feeling crap right now."

"It was a thirty-second video, Jamie." She lets out an exasperated huff but winces partway through, like every movement hurts, even just breathing. "Social media isn't real. Didn't you know that? It's called 'grinning and bearing it'. I'm a woman. We've been faking it since the dawn of time."

"Hmm." My lips curve into a slow smirk. "Now, Maisie, let's not rewrite history here. We both know those moans and cries you made the other day were one hundred per cent real."

Her cheeks flush, and she rolls her eyes so hard it's a miracle they don't get stuck. "I really don't want to talk about that right now."

Suddenly her face creases, like she's bracing for another wave of pain, and my smirk falters. Okay, maybe now isn't the time for jokes about sexcapades.

"How long is this gloating going to take?" she asks. "Any chance we can just skip to the part where you sod off?"

"But . . ." I hesitate and gesture vaguely to her midsection. "You seem like you're in quite a lot of pain."

"I *am!*" she snaps. "My periods aren't normally this bad, but they're always worse when I'm stressed, and guess what? I *have* been feeling pretty stressed lately—on account of some arse down the road opening a beer garden." She jabs a finger at me. "It's your fault I'm in this much pain!"

I blink at her tirade then take a half-step back for safety reasons (lest that hot water bottle become a projectile). "Aw, shit. Er . . . sorry?"

She slumps back against the cushions. "This is such terrible timing. My first video blew up—it went viral—and now I've got this amazing chance to keep the momentum going. I should be posting new content while people are still hooked, but right now the last thing I feel like doing is making videos."

"Then don't! Take a break."

She glares at me like my sole purpose on Earth is to ruin her life. "Oh, you'd love that, wouldn't you? Stop making videos when folk are literally starting to come here because of them! Yesterday Da and I had a couple from Glasgow *and* a group of friends from Aberdeen stop by, all thanks to my video of the stone circle. I've had messages from people as far away as Australia saying they'd love to pop in for a pint someday. I need . . . to keep making . . . more content."

Spying her phone on the arm of the couch, I swoop in and snatch it up before she can stop me. "I'm taking this. For your own good."

"Oi!" She jerks upright. "You can't do that. Give me that back!"

"Nope, you need to rest. I'll go out and pick you up some supplies. I know just what'll cheer you up."

Her lips press into a tight line. "Oh, do you now?"

"Aye." I grin. "Because I played *Highland Legacy* with you for months, remember? And during that time, you told me a lot about what you like and don't like. Like your favourite biscuit—custard creams. A tragic choice, but it's your life. I also know you like peppermint tea. Mint choc ice cream. Dark chocolate. Gaelic Fire. Okay, you probably don't want a Gaelic Fire today, but—"

"Enough! I get the point." She shifts on the couch. "Honestly? I wouldn't say no to those things, but I can see right through you, Jamie. You're only being nice to me so you can distract me from posting more videos."

I crouch so I'm closer to Maisie's eye level. "Look, why don't we call today a truce? No bickering, no competing. You don't stress about social media, and I won't plot ways to pack the snug even when it's pouring buckets outside. Just one day where we both take a break and . . . chill."

She studies me for a beat too long, those sharp eyes looking for an ulterior motive that isn't there.

"Okay," she says with obvious reluctance before sinking back into the cushions with a little sigh of surrender. "That . . . might be nice."

"Right, then." Rising to my feet, I pop her phone up on a high shelf, well out of reach. "I don't want you touching that thing until I'm back. Just stay where you are and relax. Maybe put something on TV that'll take your mind off things. I won't be long."

CHAPTER TWENTY-SIX

MAISIE

Jamie returns to the flat with shopping bags dangling from his hands and rain dripping from his jacket. A soggy paper wrap pokes out from under his arm, and after setting the bags down, he reveals with a flourish it's a bouquet of flowers. Lupins stretch their spiky heads above clusters of sweet peas and peonies—surprisingly lovely for something that moments before was smashed against his armpit.

"A guy has to give his lass flowers on their first date, right?" His eyes sparkle with devilry.

I groan loudly, partly because of him and partly because my cramps feel like tiny goblins rioting in my uterus. "Ugh. That's the exact same line you used as LochNLoad when I took you to that spot behind the waterfall. Did you think recycling it would be charming?"

"I absolutely did," he says with zero shame. "Anyway, admit it—you liked the line then, and you like it now."

"Wrong. And I can recycle lines too, like *this is not a date*. It wasn't then, and it isn't now."

"If you say so." He crouches by the shopping bags and

unpacks them with irritating enthusiasm. "In any case, I brought snacks for whatever this is."

Custard creams come out first, followed by dark chocolate, peppermint tea, a tub of mint choc chip ice cream, and a pot of fresh fruit salad.

"Right," he says casually, as if he hasn't just unloaded my entire comfort-food wish list onto the coffee table (with a bit of token fruit thrown in, possibly to help ward off guilt). "I'll pop the ice cream in your freezer unless you want some now?"

I shake my head no—not because I don't want it but because I'm too stubborn to give him the satisfaction of gratitude just yet. "Er . . . you're not planning to stick around, are you?"

"Of course I am!" he calls over his shoulder before disappearing into the kitchen like he owns the place. When he strolls back in, he beams and says, "My last gift to you is the gift of my company." I'm about to retort that I'm not sure I want that gift when he adds, "Actually, come to think of it, that's not the last gift. I got a few other things too. More . . . practical ones."

He reaches into a bag that still has some items in it, and then . . . oh no. No, no, no, no, no—

"So, I wasn't sure exactly what sort of, er, *supplies* you might need for your current *predicament*." One by one, Jamie pulls out an assortment of sanitary products and lines them up on the coffee table like he's creating a display. Pads in all shapes and sizes. Tampons—some with applicators, some without— and a menstrual cup. It's absurdly thorough, like he raided an entire chemist aisle without knowing where to stop.

A laugh bursts out of me before I can stop it, a proper belly laugh that sends another sharp jab through my abdomen but is worth it anyway.

"There!" Jamie points at me triumphantly. "A smile! See? My presence is already working wonders."

"It's not your *presence*, idiot," I manage between giggles. "I mean, what even is that?" I wave at the shrine to period products. "You've got enough there to last a women's football team a whole season!"

He shrugs, entirely unbothered by my criticism. "The specifics of how I made you smile aren't important. The point is, you're smiling."

"You're ridiculous," I mutter, shaking my head even as another twitch pulls at the corners of my mouth.

But then he drops to the carpet and lounges back against the sofa, settling close enough that I can sense the heat of him. Close enough that my fingers itch to tangle in his messy hair. Not that I'd actually do that, obviously.

It's getting a bit too cosy here—cosy and dangerous—so I grab at the nearest distraction. "How much did all this cost?"

"It doesn't matter." Jamie waves away the question like he's swatting a fly buzzing near his ear. "It's on me."

"No." Indignation creeps in. "I'm paying you back. The last thing I want is to owe you anything."

He glances over his shoulder at me, his lips curving into that infuriating smirk of his. "Seriously, it's fine. I've actually got a bit of extra cash in my pocket right now. You see, I started this beer garden recently, and it's been doing really well."

I reach out and flick his ear. His smirk morphs into a grin— frustratingly cute, as usual.

"After that comment, I'm definitely not paying you back. Anyway, I hear the beer garden isn't doing quite so well today."

"Touché." Jamie winks then his gaze drifts to the TV, to the romcom I paused when I heard him coming in. "Interesting choice. Thought you'd be more of a *You've Got Mail* kind of girl."

"You're familiar with nineties romcoms?" I ask, genuinely surprised.

"I've seen *You've Got Mail*. It's kind of eerie how similar it is to us, don't you think?"

"Not really. *It* had a happy ending."

"You're right. I always thought it was weird that Meg Ryan's character fell for Tom Hanks's. For a good chunk of the film, he knows her identity but goes on chatting with her online anyway. That's creepy as fuck, right? I mean, what sort of person would do that kind of thing?"

I make to flick his ear again, but this time Jamie dodges. He spins back to face me and presses both hands to his chest in an exaggerated shot-to-the-heart gesture. "I opened up to you, Maisie! And yet you weren't being honest with me!"

"Is *this* your grand plan to cheer me up?" I fold my arms. "Guilt-tripping me? Because, you know what, I *do* feel guilty about that—but you're not making me feel any better about myself right now." I pause deliberately before adding, "Also, I hear you've been telling people that I said we could never work unless you shut down the beer garden."

"Well, you *did* say that," he points out. "But you're right, the aim here is to distract you from cramps, and I've got something guaranteed to take your mind off things."

He reaches into one of the shopping bags still sitting by the sofa and pulls out a laptop sleeve. With exaggerated flair, he unzips it and withdraws his computer like a magician pulling a rabbit from a hat. "Despite your betrayal, I *have* been missing playing *Highland Legacy* with you, so I was thinking . . . you know . . ."

"I told you that the days of us gaming together were over."

"You did, but c'mon, you know how immersive *Highland Legacy* is. It'll distract you better than this romcom you've probably seen twenty times already." He sets his laptop on the coffee table, beside the mountain of tampons, and opens it up. "And it'll be fun playing in person for once."

"You're unbelievable."

"But irresistible too?"

"I never said that, but all right, we can play. But only because it's better than stabbing myself in the eye to distract myself from the pain in my uterus."

"Fair enough." Jamie claps his hands together as if sealing some sacred pact then jumps to his feet. "Right then, where's your laptop? I'll go fetch it."

"It's in my bedroom."

"Great! I know where that is—on account of the deliciously filthy sex we had there the other day." He shoots me a cheeky grin.

"Bloody hell. Did you really need to say that?"

"What?" He shrugs innocently. "I'm just stating facts. Anyway, back in a mo."

I hurl a cushion at him, but he's already stepped out into the hall, laughing like the devil he is.

◆ ◆ ◆

Jamie and I sit side by side on the sofa, our laptops balanced on our knees as we explore a dense forest in the northern region of *Highland Legacy*'s map. Our shoulders brush occasionally as we play, and each time it happens, my stomach does this stupid little flip that has absolutely nothing to do with my cramps.

Jamie keeps on stealing glances at me when he thinks I'm too focused on my screen to notice. His shirt sleeves are rolled up to his elbows, and against my better judgement, my gaze has on several occasions wandered to his forearms. There's something inexplicably hot about the way his muscles shift as his fingers dart over the keys.

"Tea?" Jamie asks, already reaching for my mug.

"You don't have to keep—"

But he's up and off before I can finish speaking, apparently determined to top up my peppermint tea. Again. As though leaving me with an empty mug would be an unforgivable crime.

When he returns, he brings not just my tea but also a bowl of ice cream. I snatch it greedily from him and dig in.

"Your shoulders look tense," he observes. "Want me to—"

"If you're about to offer me a massage"—I point my spoon at him like a weapon—"don't even think about it."

He shrugs. "Can't blame a guy for trying."

Shaking my head at his audacity, I shovel another spoonful into my mouth and try to refocus on the game, although it's hard when his stupid grin lingers in my peripheral vision. Our characters are stalking through the gloomy forest in search of a legendary weapon, the Staff of the Storm Witch, which supposedly grants its wielder the power to control the weather. Jamie's warrior leads the way while my mage follows close behind.

"Watch out for that—" I try to warn him, but it's too late.

A giant spider drops from the canopy like something out of a nightmare, landing square on top of Jamie's character and flattening him to the ground.

"Shit, I've been pancaked by Shelob's uglier cousin!" Jamie mashes his keyboard. "Little help here?"

"Relax." I cast a fire spell, and the spider explodes in a satisfying burst of embers and ash. "What would you do without me?"

He shoots me a sideways glance, his lips curving in a way that spells trouble. "I don't know. We make a good team, you and me. On the battlefield *and* in the bedroom."

"Oh God! Just stop. Else the next time a spider flattens you, you're on your own."

"Understood. I promise to make no further references to how I had you moaning in ecstasy a few days back. Nope, that topic is completely off limits. Although . . . did I mention on Sunday that your tits are fantastic? I mean, they're not the biggest, but they felt really delightful in my hands and—"

"*Jamie!*" I grab a cushion and wallop him square in the face. "You're *such* a tosser! I cannot believe you just said that."

He takes the hit like a champ, laughing and rubbing his jaw. "What? It was a compliment!"

"Do you want me to hit you again?" I hold the cushion aloft to prove I'm not bluffing.

"Er . . . no? All right, no more chat about your itty bitty titties, then. Although, just so we're clear, I like them. A lot. They're really pretty amazing."

"Wow. Okay, since we're sharing unsolicited opinions, maybe I'll start listing *your* best features. Starting with . . . er . . . give me a minute . . . nope, I've got nothing."

"Ouch!" He chuckles. "You know, SassyLassie always had the best banter. It's fun getting to chat to you like this in real life."

"You do realise I'm literally asking you *not* to talk about this stuff with me, don't you? Besides, it's not like I'm giving you feedback on your cock."

"True. Although, if you *were* to . . . what would you give it out of ten?"

That gets him another whack of the cushion. Again, right on the noggin. This time, he blinks quite a few times afterwards. He still laughs it off, but I wonder if it was maybe a tad too hard—and, annoyingly, that makes me feel a bit guilty. Still, it doesn't stop me from saying, "Seven."

The number lands with just the right amount of sting, and his head jerks back like I've hit him a third time. It's high enough to seem genuine and yet low enough to chip away at his fragile male ego. Is that really mean of me? Nah, it's about time I put him in his place. Anyway, I'm not so crass as to actually rate a guy's penis. (Although, if I *had* to, I'd definitely give Jamie a higher score than seven.)

Jamie tries to brush off my judgement with a smile—a thin, strained thing—but I can tell I've hit a nerve. Still, at least he doesn't offer to whip it out and give me an opportunity to re-evaluate it. I wouldn't have put that past him.

"All right, fine," I say. "Maybe a seven point five."

This sympathy half point does nothing to improve his mood. If anything, it makes him look more affronted.

"Anyway . . ." I say. "Seeing as you raised the subject of . . . well, *that part of your anatomy*, can I ask you a serious question?"

He raises an eyebrow. "You want to ask me a serious question about my dick?"

"Kind of, aye."

"Er . . . okay?"

I really shouldn't be this entertained by how adorably confused—and perhaps a little panicked—he looks right now. But apparently I'm deeply flawed. Besides, there *is* something I want to get off my chest, and it's been bothering me for ages. Two years, in fact.

"At Emily and Ally's engagement party, I asked you to dance with me, and you said no."

"Oh. Aye . . . I did."

"But when we were driving back from the distillery?" I pause for effect then point at his crotch. "Boner."

Jamie chokes. "Jesus Christ!"

"And *then*," I barrel on mercilessly, "that kiss in your garage? Boner."

"Maisie!" He laughs now despite himself, his ears going red as sin.

"And obviously," I finish grandly, "when we finally had sex . . . boner bonanza."

Jamie groans through another chuckle and runs a hand through his messy hair. "*Boner bonanza?* Really?"

"What?" I fold my arms. "That's what it was! You've got a very reliable track record of pointing north around me. Which means"—I stab a finger at him—"you can't find me *that* hideous. So why did you knock me back at the engagement party?"

He glances at the ceiling as if it might have the answer then finally meets my gaze. "You didn't seriously think I thought you were hideous, did you?" He asks it as if the very idea is baffling beyond words.

"Well . . ."

I don't have major hang-ups about my looks, but I've never exactly been brimming with confidence either. I'm no curvy Iona, and I certainly don't have Cat's endless legs.

"Bloody hell." He shifts on the sofa, folding one knee up between us. "Maisie, it wasn't about how you looked. God knows *that* wasn't the issue. I mean . . . you've seen yourself in a mirror, right?" He lets out a small huff of laughter, like this should all be obvious. But then his smile falters, morphing into something more uncertain as one hand rubs absently at his left thigh. "It's just . . . dancing makes me self-conscious sometimes."

I raise an eyebrow. "Pretty sure you're not the only guy who feels like that."

"Aye, well, not every guy has a metal pin in their leg that makes everything feel off kilter when they try to move with rhythm." He shrugs like he's brushing it off but doesn't quite succeed. "Gaming? That feels easier."

I nod, not because I'm going soft or anything—well, maybe just a little—but I can see where he's coming from. Breezily I say, "Gaming is way better than dancing anyway. Speaking of which, we've been loitering in this forest clearing for ages. Shall we crack on?"

"Let's do it."

We return to the game, our characters venturing deeper into the tangled forest. His warrior charges ahead with abandon, hacking through thorny vines and dispatching low-level enemies like they're nothing more than minor inconveniences. Meanwhile, my mage hangs back, methodically gathering herbs and enchanting Jamie's gear.

"Are you seriously picking flowers right now?" Jamie asks, glancing sideways at my screen. "We're supposed to be hunting down a legendary weapon."

"These flowers will save your arse when you inevitably get pancaked by another spider. No mana, no magic."

He chuckles softly, the sound laced with a smile I can hear even without looking his way. "Can't argue with that."

We continue on until we're swarmed by shadow sprites, once-beautiful creatures corrupted by magic gone wrong. Their glowing green wings shimmer faintly against their skeletal frames, and high-pitched giggles echo disturbingly as they dive-bomb us like homicidal dragonflies. Lochie swings his blade efficiently, attacking them and deflecting the tiny darts they shoot with flawless precision. Even in the midst of battle, I can't help sneaking a glance at Jamie. His eyes are locked on the screen, his brow furrowed in concentration, his tongue poking out slightly—a detail so disarmingly cute I almost miss a sprite that lunges at me from behind.

"Shit!" I conjure up an inferno spell just in time to roast it in midair.

Jamie's phone buzzes on the coffee table, but he doesn't pick it up until all the sprites are defeated. When he does check it, he puts it back down again a moment later.

"Anything important?"

"Nah, just Lewis. He's wondering when exactly I'll be coming back to the hotel, but I reckon I've earned a bit of time off. Besides, it's still bucketing down and no one is daft enough to sit outside in this. Let's push on and find this storm witch's staff."

"Sure thing. Imagine if it were real—I'd use it to keep your beer garden so soggy it could double as a duck pond. Meanwhile, sunbeams would shine down on the Pheasant all day, every day."

"Wow, you'd go full evil overlord with it? Like, twirling a sinister moustache and cackling on a throne made of tampons and custard creams?"

"Yes, Jamie. Because if I had magic powers, the first thing I'd do is grow a handlebar moustache. I'd even grab a monocle to go with it, just to really complete the look. I don't hate the idea of a throne made of custard creams, though."

We both laugh then the game pulls us back in. For a while, we lose ourselves in *Highland Legacy*, delving deeper into the dark forest and fending off increasingly challenging enemies. Jamie charges ahead without an ounce of caution, hacking his way through monsters like a berserker on speed. Meanwhile, I trail behind, stringing together spells to keep him alive because apparently someone has to be the responsible one.

"You know," I mutter, "if you spent even a few points improving your defence stat rather than always trying to max out your strength, I might not have to babysit you."

"But where would the fun be in that?" Jamie quips. "Besides, you're amazing at keeping me alive. I wouldn't want to rob you of your chance to shine."

We're just about to reach some creepy ruins that have boss battle vibes when Jamie's phone buzzes on the coffee table again. This time, Lewis is calling him. Jamie lets out an exaggerated sigh before snatching up the phone. "Aye? What is it?" A pause follows, during which he stares up at the ceiling like his brother's voice is personally offending him. "Where am I? I'm at Maisie's flat . . . Jesus, no, we are *not* having sex! She's feeling rubbish, and I'm looking after her."

A surprised snort escapes before I can stop it.

Jamie winks at me even as Lewis continues talking, his voice faint but distinct enough for me to make out snippets, and one word in particular: *Kyle*.

At the name, Jamie sits up straighter. "You did *what*? Why? Actually, nope, never mind, don't answer that right now." He briefly glances my way. "We can discuss this later, Lewis. I've got to go." He hangs up.

"What was that about?" I ask.

"Nothing."

"Really? Because you got upset when Lewis mentioned Kyle."

Jamie flinches then gives me a look that says, *How much did you hear?* He clears his throat. "Really, it was . . . nothing for you to worry about."

I narrow my eyes at him, getting the distinct impression it was something I probably *should* be worried about. Honestly, though? Between my cramps and the painkillers I've been taking, I don't have it in me to interrogate him right now. In fact, I think *Highland Legacy* has been masking just how bone-tired I am. Out of nowhere a wave of exhaustion washes over me.

Jamie rubs at his jaw, his gaze roaming the room, presumably searching for a change of subject. It soon lands on a framed photo hanging near the TV—a picture of me, aged about six, with my da and maw.

"She was really pretty," he says after a beat of silence. "Your maw, I mean. I don't remember her well—you must've been wee when she passed—but you obviously inherited her good looks."

It's such an uncharacteristically sweet thing for him to say that, for a moment at least, my doubts melt away. "Thanks."

I let my head fall back against the sofa. My eyelids are growing heavy, fatigue pressing down on me like an anchor sinking slowly through water. "I think . . ." A yawn sneaks its way out. ". . . I think I need a wee break from the game. The Staff of the Storm Witch will have to wait."

"Oh?" He straightens. "Shall I go?"

"No." I fold over my laptop and place it on the coffee table.

"Don't take this the wrong way, but you're kind of reassuring to have around. Just . . . give me five minutes. I'll be good to go again in no time."

I only intend to shut my eyes for a little while, but the next thing I know, I'm drifting off, my head coming to rest on Jamie's shoulder. The last thing I register before sleep takes me completely is the gentle pressure of him shifting closer, making sure I'm comfortable.

◆ ◆ ◆

I stir, my eyes fluttering open. I'm nestled against Jamie, his arm draped around me, his warmth seeping into me. For a moment—a fleeting, dangerous moment—I let myself sink into the comfort of it.

"Hello there, Sleeping Beauty," he murmurs.

I blink and sit up, stretching out the stiffness in my shoulders. His arm slips away.

"How long was I out?"

Jamie checks his phone. "About an hour. You obviously needed it. Feeling any better now?"

I nod, surprised to find that I do. My body is heavy with sleep, but the cramps have eased.

Our eyes lock for a moment too long, and just as I'm about to look away and break whatever is brewing between us, Jamie reaches out and tucks a stray strand of flame-coloured hair behind my ear. As he does so, his fingers lightly brush my skin, sending a shiver racing down my spine.

He leans back, almost as if gathering himself. "I should probably get going." He stands and stretches. "Lewis has sent me about twenty messages, and judging by the last one, he may stage a rescue mission if I don't check in. I hope you're back to full health soon, all right?"

I should leave it there. Let him go. But instead I catch a hold of his arm. "Wait."

He turns back to me. "Aye?"

"I just wanted to say . . . thanks for today." The words come out stiffly, like they're being dragged from the depths of my pride. "Despite the cramps and your general tendency to be insufferable, it was . . . nice."

He breaks into a grin that's far too charming for his own good. "I had a nice time too, Sass."

The use of my online nickname sends a strange flutter through my chest. I release his arm then watch him walk away, torn between wanting to call him back and knowing I probably shouldn't.

CHAPTER TWENTY-SEVEN

MAISIE

I set the bold red cocktail on the bar, its rim adorned with a cheeky wee chilli pepper. "There you go! Highlander's Secret—local whisky, raspberry liqueur, ginger syrup, and a touch of chilli for a bit of a kick."

The tourist's eyes light up. "Wow! It's gorgeous." She takes out her phone and tilts it just so to snap a photo.

"Feel free to share that on social media, if you like," I say casually.

"Absolutely! I'll tag you." Picture taken, she raises the glass to her lips. "Oh my God, it tastes amazing!"

Pleased, I leave her to enjoy her drink and rinse out the cocktail shaker. My crappy period is over, and I'm feeling *so* much better.

Within moments my phone buzzes. It's the photo that was just taken, along with the caption:

The Highlander's Secret: piping hot, fiery, and oh-so-delicious! 🌶️🔥🍹 @ThePheasantPub #ScottishHighlands #CocktailTime

I shoot the tourist an appreciative smile, then a second notification pops up.

Bloody Jamie. I roll my eyes, but my lips twitch all the same. Since he came over to the flat three days ago, we've exchanged a few messages back and forth—mostly him checking if I'm okay, with a wee bit of banter thrown in. It's been nice to see the same kindness in Jamie that I always saw in LochNLoad.

Not that I'd ever tell him, but getting these silly messages always makes me smile—just a little.

Scott, one of our regulars and the drummer for Thistle and Reel, sidles up to the bar with his usual easy-going grin.

"Afternoon, Scott," I say. "Feeling adventurous enough for a cocktail or will it be the usual?"

He chuckles. "Maybe another time, but I'll stick to my Glen Garve today."

"Surprising absolutely no one," I tease, pouring the whisky and sliding it over to him. "I'm expecting big things from you tomorrow, by the way. I reckon the music round could be yours for the taking."

Instead of offering some cocky quip about his encyclopaedic knowledge of obscure eighties hair bands, Scott winces.

"Oh . . . you haven't heard?" he says cautiously, as if bracing to break bad news. "The Bannock Hotel is doing a whisky tasting tomorrow night. Kyle from the distillery is running it."

My chest tightens, but my smile stays firmly in place—practised and pleasant as ever. "Oh." I hand him the card reader to settle up. "Well, guess I'll see you at next week's quiz, then."

Scott offers an apologetic smile before wandering off with his drink.

Un-bloody-believable. A whisky tasting? On quiz night? Just when I was starting to warm to Jamie, he pulls a stunt like this? It's funny how he's got all the time in the world for koala jokes, yet he omitted to mention his plan to sabotage a Pheasant—no, a *Bannock*—institution.

Monday night has *always* been quiz night. End of discussion.

Da pushes through the kitchen door, carrying a tray of clean glasses. In a low voice, I tell him the news, expecting a calm shrug and the same nonchalant response he's had to everything Jamie-related recently. Instead, his face clouds, and for once he looks more upset than I am.

"Your maw loved running that quiz."

"I know, Da." I reach out and squeeze his shoulder.

"When she passed . . ." He hesitates, his gaze dropping to the floor. "I couldn't do it myself—it wasn't my thing—so for years there was no quiz. But when you picked it up again—when you made it yours—I was proud. Still am." His jaw tightens as he places the tray on the counter with deliberate care. "And now that bloody lad thinks he can—" He breaks off, turning away to regain his composure.

I stare at him in stunned silence. Da's not one for big displays of emotion. Grumbles? Sure. The occasional (or not so occasional) flare of stubbornness? Absolutely. But this? This feels different. Seeing him like this stirs something sharp and fiery in my chest—a mix of protectiveness and simmering rage.

Jamie riling me up is one thing, but upsetting my da? That's a whole other game entirely.

It's time for me to have words with him.

"Da, I'm going to pop out for a quick break, okay?"

Moments later, I'm power walking down Main Street towards the Bannock Hotel, fury fuelling every stomp of my trainers on the pavement. The sound of laughter drifts from the beer garden, and it grates on my nerves like fingernails on a chalkboard. Without hesitation, I push through the main entrance and into reception, aiming for the garden—but stopping when I spot Jamie behind the bar in the snug.

I go in. There are no customers in here—they must all be outside—but Jamie is in the middle of preparing an order. He spots me, and his eyes light up. Oh, he thinks I'm here for a friendly chat? That's hilarious. Time to wipe that smile off his face.

"You absolute arse." I plant both hands on the counter. "A whisky tasting? Tomorrow?"

"Aye. Fancy coming along?" That devilish glint in his gaze. Doesn't he realise he's playing with fire? That this time, he's gone too far?

"You know fine well Monday nights are quiz nights!" I jab a finger in his direction. "You're messing with years of tradition. You came over to my flat and acted all pally with me, and all the time you were plotting this?"

"Actually," Emily's voice cuts through the tension, "Jamie wanted to do the tasting on Wednesday."

I turn to see her walking into the snug. "What?" I say.

"He even planned to call it 'Whisky Wednesday', if it became a more regular thing. Quite catchy, don't you think? But Kyle from the distillery called and asked to change the event to Monday instead. It was Lewis he spoke to since Jamie was out, taking care of you, if I'm not mistaken?" Emily folds her arms and gives me a pointed look. "When Jamie got back, he wasn't best pleased with Lewis. Got pretty grumpy with him, in fact. He knew about your quiz. But it was too late to change things."

I glance back at Jamie, who's watching this exchange with maddening calm. "That true?"

He shrugs and offers a curt, "Aye."

Oh. Well . . . that does change things a bit, not that I'm about to let him off the hook entirely.

"You could have at least bloody told me," I say. "A bit of common courtesy wouldn't kill you."

"Well then, Maisie." He leans forwards slightly, his voice low and measured. "It'd probably be *courteous* of me to let you know I've organised a beer and whisky tent for this year's Highland Games."

My breath catches in my throat. "*What?*"

Emily groans. "Jamie, seriously? I was trying to defuse the situation. How could you possibly think it was a good idea to break the news like that?"

"I know what I'm doing," he says, his eyes remaining fixed on mine. "Thanks for your input, Emily, but this is between me and Maisie."

Emily flings her hands up as though washing herself of this

mess entirely. "Fine! Is this ready to go out?" She gestures towards the tray of drinks Jamie has been prepping.

"Aye." He still doesn't look away from me. "Table five."

With an exasperated sigh, Emily grabs the tray and disappears, heading out to the beer garden.

The moment she's gone, Jamie rounds the bar, closing the space between us like a predator stalking its prey. He stops less than a foot from me. "You can't just storm in here and tear strips off me when something doesn't go your way."

I lift my chin defiantly. "I can do whatever I damn well please."

Jamie's chest rises and falls faster than before, irritation smouldering in his gaze. But there's something else there too—something darker, hotter.

His eyes dip briefly to my lips, and when they rise again, there's no mistaking what's about to happen. For one taut second we hover on the edge—then he snaps like a breaking storm. His mouth crashes onto mine with raw intensity, silencing everything but the roaring wildfire spreading through me. The kiss is fierce and frenzied: all clashing tongues and teeth grazing lips as though we're both trying to win some unspoken battle neither of us intends to lose.

My fingers tangle into his hair—soft but thick beneath my touch—and his hands grip my waist firmly, heat flaring where he touches me.

For one blissful eternity we're utterly consumed . . . until Jamie tears himself away with a sharp inhale that borders on a growl.

"We can't argue here." His tone is rough-edged—almost feral—as though barely restraining himself from diving back in for more. "It's unprofessional. A customer might overhear us."

"Where do you suggest we argue, then?" I'm practically panting.

"My room." His voice drops lower, darker. "I can really give you a piece of my mind there."

"I'd love to see you try."

Jamie leads the way and I follow behind, the climb up two flights of stairs giving me ample opportunity to admire the way his jeans hug his taut, perfect arse. Meanwhile, the short sleeves of his polo shirt showcase the lean muscles of his forearms and the sexy veins.

When we reach his floor, he holds his door open and stands aside. I brush past him, my gaze sweeping over his room—an unmade but inviting double bed, cool-looking books on a shelf, gaming equipment on his desk. That's all I notice before the door clicks shut and Jamie spins me around, his mouth capturing mine in a kiss so searing it makes my pulse thunder and rational thought evaporate.

I return the kiss with equal fervour, sliding my hands down to Jamie's arse and giving each cheek a good, hard squeeze. He groans against my mouth, and the sound shoots straight through me, igniting every nerve. Our kiss grows more heated, both of us pouring all our pent-up tension into it.

When we finally break apart for air, I waste no time lifting Jamie's polo, exposing his abs first—taut, with just enough definition to look utterly lickable. A light dusting of dark hair trails from his belly button and disappears beneath his jeans. I tug the polo up and over his head, and his chest comes into full view—broad with a tempting sprinkle of hair across it.

"I heard you've been hitting the gym a lot lately." I bite my lip. "It's paying off."

I trail my fingers over his chest, exploring each ridge and

curve of muscle like I'm following a map leading straight to temptation. His skin is warm, and his hair tickles my palm. My fingers brush over one small, firm nipple, and he sucks in a sharp breath through his teeth. Oh? That got a reaction. I do it again—just to see—and sure enough, his body tenses under my touch.

I let my hand slide lower, and his abs tighten beneath it. With one finger I follow the line of hair that leads from his navel to his belt. By the time I reach for the buckle, Jamie is watching me like a man on the brink. And yet when I start to undo it—

"Wait!" His breaths come fast and shallow. "I don't want this to be like last time."

"What do you mean?"

"I . . . want us to take our time."

Something flutters in my chest. "Oh."

Jamie's thumb lightly traces my bottom lip, his eyes searching mine. "Is that okay?"

I nod, and his answering smile is tender. He leans in for another kiss, and this time it's slower, deeper—and somehow it sends me reeling even more than before.

Soon his hands glide under my top, warm against my skin, and I lift my arms so he can remove it. His gaze then roams over me, lingering on my lacy bralette. Heat pools in my belly.

"You look . . ." His Adam's apple bobs, his voice husky and roughened with desire. "Delicious."

My cheeks flame at the rawness of his words, but there's no time to feel self-conscious. His fingers fumble with the clasp at my back. I reach behind to help him out, unhooking it myself and letting the bra fall to the floor.

Jamie drinks me in, his gaze shameless and scorching

enough to make my skin prickle with awareness. His large hands come up and cup my breasts, the heat of his palms seeping into me, and his thumbs start a slow, teasing rhythm over my nipples. With each gentle stroke, it's harder and harder to breathe steadily.

"Beautiful," he murmurs, his voice low and reverent, like I'm a rare work of art he can't look away from. Then he dips down, capturing one taut peak with his mouth. The heat of him—the wet warmth of his tongue against such a sensitive spot—has me gasping. My fingers tangle reflexively in his hair as he alternates between soft flicks and gentle sucks that shoot sparks straight to my core.

My other nipple receives the same treatment, then Jamie stands upright again and draws me fully into his arms until we're pressed together, bare skin to bare skin.

The contact is electric. Everywhere we touch feels alive, and his heart hammers against me, each beat resonating through me. One strong hand splays across the small of my back while the other cradles my jaw, tipping my face up so our eyes meet.

"You drive me crazy," he says quietly.

We linger like this for a few seconds more, our bodies pressed together, before Jamie sinks to his knees. He undoes the zip of my jeans, the sound loud in the quiet room. Then, agonisingly slowly, he tugs them down. The fabric clings stubbornly to my hips at first, and he lets out a soft chuckle. Somehow it only makes the moment more intimate. Then the jeans are off, and there's only a small scrap of lace still between us.

With one hand, Jamie cups me through my thong, his palm pressing just enough to make me gasp. He looks up at me, a wicked gleam in his eyes. "Bloody hell." His lips curve into that devilish smile of his. "You're already so warm . . ." He leans in closer, and I can feel the heat of his breath against my thigh. ". . . and so wet."

My skin burns with mortified excitement at the rawness of his words, but then he strokes his thumb over me—slow and deliberate—and all coherent thought dissolves into a white-hot haze.

He peels away my thong and leaves me utterly bare before him. Just like the other day, he appears mesmerised by what he sees—by my pussy. Reaching out, he brushes his fingertips over me with such gentleness that a shiver races through my entire body. His touch is exploratory and maddeningly light at first— a teasing graze along my seam—but when he strokes me more deliberately, a low moan escapes me. Then one finger dips just slightly inside me, and I let out a sharp gasp that makes him pause and watch me intently.

"Is this okay?" he asks softly.

"Incredible," I pant. "But . . . your jeans need to come off now."

The corner of his mouth lifts. "Oh aye?"

"Aye. Stand up."

He obeys and rises to his feet, but not before dragging one final slow stroke through my centre. A whimper escapes me despite myself, and his grin spreads wider—utterly cheeky and completely infuriating.

"You make the best noises," he says. "They're so fucking hot."

"Is that right?" I manage to sound a lot calmer than I feel. "Bet I can make you groan even louder."

"Ha! You're so competitive, Maisie."

"It takes two to tango."

When I drop to my knees before him, his smirk fades into something heavier—hungrier. His hands fall loosely to his sides, but tension rolls off him in waves as I undo his button then tug down the zip of his fly. My movements are unhurried; I want him to feel every second of this. I slide his jeans down first. Jamie steps out of them and kicks them aside. Then his boxers follow.

I pause for a brief moment, taking him in, and holy hell if the sight doesn't leave me breathless all over again. It may be the second time I'm seeing Jamie like this, but the view is no less striking. He's big—thick *and* long—and impossibly hard already.

But as my eyes trail lower, something else catches my attention, something I didn't notice last time: a long pale scar running along Jamie's left thigh. A quiet reminder of what he's been through.

I reach out instinctively, but Jamie stiffens.

"Does it hurt when someone touches it?"

He shakes his head. "No. It's . . . more that I don't really let anyone see it. It's not exactly something I show off." A faint touch of shyness colours his words—a surprising contrast to his usual demeanour—and it absolutely undoes me.

With deliberate care, I let my fingertips graze the scar lightly, tracing its length. Jamie doesn't flinch or pull away, so I lean in and press soft kisses along its path—gentle pecks that linger just enough to let him feel them fully.

When I lift my lips away, Jamie breathes out shakily, but I'm not finished with him yet. I trail kisses upwards, faint brushes of my mouth against his legs, teasing him without rushing towards what waits just above. When I reach the base of him, I press one kiss to each of his balls—soft and deliberate—and his breath hitches in response. The sound sends sparks through me.

I continue up, exploring his length, planting kisses here and there, lingering in places as though committing him to memory. Finally, my lips find their way to the head. I press a featherlight kiss against it, then I take him into my mouth, swirling my tongue around him in slow, deliberate circles. He tastes salty and somehow just a bit . . . Jamie. Like trouble wrapped in temptation.

He takes a sharp inhale, then a deep, broken sound rumbles from him—a cross between a groan and a growl.

I release his cock with a soft *pop* and lick my lips. "You were definitely louder," I say smugly, looking up at him. "I win."

His eyes are molten—dark and hungry—but even so, a trace of his trademark mischievousness lingers. "Aye, you fucking win. But are you forgetting the part where we agreed to take this slow? Because how do you expect me to last when you go and do that?"

Grinning, I rise to my feet, sliding my hands over his torso as I do. My fingers draw lazy patterns across his skin—an idle swirl over a pec here, a light sweep below his ribs there—and I don't miss the ripple of tension that rolls through him at my touch.

He watches my fingertips wander. "Are you . . . thinking of painting me right now?" His lips twitch. "You really do like that body-painting scene in *Highland Legacy*, don't you?"

"Aye, well . . ." I tilt my head playfully. "What can I say? Your body is quite the canvas."

Jamie arches an eyebrow, amusement sharpening his smile as both his hands slide down to cup my backside. He pulls me firmly against him—his cock pressing insistently against my belly—and the pressure draws a soft gasp from me. His fingers dig into the curve of my arse just enough for heat to spark along every nerve ending.

"And . . . what about your power-play kink?" I ask breathlessly, trying not to lose focus. "Is it about you being in control? Or do you prefer being at someone else's mercy?"

He leans closer to me until his lips hover just above mine, his grin downright maddening. "A little bit of this," he murmurs, "and a little bit of that."

A quiet laugh escapes me. Going up on tiptoes, I brush my mouth close to his ear and, in the sultriest tone I can manage, whisper, "All right, then. Let's say I buy a pair of handcuffs, and on the morning of the Highland Games, I lure you into bed just long enough to tie you there." My teeth graze the shell of his ear. "Do you think anyone would find you before the Games are over?"

Jamie chuckles, a deep, decadent sound that rolls through his chest and reverberates into mine, igniting a fresh wave of heat. "You're evil," he says softly, but there's admiration in his voice. "Sass."

The nickname falls from his lips like honey, and hearing it now—in such an intimate moment—floors me more than any smirk or teasing quip ever could.

Before I can even process how much that single syllable unravels me, Jamie bends down and captures my mouth in another searing kiss that makes thinking impossible. He scoops me up effortlessly—one arm firm beneath my legs while the other holds fast around my back—and carries me to his bed. He lays me down gently, then I tug his arm, guiding him onto the mattress beside me.

For some time neither of us moves nor speaks. We just lie there, gazing at each other, studying every detail. Then Jamie's hand begins its exploration, his fingers brushing over the curve of my hip before tracing the dip of my waist. His movements are slow and deliberate, igniting tiny sparks across my skin, goosebumps rising in their wake. I mimic his touch, sliding my hand over the flat plane of his chest where lean muscle shifts beneath smooth, warm skin. My fingers drift through the light dusting of hair there before skimming lower, exploring the ridges of his abdomen.

We remain like this for a while, mapping each other with careful caresses, until Jamie's fingers skim the inside of my thigh, brushing higher and higher—slowly, teasingly. When he reaches the heat between my legs, I gasp softly, my body arching involuntarily towards him. His eyes lock on mine, his mouth curving into the faintest smile as though cataloguing every hitch of my breath, every sound I make.

At last, he murmurs, "Your choice, Maisie. My fingers? My tongue? Or my cock?"

The words alone are enough to set me ablaze. "Your cock. I want *you*."

Jamie nods once then slides a hand down to grip my thigh firmly, drawing it up and over his hip as he positions himself against me, both of us on our sides, face to face.

He pushes in slowly at first, and I'm transfixed by the sight of him disappearing into me. There's something primal about it, something raw and achingly beautiful in the way we come together so completely.

He presses a hand against the small of my back, guiding our bodies closer still, then the same hand reaches to cup my cheek tenderly. Every nerve in my body hums with awareness as we move together. Each roll of his hips sends delicious waves of heat flooding through me.

Our eyes lock despite the closeness of our bodies, although occasionally his forehead lightly presses against mine, and our breaths mingle in the narrow space between us.

Jamie's movements grow deeper, more purposeful, the slow drag of him inside me sending tremors of pleasure rippling through me. Each thrust builds a sweet and steady tension low in my belly. His thumb brushes a soft rhythm across my cheekbone, grounding me even as I feel like I might come undone completely.

"You're perfect," he murmurs hoarsely.

The raw sincerity in his words sends a fresh surge of heat through me. I arch into him instinctively, my leg tightening around his waist to pull him closer still. He takes the cue, his pace quickening, his hand trailing down to grip the back of my thigh. The angle shifts just enough for him to hit something devastatingly perfect—a spot that makes stars burst behind my eyes and a strangled cry spill from my lips.

The pressure builds impossibly high now, cresting like a wave rushing towards its peak. I cling to him, my nails digging into his back, barely able to process anything beyond the spirals of ecstasy curling tighter and tighter inside me. When he rocks into me again—deeper this time—it's enough to tip me over the edge.

Pleasure floods every inch of me, stripping away everything until there's nothing left but trembling limbs and Jamie's name tumbling from my lips. But he doesn't stop, doesn't let go. His breaths grow rough and ragged, my climax drawing him closer to his own breaking point.

"Maisie!" he groans at last. He buries his face against my

neck, his cock pulsing deep inside me, spilling into me. His grip on me tightens briefly before softening into a tender embrace.

◆ ◆ ◆

Afterwards, we lie wrapped in each other's arms, skin against skin, as though the world beyond this moment doesn't exist. The steady rise and fall of his chest soothes me as his fingers trace lazy circles on my shoulder. I wish I could freeze us here forever—no complications, no rivalries, just this intoxicating closeness.

But reality has a way of creeping in, no matter how tempting it is to linger in fantasy.

Still, while I'm here, in his room, I can't resist the pull of curiosity and the opportunity to have a snoop. I slip out from under his arm as gently as I can. Jamie murmurs a low sound of protest but doesn't stop me.

Cool air kisses my bare skin as I pad across his carpet, my gaze flitting over his things: bookshelves crammed with fantasy and sci-fi titles, gadgets and wires on his desk, little glimpses all over into the man who normally hides behind a cheeky grin and his jokes.

And then I spot her: a figurine. A female mage from *Highland Legacy*, her fiery-red hair strikingly similar to that of my avatar in the game.

A small smile playing on my lips, I take her down and turn her over in my hands. "This is a pretty good likeness. You know, I don't remember you ever telling me that you have a miniature version of me. Should I be flattered or creeped out?"

Jamie props himself up on one elbow. "Tease all you like.

Doesn't change the fact you're standing naked in my room. I could watch you all day." His gaze rakes over me.

I roll my eyes then grab my clothes. As much as I'm enjoying this momentary reprieve from the mess outside these walls, it can't last. Nothing about this can.

"To tell you the truth," I say as I pull on my jeans, trying to sound casual, "I thought you'd be more upset than you were when you found out I'm SassyLassie. You took it reasonably well."

Jamie pulls himself upright and rests back against the headboard. "Aye, well . . . it *was* a shock. And sure, I was pissed off. At first. But then . . ." He breathes out slowly. "It's kind of amazing when you think about it. All those hours we spent gaming together, and SassyLassie—the girl I was talking to— was right here in Bannock all along? That's . . . incredible."

Something inside me twists at his words, and for one reckless second I almost let myself believe there could be more between us than this fiery push-and-pull. But no, no amount of chemistry or gaming history can change what we are: rivals tied too deeply to our competing ambitions.

I tug my top over my head. "Incredible or not," I say evenly, forcing emotion from my voice, "it doesn't change anything."

Jamie's smile slips, and a flicker of confusion crosses his face. "Shit. You're not going to do what you did last time, are you?"

"Nothing has changed," I say firmly but not unkindly. "You and I are still in competition with each other."

For a moment he looks like he might argue, but then he says nothing at all. His silence pushes me further.

"While you're setting up collaborations with the distillery and having secret talks with the Highland Games organisers,

I'm putting out videos promoting *my* pub and creating cocktails that cheekily poke fun at yours. Does any of that sound like it could end with a happily ever after?"

"Maisie . . ." A plea hides somewhere in that one word.

But now that I've started, I keep on going. "The spark between us? The fire? That's because we're always clashing heads! Each time we've kissed or ended up in bed, it's started with an argument. We're only good together because we thrive on winding each other up! That can't evolve into a normal, healthy romantic relationship."

"You don't know that."

"Oh, really?" Bitterness edges into my tone before I can stop it—not directed at him, exactly, but at how bloody hard this situation is. "It's just sex, Jamie. Incredible, mind-blowing sex—sure—but nothing more."

He flinches, and damn it! Seeing that flicker of hurt in his eyes is gut-wrenching. But what else can I do? This isn't about punishing him—it's about being honest with both of us. His drive to make the snug successful is admirable, but it's also the thing that makes us impossible. If either of us had a solution, we wouldn't be caught in this stalemate that feels more unbearable with each passing second.

"I . . ." Jamie starts, his voice quiet but thick. "I told you about my panic attacks. I don't open up about that stuff to *anyone*. But I told you." His Adam's apple bobs, and when he speaks again, there's an ache in his words that cuts right through me. "Doesn't that mean something? I want this—*us*—to work."

His appeal is raw, vulnerable, and so utterly sincere that it takes everything in me not to throw caution to the wind and fling myself into his arms. To tell him we'll figure it out somehow, whatever it takes.

But no matter how intense the spark is between us, no matter how much I care about him, it doesn't magically erase the things working against us. The rivalry between our businesses isn't just some petty spat; it's foundational to who we both are right now. If we try to build a relationship on top of all this chaos, it'll only backfire spectacularly. And then we'll both end up hurting even more than we already are.

Rather than give Jamie hope where there isn't any, the kindest thing—the only thing—is to be honest and direct with him. Which is why I say, "We can't work, Jamie. We just can't."

The finality of my words settles between us, sharp and suffocating.

"Anyway . . ." My throat tightens painfully. "I should go."

And so, before I lose my nerve completely, I turn my back on him and leave.

CHAPTER TWENTY-EIGHT

JAMIE

The rain patters against the snug's window, a steady drumbeat that matches the throbbing in my head. I've spent the last hour pretending to focus on my laptop, but my thoughts keep circling back to Maisie. Always Maisie.

I pour myself another dram of Glen Garve, the whisky sliding down smoothly and warming my chest, though it does nothing for the hollow ache inside me. It's not like Maisie and I were even an item. There was no big dramatic breakup because we were never together in the first place. And *yet*, those months we spent gaming—laughing at stupid jokes, learning each other's quirks, saving each other's arses in boss battles—felt like something. But now . . .

I tried working it out of my system earlier, powering through an extra-punishing session at the gym. My muscles are screaming from it, but my head is just as much of a mess as before.

Even last night's whisky tasting, which everyone agrees was a roaring success, couldn't distract me. Not really. Kyle's presentation was spot-on—no surprise there—and we shifted a decent number of bottles. But I couldn't enjoy it, not knowing Maisie's pub quiz was quieter than usual because of us. God, I'm pathetic.

And today—without an event to pull people in—we're quiet again. Not that I mind right now. The state I'm in, I probably shouldn't be talking with customers.

My phone pings with a notification: *SassyLassie has posted a new video.*

I shouldn't watch it.

I really shouldn't.

But I do.

Maisie appears on screen, her flame-coloured hair gleaming under the glow of a ring light. Her warm, easy smile lights up the frame as she speaks with that calm, self-assured charm she has down to an art. "Right, a number of you said you'd like to see me play *Highland Legacy*, so here it is: my first gameplay video! And to mark the occasion, I thought I'd do something a wee bit special."

She explains she recorded the footage earlier with an American streamer called LevelUpLucas, some big shot with hundreds of thousands of followers. "All right, without any further ado, here we go!"

Maisie disappears, and we're now in *Highland Legacy*. A bard—easily the most annoying of the game's classes—prances about like an idiot, singing something daft. The avatar's bright purple hair doesn't fit the game's gritty vibe *at all*. But do you know what it does match? The ludicrous purple hair of the streamer who pops up in a corner of the screen.

LevelUpLucas, I presume. God help me.

Am I just jealous because he got to play with Maisie when that's exactly what I want to be doing? Of course. Would I have any issues with his hair in literally any other situation? Doubt it. But I never claimed to be above pettiness.

"Hey, levelheads!" His voice is bright with that fake enthusiasm that always grates on my nerves. Ugh. "Guess what? Today I'm going to be playing *Highland Legacy* with an actual Scottish person. Like, from Scotland—for real. And her accent? Oh man, just wait till you hear it. You're gonna love it. Some of you might already know her—she went viral last week with her very first video. How crazy is that? She lives near that stone circle from the scene we all freaked out over. Isn't that wild? Anyway, say hi to my co-op buddy for today . . . SassyLassie!"

Her avatar materialises beside Lucas's—the same avatar I've spent countless hours adventuring alongside. Then Maisie appears in a little box in the opposite corner, adjusting a massive pair of headphones.

"Hi, everyone!"

Of course, just like LevelUpLucas, Maisie's brightly coloured hair matches her avatar's. When she does it, though, it's clever and endearing, and that's a totally impartial observation. Definitely not driven by feelings or anything.

The video is snappily edited: quick cuts of them bantering as they track down a group of kelpies accused of dragging villagers into their loch lair. The action is perfectly paced, their avatars leaping between moss-covered stones as tendrils of enchanted water whip towards them. Maisie delivers the final blow—a streak of lightning erupting from her staff—and Lucas whoops loudly, "Are you sure you're not *really* a mage?"

Wow. *That's* his banter? And this guy has how many followers? Maisie and I do so much better when we play together.

"Normally I just set everything on fire," Maisie admits. "It's kind of my thing. But I do have a few other tricks up my sleeve, and kelpies call for something with a wee bit more zap."

"Fire magic, eh?" Lucas's avatar whips out a lute and strums it. Oh God. "That's not all that can spark things up in this game, right? Have you, uh . . . ever explored the game's romance mechanics? Asking for a friend." He winks at the camera like he thinks he's hilarious.

"No, not really my thing." Maisie laughs lightly, but it's the kind of laugh you give when you're trying to smooth over an awkward moment. Her smile wavers for just a fraction of a second—not enough for someone like Lucas to notice, but enough for me.

"Oh, come on!" Lucas presses. "Maybe you and I should give them a shot! Give the people what they want, right?" His avatar sidles up close to hers, an exaggerated pantomime of intimacy. "We all know why the TV show is so popular—and why your stone circle video went viral."

Maisie lets out a chirpy laugh then redirects their conversation back to their quest. But her expression flickers—just for a beat—and there's something behind her eyes, something shuttered and uneasy that anyone less attuned to Maisie's every microexpression would probably miss altogether.

She doesn't like this. Not at all.

Something sharp twists inside me at the idea of her playing with this guy for views or clicks or whatever else, and having to put up with his nonsense. Before I know what I'm doing, I slam my phone facedown on the bar, hard enough to rattle a few glasses. Then I pour myself another dram and down it in one.

The burn hits harder this time—sharp and unapologetic—and golden streaks crawl around my vision like fireflies trapped in my skull. Of course, *this* is when Lewis shows up and ruins my pity party by crossing his arms and glaring at me.

"Jesus Christ, Jamie. How much have you had?"

"Not enough," I mumble, but even I can hear how pathetic I sound. The words come out of my mouth half-slurred and barely human. Still, I try adding, "I'm fine."

Naturally, Lewis doesn't buy it for a second. "Go to your room!" he snaps, like I'm a misbehaving teenager and he's my father, even though he's only three years older than me. "Lie down before you keel over—or worse, make a fool of yourself in front of guests. I swear, Jamie . . ." He drags a hand down his face like I'm the bane of his existence.

He takes a breath and, when he speaks again, his voice is gentler—just by a notch. "Look, I spent years pining after Iona. *Years.* So trust me, I know what it's like. If it's meant to be, it'll happen, okay? But right now, you need to sleep this off."

Okay, but what if it's not meant to be? Because sometimes things don't work out, no matter how much you want them to. I want to point this out to Lewis, but the words get stuck in my throat and maybe that's for the best.

I stumble upstairs to my room, fumbling with the key until it finally slots home. But, once inside, my chest of drawers beckons like an old conspirator, and I pull out the bottle I keep hidden there. A quick twist of the cap, then the burn of the first swig lights up my throat—hot and unforgiving. By the third, those golden streaks from earlier have scattered into shapeless smears, blurring everything into one hazy mess. Like my head has been dunked underwater.

And yet the video keeps playing over and over in my mind: Maisie's laugh, that tosser with the ridiculous purple hair hitting on her, her smile wobbling for half a second. Before I know what I'm doing, my phone is in my hand and I'm watching it again, torturing myself with every moment. My jaw clenches tight enough to give me a headache.

Fuck this.

My legs move before my brain catches up with them. Downstairs again—staggering slightly, walls tilting and swaying as if they're alive—and then out into the drizzle. The cool air hits my face, but it doesn't clear my head like I hoped. Instead my feet carry me down the street towards the warm glow of the Pheasant's windows.

And there she is.

Maisie is behind the bar, her flame-bright hair catching the light as she laughs at something a customer has said. She's so at ease, so bloody perfect, and for a second or two, I just stand outside like an idiot watching her through glass panes streaked with rain.

She looks happy. Properly happy. Like she hasn't once thought about me all day—or maybe even longer than that. Like all those hours we spent gaming together meant nothing to her. Like those times we got tangled up in each other's arms were just . . . meaningless.

I want to go in, to march right up to the bar and . . . and what? Lay myself bare in front of everyone in the pub? Tell her how much this hurts?

No. She already knows.

And she doesn't care—not really. Not enough.

My feet move again, slow and aimless, carrying me along Bannock's rain-slicked Main Street. The world around me blurs—buildings fading into shadows, streetlamps smearing gold across the wet pavement. The old stone bridge looms ahead through the gloom, and I find myself drawn to it, to the rushing water below.

The rain is heavier now, pouring in relentless sheets that drum against the stones. My clothes cling to me, water running down my neck, but I barely feel it. All I can hear is the roar of the river, and just like that, I'm eighteen again. The rain pounding on the car roof as tyres screech, the world spinning sideways—the crunch of metal and glass—

The roar of a motorcycle engine cuts through the memory. Tyres hiss as they glide to a stop, pulling me back into the present. Footsteps splash closer behind me.

"Oi, mate, are you all right?" A pause, then sharper: "Christ, Jamie—is that you? What the hell are you playing at? You're soaking wet."

I turn my head towards the voice. Robbie MacDonald stands a few feet away, rain dripping off his battered leather jacket. His motorcycle helmet is tucked under one arm; his other hand rakes back damp black hair from piercing blue eyes. They seem to cut through the rainy haze.

"I'm fine," I mutter, though the words slur together, barely audible even to me. My legs wobble beneath me, and I teeter closer to the low stone wall separating me from the river below.

Robbie lunges forwards and grabs a hold of my arm. "Like hell you are." His voice is low but firm, punching through the deluge. "Come on, out of this bloody rain before you hurt yourself."

I try shaking him off, but his grip is steady as stone. He's not letting go.

"Why d'you care?"

For a split second, something flashes across Robbie's face—something raw and unguarded. Pain? Regret? Whatever it is, it doesn't belong on the face of Bannock's resident "bad boy", yet there it is. But then it's gone as fast as it appeared, replaced by a furrowed brow and a flicker of frustration.

"Look," he says after a beat, his voice quieter now but no less resolute, "that night . . . when I came across the crash . . . " He trails off as if waiting to see if I'll interrupt him. I don't.

"You were bleeding badly—barely conscious—and your parents . . ." He pauses again. "Well, they were already gone. When I called for the ambulance, I didn't know if you'd make it."

My chest tightens until breathing feels impossible. This isn't something we talk about. Ever. Don't get me wrong: that night changed everything between Robbie and me. Before then, he was my brother Ally's mortal enemy—they could barely be in the same room without trying to start a fight. Naturally, loyalty meant I sided with Ally growing up, but after someone saves your life? Old grudges disappear.

Still, we've never spoken about that night—not properly—and suddenly he's tossing it into the open like it's no big deal?

"Your life is precious, mate." A faint shrug accompanies the statement, like even he knows how uncharacteristic the words sound coming out of his mouth. His grip on my arm tightens—not harsh or forceful, just enough to anchor me in place against the pull of whisky-drunk thoughts. "So, like I said, let's get you out of this rain, eh?"

He steers me towards the nearest bus shelter. I slump onto the weathered bench, protected now from the rain pattering against the arched wooden roof, though I'm already drenched to the bone.

Robbie leans casually against the shelter's wall, scrutinising me with eyes that feel like they can peel back layers I'd rather keep hidden. "Right, what's going on?"

I drop my head into my hands. "Everything is a bloody mess. Maisie . . . the beer garden . . . everything."

"Maisie Kerr? What's the story there?"

I huff out something between a laugh and a breath—not quite sharp enough to sound bitter, but nowhere near strong enough to sound okay either. "We've been gaming together for months. For a lot of that time, as crazy as it sounds, we didn't realise we knew each other in real life. Then Maisie figured it out, but she didn't tell me who she was—not until everything blew up because of the new beer garden." I shake my head as if that'll help untangle the knot in my chest. "Then today she posted a video with this guy—some American streamer—and I know I shouldn't care, but . . . God, it stings."

"Sounds like you've got it bad for her."

"Maybe. Actually . . . okay, aye, I do."

"And she doesn't feel the same?"

"She says we can't be together because of the beer garden." The words taste sour in my mouth. "She says it's hurting her and her da's pub too much. Even though, on days like today, there's not a bloody person in the garden."

I glance up and see Robbie nod slowly, his expression unreadable except for a faint crease forming between his brows. He pushes off from the wall and scrubs a hand through his hair, scattering droplets of rain. "Look, mate, I'm not exactly your go-to guy for relationship advice. I don't get attached. I've no interest in messy feelings tangling me up or business rivalries screwing everything sideways. But your brothers have found love, right? Maybe you should try talking to them. When you're sober, I mean."

"Hmm. Maybe." My stomach churns, a sharp lurch reminding me just how much whisky I've had.

The way I'm feeling must be written all over my face because Robbie says, "Right, let's get you home before you puke all over your shoes—or worse, mine. Besides, Ally would murder me if I left you out here in this weather."

I agree to go, but when I push up from the bench, my legs buckle. Robbie catches me with ease, his arm sliding around my back to steady me. "I've got you. C'mon, this way."

Together, we head back along Main Street to the hotel. The rain has eased into a steady drizzle now. Robbie steers us towards the main entrance, but I say, "No, guests can't see me like this. Around the back."

He doesn't argue, just adjusts his hold on me and leads me along the driveway instead, past the garage in which I kissed Maisie (the memory of it scraping at my ribs like broken glass), then through the gate and into the beer garden. Rain pools on empty tables while fairy lights sway beneath dark skies overhead. It's a far cry from how it was on opening day.

"I can take it from here," I say.

"You sure?" Robbie doesn't loosen his grip just yet. One eyebrow lifts in doubt.

"I'm fine," I insist, wriggling out of his hold and tottering a few unsteady steps to prove my point.

Robbie watches me walk a little further before relenting. "All right. Go inside and change into something dry before you catch your death out here."

I smirk despite myself. "Didn't realise you cared so much."

"Aye, well, I've already saved your life once. Try keeping yourself alive from now on." With a nod, he turns and strides off into the night.

I make my way towards the rear entrance but hesitate when my gaze falls on Maw and Da's bench. The brass plaque catches what little light spills from the hotel windows, its inscription gleaming faintly through streaks of rain: IN MEMORY OF ANGUS AND MAIRI MCINTYRE, SORELY MISSED BUT FONDLY REMEMBERED. Before I know it, I've sunk down onto the wet wood.

It's funny, really. All those days spent setting up this place—hauling furniture around, stringing up lights—and not once did I ever take a break on this particular bench. Ally installed it a couple of years back, and I know he, Lewis, and Cat all use it now and again to have a quiet moment with our parents. Me? I usually steer clear.

But tonight? Tonight it feels like exactly where I need to be.

Rain drips from my hair and trickles down my face—not that it matters much when I'm already soaked through. Somehow, though, sitting here feels steadier than wading through the mess in my mind. I tilt my head back and close my eyes.

"I'd like to believe you can hear me," I say, "but . . . I'm not sure you can." My throat tightens. "Either way, there are some things I want to get off my chest."

I draw in a shaky breath that feels like it's scraping through my lungs. "I . . . don't think I've been living my life since I lost you. Not properly. If anything, I've been hiding from it—dragging myself from one day to the next but never really moving forwards."

I swallow hard. "What happened—losing you—hasn't been easy for any of us. Ally, though, is doing all right for himself these days. You'd be pleased, Da—he finally went and set up his outdoor-activities business with Aidan. Needed Emily to give him a good shove in the right direction, but he got there.

"And Lewis . . . he's with Iona now. Took them long enough, didn't it? He's doing a good job of keeping your legacy alive—the hotel looks better than ever. If you could see it, you'd both be so proud of him.

"Cat's also doing well. She's an English teacher—in Wick, if you can believe it. Aye, we never thought she'd last a day somewhere quieter than Bannock, but she's up there holding her own with a classroom full of teenagers. She's talking about moving back here soon, though. It'd be good if she did—all four of us together again."

I pause for a moment and shift on the bench. Water squelches beneath me, and my jeans cling uncomfortably tight to my thighs. Goosebumps prickle on my arms, but I don't move just yet.

"As for me?" My laugh is low and humourless. "Well . . . where do I even start? For years after losing you both, it was like . . . like I froze everything inside me so nothing could hurt as bad as that again. Gave up rugby—it wasn't really an option after the crash—but did I find something else worth doing with my life? Nah, couldn't be bothered." My voice catches. "Ally started his business; Lewis renovated the hotel; Cat found her path teaching kids—and what did I do? Sat in the snug and, as often as I could get away with it, played games on my laptop and ignored the world outside."

Guilt trickles through me like icy rainwater, and I clench my hands into fists. "That's not what you'd have wanted for me, I know that. But lately . . . things have shifted. Putting together this beer garden gave me a purpose I hadn't felt in years. And seeing folk enjoy themselves here? Families laughing together over pints and burgers? You'd have loved it, I'm sure of it. And, aye, I know it's not much to look at right now, but seriously, you should have seen it on opening day." A small smile tugs at my mouth.

"I've even started going to the gym again. For so long after I had to give up rugby . . ." A lump rises in my throat, making the words harder to push out. "God, Da, I know how much you wanted me to play for Scotland someday. And I wanted it too. But after the accident, it was like . . . I don't know, like everything inside me just ground to a halt."

I rub my hands together, warming them against the bite of the night air. "Instead of focusing on myself—on what was real—I threw myself into gaming. It was easier, I suppose. Fun too. Levelling up a character? Completing quests? That felt manageable in a way real life didn't. And gaming isn't bad— don't get me wrong—it's brilliant, actually. And it's because of *Highland Legacy* that I got to know Maisie really well, even though she and I have lived just a few minutes away from each other our entire lives. But . . . that's a story for another day.

"Anyway, I've been mulling over the idea of doing something more hands-on—something that takes me back to the rush of you cheering me on from the sidelines, back when rugby was my whole world." I can still picture Maw jumping up and down whenever I scored a try, and Da bellowing encouragement even when we were losing by a mile.

"Don't worry, I'm not daft enough to try diving back into contact sports—not with this pin in my leg—but there must be something else out there for me."

The faint buzz of my phone cuts through my thoughts. Reluctantly I dig it out from my pocket and squint at the screen.

About the Highland Games—just wanted to say I'm happy to help run the tent. We can take shifts so we both get some time to enjoy the day.

A wry chuckle escapes me, and I slip my phone away. I'll reply later when I'm out of this rain.

"Well, I'm not normally one for superstition, and—sure—that was probably just a coincidence. And *yet* . . . I'm going to interpret it as a wee nudge from you two. If you *were* here, I can imagine you encouraging me to sign up for one or two events at the Games. So that's what I'm going to do."

I push myself up from the bench and onto unsteady legs. "Anyway, time to go in, I think. I better get out of these wet things. This was nice, though—I can see why the others do it. I think I'll try it again sometime, maybe even when I'm sober. Anyway . . . night, Maw. Night, Da."

CHAPTER TWENTY-NINE

MAISIE

Bagpipes wail over the warm buzz of conversation and laughter, occasionally drowned out by roars of cheering and enthusiastic clapping. Today is our annual Highland Games, which means a usually quiet field outside town has been transformed into a sea of sunhats and tartan-clad chaos. Just about everyone from Bannock is here, alongside residents of neighbouring villages and a number of folk from further afield too. It's nice to think that I've had a hand—albeit a small one—in attracting visitors.

Throughout the day people have stopped by the Pheasant's beer tent to tell me they're here because of my videos. I'm hardly claiming to be the next big influencer, but it's happened more times than I have fingers, so we're talking double-digit numbers.

Not that I can take all the credit. Sure, I did a wee video hyping up the Games, but let's be honest, with weather like this—blue skies and sunshine that feels almost Mediterranean—it wasn't exactly a tough sell. Still, three strangers have asked me for selfies so far (three!), and one woman told me that my hair looks just like it does in my videos. The attention has been flattering, but also slightly weird. There's something about hearing comments face to face that hits differently than reading them on an app.

Da and I have rigged up a stall in front of our tent, and from it we're churning out drinks like nobody's business. Plastic cups foam over with ales, lagers, and the odd cider as we pass them over to thirsty customers. Some folk duck into the tent for a quick break from the sun, but most wander off with their drinks, either heading back to spectate or else flopping onto the grass to bask in the kind of sunshine that feels almost too good to be true.

Business really has been booming—so much so that I had to ditch my earlier plan of making cocktails because they were slowing everything down too much. It's all about keeping customers happy and queues moving. And that's fine! We adapted—that's what a good business does.

From where we're stationed, our view of the events isn't exactly stellar. I can just about glimpse the tug-of-war if I stand on tiptoes and crane my neck—although all I really see are broad shoulders and red faces straining like their lives depend on it. Later, though, Da and I have an extra staff member swinging by to help us out. When she arrives, I'll sneak off for a proper wander and film a bit of footage for tonight's video. A surprising number of my followers who couldn't be here made me swear I'd give them a wee peek of what they're missing. And who am I to deny them?

With the sun shining and the money rolling in, it's almost a perfect day. There's just one problem, and that comes in the form of the competing beer tent only a stone's throw away, literally opposite me and Da. Outside it is Jamie, operating at a stall like ours, and he's doing brisk business too. But he isn't just serving drinks. Oh no, he's got theatrics going on over there. The "exclusive collaboration" with the Glen Garve Distillery he keeps banging on about? Please. And of course, he *would* put on a kilt today, wouldn't he? And he had to go and look bloody sexy in it too, especially with that white polo shirt clinging to his chest like it's been tailored just for him. Ugh.

His presence wouldn't bother me so much if he wasn't making it his life's mission to poach every customer who so much as glances in his direction. Right now Morag from the bakery is hovering between the two tents, clearly torn, like she's facing an impossible dilemma. My queue has died down for the moment—just enough to wipe my brow or have a sip of water—but instead of enjoying the rare reprieve, I strike before Jamie can.

"Morag!" I call cheerfully. "What can I get you?"

Jamie doesn't miss a beat. "Over here, Morag! I've got some incredible whiskies today, exclusively available at *this* tent! Don't miss your chance—they're selling fast! Come on over!"

Morag throws her arms up. "I just want a drink! This is supposed to be a fun community event, not World War Three!"

I laugh—until she goes over to Jamie's stall. Damn it!

Not that it *really* matters, or so I keep telling myself. Da and I are doing well, and business is steady, but it still smarts every time someone heads for Mr Beer Garden instead of us. Especially since, let's be honest, Morag didn't go over there for a whisky. No, she went for a close-up view of Jamie in a kilt. And who can blame her? Those calves could probably crush a watermelon. Not that I've been imagining things like that.

Nope, I've absolutely not let my mind wander into fantasy land when it comes to Jamie and that bloody kilt. I've barely even mulled over the question of his underwear situation—or, hopefully, his lack-of-underwear situation. Which is ridiculous because I've already seen what's under there. It's not like it's a mystery to me. But . . . that doesn't mean I wouldn't mind refreshing my memory.

Have I debated staging some sort of "accident" that might require me to crawl around nearby him? Look, I'm only human. But no, I have *not* spent the past five minutes calculating the exact speed and trajectory required to fling an empty cup over there so I'd have an excuse to retrieve it. That would be ridiculous. And pathetic.

Would it work, though?

"Earth to Maisie!" Cat's voice breaks through my thoughts like a bucket of ice-cold water. She strolls over, grinning, with Iona and Elspeth in tow.

Cat is back in Bannock, not just for the summer holidays but for good. She landed a job at the high school and will be starting there in August.

I hug her first and then Iona, then Elspeth too. All three of them look gorgeous in sundresses, making me wish I'd worn something breezier than my denim shorts and button-up blouse.

Elspeth goes over to natter away with Da, so I pour Cat and Iona a white wine each. I don't bother asking if they want one—I've never known either of them to say no.

Cat gratefully accepts the drink then places her sunglasses on her forehead. "So, this is a bit awkward but . . . I couldn't help noticing you eyeing up my brother like he's your next meal." Her eyes sparkle mischievously.

"I wasn't eyeing him up!" I splutter. "I was just trying to stay on top of the competition."

"Oh, right," Iona says with a teasing smile. "Staying on top of Jamie—that sounds completely innocent."

Good God! If this is what we're going to be talking about, I don't want Da overhearing, so I glance his way and say, "While it's quieter, why don't you head into the tent for five minutes and have a seat? You and Elspeth can catch up. I'll chat to the girls out here and handle any orders."

To my surprise, for once he doesn't put up a fight but nods, pours a couple of glasses of wine, for himself and Elspeth, and disappears into the tent with her. Wow, he must be tired. He willingly took a break without muttering some sarcastic comment about not being ready for a care home yet. That's not like him at all.

"Right, where were we?" Cat says once it's just the three of us. "Oh aye, you were—"

"Don't say on top of Jamie!" I interrupt before she can. "There's nothing going on between us."

Iona raises an eyebrow. "But that's not exactly true, is it? Remind us, how many times have you had sex? Four times? Five?"

"Twice," I say drily. "And you know it was twice. It won't be happening again—I can guarantee that."

Note to self: think carefully before sharing gossip with Iona and Cat in the future.

"Hmm," Cat says. "I hate to quote Shakespeare at you, but *the lady doth protest too much, methinks.* Anyway, I know he's my brother, so I can hardly evaluate the situation objectively, but . . . Jamie? Isn't he, like, the most annoying person in all of Bannock? Iona is with Lewis, and I can *kind of* see that. I can also see why Emily might find Ally appealing. But Jamie? Really?" Cat glances at Iona. "Am I missing something?"

"Honestly?" Iona says. "I'm with you. Aidan and I pretty much grew up in the Bannock Hotel—it was like a second home—so Jamie is practically a wee brother to me." Iona pauses then adds, "An incredibly annoying wee brother."

I raise my hands in surrender. "I'm with you two, all right? It was a mistake—one I won't be repeating."

"Except you already did," Cat points out. "Seeing as you've done the deed with him twice. Plus, nowadays Jamie is almost as obsessed with the gym as Lewis. Could it be that he's seeking out a six-pack and bulging biceps to impress a certain barmaid?"

"Oh, look, here come some customers. Drat! Oh well, bye-bye, you two!" My dismissal of them is only a joke, but actually, just then a couple from Newcastle do come over, and they want to chat to me about my videos, so it ends up being a natural time to say goodbye to Cat and Iona.

After the Geordie couple leave, the stall is nonstop busy for a while, and I'm run off my feet trying to take all the orders by myself until Da eventually emerges from the tent.

I appreciate having him back to help, until suddenly *he* decides he wants to talk to me about Jamie too. I don't know what's got into him—or, more to the point, what Elspeth has been saying to him.

As we pour drinks, take money, and hand out change, Da says in a low voice that Morag's World War Three comment wasn't far off the mark. He reckons the situation between me and Jamie has gone on long enough and that the two of us just have to jolly well learn to get along—because that's what people do in Bannock.

I'm willing to half listen and let his words drift past without sinking in. Until, that is, he accuses *me* of being stubborn—the very epitome of the pot calling the kettle black! Then he really takes the biscuit by saying I need to show a bit of *maturity*.

That's when I snap. Maybe the relentless heat of the sun has fried my patience today, or maybe it's simply that the sheer, jaw-dropping unfairness of what he's saying pushes me to breaking point. Whatever the reason, I hiss, "Has it occurred to you, Da, that maybe Jamie and I are fighting because I'm stressed—and that maybe *you* have something to do with that?"

I *never* talk to Da like this, but now that I've started, the words tumble out. "You won't admit it, but you can't do everything anymore. And since you refuse to hire someone else to help us out, I'm left to pick up all the slack. Longer hours, more pressure, worries about the future . . .

"So please, Da, before you talk to me about showing a bit of maturity—or about being stubborn—maybe take a look in the mirror first."

For a fleeting moment Da's face is an open book. Surprise, hurt, and anger all ripple through his expression. But then, as quick as a blink, he pulls himself together again, his features settling into that familiar, unyielding mask.

And then comes the silent treatment. Because that's how my da deals with conflict—or at least, conflict with me. It's different if it's a young man in the pub who's had too much to drink and is making a fool of himself. Oh, Da doesn't hold back then—I've seen him really let rip. But with me? No. We bicker, of course, but when things get heated? He doesn't argue back or shout. He just shuts down.

The strained silence stretches on for several minutes, not that anyone who comes over to buy a drink from us picks up on it. Oh no. Da and I happily chat away to customers as we pour them their pints. It's all very professional. We just don't talk to each other.

Eventually I can't take it anymore. "Okay! You were right. This is supposed to be a fun community day, and . . . well . . . maybe this rivalry with Jamie isn't exactly in the spirit of things."

No response from Da.

"So . . ." I say reluctantly. "I'm going to go over there and try to bury the hatchet." And maybe then Da and I can get past this awful silence.

I head across the field to Jamie's stall, genuinely intent on making peace. But as I draw closer, I overhear him chatting with some tourists about the Bannock Hotel's beer garden and how bloody perfect it is on sunny days like today. The best place in Bannock to go for a drink, apparently.

At this, all thoughts of reconciliation vanish from my mind. So much for burying the hatchet—unless we're talking about into Jamie's skull, of course.

He's grinning like an idiot—looking far too pleased with himself, as usual—and that stupid kilt sways enticingly in the light breeze as he gestures animatedly during his sales pitch. The tourists lap up his every word, nodding along eagerly as if they've just discovered Scotland's best-kept secret.

By the time they walk away clutching their whiskies, I'm ready for war.

"Maisie," Jamie says smoothly. "Here to admire my kilt?"

"Fat bloody chance!" I say. Even though, yes, I've been shooting admiring glances at it all day.

"Oh! I'm sensing a bit of tension from you." He tilts his head as though pondering why this might be, then snaps his fingers like he's cracked the case. "Ah! I know what you're after, but I can't help you right now, I'm afraid. I'm too damn busy for one of those arguments that ends with us tangled up together and doing all sorts of naughty things to each other."

"Jamie!" Heat rushes to my cheeks.

"*But*," he goes on, "I'd love to catch up with you later. Maybe at some of the events? Yours truly will be competing in a few."

"Oh joy," I say, the words dripping with sarcasm.

He either doesn't hear me or pretends not to because he presses on with far too much enthusiasm. "I know you liked to hang out with LochNLoad because of his rippling muscles and how hot he looked swinging a sword about. Maybe I'll look just as good throwing a hammer or tossing a caber, eh?"

The man is insufferable. Absolutely bloody insufferable.

"I . . ." No other words come because I honestly don't know where to begin. Will I be hurrying to watch him compete in his events like some tragic, hormonal teenager off to her first boy band concert?

Of course I will. But I don't want to give him the satisfaction of knowing that.

Some customers arrive, saving Jamie from the clever, biting retort that I'm sure would have come to me any moment.

"Excuse me," Jamie says, flashing me that charming grin of his before turning his attention to them.

I spin on my heel and storm back to the Pheasant's stall. I don't meet Da's eye but I do yank my phone from my pocket. I've never done a livestream before—normally I carefully edit and check each video before uploading it. Desperate times call for desperate measures, though. I tap to go live.

"Hi, everyone!" I wave to my phone's camera. "I know some of you were eager to see what the Highland Games is all about, so I thought I'd do my first ever livestream. I'll show you around the field in a moment, but before that I have an important message for any of you who may be visiting in person today. Please come see me and stop by for a drink! The tent to come to is this one." I angle the camera to get me, Da, and our sign in the shot. Then, switching to the rear camera, I add, "Under no circumstances go to *that* tent. No matter how good that man looks in a kilt!"

CHAPTER THIRTY

I stretch, rolling my shoulders and shaking out my arms, preparing for the caber toss—my first event of the day. The sun beats down on the field, and the Highland Games are in full swing around me. A few months ago I wouldn't have dreamed of doing something like this. Gaming was my escape, a way to feel strong without actually having to be strong. But things are different now. I'm different now. We'll see how I get on.

I'm towards the end of the line of kilt-clad participants, which gives me plenty of time to overthink and watch the others go before me—their faces flushed with effort, the thud of the caber landing echoing across the field.

It's not about how far you can throw the massive log. It's about getting it to flip perfectly and land straight, like twelve on a clock face. That's what gets you the points. Sounds simple in theory. In practice, not so much.

As my turn inches closer, nerves tangle in my stomach. This is me putting myself out there in a way I haven't done in years—a very public test of whether I measure up.

The crowd whoops and claps for a particularly impressive

throw. I scan the faces for Maisie. Is she here? She's a big part of why I'm doing this, after all. Not that chucking a tree end over end is going to change her mind about me. Life isn't some cheesy film in which the hero flexes his muscles and the girl melts into a puddle of desire.

Still, a guy can hope.

And then I spot her, recording one of her selfie videos beside a hulking giant of a man who looks vaguely familiar. She's laughing at something he's said, completely oblivious to me standing here like an idiot with my caber-related nerves and misplaced daydreams.

Wait—no way.

Cammy Morrison.

Aw, hell. I used to play rugby with him. The career I once wanted so badly? He's got it. He went on to do everything I couldn't. Since the crash, I've tried to avoid rugby news as much as possible, but even I've heard about Cammy's meteoric rise.

God, jealousy burns hot and fast. My brain helpfully supplies an image: an alternative timeline where everything was different, where my femur didn't snap like a twig, where Maw and Da lived to see me play professionally. Maybe then Maisie would've fallen at my feet. Maybe then everything would have been easy.

Even as envious thoughts spiral through my head, Cammy turns and notices me.

Shit.

I look away like some starstruck fanboy caught staring at his idol. Not embarrassing at all.

It's been seven years since I turned my back on rugby, seven years since I cut all ties with that world after everything went wrong. It wasn't just the injury—it was losing Maw and Da. Rugby was how Da and I bonded, and without him . . .

Cammy probably doesn't even recognise me. Why would he? He's got bigger things to think about than some washed-up ex-teammate skulking around a field pretending he knows what he's doing with a caber.

Right then, only five more guys ahead of me before it's my turn. No big deal. Just me and a literal tree trunk in front of pretty much the entire town. The guy up now is a bloody beast—he looks like he could bench-press a car. Sure, I've been grafting away at the gym these past few months, but there's just no comparison between me and him. What if I go to lift it and it doesn't even budge?

I can hardly lean over to one of the other guys in line and say, "I'm feeling a wee bit nervous. How about you?" It's all gruff nods and testosterone around here. But alongside the nerves, there's a faint thrill thrumming in my chest—yet another callback to my rugby years. That mix of dread and adrenaline before kickoff. The itch to do something impressive. To prove, to everyone else and myself, that I have what it takes.

A firm hand lands on my shoulder, startling me. I turn around and, shit, it's Cammy.

"Jamie McIntyre! I thought it was you." He pulls me into a bro hug even though I've not once spoken to this guy in seven years. Well, seems he remembers me after all. He claps me on the back hard enough to rattle my teeth and maybe two or three internal organs. Thank God I've been hitting the gym again. Otherwise, I'd be lying in the dirt trying to remember my own name.

"How the hell are you doing?" he asks, pulling back to look at me.

For a second I freeze. What's there to say to someone who represents everything I once wanted? But then I find my voice. "Good to see you, Cammy." And because that seems woefully insufficient: "Congrats on all your success."

"Cheers." He grins then shifts his weight slightly. "Listen, mate. I always felt bad about . . . you know, the accident. You were going to go all the way. Everyone knew it back then."

Christ.

"And your parents," Cammy adds after a beat. "Your da was such a great supporter of the club."

"Thanks." My voice comes out steadier than I expected. Cammy just brought up the crash, my injury, and the death of my maw and da—all in just a few sentences—and . . . I've not fallen apart. I'm still looking him in the eye. "To be honest, it's been a long time since I've done anything like this. But aye, it feels good to push myself again."

He playfully punches my arm. "Good man! Listen, if you ever fancy coming along to watch us play, you let me know. I'll sort out tickets."

I find myself smiling despite everything—a real smile. "You know what? Aye, I'd like that."

Shit. What's happening to me? Any time the rugby comes on the TV, I immediately switch it off. But now I'm considering going to see a game in person? Somehow, though, the idea sits okay with me. I'm not just brushing Cammy off—I really would quite like to do it.

Cammy leaves with a wave, and I shake myself. Okay, not long now until my turn. Time to get into the right frame of mind. These things are as much about mental focus as they are about physical strength.

I bounce on the balls of my feet, rolling my shoulders,

trying to drown out the noise of the crowd and channel my adrenaline into something useful.

And then a voice says, "I thought LochNLoad was over-compensating with the Claymore of the Clan Chiefs. But a caber? That takes phallic symbolism to a whole new level."

Maisie steps into view, in denim shorts that show off slim legs and a white button-up blouse knotted at her waist. It teases just enough skin to drive me quietly insane.

She's come over to speak to me. Even though my rival beer tent made her so mad earlier.

I can't help the grin that spreads across my face. "I bet you've been dying to make a joke about my wood, haven't you? Well, just wait till you see me toss it."

Smirking, she slides her phone from her pocket and taps its screen. "I look forward to it. Fancy being immortalised on social media?"

Shit. No pressure or anything. As if hurling this bloody tree wasn't nerve-racking enough already.

But her attention stirs something in me—a flicker of pride buried beneath the anxiety. If Maisie wants to film me for her followers, then I'll make damn sure I give them something worth watching.

"Go ahead. Just make sure you get my good side."

She rolls her eyes but lets out an amused snort. "Seriously, though . . . good luck." The teasing tone in her voice is gone, replaced by sincerity, and it grounds me.

"Thanks."

And now there's no more time to chat because it's my turn.

The caber is heavier than it looks—and trust me, it looked bloody monstrous—but weeks of training pay off: I manage to hoist it vertical against my shoulder. My muscles scream their objections as I take one step forwards . . . then another . . . then one more for good measure and I launch the beast with every-thing I've got.

It tumbles end over end through the air before hitting the ground with a satisfyingly solid thud. It's far from a perfect twelve o'clock—not good enough to win—but it's a decent attempt. Respectable. I can hold my head high.

The crowd erupts in cheers, a wave of noise crashing over me. It might be my imagination, but it sounds louder than it was for anyone else—even the guys who did better. There's something in the sound, something deeper than polite applause. Like the whole town remembers where I've been and can see exactly how far I've climbed to get here.

A wolf whistle cuts through it all. I glance around in time to see Maisie lowering a hand from her lips. She shoots me a wink—bold and cheeky—and it sends a crackling spark straight to my chest.

Winning? Pah, who needs it when I've got Maisie Kerr whistling for me like I'm the only guy on this field worth noticing?

◆　◆　◆

I do pretty well in my two other events, the hammer throw and the stone put, although I don't come away with a win. Still, there's something deeply satisfying about the ache in my muscles and the hearty slaps on the back from locals. It's a kind of respect that feels earned, raw and real in a way I haven't expe-rienced in years.

"You weren't too shabby out there," Maisie says, appearing out of the crowd and passing me a water bottle. "Not bad for a bloke who used to think heavy lifting meant carrying his laptop upstairs."

I take the bottle like it's some sort of trophy—and let's face it, it's the closest thing to one I'll be winning today. After a long swig, I press the cold plastic against my neck to cool off, although I reckon Maisie's presence might be heating me up more than any feat of strength ever could.

Meeting her gaze, I see she's got that look in her eye—the one that dances between teasing and something softer—and before I can stop myself, I admit, "I really wanted to win one of the events. For you."

She tilts her head, eyebrows lifting like she's not sure whether to laugh or take me seriously. God help me if she laughs.

"Is that so?" she says eventually. "Well, you've still got one more chance to impress me."

I know what she's referring to. The hill race.

Most people think the Highland Games are all about raw strength, but they began with a simple race. Back in the eleventh century, King Malcolm III held a competition to choose his royal messenger. The first man to reach the summit of Creag Choinnich and return won the title. Here in Bannock, we honour these origins by ending each year's Games with a race up and down Ben Garve.

I used to take part every year, and I remember it well: an uphill battle so punishing it makes you question every life choice, followed by a downhill sprint with your lungs screaming for mercy. I won it when I was seventeen. And again at eighteen. Then life happened, and I never ran it again.

My smile wavers, just slightly, but enough for Maisie to notice.

Speed was once my greatest asset—the thing that made me special on the rugby pitch. Back then, nobody could catch me if I had open space in front of me. My legs were lightning bolts wrapped in muscle.

After the accident—after they placed that damn pin in me—nothing was ever the same. I knew that no matter how hard I worked at it, I could never be as good as I once was. And if you can't be as good as you were at your best, then what's even the point?

Maisie doesn't push me. She just waits quietly as if daring me to work through whatever excuse is forming in my head.

And maybe she's right because why put limits on myself? If these last few months—and these Games especially—have taught me anything, it's that I'm stronger than I give myself credit for.

Sure, my training has been almost entirely focused on strength—cardio, not so much—but who cares? This isn't about being perfect or winning some prize. This is about proving something, even if only to myself.

Besides . . . maybe impressing Maisie one last time wouldn't be so bad either.

"All right," I say finally. "Why not?"

Her face lights up with triumph.

◆　◆　◆

A large group of competitors gathers at the base of Ben Garve, and I'm among them. I stretch my leg, wincing slightly at the dull ache that's settled in following the strength events. It's nothing serious—just a reminder that I've already pushed my body today. Beside me, my brothers, Ally and Lewis, limber up too.

The three of us used to do this race every year as lads, sprinting uphill like we were invincible. Then came the accident, and I stopped. So did they—out of sympathy, although they never outright admitted it. Lewis muttered something about a knee niggle once, while Ally claimed work commitments got in the way, but I knew better. When I suggested fifteen minutes ago we all run it again for old time's sake, they barely hesitated before agreeing.

The field is packed with maybe fifty or sixty runners—more men than women but a decent mix. Some look like seasoned athletes ready to dominate the course, while others appear to have wandered in on a dare after one pint too many. It's entirely possible. Unlike the strength events, which require advance sign-up, the hill race is open to anyone brave (or mad) enough to give it a go.

The atmosphere is buzzing, infectious. The crowd has turned out in force too, lining up to cheer us off and welcome back whoever returns first.

I spot Emily in the throng with wee Ru perched on her hip, while Iona keeps Bruce calm on his lead. Aidan bounces Callie on his shoulder—Grace is off somewhere running a yoga taster session for those who'd rather stretch than sprint. Cat waves when she spots me looking and calls out, "Don't fall on your face!" When I remind her it's not too late for her to take part, she just smirks and says she looks too nice today to ruin it by getting sweaty.

The starting gun fires with a sharp crack, and suddenly there's no more time for banter—we're off.

Chaos erupts as everyone jostles for position on the uneven

ground. Elbows bump; feet stumble; someone curses loudly as they almost lose their balance. But soon enough the pack begins to thin out, and I find myself near the front, alongside Ally and Lewis. I'm not surprised to see either of them here—Lewis practically lives at the gym, all protein shakes and deadlifts, while Ally spends half his life scaling cliffs or rafting rivers like some sort of Highland action hero.

We charge past a group of grazing sheep, who lift their heads, bewildered by the parade of kilted daredevils storming through their patch of tranquillity.

The climb gets steeper—brutally so—but I push forwards. My breath comes hard and fast, and every stride burns in my thighs, but there's something exhilarating about this. The rhythm of my feet pounding against the grass. The wind whipping past my face. That raw, primal drive to go faster than everyone else.

It floods back—the freedom I used to feel when running flat out during a rugby match. God, I'd forgotten how much I loved this.

Finally, blessedly, the summit comes into view. A steward stands at the top, and as I close the gap between us, he raises a smoke flare high. I dig deep—legs screaming, lungs about to burst—and reach him first. He grins and lets off the flare. It hisses violently before erupting in the sky in a plume of orange smoke.

First one up! Despite everything—my leg, all those years spent doubting myself—I might actually win this.

The downhill is where things get risky. Momentum builds fast on these steep slopes, gravity pulling you forwards whether you like it or not. Soon you're not so much running as hurtling downwards at breakneck speed with only your legs—which are screaming bloody murder—to keep you upright.

I pass runners still climbing uphill. Their shouts of encouragement blur into white noise as my pulse hammers in my ears. This is incredible—like flying without wings or engines or parachutes.

And then disaster strikes.

My foot catches on something—a root or rock maybe—and before I can stop myself, I'm pitching forwards into empty air. I hit the ground hard enough to knock the wind clean out of me, pain exploding through my leg.

Shit.

For a second all I can do is lie there stunned while agony radiates from my leg and up into my hip.

No, this isn't how this was supposed to go. I wanted to charge across the line triumphant, arms raised like a bloody champion. I've no interest in some *Cool Runnings* underdog moment where everyone claps out of pity while I limp across the finish line.

Ally and Lewis streak past without stopping—not because they don't care but because this is a competition. They'll check on me later, I know that, but right now this is about the race. And that's how it should be.

I force myself upright, a groan escaping my throat, which quickly morphs into a growl of sheer determination. The pain in my leg pulses like a drumbeat, but I shove it to the back of my mind. No bloody way am I letting it stop me now.

I start running again, each step a battle against the screaming protests of my muscles. The gap between me and my brothers is significant, but I don't care. I'm not done yet.

Up ahead, Lewis has edged past Ally. My lungs are on fire

and my injured leg feels like it might give way any second, but I dig deep. Deeper than I thought possible. I pass Ally first, sparing just enough breath to yell over my shoulder, "You're looking great back there—like a majestic, panting tortoise!"

Ally's bark of laughter follows me. "Torn between being pissed off and proud of you, ya wee shite!"

I'm closing in on Lewis now, his powerful frame powered by years of gym sessions and protein-fuelled stubbornness. "Oi, Lewis! Ally said you curl like you're scared to break a nail. You better stop running and sort him out!"

The gibe riles him up—enough, apparently, for him to reach out and grab a hold of my kilt as I pass him.

"Oi! Let go!"

I shouldn't really be surprised—we still wrestle like we're twelve, after all—but seriously? Grabbing my kilt mid-race? Who does that? I can't win with Lewis hanging onto me like an anchor.

Well, desperate times and all that.

With grim resolve, I unfasten the left strap of my kilt. And then the right. Gravity takes care of the rest.

The fabric falls away entirely, and so does Lewis's grip. He stumbles back in shock. "What the—Jamie!"

I don't stick around to hear any more because I'm already pelting towards the finish line like a man possessed. I cross it first, punching the air triumphantly, and the crowd erupts into cheers mingled with gasps and laughter.

And then reality catches up with me. Shit.

Suddenly aware of just how much I'm exposing—and how little there is left to people's imagination—I use both hands to shield myself while grinning sheepishly at the crowd, my face burning hotter than a bonfire. Lewis barrels across the finish line next. He throws me my discarded kilt, his face almost as red as mine.

Ally comes in third and gives me a clip across the back of the head. "Would it have killed you to wear boxers today, you bloody eejit?"

"Wait, you aren't trying to blame this on me, are you?" I protest, frantically fumbling to get decent again. "Lewis grabbed my kilt! Such poor sportsmanship. If anyone deserves a lecture, it's him."

"Oh aye?" Ally says. "And what about you? Flashing your bits to half the town like you're auditioning for *Magic Mike: The Highlands Edition*? Don't you think *that* warrants a word or two?"

I steal a glance at the crowd. There are way too many wide grins and stifled giggles for my comfort. A few people even have their phones out. Great. Just great.

"Well, it got the job done, didn't it?" I quip, feigning nonchalance. "I won." I lift a hand to the onlookers in a sort of apologetic wave. "Sorry if some of you got more—well, *saw* more—than you bargained for. Blame *him*!" I jab a thumb over my shoulder at Lewis because deflection is clearly my best bet here. "He's the one who grabbed my kilt!"

A fresh wave of laughter ripples through the crowd, and Lewis's face flushes beetroot red.

Ally leans in close to me. "You do realise you're never living this one down, right?"

"Oh. Do you think there's any chance people will remember me as the comeback hero rather than the guy who finished without his kilt?"

Ally smirks and claps a hand on my shoulder. "Aye. I'm sure

the kilt thing will barely come up at all . . . aside from at every wedding, ceilidh, and funeral for the rest of your days."

I groan. And yet, honestly? I can't help but feel proud of myself for winning. Even if no one else remembers me as the comeback hero, *I* will. And, at the end of the day, it's just a cock, isn't it? Half the population has one. Sure, I'd rather not have waved mine at what feels like the entire bloody town, but all things considered? Worth it.

The crowd is still buzzing with sniggers and chatter. I shift awkwardly, scanning the sea of faces properly now. Old Hamish is doubled over, laughing so hard I'm genuinely worried he might need medical attention. Morag from the bakery is in fits, crying actual tears, her shoulders shaking as she attempts (without success) to pull herself together. Then there's Cat, whose face has turned a shade of red usually reserved for stop signs or emergency buttons. Aidan, meanwhile, is grinning like *he's* the one who won the race, perhaps because he now has fuel for an entire decade of piss-taking.

But it's not any of these people I'm looking for. Where is she?

Finally my gaze lands on her, and whatever trace of good humour I've managed to cling to nose-dives faster than I did on that bloody hill.

Everyone else is busy peeing themselves laughing, but Maisie is not amused. She's off to the side, her phone aimed at her face, her lips moving a mile a minute. But this isn't playful-banter Maisie; this is panicked-apologies Maisie. Hell, it might even be preparing-for-an-online-backlash Maisie.

Oh no.

Was she . . . livestreaming?

The ground might as well open up beneath me because *fuck*.

Finishing her video, she shoves her phone into her pocket then locks onto me like a heat-seeking missile. Before I have time to fully process just how catastrophic this could be, she's storming towards me.

"What," she hisses through gritted teeth, "were you *thinking*?"

"Hey," I reply brightly as if sheer optimism can undo public humiliation on this scale. "I wanted to win—and I did! By the way, I'm accepting congratulatory hugs. Fancy giving me one?" I hold my arms out in what I hope reads as cheeky charm but probably comes across as desperation.

Maisie stares at me, unblinking, daggers in her eyes sharp enough to cut granite. "Oh sure," she snaps, sarcasm dripping from every syllable. "Let's throw a celebratory party—pop some champagne! And while we're at it, why don't you explain to me why my followers just got an eyeful of your cock and balls?"

I blink then lower my arms awkwardly back to my sides. "Er . . ."

She waves her phone in my face like it's Exhibit A in a murder trial. "I was live when you decided to re-enact *The Full Monty*!"

The mounting fury in her voice draws attention from some of the nearby spectators. Their grins give way to looks of concern—or maybe just curiosity about whether she's going to deck me here and now or do it later. Her ferocity really is a sight to behold. Maisie Kerr yelling at me isn't exactly new territory, but I've never seen her quite this rattled before.

"Do you have *any* idea what people are saying in the comments?" she demands.

Stupidly gambling that humour might somehow fix this, I say, "Nice things, I hope?"

Her silence cuts even deeper than her glare did. When she finally speaks again, her voice is clipped, like her words are barely holding back an avalanche of rage. "Do you know what kind of damage this could do? To me? To my account? If this mess gets me banned or ruins my reputation then—ugh!" She throws up her hands and, without another word, spins on her heel and storms off.

"Maisie, wait!"

But she doesn't stop or even slow down. She disappears into the crowd, and just like that, triumph turns into utter catastrophe.

CHAPTER THIRTY-ONE

MAISIE

I haul the last crate of empty glasses out of the beer tent and dump it into the back of the van. My hands are steady as I tidy up after the Games, but my brain is a riot—spinning and tumbling through every worst-case scenario I can dream up. What if Jamie's full-frontal race win ruins everything? My followers, my profile, all the plans I've made for future content—it could all come crashing down.

Near me, Da works efficiently in his usual no-nonsense way, folding up tables and stacking chairs into neat piles. I've reminded him on multiple occasions to take a break whenever he needs one, but he claims he's all right. We mostly work in silence, the tension from our earlier clash hanging unspoken between us.

The clean-up is repetitive and methodical—the kind of task that *should* soothe me—but my nerves are frayed too thin for that. I still can't believe Jamie crossed the finish line stark naked for all the world to see. And by "the world", I mean *my* world: my followers, who now probably think I'm running some kind of OnlyFans-lite account for accidental-nudity enthusiasts. The sound of laughter from another part of the field floats past—other stallholders tidying up, buzzing with gossip and no doubt replaying the day's events. I can only imagine what they're saying about Jamie's grand finale.

The one small mercy is that Kyle and other staff from the distillery have taken charge of cleaning up Jamie's tent. Emily is there too—more to supervise than to lend a hand, given her bump. She's cast a few glances my way, clearly trying to catch my eye, but I've made a point of looking anywhere but at her. I'm sure she's figured out by now that I'm not ready to go over the whole fiasco quite yet.

What hurts the most is how perfect it all was up until that moment. Jamie charging up the hill, his kilt swishing with every powerful stride, his calves flexing as if sculpted by some divine hand. He reminded me of a Highland warrior—of LochN-Load. And he was running for me—no, for *us*. But instead of a triumphant ending, we got . . . well, more of Jamie than anyone asked for.

Once the beer tent is empty, it's time to dismantle it. Da gestures to the nearest peg. "Start there."

I kneel and wrestle the peg loose from the ground. I've had enough of being at odds with both my father *and* Jamie, so I say, "About what I said earlier . . ."

"It needed saying." Da doesn't look at me but instead focuses on pulling out a peg of his own. "I've been too damned stubborn for too damned long. You were right to call me out on it."

A lump rises in my throat but I swallow it back and grip another peg. "I love you, Da. You know that, right? If I've been stressed lately, it's only because I care—about you and about keeping the Pheasant going strong."

He keeps his gaze down but nods once, a small gesture of understanding. "Aye, I know. And you're right—we need to face things head-on. I can't go on burying my head in the sand like some daft old fool. We'll sit down soon and figure everything out. Together."

The weight in my chest eases—not gone, but shifted enough that I can take a proper breath for the first time in hours. That's one problem chipped away, at least.

Straightening, I study Da—his thinning hair flecked with silver, his hands calloused from years of work—and my throat tightens again, this time for entirely different reasons. I step closer to him and squeeze his arm gently. "Thanks, Da."

Not everything is fixed—not even close—but it's a start.

We work in companionable silence after that, peeling away the canvas bit by bit until only the bare skeleton of the tent remains. Elspeth appears as we're folding the canvas up. She exchanges a few words with Emily across the way before coming over to see us.

"I'm not going to bring up what happened at the race!" she announces pre-emptively, with a glance at me. "I'll leave that for you young folk to sort among yourselves. But, Bryce, do you have a few minutes for a chat?"

"Aye," Da says. "It's the perfect moment for a wee break."

Oh, is it now? It's funny how any time *I* suggested he have a rest, he didn't want to hear it, but now that Elspeth is here, it's a brilliant idea.

I can't help but remember Jamie's claim at my Bannock-themed pub quiz—that Da and Elspeth were giving each other dreamy looks. At the time I assumed it was one of Jamie's usual wind-ups, but maybe he was on to something. Still, I've got more than enough on my plate at the moment without wondering if Da has a thing for Elspeth. That's a mystery for Future Me to dig into. For now, a quick break sounds like just what I need, especially as it'll give me a chance to check in on social media.

I've been putting that off—I wasn't exactly in the right headspace earlier. I saw a few shocked comments come in during the live, but otherwise I'm not sure how my followers have reacted. For all I know, there's been a huge backlash. Well, whatever has happened, it's about time I faced the music.

Da and I agree to continue in ten, then I wander off to a quiet spot near the edge of the field. Sitting on the grass, I pull out my phone, take a deep breath, then check my profile.

Oh no. Oh, bloody hell.

Things are even worse than I feared. A lot worse.

Apparently, after the livestream ended, the video automatically uploaded to my timeline for people to rewatch. I didn't know it did that! Today was my first time going live—I'm still learning how it all works.

My stomach lurching, I stare wide-eyed at the stats. The number of views is astronomical—the highest I've seen since my very first video, about the stone circle. *And* there's been an explosion of new followers since earlier today.

Normally, I'd be thrilled by this kind of attention, but not for this. What exactly do these new followers think they've signed up for? Are they expecting more content like this?

And then there are the comments. Hundreds and hundreds of them.

The laughing emojis alone could probably fill a short novel. Then come the jokes—terrible, shameless jokes that somehow still manage to coax a reluctant laugh from me:

Well, that's one way to cross the finish line!

Now we know where the Loch Ness Monster has been hiding!

Came for the race, stayed for the unexpected show!

It's a shame the title Free Willy is already taken. 🐋 It's perfect for this video.

A Scottish underwear company has even chimed in uninvited, tagging the post with some a bit of marketing about how their boxer briefs are an essential investment for Highland Games competitors everywhere. Honestly? Fair play to their social media manager—that was quick work.

I scroll faster, expecting outrage or complaints buried somewhere in the flood of hysterics but . . . there's nothing. Not one hint of public fury or even a sniff of controversy. No accusations of indecency or cries to cancel me—or Jamie, for that matter. If anything, everyone seems delighted by how ridiculous and utterly human it was. They're laughing *with* him, not at him, and they understand that my broadcasting of the moment was entirely accidental.

This revelation puts a dent in my panic—not enough to completely calm me, but enough for me to start believing that I might just survive this.

There's only one sensible thing left to do: delete the video before anyone else has time to share it—or worse, download it for posterity.

My finger hovers over the delete button . . . and stops.

Would it be bad if maybe, just quickly, I give it a watch? It's not like I properly registered what was going on at the time—I was too busy careening headfirst into sheer panic. And now that everyone else has seen it anyway . . .

I tap play before my brain can talk me out of it.

The video starts innocently enough—crowds cheering as

competitors hurtle down the hill. Jamie, Lewis, and Ally lead the pack. But then Lewis is grabbing Jamie's kilt, Jamie is loosening it, and . . .

Oh God. His bits! The flapping is almost hypnotic, and yet he charges on, utterly undeterred.

A snort escapes me before I can stop it, followed by another, and soon I'm laughing so hard my ribs ache. Because honestly? It's absurdly funny watching someone so committed that they barrel through social norms with utter abandon. As ridiculous as it is, there's also something weirdly admirable about it—about him.

And suddenly I see it: Jamie being exactly who he is in this moment—bold to the point of reckless, too stubborn to quit even when he probably should have, and somehow managing to laugh at the chaos of it all without breaking stride. Only Jamie could make utter humiliation look this damn charming.

And, what's more, he did it! He won the bloody race, against all odds and after everything he's been through.

I think back to how I acted afterwards, and shame washes over me. He held out his arms to me for a congratulatory hug, but I didn't give it to him. Instead I snapped at him, wiping the proud grin right off his face. It was his moment, but I made it all about me and my stupid social media account. Why couldn't I just have laughed along with everyone else? Thrown my arms around him and told him how bloody incredible he is?

God, I'm such an idiot.

My finger once again hovers over the delete button. Part of me doesn't want to press it, not because of what's *in* the video but because of what it represents: Jamie being so unapologetically Jamie. That maddening streak in him that drives me up the wall but also makes me ache with something I'm not quite ready to name yet.

But this clip can't remain on the internet for all eternity, and Jamie deserves a bit of his modesty back. I hit delete then lay my phone down on the grass beside me.

I should really head back soon and help Da finish tidying up, but later today I've got my work cut out. First: damage control. My followers might think the whole fiasco was comedy gold—and fair enough, it was—but I'll need to post a new video to get things back on track. I don't want anyone expecting more of that type of content from me.

Second, and far more importantly, I owe Jamie an apology. Because if the man is willing to win a race for me—with his dick out, no less—then maybe it's time I stop focusing on why we wouldn't work and start thinking about why we could.

Aye, his beer garden rubs me up the wrong way. But am I really going to let a business grudge keep me from someone who might be my shot at happiness?

No. Not anymore.

I have to stop being too scared—or too proud—to admit how I actually feel.

And maybe, just maybe, there's a way to deal with my followers and my feelings in one bold move. Because in every romcom film, it all boils down to the grand gesture, right?

If Jamie can bare it all—literally—for me, then surely I can muster the courage to bare my heart for him.

◆ ◆ ◆

It's evening and I'm back on Ben Garve. After the chaos of earlier, the hill feels eerily still, save for the occasional bleat of a sheep and the soft whisper of the breeze through the grass. No racers or spectators now—just me, the heathery slopes, and an increasingly ominous grey sky.

A fat droplet of rain splashes onto my head. Brilliant. So much for the perfect weather we had earlier. I glance upwards as more droplets begin to fall, speckling my hoodie. Hopefully it won't turn into a full-on downpour.

All right. Here goes nothing.

I pull out my phone, run a hand through my hair—useless, it's already curling in the damp air—then tap the Go Live button before I can second-guess myself. Viewers join quickly, one after another. I wave at the screen, a nervous smile tugging at my lips.

"Hi, everyone! Thanks for joining," I say cheerily, watching the numbers rise. My stomach performs little somersaults as usernames I recognise pop up alongside new ones. But there's only one name I'm looking for—and it's not here yet.

The rain intensifies into a steady drizzle. I shield my phone with one hand and force a laugh. "Ah, Scotland in summer," I quip. "If you were watching earlier today, you'd have seen how gloriously sunny it was. It's amazing how quickly the weather can change."

At this, comments flood in:

I was watching earlier 👀👀👀

Sunny? Didn't notice. Was too distracted by other things. 😉

#TheHighlandFlash 4eva!

I bite back a groan and do my best to keep my expression light-hearted, despite all the innuendo.

The longer I wait for him to appear in the viewers list, the harder it is not to get discouraged. Maybe he doesn't want to watch this nonsense—maybe he's avoiding me altogether after the way I snapped at him earlier.

No. Stop spiralling, Maisie. You're here for a reason. Do what you need to do.

Clearing my throat, I press on. "So . . . aye . . . there are some things we have to talk about. Like a certain unexpected event that occurred during today's race."

Predictably, the comments explode with laughing emojis.

Where's the guy who won? Asking for a friend. 👀

I NEED tickets for next year's kilt run. When is it?

That guy had balls . . . literally AND figuratively! 🏃

Can we get a slow-mo replay, please?

My eyes catch on that last comment, and suddenly my brain is unhelpfully obliging, flashing me a crystal-clear mental image of slow-motion Jamie: his arms and legs pumping, his (not so) private parts bouncing—like some wildly inappropriate sports highlight. A snort-laugh slips out before I can stop it, although I quickly smother it with a cough. *Oh God. Get it together, Maisie. Focus.*

And then I see it: LochNLoad. His name appears in the list of viewers.

Right. This is it. No turning back.

"So," I say, trying to steady my voice as both the rain and my heart pound harder. "First off, thank you to everyone who tuned in earlier for having such a good sense of humour about . . . well, everything. I had no idea the race would feature full-frontal male nudity—that was a bit of a surprise! And while I'm glad the video gave many of you a good laugh, I want to make one thing absolutely clear: it was an accident and you won't be getting any more content like that from me."

The comments come fast and furious:

Booooo! Bring back #TheHighlandFlash 🏃

SassyLassie blushing while talking about nudity—she's so pure! 🤍

Did you really delete it, though? Or is there a secret archive somewhere? 👀

No more nudity? Unfollowing immediately (joke!)

Girl, you could have charged £5 per view for that video and retired tomorrow. 😉

I can't stop my lips from twitching at some of them—God help me, the internet is relentless—but I push on. "There's something else I want to say . . . something important. And, believe it or not, it involves the man you all saw today . . . saw rather a lot of, in fact."

My heart thuds against my ribs as I glance again at his username. He's watching. He's actually watching this. And, oh God, the comments keep rolling in—playful, cheeky, some downright naughty.

Suddenly it occurs to me that this might not be the best time to declare my feelings—not when strangers on social media are making jokes about his rather unorthodox victory. Maybe this was a mistake. And, anyway, what if he doesn't feel the same way about me?

Maybe I should just stop this right now. Make a quick joke then pivot into something safer. God knows it wouldn't be the first time I bottled up what I really wanted to say because it felt easier than taking a risk.

But no. After everything that's happened today—Jamie's boldness, his utter determination—I can't chicken out. This is about taking my own leap.

It's at this point that the rain goes from heavy drizzle to torrential downpour in about two seconds flat. It drips off my nose and spatters the phone screen even as I try to shield it.

"Jesus!" I yelp with a laugh. "Is this nature's way of telling me this is a bad idea? Because, if so, tough luck—I'm not listening! There's something I need to say and I can't hold it in anymore."

The viewers are eating this up:

Spill already!

Go on, SassyLassie. Don't leave us hanging!

I pull my hood up as much as possible then start walking—for no reason other than my nerves making it impossible to stay still. The hillside stretches out around me in misty greens and purples as the rain somehow turns even heavier.

"That man you all saw today—the winner of the hill race—is someone I know very well," I say carefully. "He runs a small bar just down the road from where I work at the Pheasant. He recently opened a beer garden there, and it has been the bane of my existence." My steps quicken, adrenaline surging through me.

"There's been plenty of rivalry between us these past few months, but also something else." My voice catches.

Comments come in, people excitedly guessing where this might be going.

"Anyway, I have a confession to make. After the race, I wasn't happy with him—with Jamie. That's his name, by the way. Jamie. I'm not proud of myself for this, but I lost my temper with him. And now, well, I feel bloody terrible about that. So, Jamie, if you're watching this"—my eyes flick to the viewer list, confirming LochNLoad is indeed still there—"I want to say I'm sorry. From the very bottom of my heart."

I tighten my grip on my phone, nervous energy propelling

me further along the hillside, my trainers squelching against the sodden grass. "Jamie, I also want—no, *need*—to say something else to you. Something . . . bigger."

But before I can get the words out, my foot betrays me. It slides on a patch of slick grass, sending me stumbling forwards with a yelp. I catch myself before I faceplant—and then whisper, "Holy shit!" Because just a few inches beyond my toes is a *very* steep drop.

That was close. Too close.

"Right," I say to the camera, aiming for calm and perhaps overshooting into manic cheerfulness. "Quick tip for all you lovely viewers: when livestreaming your romantic confessions from an extremely wet hillside, please do watch where you're going. Don't do what I just did and—"

Something snaps beneath me with a loud *crack*. The next thing I know I'm lurching forwards, my arms flailing wildly, my phone flying out of my hand—

CHAPTER THIRTY-TWO

I've finally figured out how to pack the snug wall-to-wall. It's simple, really. All I have to do is strip off and win a race with my bollocks bouncing around for all to see. Crowd-pleaser, that one. Now every guy in Bannock seems to think it's his personal duty to pop in, order a pint, and crack the best joke he can come up with.

Some recent attempts at humour include:

"Next year you should take part in the 100-metre flash. Oh! I mean dash!"

"Did someone tell you to give it your all? Because, mate, that wasn't what they meant."

"Well done! You didn't just come first in the race—you also came first in giving zero fucks."

"I was like, *Is it a bird? Is it a plane? No, it's . . . oh God!*"

Three different men have congratulated me on going "balls out" in the race, and each of them was so proud of themselves for coming up with that pun. Don't get me wrong, if folk want to take the piss about what happened, fair enough—I'd absolutely do the same thing in their shoes. But at least put in the effort and come up with something original, eh? I mean, try a bit harder!

Oh, and another thing that keeps happening? The mock toast. I hand them their freshly poured pint, then they raise it with a smirk and say something like, "To the fastest arse in the Highlands!"

Aye, it was funny the first time I heard it, mate.

But you know what? Beneath all the ribbing and piss-taking lies something real. These guys have known me since before the crash. They know what I've been through. And a Scottish man doesn't *say* he's proud of you—he shows it by ripping into you while raising a pint in your honour. The sentiment is there, even if it's unspoken, and I appreciate it. That being said, if one more guy claps me on the back and says I really went "balls out", I might just lose my patience.

For now, though, I'm all chuckles and grins, even though my leg aches like hell. I wasn't prepared for a race today, and the fall didn't help. But you know what? I won, so I'm not about to let a bit of pain get to me.

What *is* getting to me is the knowledge that I've royally cocked things up with Maisie. God, I'm such a bloody idiot. What the hell was I thinking? Charging ahead like that, as if crossing the finish line first was more important than using my brain for half a second.

I've just poured Roddy and Hugh their usual order. I thought these two liked it when the snug was dead, but even they've come along to say their piece, which is . . .

"To winning gold and mooning the competition in style!" Roddy raises his pint high.

"I'll drink to that!" Hugh lifts his too.

"To be fair, a better toast than some I've heard tonight," I admit. "You two old buggers enjoy your drinks now, you hear me?"

"Ach, you may have won the race, Jamie, but you're still a cheeky sod," Roddy observes.

"Whatever happened to respecting your elders, eh?" Hugh adds.

I wink at them then notice my phone lighting up with a notification. As I go to reach for it, David and Johnny make an appearance, and before David even opens his mouth, I just know he's going to be the first person this evening to make me blush. I'm not wrong.

"And *that*, Jamie, is why I moved to the Highlands. Thank you!" He throws his arms around me and pulls me into the tightest hug.

"Er . . . didn't you move to the Highlands for *me*?" Johnny asks.

David releases me and pats Johnny's chest affectionately. "Oh, right, of course. But, c'mon, you've got to admit—the end of that race?" David fans himself. "It wasn't just the sun that got me hot and bothered today!"

Johnny rolls his eyes in that way people do when they pretend they're irritated but they really think the world of you. Honestly, I'm not sure what's more nauseating—the lovesick puppy eyes that Lewis *still* gives Iona (even though they're together now) or the way Johnny gazes at David like he hung the moon in the sky.

"Anything you want to get out of your system?" I ask Johnny. "Because every other guy here has made a joke at my expense. You may as well go ahead too."

Johnny taps his chin. "Well, this isn't a joke, but I do want to say congratulations. That was an incredible performance."

David grins. "It was! Jamie, trust me, Johnny and I have already discussed your *performance* in great detail. We were both *very* impressed by it."

Now it's not just me who's blushing but Johnny too.

"All right, now that you two have had your fun, what can I get you?" I say, trying to get things back on track. "Oh, and be warned: you get one attempt at embarrassing me per drink. So if you want to have another go, you'll have to wait till your second round. House rules, I'm afraid."

Once I've served them, I get a chance to check my phone. The notification says: *SassyLassie has gone live.*

I don't even hesitate. I tap to join the stream, and there she is, looking as stunning as ever, raindrops dotting her face.

The landscape behind her is familiar, not least because I was there myself earlier today. I'd like to know what Maisie is up to on Ben Garve, but unfortunately it's too bloody loud in the snug to hear a thing. That's the downside of the place being so damn busy for once.

Deciding I deserve a brief break, I make for the door, squeezing past folk and enduring a few more hearty slaps on the back. I check the office: empty. All right, I'll have a very quick breather. If anyone needs another drink, they can wait a minute or two.

Dumping myself in a chair, I prop my elbows on a desk and hold my phone in front of me. Maisie's voice fills the room, clear as day now that I'm away from the chaos.

"There's something else I want to say . . . something important." Damn, I must've missed whatever her first point was. That worry takes a back seat when she adds, "And, believe it or not, it involves the man you all saw today . . . saw rather a lot of, in fact."

Wait, she's talking about *me*? Ah, I get it. She'll want to apologise to her followers for what I did earlier. That makes sense. Well, I hope they forgive her.

Comments flash up at the bottom, like:

It's raining, but SassyLassie still brings the sunshine 

That's nice. These people really do love her.

Also:

Saw rather a lot? More like saw EVERYTHING! 😂😂😂

I blink at this comment, my brain slowly catching up to the fact that strangers on the internet are now cracking jokes about having seen every last bit of me. Getting roasted by the local lads was one thing . . .

A laugh bursts out of me before I can stop it. Ah, well—no point losing sleep over it. At least I made an impression.

"Jesus!" Maisie yelps, snapping my attention back to her. The rain has turned torrential, plastering her hair to her face and moulding her hoodie to her like a second skin. "Is this nature's way of telling me this is a bad idea?" she wonders. "Because, if so, tough luck—I'm not listening! There's something I need to say and I can't hold it in anymore."

Wait, what might be a bad idea? Have I missed something?

More comments come in:

Came for comedy, staying for drama!

Does Maisie secretly fancy him? Place yer bets!

Hold up! What's this about Maisie secretly fancying me?

Maisie is walking now. "That man you all saw today—the winner of the hill race—is someone I know very well." She tells her viewers about my beer garden—the bane of her existence, apparently—then adds, "There's been plenty of rivalry between us these past few months, but also something else."

I lean closer to my phone, my pulse quickening. Why

exactly is she telling all this to her followers? And, more to the point, where is she going with this? My knee bounces beneath the desk.

Next, Maisie addresses me directly and . . . she apologises to me. For losing her temper with me after the race.

Why is *she* apologising? I'm the one who messed up! She doesn't have to say sorry for anything.

But apparently she's not done. "Jamie, I also want—no, *need*—to say something else to you. Something . . . bigger."

Jesus Christ. Is she about to say what I think she's about to say? No. There's no way. And yet the comments are going wild, heart and flame emojis lighting up my screen. Clearly, I'm not the only one thinking—or maybe just hoping—that this might be heading in a . . . romantic direction.

The way she's looking at me through my screen, it's like there's no camera, no distance—just her eyes locked on mine, as if I'm the only one who matters.

It's an intense moment—so intense I barely register Maisie slipping at first. She stumbles, arms windmilling, but mercifully she catches herself. "Holy shit!" she mutters. Then, with a grin that doesn't quite mask the alarm in her eyes, she jokes, "Right, quick tip for all you lovely viewers: when livestreaming your romantic confessions from an extremely wet hillside, please do watch where you're going."

Damn right you should watch where you're going! You're precious, Maisie. Don't you—

Hang on. Did she just say "romantic confessions"? Did I hear that right?

"Don't do what I just did and—"

One second she's there, and the next she's gone. She lets out a startled cry, and the feed spins wildly—a sickening blur of sky and hillside. Then there's a hard *thud*. The livestream continues, the camera now capturing nothing but clouds and rain. Maisie is nowhere to be seen.

My stomach drops clean out of me. Scarcely breathing, I stare at the screen like if I will it hard enough, she'll pop into view. Any second now she'll surely swoop in to grab her phone, laugh, and say, "What am I like?"

Won't she?

Rain keeps falling from a grey sky. There's no sign of Maisie.

Comments flash across the bottom of the screen:

OMG! Is she okay?

Did she fall?!

SOMEONE HELP HER!!

Cold dread claws up my spine. My body moves before my brain has even caught up—I shove my phone into my pocket, shoot out of the chair, and stride for the door.

Out in reception, I meet Aidan, who saunters in through the main entrance with a cheeky grin plastered on his face. He's clearly gearing up to deliver some punchline or other, but I don't have time for that.

"She's on Ben Garve!" I bark, already heading for the back exit.

"What?"

"Maisie! She's hurt, I think. Get help! I'll be ahead of you."

I don't wait for a response. I head outside into a storm so fierce it feels like a living thing. The rain lashes down in heavy sheets, soaking me within seconds as I race through the beer garden, out the back gate, and to my car.

Key in the ignition. The engine growling to life.

Rain pounds the bonnet like fists on a door, each strike reverberating in my skull, dragging me back—

Twisted metal. Shattered glass.

Maw. Da.

My chest tightens so suddenly, so viciously, it's like a fist clamping around my lungs. I can't get air in properly, just shallow gasps that don't seem to go anywhere.

No, no, not now. Not fucking now. Maisie could be hurt—badly. She needs me.

"Come on," I mutter, gripping the wheel tight, like it's the only thing anchoring me to reality.

Deep breaths. Focus. In for two . . . out for two . . .

The pressure eases just enough that I can push past it. My hand trembling, I find the gear stick and shift it into place.

I pull out of the driveway and make my way down Main Street, the wipers whipping frantically across the windscreen. Before long, Bannock is behind me and the narrow country road twists and turns ahead, treacherous in this relentless deluge. But adrenaline propels me forwards with single-minded determination. *Just get to her.*

"That's it," I say, my voice strained. "Almost there . . ."

Ben Garve looms through the haze of grey, an ominous shadow shrouded in rain and cloud.

A fresh spike of dread drives through me. What if she's lying there alone? Injured and scared? Or worse?

No. Don't think like that.

I tug the handbrake into place and fling the door open. Before I've even registered the cold bite of the rain, I'm tearing up the hill, pushing myself even harder than I did in the race—harder than I thought possible.

My leg screams in protest with every step—pain shooting

from knee to hip—but nothing can stop me now, not when Maisie could be hurt.

I can barely see a thing, the rain blurring everything, the ground soggy and uneven underfoot, but I have to keep going. I have to find her.

"MAISIE!" I yell. "Maisie, where are you?"

Nothing.

"MAISIE?"

Still nothing but rain hammering down and wind whipping against me.

And then: "Jamie?"

Her voice is faint but unmistakable. Relief crashes over me like a wave, but I don't stop—I can't stop—not yet.

"Maisie!"

I run on until, through the haze, I finally spot her—a small figure moving towards me down the hillside. Her tentative steps grow faster when she spots me too. I don't stop running until she's in my arms, soaked to the bone but alive, miraculously alive. I hold her tight, like I'll never let her go again.

When I eventually pull back just enough to look at her properly, my words tumble out: "Did you fall? Where are you hurt? Should you even be standing? Christ, let me carry you." My arms move instinctively, already preparing to lift her off her feet.

"Jamie!" She slaps my hands away, laughing—a real laugh full of warmth and life. It washes over me like a balm to raw nerves. "I'm fine!"

I'm happy but also confused. I don't understand. The livestream—

"I was so bloody lucky! See that cliff?" She points up to a crag that must be twenty-five, maybe thirty feet high. "I wobbled right on the edge of it. I won't lie, it scared me shitless, but I managed to keep my footing."

I pull her into another hug because . . . well, I can't help it. "You need to be more careful!"

"Aye, don't worry, I've learnt my lesson. Well aware I could've gone the way of my phone. It went tumbling right down. I've been trying to look for it—safely, obviously. It must be around here somewhere. It's probably smashed to bits anyway."

"I'll help. In fact, let's get you somewhere dry first, then *I'll* look for it."

I make to lead her back down the hill, but she says, "Hold your horses! Before anything else, there's something I need to say and it can't wait."

I glance up at the sky, at the endless rain still pouring down. "Can't it? I don't want you catching a cold out here—or worse, slipping again."

"No, it can't wait." A gust of wind catches her hair, plastering it across her face. She sweeps it away then tilts her head. "Actually, first, a question. How did you get here so fast? I swear it's only been a few minutes since I narrowly averted disaster."

I shrug, water dripping from the tip of my nose. "I drove. Then ran."

"Whoa, whoa, whoa! First, you *drove*? In this? This rain is wild! I thought with weather like this, you—"

"Aye, well," I interrupt. "I needed to get here, didn't I?"

Maisie studies me intently. Reaching up, she brushes my wet fringe from my face with gentle fingers.

"And the run? You've already sprinted up and down this

hill today—more than that leg of yours has done in a long time. You shouldn't be pushing it even more."

"Same answer as before," I say simply. "I needed to get here. For you."

She rests a hand against my chest. "And I came here because there's something I need to say to *you*. I wanted to lay out my feelings on that livestream—for everyone to hear—because I've been a fool for far too long. I don't care if you run a rival business. Hell, I don't care about *anything else.* The only thing that matters is you." She swallows hard. "And I want you, Jamie McIntyre."

"Aye? Well . . ." My voice deepens into something rougher, the weight of everything boiling over inside me. "I want you too." My hands find their way to her waist without thought or hesitation, and I pull her closer. "Because you, Maisie Kerr, are fucking perfect."

As if on cue, the rain begins to ease—not stopping entirely but softening to a gentle drizzle—and a single ray of light breaks through the thick clouds above us.

"Can I kiss you?" I ask.

Her lips curl into a slow smile. "I've never wanted anything more."

Without waiting another second, I angle my head and press my rain-soaked lips to hers. Despite the damp chill clinging to us both, Maisie's mouth is soft and deliciously warm. I cup her cheek with one hand, and we lose ourselves in each other beneath the Highland sky. What starts off slow and searching changes into something deeper, bolder. Her hand clutches my drenched shirt, and the subtle scent of rain and heather wraps around us.

When we finally pull back, I can't resist a cheeky wink

through our shared breathlessness. "Well," I say with a laugh that feels lighter than it has in years, "that was officially the best kiss of my life—and that's saying something considering how bloody drenched we both are."

I want to take Maisie to my car, to crank up the heat and get her warm, but she's determined to hunt for her phone for a little bit longer. So we both look, and I find it after just a couple of minutes. It actually wasn't far from where we were both standing. What's more, when I pick it up from the patch of thick grass it landed in, by some miracle it's intact.

Even more unbelievably: the livestream is still running, and people are still watching it. The moment my face comes into view on the screen, a deluge of comments floods in.

It IS him! The voice we heard is #TheHighlandFlash guy!

OMG, SassyLassie's livestreams are THE BEST!

First he wins the race, and now he wins her heart? Someone stop this man!

SassyLassie + #TheHighlandFlash = couple goals 💜

"Er . . . did you guys hear what we were just saying?" I ask.

YES! WE HEARD EVERYTHING!

I grin at the camera, rubbing the back of my neck, feeling like a proper daftie. "Wow. So now I've laid myself bare to you all literally *and* figuratively, huh?"

More comments fly in, too fast to read, though I catch plenty of laughing emojis, hearts, flames . . . and a fair few eggplants too.

"Wow. It's really still working?" Maisie appears beside me on the screen—and in real life too, of course.

"Aye," I confirm with a nod. "Now, dear followers of Sassy-Lassie, if you guys will excuse us, I really want to kiss this woman again. And since I'm sure you'll agree we've both shared more than enough of ourselves today, I think it's time to end this livestream so we can do that in private." I wave at the camera.

Maisie waves too. "Bye, everyone!"

I tsk lightly. "Even *I* know you're supposed to say, *Don't forget to like and subscribe!*" And with that, I tap to end the stream.

CHAPTER THIRTY-THREE

MAISIE

"Is the blindfold really necessary?" I try to sound casual, even though adrenaline is surging through my veins.

"Aye, it is. Can't have you sneaking a peek. That would spoil the surprise."

Jamie hasn't even started painting me yet, but I'm already a live wire, every nerve sparking in suspense, waiting for that first stroke. My heart is pounding—I suppose it would be weird if it wasn't, given I'm lying here naked, blindfolded, and tied to the bed.

"Besides," Jamie continues, "depriving one sense makes the others stronger." He leans close so that I can feel his breath on my ear. "I reckon you're hanging on every word I say. And"—his lips brush my throat, soft as a whisper—"what about that kiss, eh? I bet you *really* felt it."

My breath catches. "I . . . I did. But, you know, being tied up like this . . . it requires a lot of trust."

"Aye, it does. But you trust me, right?"

I give the silky scarf knotted around my wrists a little twist and pull. The headboard doesn't so much as creak. I'm well and truly stuck, my body laid out at his mercy. Aye, I'm nervous, but it's also not the worst place to be.

"I suppose I do—no, I *do* trust you. But, when it's your turn, will you let me blindfold you, tie you up, and strip you naked?"

"Of course. But for now I really need to be getting on with my masterpiece. Are you ready?"

I swallow and nod.

He begins at my neck, the first stroke of the brush soft and ticklish, like a feather drifting across my skin. The cool paint contrasts with the warmth of Jamie's body as he leans close, his breath teasing my collarbone. My senses are on overdrive, every brushstroke magnified, like ripples spreading through a still pond. He trails the bristles down my throat, and my back arches instinctively when he guides them lower, tracing a path between my breasts.

"How does that feel?" he murmurs.

"Good!" It comes out as little more than a breathless whisper.

He traces a lazy circle around my left nipple then flicks the tip of the brush over the sensitive peak, back and forth, back and forth, in barely-there strokes, coaxing it to tighten. Then, with tantalising precision, he gives my right nipple the same exquisite treatment.

Jamie lingers at my chest a while longer before sweeping downwards in a slow, deliberate descent then swirling around my belly button. The sensation sends an unexpected shiver rippling through me.

"Ticklish, are we?" He proceeds to dip into the shallow hollow of my navel.

I let out a shaky laugh that turns into a gasp when he stays there, drawing lazy spirals that make my stomach tighten and quiver. My toes curl involuntarily.

Then he shifts his focus lower still, teasing over the curve of my hip and downwards. My breath falters when he skims over my most intimate place in a delicate caress that sets everything alight. The brush continues along the tender skin of my inner thigh to my knee.

By now I'm a quivering mess, every inch of me attuned to him. He swaps sides, starting at my other hip and repeating the torturously delicious path down my other leg. Again the brush grazes over my core, and a desperate little sound escapes my throat, my hips instinctively lifting towards him. But he's already moved past it, again following a trail to my knee.

But then . . . then he circles back.

Slowly. Intentionally. Dragging the brush in slow spirals that bring him closer and closer to where I'm aching for him most.

He lets out a low, wicked chuckle. "This might just be my favourite bit."

The bristles tickle my pussy—soft at first, then firmer with calculated strokes that send sparks shooting straight through me. He spends longer there than anywhere else, stroking, swirling, and driving me absolutely mad.

"Jamie!" I whisper. It comes out as barely more than a gasp.

"Aye, lass?" he says with a grin in his voice. "I can't rush perfection. You'll just have to be patient."

It's a ridiculously small patch of skin for Jamie to fuss over with such precision—but, let's be honest, painting probably isn't what's on his mind anymore. Not that I'm complaining. If this is his idea of art, he can take all bloody day to finish.

Finally the brush stills and my whole body trembles with the loss.

"Well?" I murmur, my voice tight with equal parts need and curiosity. "How does it look?"

"Hmm . . ." He pauses like he's truly considering the question. "It's a masterpiece. But only because I had such a beautiful canvas to start with."

He unties the scarf around my wrists, followed by the blindfold. I blink, adjusting to the light, then get up to inspect myself in the mirror. Across my skin, in loops and swirls, are Celtic patterns. I'd half expected Jamie to slap on a smiley face or something equally daft, but this is actually pretty good. It's not far off how the actors looked in that famous scene in *Highland Legacy*, the one I may or may not have paused and stared at for far too long.

And then I notice what he's done on my chest. Right over my heart are the initials LNL and SL—LochNLoad and Sassy-Lassie—woven into a braided heart. Something warm blooms inside me.

"Jamie," I whisper. "It's perfect."

I turn to him. He's still in his boxers, although they're doing a piss-poor job of hiding just how . . . *enthusiastic* he got during our little art session. My lips twitch into a grin.

"Someone's keen," I remark, letting my gaze linger meaningfully.

"That," Jamie says with a cheeky raise of his brows, "is entirely your fault."

"Oh?" I step closer and run a finger lightly along his waistband. "Well, guess what? It's your turn now." I push him onto the bed.

His eyes gleaming with anticipation, he stretches his arms lazily above his head, ready for what's coming.

"Blindfold first," I say.

He smirks but doesn't protest as I slide it over his eyes.

"And now for this." I reach for the scarf he used on me and loop it around his wrists, tying them to the headboard just as securely as he tied me earlier.

I lean down to press a kiss to his jawline. Then, with one smooth motion, I pull down his boxers and toss them aside, leaving Jamie completely bare. I take a moment to survey my canvas: broad, sculpted shoulders; lean muscles that ripple ever so slightly as he shifts beneath me; and taut abs leading down to . . . well, yes.

"See anything you like?" Jamie quips, as if somehow he knows exactly what I'm looking at despite the blindfold.

"Aye, but it'll look even better once I'm finished with you."

Picking up a fresh brush, I decide to have a bit of fun before starting properly. Without warning, I trail the bristles ever so lightly across a very sensitive spot: his balls. It's more of a tickle than anything else—scarcely there at all—but the effect is immediate and hilarious.

Jamie lets out the most undignified squawk I've ever heard—which sends me into fits of giggles—and jerks against the silk knots, hips twitching away from the offending brush.

"What the bloody hell was that?"

"What?" I ask innocently. "You painted *me* down there."

"Aye, but that was different!" he protests, squirming when I flick the brush against him again for good measure. "There are rules! You can't *start* there! That's cheating!"

"Oh? Well, I just wanted to check something, and . . . aye, it seems I'm not the only one who's ticklish. You've gone all squirmy."

"Lass," he warns in a tone that would probably be intimidating if he wasn't tied up and blushing furiously.

Deciding not to push my luck (too much), I leave his balls alone. For now. But oh, don't you worry, lads—I'll be back. Like a villain in an action film, I'm already plotting my triumphant return.

I dip the brush into one of the pots of paint instead—a deep blue. I hover it above Jamie's chest in preparation for stroke number one. But before I can begin, there's a loud knock at the door.

"Don't come in!" we both shout at exactly the same time— my voice high-pitched with panic while Jamie sounds more irritated than anything else.

The awkward silence that follows makes me want to dive under the duvet and never come out.

"Oh . . . okay," Da eventually says from the other side of the door. "Well, when you're decent, could the two of you come downstairs? I'd like to have a chat."

His footsteps fade away, leaving behind another silence, which is only broken when Jamie says, "Well, I'm glad he knocked."

I giggle at the thought of Da bursting in here with Jamie stark naked, tied up to my bed, and sporting an erection. Laying a hand on Jamie's chest, I say, "Sorry about this. I'm too old to still be living with my da."

He manages a brave smile. "It's all right. Trust me, I know all too well what living with family is like. Anyway, I suppose you better untie me."

"Aye, I suppose I should." And *yet* . . . I've already dipped my brush into the paint. Seems a shame to waste it, doesn't it? So I quickly scrawl my signature. On his cock.

It twitches as I do so, and Jamie takes in a sharp breath, which is followed by a low, rumbling laugh—a sound somewhere between amusement and disbelief.

When I remove his blindfold and he sees what I've done—signed my name on *that*—I expect him to crack up or come up with some cheeky remark. But instead? He looks at me like I've just given him the greatest gift in the world.

To have my name. On his cock.

Men are so bloody weird sometimes. Like, *now* you show me your emotions?

"I hope we're clear that there are to be no more kilt-dropping incidents." I point a warning finger at him. "Because next time, I'll skip the paint and get my name tattooed down there. So everyone will always know you're mine."

Jamie winces but then breaks into a wicked grin. With a casual shrug, he says, "So long as you put wee hearts over the *i*'s, I'm game."

◆ ◆ ◆

After I have a shower and pull on some fresh clothes, and after Jamie waits for the paint to dry then pulls on his (because, apparently, he's not quite ready to wash off my name), we head downstairs.

The pub is empty, save for Da and Elspeth, who are at a table near the bar. I didn't realise Elspeth would be joining us for this chat.

Da motions for us to sit opposite them, and Jamie gets to the table first so he can pull out my chair for me. It's a ridiculous, gentlemanly, and very un-Jamie-like gesture, but kind of sweet. I think he's trying to impress Da.

"Looking nice and clean." Elspeth smiles sweetly at me as I sit, but there's a hint of mischief in her eyes. "Did you decide to have a quick freshen-up before coming down?"

My cheeks warm. "Er . . . aye." Please don't let there be any follow-up questions.

"Oh, Elspeth." Jamie tuts and shakes his head. "Don't go embarrassing Maisie. Not when you and Bryce have been sneaking around like teenagers getting up to who knows what."

This comment is followed by several seconds of stunned silence. Okay, so maybe Jamie isn't trying *too* hard to impress Da. He wasn't on his best behaviour for long—he never is. But that's just Jamie, isn't it? God knows he makes me laugh, and the surprised glance Da and Elspeth give each other is pretty priceless.

Smug, Jamie leans back. "Is that what this chat is about? Were you going to blow our minds by telling us you're an item? Were Maisie and I meant to gasp and say"—he presses his hands dramatically to his cheeks—"*Oh my God! We had no idea!*"

"You knew?" Da sputters. He looks to me. "Both of you?"

"I didn't *know*," I say. "But I suspected, yes. I didn't want to pry, though. I knew you'd tell me when you were ready."

"You see, *some* people have class," Jamie teases. "We don't all gossip when someone goes upstairs with another person then returns with dishevelled hair." He stares at first Elspeth then Da with mock disapproval. "Maisie and I? We know how to be subtle."

Da snorts. "And I suppose nothing screams subtle like the two of you yelling, 'Don't come in!' when I knock on Maisie's door?"

"Or finishing a race minus a kilt and with your bits on show for all to see?" Elspeth adds.

Jamie pauses. "Touché," he offers eventually. "You've got me there."

"Can we please get back on track?" I say. "I may have guessed something was going on, but I still want to hear it directly from you. So, spill. What was it you wanted to tell us?"

Elspeth and Da exchange a look, and just from the way their eyes meet, I can tell this isn't a fling—it's something real.

Da places his hand over hers on the table, the gesture uncharacteristically tender for him. "We've been seeing each other for quite a number of weeks now. We kept it quiet because . . . well, you know how folk in Bannock talk. We didn't want anyone making assumptions before we were ready to say something."

"But we're ready now." Elspeth smiles warmly at me and Jamie then turns to Da. "And Bryce and I . . . well, we're rather taken with one another, aren't we?"

Da chuckles, his eyes crinkling at the corners. There's a rare softness about him that makes his whole face lighter somehow. He looks so . . . content, and seeing him like this tugs at something deep inside me.

I get to my feet, round the table, and hug them both in turn. "It's wonderful news. Really, it is. I'm so happy for you."

Jamie stands too and clasps Da's hand in a firm shake, then he gives Elspeth a hug. "Aye, congrats. Just look at the four of us! Me and Elspeth from the Bannock Hotel, you two from the Pheasant. Our business rivalry should have kept us apart, but it didn't. It just proves what I've always said: our sex drive conquers all."

I swat his arm. "Love, Jamie. Love conquers all."

"Whoa! Let's not get ahead of ourselves." He winks at me. "I'm still very much in the infatuation stage. Could be bored of you come tomorrow."

I smirk at him because I know he's all talk. This is the man who couldn't bring himself to wash my name off his penis.

"And, er, you're sure about this one, are you?" Da asks me with a nod at Jamie. "Even when he says things like that?"

"Aye, Da. Because even though he can be a bit of an arse, he's my arse." I sling an arm around Jamie, who grins and pecks my cheek.

"All right, then," Da says. "Well, that's the first item ticked off the agenda, but there's still more to discuss, so let's all take our seats again."

Oh? When I spotted Elspeth, I guessed Da was going to tell me about his secret relationship, but I didn't realise there would be more to this meeting than that. I sit, wondering what's next.

Da takes a deep breath. "Well, with my health being what it is, I've been thinking it might be time I stepped back a little. Not completely, mind! More of a semi-retirement. But, aye, I'd like to gradually transition more responsibility over to you, Maisie."

My heart stutters. This is what I've wanted, for both me and him. It's time he slowed down, and I wouldn't mind having more of a say around here. I know what a big deal this is for him, though—letting go of the reins of this place he's worked so hard at over so many years.

"I won't let you down," I promise him.

"I know that. The Pheasant will be in safe hands with you running things day to day." Da's gaze briefly flickers to Jamie before returning to me. "It's not my place to meddle, of course, but maybe at some point down the road, the Pheasant and the

Bannock Hotel might even work together rather than against each other, eh? There could be advantages. The beer garden, the snug, and the Pheasant all offer something unique—an outdoor space, a cosy indoor space, and a lively pub. If you two collaborated rather than constantly being at loggerheads, maybe something amazing could come from it."

Jamie and I exchange looks, and he raises an eyebrow. It's certainly an interesting idea.

"Anyway, I probably shouldn't be tossing out ideas like that quite yet and putting pressure on your relationship. Especially as Jamie here is still in the 'infatuation stage'. It was just a thought, that's all."

Jamie chuckles a little nervously. "To be clear, Bryce, the infatuation thing *was* a joke. I do, you know . . ." He waves a hand vaguely. "Have feelings for your daughter."

Da smirks. "Aye, I know. Maisie explained to me that, when you got your tackle out in front of the whole town, it wasn't so much an act of public indecency as it was a declaration of sorts."

Jamie scratches his chin, his cheeks growing pink. "Er, aye. Anyway, was there anything else? Because this conversation is getting a wee bit painful now."

It takes a lot to embarrass Jamie, but apparently my da is one of the few people who can make him squirm. And honestly? I kind of love seeing Jamie act sheepish around him. He may never admit it, but it shows Jamie cares what my da thinks.

"As a matter of fact, there is something else." Da shifts his gaze back to me. "Maisie, I'm sure the last thing you want is your old man knocking on your door when you're trying to have some, ahem, *private time*. You won't want to be living with me forever."

"Oh God. Is this your way of kicking me out?"

Da laughs. "Not at all! Quite the opposite, in fact. You see, if I'm going to be semi-retiring, I wouldn't mind a bit of peace and quiet on the days I'm not working. But in the flat upstairs, you can always hear the hubbub of conversation in the Pheasant. Elspeth, though, has a lovely wee place nearby, and . . . well, she asked if I'd like to move in with her, and I said yes. So . . . the flat is yours, love."

"Oh." This announcement catches me so completely off-guard that I'm not sure what to say. I glance at Jamie, and his grin is positively wicked. I know what he's thinking: no more interruptions for any future sessions involving blindfolds and scarves.

I stand and fling my arms around Da, holding him tight. "Thank you! For everything. I love you so much."

EPILOGUE
MAISIE

"And at the end of that round, the Bannock Brainiacs are *still* in the lead, now with twenty-four points!" Jamie announces into the mic. "As for the rest of you, remember, it's not about the winning or the losing, it's about . . . oh, who am I kidding? It's totally about the winning. Step up your game!"

From a corner of the busy pub, Scott calls, "We all know *you'll* do anything to win, Jamie, but some of us have a wee thing called dignity!"

Laughter ripples through the Pheasant.

Jamie grins, not embarrassed in the slightest. "You don't have to tell us its name, Scott, or that it's wee—just keep it in your trousers, please!"

The laughter explodes this time, and Scott's cheeks go pink, although he chuckles good-naturedly.

It's Jamie's first ever time running the quiz, but you wouldn't know it by looking at him. Microphone in hand, grin on his face, and oozing confidence, he has folk hanging on his every word. If he wasn't so bloody charming—and sexy—I might even be a little jealous. After all, Monday quizzes are *my* domain.

But no, I can't be jealous—not when I get to take this man upstairs later and have my wicked way with him. If anything, seeing him hold his own in front of everyone, and banter with them so naturally, only makes him more attractive. I can't wait to wipe that cheeky grin off his face after we close up—and coax a few noises out of him that he didn't even know he could make.

"Check out the way she's looking at him," Iona comments.

"Aye, she's absolutely smitten," Cat agrees.

I'm behind the bar while the two of them are on stools opposite me with wine glasses in hand. I don't deny the accusation—why would I? Instead, leaning casually against the counter, I say, "Cat, if *you* had a man who can go three rounds in one night and still have the energy to make you breakfast in the morning, you'd be smitten too."

She chokes on her wine, eyes bulging. "Jesus Christ, Maisie! That's my brother!"

"What?" I say innocently. "Making breakfast is a very attractive quality."

Cat fixes me with a dry stare. "That wasn't the bit I objected to, and you know it."

Before I can tease that there's nothing sexier than a man who can cater to a woman's *every* need, Jamie speaks into the microphone again.

"Before the next round, I have a few important announcements. If I could have everyone's attention, please."

The chatter throughout the pub dies down, and people turn to Jamie expectantly.

"First off, look at this, eh?" Jamie holds one arm out wide, like an MC introducing a headline act. "Me, hosting quiz night at the Pheasant! Who'd have thought it? Especially after the rumours that Maisie and I were set to start World War Three with our competitiveness. But here we are, working together! And this is just the beginning of a more collaborative approach between the Bannock Hotel and the Pheasant."

There's an approving murmur from the crowd, followed by clapping.

I won't be letting Jamie run the pub quiz every week, of course, but tonight is something of a symbolic gesture, marking the start of this new partnership of sorts between our businesses. A lot of the details still need to be figured out, but we'll hash things out as we go. One thing we *have* decided is that Jamie sleeps in my bed now. He hasn't spent a single night in the hotel since Da announced he was moving in with Elspeth. In fact, because Jamie's room has been vacant for a wee while, Lewis has started dropping increasingly unsubtle hints about converting it into a guest room.

"Next up," Jamie says, "I regret to say I've actually had a number of complaints tonight. About you, Iona Stewart."

All eyes turn to Iona, who blinks in confusion. "Er . . . you have?"

"Aye," Jamie says solemnly. "If you could *please* stop waving around that sparkly engagement ring quite so smugly, then people might be able to concentrate on my questions. Thank you."

The room erupts into laughter again, and Iona defiantly holds her hand aloft and wiggles her fingers. She and Lewis got engaged just over a week ago, and she couldn't be happier.

"And in other news," Jamie says, continuing smoothly, "Ally and Emily welcomed their second child—another wee boy—into the world just yesterday. Baby and mother are both doing great, and Ally is . . . well, still Ally. So, I hope you all have a drink to hand—and if not, stop being a cheapskate and go order something off Maisie! This is a pub, people! *Anyway*, I'd like to ask you all to raise a glass to wee Ciaran."

There are chuckles, and glasses are raised. "To Ciaran!" we all say.

Jamie's eyes find mine, and his gaze softens. "One last thing. Can we please all take a moment to appreciate how stunning Maisie looks tonight? That lilac hair suits her perfectly—not that there's any colour she couldn't pull off."

The room lets out a collective, "Aww!"

With a dramatic flourish, I flick my hair over one shoulder and give the pub a queenly wave that has the regulars hooting with laughter.

But Jamie isn't done. "Of course, there are a lot of people around the world who adore Maisie's videos, but let's not forget, she was ours first!"

More awws, and cheers this time too. Then, from the table he's sitting at with Elspeth, Da bellows, "Damn right!"

The warmth of everyone's reaction sneaks past my defences, and my throat tightens just a smidge. I resist the urge to blink too much. Nope, not going to get emotional in the middle of quiz night. That's not happening.

Jamie throws me a cheeky wink before turning back to the quiz.

"I *still* can't believe you're with Jamie," Cat says when he starts reading out the next question. "I'm happy for you," she adds quickly. "I just . . . can't wrap my head around the appeal."

"I can see it now," Iona says, setting her wine glass down on the bar. "I couldn't at first, but now I reckon they're perfect for each other. Jamie's met his match in Maisie." She gives me an approving nod. "No one can keep him in line like you can."

Cat cocks her head before admitting, "That *is* true."

I glance back at my former nemesis, enjoying the way his eyes sparkle when he delivers another cheesy line.

"You know, we're practically family now," Iona muses, pulling my attention back to her. "What with our parents being together."

Da has a pint in one hand and his other arm around Elspeth's shoulders. It's so nice seeing him relaxing and enjoying himself. He's earned it.

"Aye." I shoot Iona a little smile. "Plus, when you marry Lewis, you and Cat will become sisters."

"And if you and Jamie ever get hitched," Cat adds, "we'll *all* be sisters. One big happy but slightly weird family."

"True! It's funny how everyone is pairing off now." Something clicks in my brain half a second too late, and I wince. "Oh! Sorry, Cat. Not you, obviously, but—"

"Ha!" Cat waves off my faux pas, swirling what's left of her wine like she couldn't be any less bothered. "That's okay. I'm not exactly looking to settle down. *Although* . . ." Her lips tug upwards, mischief written all over her face. "I *may* have my eye on someone I could have a wee bit of fun with."

Iona leans in eagerly. "Oh? Spill!"

"Well . . ." Cat pauses for dramatic effect. "Let's just say I have a thing for a certain . . . bad boy."

A NOTE FROM THE AUTHORS

We hope you enjoyed Jamie and Maisie's story. Want more of the pair? Subscribers to our free email newsletter can download a cheeky wee bonus epilogue.

The *True Scotsman* series concludes in *The Highland Bad Boy*, Robbie and Cat's story. You won't want to miss it!

For more information about the bonus epilogue and *The Highland Bad Boy*, visit amymcgavin.com.

Bonus Epilogue

Next Book

The True Scotsman Series
The HIGHLAND BAD BOY
AMY McGAVIN